Praise for Carrie Vaughn's Amaryllis and Other Stories

"Carrie Vaughn's stories are by turns fu
soling. For brilliance and versatility, I p
with Gaiman and Martin."
—Daniel Abraham, au

"Carrie Vaughn's approach to fiction is altogether adventurous, entertaining and joyous in the way each story shines a new light on a different part of humanity. Whether we share in the life of a princess or
an astronaut—Vaughn knows just exactly how to hit each note with
perfection and embrace the love of the written word. And through her
characters we discover new things about ourselves."
—Ann VanderMeer, co-editor of *The Weird*

"Bold, risk-taking, mold-breaking SF, with strong heroines and heroes.
Prepare to have your boundaries pushed, and your heart and mind ex-
panded. Highly recommended."
—Ramez Naam, author of the Nexus Trilogy

"A superior fiction collection. Every story showcases her talent and
stays with you long after you've finished reading. This one is a keeper."
—Jennifer Brozek, author of *Never Let Me Sleep*

"Vaughn's second collection (and first without her series protago-
nist, Kitty Norville) displays impressive talent across a range of both
styles and subgenres. The Hugo-nominated title story, unsurprisingly,
is among the best here, a short tale filled with emotional moments
and impressive worldbuilding in a future in which families are created
by committees, and one woman is dealing with the consequences of
her mother's rebellion. A prequel, 'Bannerless,' is also impressive, as
are the Prohibition-era 'Roaring Twenties' and 'Draw Thy Breath in
Pain,' which relates the secret origins of Shakespeare's works. 'For Fear
of Dragons' is another highlight, an update of the virgin-sacrifice-to-
dragons trope that avoids the snark of so many contemporary revamps
. . . fans of Vaughn who only know her urban fantasy will be impressed
by just how far she can stretch her wings."
—*Publishers Weekly*

Also by Carrie Vaughn

The Kitty Series
Kitty Saves the World
Low Midnight
Kitty in the Underworld
Kitty Rocks the House
Kitty Steals the Show
Kitty's Big Trouble
Kitty Goes to War
Kitty's House of Horrors
Kitty Raises Hell
Kitty and the Dead Man's Hand
Kitty and the Silver Bullet
Kitty Takes a Holiday
Kitty Goes to Washington
Kitty and The Midnight Hour
Kitty's Greatest Hits (short story collection)

Other Books
Dreams of the Golden Age
After the Golden Age
Discord's Apple
Steel
Voices of Dragons
Straying from the Path (short story collection)

AMARYLLIS

AND OTHER STORIES

AMARYLLIS

AND OTHER STORIES

CARRIE VAUGHN

FAIRWOOD PRESS
Bonney Lake, WA

AMARYLLIS

A Fairwood Press Book
August 2016
Copyright © 2016 Carrie Vaughn, LLC

Fairwood Press
21528 104th Street Court East
Bonney Lake, WA 98391
www.fairwoodpress.com

Cover by Elena Vizerskaya
Book design by Patrick Swenson

ISBN: 978-1-933846-62-0
First Fairwood Press Edition: August 2016
Printed in the United States of America

For Robin McKinley and Ray Bradbury
whose work made me want to write.

CONTENTS

THE BEST WE CAN

In the end, the discovery of evidence of extraterrestrial life, and not just life but intelligence, got hopelessly mucked up because no one wanted to take responsibility for confirming the findings, and no one could decide who ultimately had the authority—the obligation—to do so. We submitted the paper, but peer review held it up for a year. News leaked—NASA announced one of their press conferences, but the press conference ended up being an announcement about a future announcement, which never actually happened and the reporters made a joke of it. Another case of Antarctic meteorites or cold fusion. We went around with our mouths shut waiting for an official announcement while ulcers devoured our guts.

So I wrote a press release. I had Marsh at JPL's comet group and Salvayan at Columbia vet it for me and released it under the auspices of the JPL Near Earth Objects Program. We could at least start talking about it instead of arguing about whether we were ready to start talking about it. I didn't know what would happen next. I did it in the spirit of scientific outreach, naturally. The release included that now-famous blurry photo that started the whole thing.

I had an original print of that photo, of UO-1—Unidentified Object One, because it technically wasn't flying and I was being optimistic that this would be the first of more than one—framed and hanging on the wall over my desk, a stark focal point in my chronically cluttered office. Out of the thousands of asteroids we tracked and photographed, this one caught my eye, because it was symmetrical and had a higher than normal albedo. It flashed, even, like a mirror. Asteroids aren't symmetrical and aren't very reflective. But if it wasn't an asteroid . . .

We turned as many telescopes on it as we could. Tried to get time on Hubble and failed, because it sounded ridiculous—why waste time looking at something inside the orbit of Jupiter? We *did* get Arecibo on it. We got pictures from multiple sources, studied them for weeks until we couldn't argue with them any longer. No one wanted to say it because it was crazy, just thinking it would get you sacked, and I got so frustrated with the whole group sitting there in the conference room after hours on a Friday afternoon, staring at each other with wide eyes and dropped jaws and no one saying anything, that I said it: It's not natural, and it's not ours.

UO-1 was approximately 250 meters long, with a fan shape at one end, blurred at the other, as if covered with projections too fine to show up at that resolution. The rest was perfectly straight, a thin stalk holding together blossom and roots, the lines rigid and artificial. The fan shape might be a ram scoop—Angie came up with that idea, and the conjecture stuck, no matter how much I reminded people that we couldn't decide anything about what it was or what it meant. Not until we knew more.

We—the scientific community, astronomers, philosophers, writers, all of humanity—had spent a lot of time thinking about what would happen if we found definitive proof that intelligent life existed elsewhere in the universe. All the scenarios involved these other intelligences talking to us. Reaching out to us. Sending a message we would have to decipher—would be eager to decipher. Hell, we sure wouldn't be able to talk to them, not stuck on our own collection of rocks like we were. Whether people thought we'd be overrun with sadistic tripods or be invited to join a greater benevolent galactic society, that was always the assumption—we'd know they were there because they'd talk to us.

When that didn't happen, it was like no one knew what to do next. No one had thought about what would happen if we just found a . . . a *thing* . . . that happened to be drifting a few million miles out from the moon. It didn't talk. Not so much as a blinking light. The radiation we detected from it was reflected—whatever propulsion had driven it through space had long since stopped, and inertia carried it now. No one knew how to respond to it. The news that was supposed to change the course of human history . . . didn't.

We wouldn't know any more about it until we looked at it up close, until we brought it here, brought it home. And that was where it all fell apart.

I presented the initial findings at the International Astronomical Union annual meeting. My department gathered the data, but we couldn't do anything about implementation—no one group could implement *anything*. But of course, the first argument was about whom the thing belonged to. I nearly resigned.

Everyone wanted a piece of it, including various governments and the United Nations, and we had to humor that debate because nothing could get done without funding. The greatest discovery in all of human history and funding held it hostage. Several corporations, including the producers of a popular energy drink, threatened to mount their own expeditions in order to establish naming and publicity rights, until the U.S. Departments of Energy, Transportation, and Defense issued joint restrictions on privately-funded extra-orbital spaceflight, which caused its own massive furor.

Meanwhile, we and the various other groups working on the project tracked UO-1 as it appeared to establish an elliptical solar orbit that would take it out to the orbit of Saturn and back on a twenty-year cycle. We waited. We developed plans, which were presented and rejected. We took better and better pictures, which revealed enough detail to see struts holding up what did indeed appear to be the surface of a ram scoop. It did not, everyone slowly began to agree, appear to be inhabited. The data on it never fluctuated. No signals emanated from it. It was metal, it was solid, it was inert. We published papers and appeared on cable documentaries. We gritted our teeth while websites went up claiming that the thing was a weapon, and a survivalist movement developed in response. Since it was indistinguishable from all the existing survivalist movements, no one really noticed.

And we waited.

The thing is, you discover the existence of extraterrestrial intelligence, and you still have to go home, wash up, get a good night's sleep, and come up with something to eat for breakfast in the morning. Life goes on, life keeps going on, and it's not that people forget or stop being interested. It's that they realize they still have to change the oil in the car and take the dog for a walk. You feel like the whole world ought to be different, but it only shifts. Your worldview expands to take in this new information.

I go to work every day and look at that picture, *my* picture, this satellite or spacecraft, this message in a bottle. Some days I'm furious that I can't get my hands on it. Some days I weep at the wonder of it. Most days I look at it, sigh, and write another round of emails and make phone calls to find out what's going to happen to it. To *make* something happen.

"How goes the war?" Marsh leans into my office like he does every afternoon, mostly to try to cheer me up. He's been here as long as I have; our work overlaps, and we've become friends. I go to his kids' birthday parties. The brown skin around his eyes crinkles with his smile. I'm not able to work up a smile to match.

"The Chinese say they're sending a probe with a robotic arm and a booster to grab it and pull it back to Earth. They say whoever gets there first has right of salvage. It's a terrible idea. Even if they did manage to get it back without breaking it, they'd never let anyone else look at it."

"Oh, I think they would—under their terms." He doesn't get too worked up about it because nobody's managed to do anything yet, why would they now? He would say I take all of this too personally, and he'd be right.

"The IAU is sending a delegation to try to talk the Chinese government into joining the coalition. They might have a chance of it if they actually had a plan of their own. Look, if you want me to talk your ear off, come in and sit, have some coffee. Otherwise, leave now. That's your warning."

"I'll take the coffee," he says, claiming the chair I pulled away from the wall for him before turning to my little desktop coffee maker. His expression softens, his sympathy becoming genuine rather than habitual. "You backing any particular plan yet?"

I sigh. "Gravity tractor looks like our best option. Change the object's trajectory, steer it into a more convenient orbit without actually touching it. Too bad the technology is almost completely untested. We can test it first, of course. Which will take years. And there's an argument against it. Emissions from a gravity tractor's propulsion may damage the object. It's the root of the whole problem: we don't know enough about the thing to know how much stress it can take. The cowboys want to send a crewed mission—they say the only way to be sure is to get eyeballs on the thing. But that triples the cost of any mission. Anything we do will take years of planning and implementation anyway, so no one can be bothered to get off their asses. Same old, same old."

Two and half years. It's been two and a half years since we took that picture. My life has swung into a very tight orbit around this one thing.

"Patience, Jane," Marsh says in a tone that almost sets me off. He's only trying to help.

Truth is, I've been waiting for his visit. I pull out a sheet of handwritten calculations from under a manila folder. "I do have another idea, but I wanted to talk to you about it before I propose anything." His brow goes up, he leans in with interest.

He'll see it faster than I can explain it, so I speak carefully. "We can use Angelus." When he doesn't answer, yes or no, I start to worry and talk to cover it up. "It launches in six months, plenty of time to reprogram the trajectory, send it on a flyby past UO-1, get more data on it than we'll ever get sitting here on Earth—"

His smile has vanished. "Jane. I've been waiting for Angelus for five years. The timing is critical. My comet won't be this close for another two hundred years."

"But Angelus is the only mission launching in the next year with the right kind of optics and maneuverability to get a good look at UO-1, and yes, I know the timing on the comet is once-in-a-lifetime and I know it's important. But this—this is once in a *civilization*. The sooner we can look at it, answer some of our questions . . . well. The sooner the better."

"The better *you'll* be. I'm supposed to wait, but you can't?"

"Please, Marsh. I'll feel a lot better about it if you'll agree with me."

"Thank you for the coffee, Jane," he says, setting aside the mug as he stands.

I close my eyes and beseech the ceiling. This isn't how I want this to go. "Marsh, I'm not trying to sabotage your work, I'm just looking at available resources—"

"And I'm not ultimately the one who makes decisions about what happens to Angelus. I'm just the one depending on all the data. You can make your proposal, but don't ask me to sign off on it."

He starts to leave and I say, "Marsh. I can't take it anymore. I spend every day holding my breath, waiting for someone to do something truly stupid. Some days I can't stand it that I can't get my hands on it."

He sits back down, like a good friend should. A good friend would not, however, steal a colleague's exploratory probe away from him. But this is *important*.

"You know what I think? The best bet is to let one of these corporate foundations mount an expedition. They won't want to screw up because of the bad publicity, and they'll bring you on board for credibility so you'll have some say in how they proceed. You'll be their modern-day Howard Carter."

I can see it now: I'd be the face of the expedition, all I'd have to do is stand there and look pretty. Or at least studious. Explain gravity and trajectories for the popular audience. Speculate on the composition of alien alloys. Watch whatever we find out there get paraded around the globe to shill corn chips. Wouldn't even feel like I was selling my soul, would it?

I must look green, or ill, or murderous, because Marsh goes soothing. "Just think about it, before you go and do something crazy."

I've kept a dedicated SETI@home computer running since I was sixteen. Marsh doesn't know that about me. I don't believe in extraterrestrial UFOs because I know in great, intimate detail the difficulties of sending objects across the vast distances of space. Hell, just a few hundred miles into orbit isn't a picnic. We've managed it, of course—we are officially extra-solar system beings, now, with our little probes and plaques pushing ever outward. Will they find anything? Will anything find *them*?

Essentially, there are two positions on the existence of extraterrestrial intelligence and whether we might ever make contact, and they both come down to the odds. The first says that *we're* here, humanity is intelligent, flinging out broadcasts and training dozens of telescopes outward hoping for the least little sign, and the universe is so immeasurably vast that given the odds, the billions of stars and galaxies and planets out there, we can't possibly be the only intelligent species doing these things. The second position says that the odds of life coming into being on any given planet, of that life persisting long enough to evolve, then to evolve intelligence, and then being interested in the same things we are—the odds of all those things falling into place are so immeasurably slim, we may very well be the only ones here.

Is the universe half full or half empty? All we could ever do to solve the riddle was wait. So I waited and was rewarded for my optimism.

In unguarded moments I'm certain this was meant to happen, I was meant to discover UO-1. Me and no one else. Because I understand how important it is. Because I'm the one sitting here every day sending emails and making phone calls. I ID'd the image, I made the call, I had the guts to go public, I deserve a say in what happens next.

I submit the paperwork proposing that the Angelus probe be repurposed to perform a flyby and survey of UO-1. Marsh will forgive me. I wait. Again.

I've kept track, and I've done a hundred fifty TV interviews in the last two years. Most of them are snippets for pop-documentaries, little chunks of information delivered to the lowest common denominator audience. I explain over and over again, in different settings, sometimes in my office, sometimes in a vague but picturesque location, sometimes at Griffith Observatory, because for some reason nothing says "space" like Griffith Observatory. I hold up a little plastic model of UO-1 (they're selling the kits at hobby stores—we don't see any of the money from that) to demonstrate the way it's traveling through space, how orbital mechanics work, and how we might use a gravity tractor to bring it home. Sometimes, the segments are specifically for schools, and I like those best because I can give free rein to my enthusiasm. I tell the kids, "This is going to take more than one lifetime to figure out. If we find a way to go to Alpha Centauri, it's going to take lifetimes. You'll have to finish the work I've started. Please grow up and finish it."

I call everyone I can think of who might have some kind of influence over Angelus. I explain that a picture of a metal object taken from a few million miles away doesn't tell us anything about the people who made it. Not even if they have thumbs or tentacles. Most of them tell me that the best plan they can think of is to build bigger telescopes.

"It's not the size," I mutter. "It's how you use it."

NASA thinks they will be making the decision because they've got the resources, the scientists, the experience, the hardware. Congress says this is too important to let NASA make decisions unilaterally. A half dozen private U.S. firms would try something if the various cabinet departments weren't busy making anything they could try illegal by fiat. There are already three court cases. At least one of them is arguing that a rocket launch is protected as freedom of speech. The IAU brought a complaint to the United Nations that the U.S. government shouldn't be allowed to dictate a course of action. The General Assembly nominated a "representative in absentia" for the species that launched UO-1—some Finnish philosopher I'd never heard of. It should have been me.

After a decade of international conferences I have colleagues all over the world. I call them all. Most are sympathetic. A South African cosmologist I know tells me I'm grandstanding, then laughs like it's a joke, but not really. They all tell me to be patient. Just wait.

Life goes on. My other research, the asteroid research I was doing, has piled up, and I get polite but firm hints that I really ought to work on that if I want to keep my job. I go to conferences, I publish, I do another dozen interviews, holding up the plastic model of the object that I'll likely never get close to. The ache in my heart feels just like it did when Peter left me. That was three years ago, and I can still feel it. The ache that says: I can't possibly start over, can I?

The ache faded when I found UO-1.

"JPL rejected your proposal to repurpose Angelus. Thank God." Marsh leans on my doorway like usual. He's grinning like he won a prize.

I got the news via email. The bastards can't even be bothered to call. I'd called them back, thinking there must have been a mistake. The pitying tone in their voices didn't sound like kindness anymore. It was definitely condescension. I cried. I've been crying all afternoon, as the pile of wadded-up tissues on my desk attests. My eyes are still puffy. Marsh can see I've been crying; he knows what it looks like when I cry. He was there three years ago. I take a breath to keep from starting up again and stare at him like he's punched me.

"How can you say that? Do you know what they're talking about now? They're talking about just leaving it! They're saying the orbit is stable, we'll always know where it is and we can go after it when we have a better handle on the technology. But what if something happens to it? What if an asteroid hits it, or it crashes into Jupiter, or—"

"Jane, it's been traveling for how many hundreds of billions of miles—why would something happen to it now?"

"I don't know! It shouldn't even be there at all! And they won't even *listen* to me!"

He sounds tired. "Why should they?"

"Because it's *mine!*"

His normally comforting smile is sad, pitying, smug, and amused, all at once. "It's not yours, not any more than gravity belonged to Newton."

I want to scream. Because maybe this isn't the most important thing to happen to humanity. That's probably, oh, the invention of the wheel, or language. Maybe this is just the most important thing to happen to me.

I grab another tissue. Look at the picture of UO-1. It's beautiful. It tells me that the universe, as vast as we already know it is, is bigger than we think.

Marsh sits in the second chair without waiting for an invitation. "What do you think it is, Jane? Be honest. No job, no credibility, no speaking gig for *Discovery* on the line. What do you think when you look at it?" He nods at the picture.

There are some cable shows that will win you credibility for appearing on them. There are some that will destroy any credibility you ever had. I have been standing right on that line, answering the question of "What is it?" as vaguely as possible. We need to know more, no way to speculate, et cetera. But I know. I *know* what it is.

"I think it's Voyager. Not *the* Voyager. *Their* Voyager. The probe they sent out to explore, and it just kept going."

He doesn't laugh. "You think we'll find a plaque on it? A message? A recording?"

"It's what I want to find." I smile wistfully. "But what are the odds?"

"Gershwin," he says. I blink, but he doesn't seem offended by my confusion. He leans back in the chair, comfortable in his thick middle-aged body, genial, someone who clearly believes all is well with the world, at least at the moment. "We've had fourteen billion years of particles colliding, stars exploding, nebulae compressing, planets forming, all of it cycling over and over again, and then just the right amino acids converged, life forms, and a couple of billion years of evolution later—we get Gene Kelly and Leslie Caron dancing by a fountain to Gershwin and it's beautiful. For no particular evolution-driven reason, it's beautiful. I think: what are the odds? That they're dancing, that it's on film, and that I'm here watching and thinking it's gorgeous. If the whole universe exists just to make this one moment happen, I wouldn't be at all surprised."

"So if I think sometimes that maybe I was meant to find UO-1, because maybe there's a message there and that I'm the only one who can read it—then maybe that's not crazy?" Like thinking that the universe sent me UO-1 at a time in my life when I desperately needed something to focus on, to be meaningful . . .

"Oh no, it's definitely crazy. But it's understandable." This time his smile is kind.

"Marsh—this really is the most important thing to happen to humanity ever, isn't it?"

"Yes. But we still need to study and map near-Earth asteroids, right?"

I don't tell Marsh that I've never seen *An American in Paris*. I've never watched Gene Kelly in anything. But Marsh obviously thinks it's important, so I watch the movie. I decide he's right. That dance at the fountain, it's a moment suspended in time. Like an alien spacecraft that shouldn't be there but is.

*

Two things happen next.

At the next IAU meeting an archaeologist presents a lecture on UO-1, which I think is very presumptuous, but I go, because I go to everything having to do with UO-1. She talks about preservation and uses terms like "in situ," and how modern archaeological practice often involves excavating artifacts, examining them—and then putting them back in the ground. She argues that we don't know what years of space travel have done to the metal and structures of UO-1. We don't know how our methods of studying it will impact it. She showed pictures of Mayan friezes that were excavated and left exposed to the elements versus ones that remained buried for their own protection, so that later scientists with better equipment and techniques will be able to return to them someday. The exposed ones have dissolved, decayed past recognition. She gives me an image: I reach out and finally put my hand on UO-1, and its metallic skin, weakened by a billion micrometeoroid impacts gathered over millennia, disintegrates under my touch.

I think of that and start to sweat. So yes, caution. I know this.

The second thing that happens: I turn my back on UO-1.

Not really, but it's a striking image. I write another proposal, a different proposal, and submit it to one of the corporate foundations because Marsh may be right. If nothing else, it'll get attention. I don't mind a little grandstanding.

We already have teams tracking a best-guess trajectory to determine where UO-1 came from. It might have been cruising through space at nonrelativistic speed for dozens of years, or centuries, or millions of centuries, but based on the orbit it established here, we can estimate how it entered the solar system and the trajectory it traveled before then. We can trace backward.

My plan: to send a craft in that direction. It will do a minimal amount of science along the way, sending back radiation readings, but most of the energy and hardware is going into propulsion. It will be fast and it will have purpose, carrying an updated variation of Sagan's Voyager plaques and recordings, digital and analog.

It's a very simple message, in the end: Hey, we found your device. Want one of ours?

In all likelihood, the civilization that built UO-1 is extinct. The odds simply aren't good for a species surviving—and caring—for long enough to send a message and receive a reply. But our sample size for drawing that conclusion about the average lifespan of an entire species on a particular world is exactly one, which isn't a sample size at all. We weren't supposed to ever find an alien ship in our backyard, either.

I tear up when the rocket launches, and that makes for good TV. As Marsh predicted, the documentary producers decide to make me the human face of the project, and I figure I'll do what I have to, as best as I can. I develop a collection of quotes for the dozens of interviews that follow—I'm up to two-hundred thirty-five. I talk about taking the long view and transcending the everyday concerns that bog us down. About how we are children reaching across the sandbox with whatever we have to offer, to whoever shows up. About teaching our children to think as big as they possibly can, and that miracles sometimes really do happen. They happen often, because all of this, Gershwin's music, the great curry I had for dinner last night, the way we hang pictures on our walls of things we love, are miracles that never should have happened.

It's a hope, a need, a shout, a shot in the dark. It's the best we can do. For now.

STRIFE LINGERS
IN MEMORY

My father was a wise man to whom many came seeking advice. During his audiences I'd lurk behind his chair or fetch his cup, and they called me fair, even when I was little. I grew to be golden-haired and wary. I was destined for—something.

War overwhelmed us. The Heir to the Fortress was dead—no, in exile, nearly the same. The evil rose, broke the land over an iron knee, and even my father went into hiding.

Then he came.

I was eighteen. The stranger was—hard to say. He looked young but carried such a weight of care, he might have lived many lifetimes already. He came to ask my father how he might make his way along the cursed paths that led to the ancient fortress now held by the enemy.

My father proclaimed, "That way is barred to any who are not of the Heir's blood, but that line is dead. It is useless."

Our gazes met, mine and that stranger's, and I saw in him a shuttered light waiting to blaze forth. I gripped the back of my father's chair to steady myself.

The stranger and I knew in that moment what was destined to be, though our elders needed a bit more persuading.

So it came to pass that the stranger, Evrad—Heir to the Fortress, the true-blooded prince himself—took the cursed paths and led an army to overthrow the stronghold of his enemy and claim the ancient fortress as his own. He married the wizard's daughter and made her— me—his Queen. Happily, the land settled into a long-awaited peace.

The night after the day of his coronation and of our wedding we had alone and to ourselves. When the door closed, we looked at one another for a long time, not believing that this moment had come at last, remembering all the moments we believed it would not come at all. Then, all at once, we fell into each other's arms.

He made love to me as if the world were ending. I drowned in the fury of it, clinging to him like he was a piece of splintered hull after a shipwreck. Exhausted, we rested in each other's arms. I sang him to sleep and, running my fingers through his thick hair, fell asleep myself.

I had dreamed of this, sleeping protected by him. I had dreamed of waking in his arms, sunlight through the window painting our chamber golden, drawing on his warmth in the chill of morning.

Instead, I awoke to the sound of a scream. Evrad's scream. He thrashed, kicking me. I backed away, arms covering my head. Our blankets twisted, pulling away from the bed as he fought with them. When I dared to look, he had curled up, drawing his limbs close. He was trembling so hard I felt it through the bed.

"Evrad?" I whispered. He remained hunched over and shaking, so I reached for him. "Evrad. Please."

I touched his shoulder, the slope of it glowing pale in moonlight shining through the window. It was damp with sweat.

He flinched at the touch and looked at me, his eyes wide and wild. My stomach clenched—he did not seem to see me.

Then, "Alida?"

He came to life, returned to himself, and pulled me close in an embrace. I held him as tightly as I could, but my grip seemed so weak compared to his.

"Oh, my love," he said over and over. "I thought it was a dream: you, peace—you. I dreaded waking to find you weren't real."

"Hush. Oh, please hush. You're safe."

I said those words to him many times, on many nights. I kept hoping he would believe me.

Strife lingered in the memory of what we had suffered. He defeated an army of horrors, but the demons may yet overcome him.

He kept the nightmares well-hidden. He always appeared to his men, his guards, his people as the hero, the savior, the King. He looked the part, standing tall, smiling easily and accepting gracefully the adoration of hardened warriors and toddling children alike.

He turned his best face toward the people, keeping his secret soul hidden. But he could not hide it from me. So it fell to me to keep my best face toward him, to be strong for him, and hide my secret soul away.

One night, he came to our chamber carrying an arcane-looking bottle covered with dust, the cap sealed with wax.

"I will sleep through the night," he said in much the same way he'd once said he would defeat the dark army that threatened to overrun him. Liquid sloshed in the bottle when he set it on the table.

"What is it? Rare potion?"

"Rare whiskey," he said with a grunt. "Perhaps it will make me forget the shadows."

I pursed my lips, making a wry smile. "That will inspire sweet dreams, and not the comfort of my arms?"

"Oh, my love." He touched my cheek with all the tenderness I could hope for, though his face was lined with worry. I took his hands, locking their anxious movements in mine.

Once, we needed no words, but I could not read the thoughts that clouded his expression. During the war, he had been proud, his look keen and determined. I had never seen him so careworn.

He kissed my hands and went out of our chambers. At least he left the whiskey behind.

A month passed, then came the night I awoke alone.

Perhaps the stillness woke me. Midnight—the dark chill of night when he usually began sweating, trembling as if all the fears he had kept at bay during the war came on him at once—had passed and no screams woke me. I sat up, felt all around the bed, looked when my sight adjusted to the dark. I was alone.

I searched for him. Wrapping my cloak tight around me, I went along the battlements where I could see half the realm across the plains. I searched the stables, where he might have sought the calm influence of sleeping horses. I carried a lantern through stone corridors where no one had walked since Evrad claimed the fortress.

I found him crouched in a forgotten corner, arms wrapped around his head, face turned to the wall. He had managed to tie a cloak around his middle, but it was slipping off his shoulders.

A guard walking his post from the other end of the corridor found him at the same time. "My liege!" the man cried and rushed toward him.

I interposed, stopping him with a raised hand. "Please. Stay back." Turning to Evrad I said, "My lord? My lord, are you awake?"

I touched his shoulder. He looked at me. The lantern light showed his cheeks wet with tears. "Come, my lord. Let's go to bed." I helped him to his feet, like he was an old man or a child.

To the guard I said, "You will not speak of this. You will keep this secret." And what of the next night? And what of the night the guards found him before I did? I was a wizard's daughter but I still needed sleep. I needed more eyes. "You will help me keep this secret, yes?"

"Yes, my Queen. Oh yes." Wonder and pity filled his gaze. I remembered his face, learned his name, Petro. If I ever heard rumor of the King's illness, this man would answer for it.

We had fair nights. Some nights, he only whimpered in his sleep, in the throes of visions I did not want to imagine. Some nights, drunk on wine, we threw logs on the fire until it blazed, making the room hot, and we played until we wore each other out.

Other nights, I wore my cloak, took another in case he had lost his, and searched deserted corridors by lantern light. I always waited until I had put him back to bed and he slept before I sat by the fire and cried.

*

At last, weary and despairing, I departed in the shrouded hour before dawn. I used craft that my father taught me: how to move without sound, how to turn aside the curious gaze, how to not leave tracks. I left my own horse behind and took one from the couriers that would not be so quickly missed. I rode hard, turned off the main way, and found the forested path that led through ravine and glen to my father's valley.

After the war, he secluded himself in a valley beyond the line of hills where the city lay, a day's journey away. He said he wished to be out of reach of peaceful folk who would trouble him with petty complaints now that the great matters were over. He said he was finished dispensing wisdom for people simply because they asked for it.

What a gentle place. I had traveled with him when he came to live here, but my heart had been so full of the times, of the ache of war and separation from my beloved, that I hadn't looked around me. Water ran frothing down a rocky hillside and became a stream that flowed through a meadow of tall grass scattered with the color of wildflowers. Late sun shining through pollen turned the air golden. I could smell the light, fresh and fertile.

I made a mistake. I shouldn't have run away. Or better, I should have brought Evrad here, to this peace.

The whitewashed cottage sat where the grass ended and trees began. Smoke rose from a hole in the roof.

My horse, breathing hard and soaked with sweat, sighed deeply and lowered her head to graze. I pulled off her tack, brushed her, and let her roam free. I left my gear by the cottage's door and went inside.

A fire burned at the hearth in the back of the cottage's one room. Near it were a kettle and all manner of cooking implements. A cot occupied one corner, a table and chair another, and the rest of the walls had shelves and shelves of books. My father sat in a great stuffed chair near the fire, wrapped in a blanket, gazing into a shallow bowl of water he held in his lap.

Quietly, I sat at his feet as I had when I was little.

"My Queen, is it?" he said. A smile shifted the wrinkles of his face. He was bald, but for a fringe of white hair.

"Your daughter still."

"No, I gave you away."

"Father—"

He sighed. "Why have you come here? What trouble drives you from your home?"

"Perhaps I only wish to visit you."

"I still have sight, girl." He touched the surface of the water in the basin and flicked his fingers at me, sprinkling me. I flinched, then hugged my knees.

He shook his head. "I was supposed to be able to leave the keeping of the world to its heirs."

"If you have your sight, then you know what is wrong."

"Tell me. I want to hear what you think is wrong."

I was Queen of this land, the destined love of the greatest of heroes, fortunate and blessed beyond reason, and he made me feel like a hapless child. Perhaps that was why the heroes in the stories were almost always orphans.

"The war haunts him," I said. "He has nightmares. He cannot sleep. He buries all this deep in his heart, but it is festering there. How long can he survive like this? I am afraid, more afraid than I ever was when he carried his sword against the enemy. I try to comfort him. I don't know what to do."

Grunting with the effort, he leaned over the arm of his chair to set the basin on the floor. "So, are you looking for a potion or a spell that will set all to rights?"

I hadn't thought of that, when I decided to come here. If there were such a thing I would gladly take it. But my coming here was selfish. I wanted to rest in the shelter of another, as tired as I was of *being* shelter for another.

"Or do you simply flee from what you do not understand?"

I could have cried, but I pretended to be strong. In a world where fate had ordered all our actions and brought us all to this point, I was terrified that it should leave us now. "The evil lingers. I thought he had defeated it for all time."

"He is battle weary. That is no surprise. As for a cure? Time and care. I know no magic to speed it along. We must be vigilant. Each of us has a role in the war. Now, yours has come."

"But he is the warrior and King, I am just a—" I almost said any of a dozen things: woman, child, pawn, symbol. None of the stories prepared me to be anything else.

"He is King, so he must hide his fears. It falls to you, then, to keep him sane."

"This has been a mistake. Would the true Heir of the Fortress suffer so?"

"Would one who was not the Heir have survived to suffer so?"

"I cannot do this," I said, tears falling at last.

My father smiled and touched my hair with his arthritic hand. "He said the same thing to me before he departed for the last battle. I will tell you what I told him." He held my hand. His was warm and dry. "'That may be true,' I said. 'But you must try, because no one else will.'"

I pressed his hand to my face, wishing I was a child again, able to hide behind his chair and take no part in the worries of the world.

He continued, "You may have the hardest battle of all. No one victory will defeat this enemy. This is not a beast to slay and be done with."

"And no one will sing of my battles."

I slept curled in a blanket near the hearth that night—the first night in many I had not been awakened by sleepwalking or nightmare cries. I treasured the peace of the valley. In the morning, I sat in the meadow by the stream. Since settling at the fortress and into my life as Queen, I had seldom touched living earth or smelled grass and wildflowers warmed by the sun. Here, I could pretend none of it had happened.

My father joined me. He spent a long time settling to the ground, leaning on his cane. He'd never used a cane before. Too late, I reached to help him, to give him my arm to lean on. He'd never needed help before, so I didn't think of it. He spent time arranging his cane and robes around him, gazing over the dancing water.

"When will you return to him?" he said at last.

"I don't know." I had to gather my strength. I could spend the rest of my life gathering strength and still not have enough.

"Make it soon."

I'd been picking at grass, weaving something of a tangled wreath. I threw the mess of it into the stream. "If you don't wish me to stay, I can go elsewhere."

"I want you to go to your home. Your child should know his father."

"My—" I flushed, my whole body burning from my scalp to my bare toes. Then the expected movement: I put my hand on my belly. "You don't mean—"

He smiled, a cat-wise smile of secrets. "I still have sight. You—are still learning."

A child. Me—a child. My child. *His* child. Oh, have mercy. Forgive me.

"Father, I must go."

"Yes, you must."

I caught my horse, saddled her quickly, and fled in a whirlwind. I had galloped a mile when I pulled up suddenly—I was carrying a child. I should be more careful.

What would Evrad say? Perhaps he would sleep well, with a child in his arms.

Halfway back to the fortress, a thunder of hoofbeats galloped toward me. I waited for the rider to appear around the curve in the road. The horse was a snow white charger, with a gold breastplate and gold fixings on his tack, tail flying, mane rippling. His rider pulled up hard, and his hooves raised dust as he skidded in the road.

I knew this stallion, and I knew the rider who jumped from the saddle and ran toward me.

As I dismounted I stumbled, my grip on the saddle keeping me upright. Here was my hero, my King, face uplifted, striding with strength and determination. Grim and fierce, as I had seen him ride to battle, as I had not seen him in weeks. I had not lost him to the war.

I would have run to meet him, but I had moved just a few steps away from my horse when he reached me. He caught me in his arms and held tight. His leather doublet pressed my flesh, his rough cheek brushed mine.

"I'm sorry," I cried again and again, weeping on his shoulder.

He made soothing noises. "Hush. It's enough that you're safe. I guessed where you had gone, and I meant to go and beg you to return. I meant to make promises—to tie myself to the bed so you wouldn't have to search after me at midnight anymore. To have my guards knock me unconscious every evening so I might sleep through the night."

I laughed. "No guard of yours would even try, my lord."

He touched my cheeks, wiping away tears. "I know you are a wizard's daughter. Your spirit is wild, free as the wind, and your will is strong. I have nothing that can bind you—but tell me you will never leave me again. Promise me."

Oh, how such words would bind me. Did he not know that words are nearly all that will bind a wizard, or his daughter?

"I promise," I said.

Men fight for symbols: a crown, a throne, lines on a map.

When he reclaimed the fortress and we married, our story ended but our lives didn't. None of the old stories prepared me for the battles I now fought.

I remembered the night he left my father's hall to meet the last battle, when all but I believed he was marching to his death.

I held him as long as I could. "I wish I could go with you. I wish I could do more than wait here for news."

"But you're already doing so much."

"What? What am I doing?" I said, smiling with wonder.

"You are the symbol of what we fight for: all that is beautiful."
Men fight for symbols. What do women fight for?

Again I wandered nighttime passages, my way lit by a dim lantern, searching. I moved slowly, some seven months along my child's time. I wore two cloaks and fur boots, because winter was upon us. On bad nights, when the terrors wrenched Evrad to immobility, he found dark passages and shivered there in the cold, fighting demons in his mind. I walked every corridor in the fortress and could not find him. Petro had not seen him either.

On bad nights, he hid in dark passages. This night was worse.

I found him on the battlements of the highest tower. A spire jutting above the sheer wall of the fortress, it served as a watchtower and a place for message fires. He leaned on the stone wall, gazing straight down, a hundred feet to hard earth.

I caught my breath and swallowed a scream.

"My lord? Evrad," I said softly, my voice shaking. "What are you doing?"

He climbed to sit on the lip of the wall. He looked at me; his eyes were feral, shining. He trembled. Sweat matted his hair, and his face was pale, drained of blood. He wore only breeches, and gooseflesh covered his arms.

If I reached for him, the gesture might push him over.

"Go back to bed. Why must you follow me?"

Because I loved him. Because I worried about him. Because it was my duty, and I must do it so the secret of his nighttime terrors did not spread. But I didn't say those things.

"I will follow you to the end of the world, over cliffs into fiery rifts that split the earth if I must. But I will follow you."

"Like the demons."

"I'm faster than demons. They will not reach you before I do."

"Will you follow me there?" He nodded over the wall to the long drop.

The moon shone near full, low in the sky, painting the land with shadows. Lurking behind each house and tower and city wall, stretching away from every rise in the land, every tree on the plain, black shapes reached toward the fortress.

"They whisper in my ear, *jump*. Oh Alida."

My knees gave way and I sat on the stone, lurching with my swollen weight. I couldn't shutter the moon, to chase away the shadows.

"Evrad. What did you fight for? Did you fight for this, to cast yourself off a tower? Then they've won. The enemy is dead and gone, but will still win the war. It was all for nothing. What did you fight for?"

"I don't know anymore—"

"Me, Evrad! You fought for me! Now I am yours. You don't have to fight anymore. You've won."

He shook his head. "I'm not worthy of you. You deserve better. Someone who doesn't have nightmares."

I laughed, clapping my hand over my mouth because the sound was so acrid. "I deserve better? Evrad—you are the hero of the age, the king of legends. And I deserve *better*? Who do you think I am?"

He looked at me. His frown was long, unmovable. "You are everything."

I crawled toward him. "Come down from there, Evrad. Come to me." I stretched my hand to him. I had to be stronger than the shadows. My voice had to be more alluring. "Touch me. Just touch me."

A small goal, an easy quest, well within his reach. A slender hand, poised in the dark. He leaned, lips parted in an expression of longing.

He fell off the lip of the wall and into my arms.

"I don't want better. I don't want the hero and king. I want you." We sat for many hours, hugging each other against the cold.

I brought him to bed and wrapped myself around him. He shivered. I was not blanket enough against the cold.

"Do you see them? In the shadows on the wall," he said. Candle flames flickered in a draft. The warped shadows of a cup, a candlestick, a comb danced and trembled all around.

"It's only light and dark."

"I know that—but I see memories. I see a thousand goblin warriors throwing themselves against the burning ramparts of the city. I see them pulling my men into the flames. And there's nothing I can do. I didn't destroy them. They're still here, watching us."

Almost I could see their red eyes and clawed hands. For all his army had saved, ten thousand men had perished in the war. Goblins shook spears which rippled like ocean waves above their heads. I had not been there, yet I could almost see. He lived with such visions in his waking mind. How did he endure?

I got up and blew out the candle, banishing the shadows. Returning to bed, I pressed myself against his back and whispered in his ear. "They're gone now."

He was crying.

Over time, we learned what sparked the grim memories. Bonfires. Shadows under a full moon. Then, our sons in armor. Oh, were his nightmares fierce after Biron's first day in armor. If I could have changed the world, altered the course of sun and moon, rewritten tales of destiny that had been put down by great unseen hands, our children would never have learned to fight. But they were the children of a King and must learn the ways of arms. Evrad insisted on this. Even after waking in the night and telling me that the faces of his men dying over and over in his dreams had changed, and were now the faces of our children.

Over time, nights became easier. With children to occupy him—first a son, then two daughters, and two more sons—he went to bed happy and weary. He did not notice the shadows so much.

Thus peace ruled the land for our children's time, and our children's children's time, and will rule beyond. Just like in the stories.

I sit by a window, my gray hair braided behind me, my withered hands resting on a worn blanket. Evrad is also old, but he wears his age, his gray, and his wrinkles like a prize. He still rides out, straight as a statue in the saddle, and I still wait for him.

Behind me, a door opens and closes softly. Our youngest son, Perrin, attempts to not disturb me. I don't have to look; I am my father's daughter, and I have acquired some of his sight over the years. My father is long dead.

Perrin comes to my chair and kneels on the rug. This puts him at the height he was as a boy. I look on him as if he is a boy come to beg a favor. But he is a man, with a beard and his father's bold eyes.

"Mother? I've almost finished. But I have one last question."

My other children have become warriors, diplomats, husbands, wives, parents, leaders and healers. Perrin, while he dutifully learned swordplay and manners along with his siblings, has become none of these. He is a scholar, historian, chronicler. A bard.

He has been writing an account of the great War of the Fortress and the turning of the age. I've read parts of it—what he has seen fit to show me—and hardly recognize the events and trials I lived through. It reads like the old stories.

"Oh?" I say. "Why not just invent an answer? It won't sound any more outlandish than what's there already."

"I've written no lies—"

"No, of course not. But you've painted the truth with bold colors indeed." Gah, that's something my father might have said.

He looks away, smirking. Like I might have done, kneeling at my father's chair. "I have a question about a thing I am not sure even happened."

He paused, wincing in difficult thought, trying to speak—my son the bard, tongue tied. I might have laughed, but he looked to be in pain. Finally, he said,

"When I was young, quite small, a noise woke me, and I was afraid. I thought to go to your chamber to seek comfort. The passages were very dark. I crept along the walls like a mouse, fearful of losing my way in my own home. Then, I heard crying. I turned a corner and saw a lantern. In the circle of light I saw you and Father sitting on the floor. You held him in your arms, and he was crying. I thought his heart would break. And I realized—he was afraid of something, more afraid than I was or had ever been. That sight . . . terrified me. I ran back to my own bed. I trembled under my blankets until dawn, and never spoke of it until now.

"Tell me: what I saw—was it real? Did it happen?"

Evrad and I have even managed to keep our troubles from our children. Mostly. He walks in his sleep rarely these days. No reason anyone should know.

"Yes. It happened that night and many others. The horrors of that war have haunted him for many years. It may be that the enemy left him with such visions as revenge, as a final defiance. Or perhaps it is the price for victory." I shake my head. I have invented many excuses, but the simplest is probably the truest: his memory haunts him, and there is no one to blame.

I lean forward and rest my hand on Perrin's shoulder. "You must not write of this. You must not add this to your chronicle."

"But—it means the hero's journey is not ended. It adds all the more to his victory, that he has continued to struggle and continued to win—"

"The hero must be strong, more than human, and when he becomes King, his struggles should be over. *That* is the end of the story. That is the law of stories, Perrin, however else the rest of us must live. If people saw him any different—some spirit would go out of the world, I think. People would believe in him less." I sit back and take a tired breath.

"Believe in him less because he is human?"

"Just so."

I watch Perrin thinking. As a child, his questions went on longer than any of the others' did. He was the one who wanted to know why different birds had different songs, and why water could not flow up-hill. He exhausted my ability to make answers. Even now, I hope he has no more questions.

"I understand, I think," he says at last. "The war ends, the age ends, the story ends."

"So the children can make their own stories."

He nods, and wonder of wonders I think he does understand. "One more question," he says, and I brace. "Which was harder? The battles leading into the new age, or the ones after?"

Strange. Looking back now, I only remember the ones after. The ones before happened to someone else, in another age.

I click my tongue and think of what my father might have said. "That's not a fair question. It doesn't matter which is harder, because no one will ever know of the battles after."

Shadows writhe across the floor and climb to the ceiling. They swim around the bed and my sleeping lord. One is like a laughing mouth, another like a reaching hand that touches the slope of his shoulder.

"Get away from him." I have drunk too much wine and my vision is spinning. I throw the cup. Wine flies in a spray of droplets across the floor. The silver cup drops with a ringing noise. The sound of swords striking or inhuman teeth gnashing in a cry of victory.

"He is mine!" I cry, standing. "You cannot have him."

Blood rushes in my ears like laughter. I want to scream, I open my mouth to scream, and then—

"Dear heart? What are you doing?" Sitting up, he rubs sleep from his eyes, his brow furrowed with curiosity.

"It's the light," I say in a fey mood. "You were right all along. The demons have come for us."

He searches the room, his eyes gold in the candle's glow. His face is calm, but he takes a trembling breath before saying, "It's only light. Come to bed."

"I must win you back. You fought a war and won. Now it's my turn. I will win you back!"

I clench my fists at my sides. My jaw trembles with an unsounded scream. My King watches me. Soon, the wrinkled brow eases, the tired face softens into a smile. To see him smile so, at night—but then, I must look amusing, in a rage, wine spilled around me, shift falling off my shoulders.

He says, simply as grass in summer, "I know you will. Come to bed, love."

I go to him, wrap my arms around him and kiss him, deeply, longingly. His hands press against me, inviting and warm. So warm.

He pulls away for just a moment. "I know how to chase away the shadows," he says, and blows out the candle.

A HUNTER'S ODE
TO HIS BAIT

Y ou're sure she's untouched?"
   "For God's sake yes. She's just a girl."
Duncan took the girl's face in his hands, tilted her head back, pried apart her lips and had a look at her teeth. Her frightened gaze darted between him and her mother. "Doesn't mean anything. There are whores younger than her."

She was twelve or thirteen, small and thin for her age but healthy—good teeth, straight back. In a year or so, with a few good meals in her, she'd be a beauty with golden hair and clear eyes.

Her mother stood a few steps away, wringing her hands and trying to maintain a business-like lack of expression. "I've heard men pay more for virgins."

"You heard right," Duncan said. "But you already agreed to my price. I'll take her." He tossed the pouch of silver at the woman. It landed at her feet, and she hurried to pick it up. Her husband was dead and she had eight other children to feed.

He went to where he'd tied his horse to a fence post. "Get your cloak, girl, and come on."

Barefoot, she stood in the dirt in front of the hovel and didn't move. "I don't have a cloak."

"Eleanor, go on." Her mother gestured, brushing her away like she was a wild dog.

She still didn't move, so Duncan picked her up and set her at the front of his saddle. He mounted behind her, wheeled his horse around, and rode off without a backward glance. She didn't struggle or cry at all, which worried him at first. Perhaps she was an idiot child.

Then she said, "What's a whore?"

He considered how to answer. The less she knew about such things the better, so he said nothing.

He kept her steady with an arm across her shoulders, and she was limp in his grasp.

In three days they reached the wilds of Northumbria, plunging straight into a forest of twisted oak. What few local folk there were would not enter the place because they said it was haunted. Duncan made camp in a glade where a spring flowed clear. He set the girl on the ground and left her huddled in the crook formed by an immense protruding root. He'd bought a cloak for her, and boots.

Late that afternoon, just before dusk, he took her to a glen dipped in the shadow of a hill. He carried his longbow, a quiver of arrows with varnished shafts, and his sword. He set about building a blind, a crawl space shadowed with leaves and branches that allowed a view of the whole clearing. The girl watched him with her wide, blue eyes and slack, numb face.

He bade her sit on a grassy hillock. She began to tremble, clutching the edges of her cloak and hugging herself. For a moment he doubted. What was he doing, paying silver for a slip of flesh and then dragging the poor girl out here? The prize, remember the prize. This would work.

"Don't be frightened," he said, putting a hand on her shoulder. "I'll be over there. Sit quietly, and the beast will appear. When it does, calm it."

"What beast?"

"You'll see."

He left her and went to his blind.

Wind shivered through the trees, sending autumn leaves raining.

One landed on the girl's cloak, and she brushed it off. Duncan held his bow with an arrow notched and watched all around the glen. Every whisper of leaves he took for footsteps.

Her fear passed with the time. She scratched at the dirt with a stick, played with the edges of her cloak. She started humming a country jig, a little off-tune. Over the next few days, Duncan kept the girl warm and fed, and she never complained.

After a week of sitting in the cold, the creature came.

It stepped out of the trees, out of the twilight mist, head low to the ground and nostrils quivering. A silver shadow in the form of a horse, seemingly made of mist itself. The long, spiral horn growing from its forehead reflected what little light remained in the world and seemed to glow.

The girl's gasp carried all the way to Duncan's blind. The unicorn's head lifted, ears pricked forward hard, and he feared that she'd startle the thing away. But no, her scent was strong, and its instinct was powerful. Instead of cringing in fear, she got to her knees and reached toward it with both hands, whispering to it.

It leaned toward her, like a horse would to a bucket of grain. It made careful, silent steps, not even rustling the fallen leaves. Its thick mane fell forward, covering its neck. It huffed quick breaths at her, stretching forward to sniff at her fingers. The girl cupped her hands. The unicorn rested its muzzle on her palms and sighed.

Duncan shot his arrow, striking the creature's neck.

It screamed, a piercing wail, and reared straight up like it might fly. Duncan shot again and hit the crook of its throat, where the head joined the neck. Twisting in mid-air, it tried to leap back to the shelter of the woods, crying with strained breaths. After one stride it fell, chest plowing into the earth, head and horn still raised. Groaning, it rolled to its side.

He didn't know how much it would take to kill it. The stories were vague on that point. Heart racing, Duncan drew his sword and approached. The thing shuddered, sighed quietly, the sound of air leaving a billows. He sprang at it, driving his blade into its side, through its heart, but it didn't move again. Dark stains ran from all three wounds, matting the hair of its mane and coat.

His hands were trembling. He'd done it. Bracing his foot against the unicorn's ribs, Duncan pulled out the sword, stumbling back and dropping it. Its horn was a foot long. Worth a fortune. He took his hunting knife, and it occurred to him that no one would believe where the horn came from if he didn't take the whole head.

Belatedly, he looked at the girl.

She huddled on the ground, covering her head with her hands. Slowly, her face emerged. She stared at the dead unicorn, blood congealing on its side.

"You did well," he said, attempting gentleness. His voice shook.

This was another part he had not thought to plan for—what would she do after? He expected sobbing. But she merely gathered her cloak around her and got to her feet. She seemed older, wrapped in the gloom of the forest, mist-glow turning her hair silver.

She stepped to the body, knelt by its head, and pressed her hand to its cheek. Quickly, she drew away. "It's already cold."

"It's just a beast," he said. "Just a hunt."

He started cutting, and she moved out of the way.

As he cut the final strand of muscle joining the head to the neck, the body began to shrivel, drying up, turning to dust, blowing away piece by piece. The girl put her hands in it, clutching the ash-like powder and opening her empty hands as it faded to nothing.

"It was beautiful," she said.

Eleanor gave a final tug on the cord that secured the bundle to the pack horse. The mass of it was awkward, wrapped tight in oilskin. A long, thin piece jutted out, lying flat along the horse's flank. It was the head of their ninth unicorn.

She'd grown like a weed the last five years. Regular meals worked wonders. Duncan kept her fed, and she put on weight, developing healthy curves and roses in her cheeks. He bought a horse for her, along with the pack horse. They made quite the little company now, a world of change from when he stalked the woods alone.

She scratched the pack horse's ear and went to kick dirt on the last embers of their campfire. "Do we ride far tonight?"

"Yes. I'd like to cross the border without guards watching. And— these woods are angry, I think." It was spring, but the trees still looked like skeletons, black shapes against the sky, reaching for him. He'd made a habit of killing magic, old magic, and he found himself looking over his shoulder more and more these days. "Will you be all right?"

"Of course." She said it sharply, but when he looked, she was smiling, watching him as she tightened her saddle's girth.

Of course she'd be all right, living wild in the wood and traveling like a bandit as she had. He avoided civilization as much as possible, kept her away from towns with their taverns, from people who might say a corrupting word. She was still pure; the unicorns still came to her.

They left the road before they reached the border and cut overland, picking their way through the ruins of the old Roman wall. No one saw them, and they stopped before dawn to rest.

In two days they reached their destination, where a wealthy lowland chieftain bought the horn, then opened his hall for a feast in honor of the hunter. Duncan relented. They wouldn't stay long.

Eleanor, wearing a simple gown of green wool, hair tied up in a braid, stood with him, untroubled by the great hall, the gold, the rich folk, and the stares. She had never been very excitable, but there was more to it than that. She was a creature of nature and didn't know to be wary here. She stood calmly, chin lifted, meeting every gaze that came to rest on her, refusing to be cowed by the noble company. She only gave a nod to the chieftain himself. They all saw she was proud, haughty even, and a wild beauty showed through with that pride. How had she learned to carry herself so, this waif from the hovel?

She glanced at him out of the corner of her eye and smiled.

He hadn't trimmed his beard or combed his hair to appear before the chieftain. His clothes were clean at least, but they were still hunting clothes, leather breeches and jerkin. And he, who slew unicorns, owed them no obeisance.

Then he knew: she'd learned by watching him.

That evening, he allowed himself more ale than he usually drank, to help chase away the shadows lurking at the edges of his thoughts. Sitting at the high table with the chieftain's men, he listened to conversation play around him. He only answered when someone spoke his name and woke him from his reflections.

"Duncan. The lord has given you a quarter of his wealth for that horn. You could live nobly on that."

"I hunt again in the morning," he said.

Laughing, the courtier said, "But why? You're rich, aren't you?" Several times over in fact, but he kept the money hidden. "You've a beautiful woman at your beck and call—"

Before Duncan could turn on the man to correct him of this notion, an older fellow with a white beard leaned over. "He doesn't do it for the wealth. That's what you don't understand. He does it for the power, to be able to turn his nose up at lords."

"And the girl?" the overloud courtier said. "Don't tell me you've never even touched her."

"You fool, of course he hasn't," said the older one. "She's the bait."

Across the hall, Eleanor was dancing with the chieftain's youngest son, a handsome lad of twenty with far more charm than Duncan liked. She didn't know the steps, and he was teaching her. She stumbled—Duncan had never in the last few years known her to stumble. The boy caught her waist, and she laughed. Then he took her hand and raised it to his lips.

Duncan set down his mug and climbed around the table.

He marched across the hall directly toward Eleanor and the boy, scattering the figures of the dance. The fiddler stopped playing, the drummer lost his beat, and the whole hall fell silent. Folk cleared a space for him.

Planting a hand on the young lord's chest, Duncan shoved him away and stood between him and Eleanor. He didn't say a word, only glared, and the boy backed into to the protection of the crowd.

Duncan put his hand on the back of Eleanor's neck and turned her toward the door.

"Never even think of it," he said, hissing into her ear.

"What are you—"

"If he gets what he wants from you, you become useless to me."

She ducked out of his grasp. "It was only a kiss—"

"A kiss leads to other things." He'd said too much already. How much longer would he be able to keep her? "Go to the stable. Get our horses ready. We ride out tonight."

"Duncan, there's no reason to ride out. We've a warm place to sleep tonight. A roof, for God's sake."

"We ride out tonight."

So, wrapped in cloaks and huddled in their saddles against a cold drizzle, they spent the night on the road.

Eleanor rode behind him, and her silence bothered him. He kept looking over his shoulder to make sure she was still there.

"What did he say to you?" he said.

"Who?"

"That boy."

"He told me I was pretty."

"What else?"

"What's the matter with you?"

"What else?"

She gave a long-suffering sigh, then let hoofbeats fill the silence before answering. "He asked me if I ever felt like I was betraying them. He could not believe that I would draw a creature of magic to me, then betray it."

"Well? Is that how you feel?"

"I don't know. I don't think I want to do this forever. I think I would like to marry someday."

"What do you know about marriage?"

"It's what men and women do, isn't it?"

He was so very, very close to losing her. Perhaps he should just let her go.

"Men like that don't marry girls like you, so you can stop thinking of it."

"I didn't say I'd like to marry *him*. Though—I've heard men pay more for virgins."

He might have said a hundred things to that, but he refused to be taunted.

A couple dozen strides of silence later, Eleanor said sullenly, "You may own me, Duncan, but you're not my father, so don't pretend to be."

More hoofbeats, more silence, then Duncan said softly, "You earned your way free a long time ago, Eleanor." He didn't think she heard him.

Eleanor let her hair hang loose, draping in waves down her shoulders and back. She wore a blue gown the color of sky at twilight and went barefoot. As she matured, becoming more comfortable in her own skin, she attracted older unicorns, ones not so easily enticed, the ones with the longest horns.

They might wait for weeks before drawing one close. During that time Eleanor would wander through the woods, walking, singing, making her presence known. Duncan followed, moving softly and staying hidden. Once, he'd had to stay downwind of a unicorn who followed Eleanor for five days before finally revealing itself and coming to her hand.

He never struck until the unicorn touched her, thus losing its will to flee.

This time it took three days to lure the beast. Eleanor walked into a clearing, knelt, and picked flowers, humming to herself. The unicorn emerged from the trees behind her. She paused—perhaps she felt its breath on her neck—but she didn't turn around. She kept humming, picking flowers until she had a small bouquet. Duncan crouched in the shelter of a thicket and waited.

The unicorn, a broad, muscular beast with a horn almost two feet long, stepped around her, sniffing her. She didn't move, she was in its power—with its horn leveled at her, it could stab her at any moment. So she waited until it stopped before her, then slowly offered it her flowers. It reached and brushed them with its lips.

A cry, like the whinny of a horse sounded through a trumpet, rang through the forest. On the opposite side of the clearing from Duncan, a white shape hurdled the underbrush and thundered toward Eleanor and the unicorn. It snorted with each stride.

This creature, this second unicorn, was at least eighteen hands tall, a titan that shook the ground as it galloped. Its blazing horn must have been three feet long, the longest Duncan had ever seen.

Tossing its head, it raced at Eleanor's unicorn and rammed it flank-to-flank, shoving it away from her. The newcomer screamed again, rearing at its fellow, which cried in answer and spun out of the way, tearing the soil with black hooves. The monster drove it off, and it raced into the forest.

The monster's mane shook, white hair cascading over satin shoulders. As it turned to follow the other, it let fly a kick with all the power of those massive hindquarters.

Eleanor had backed away from the fight, but not out of range of those hooves. Struck, she flew back, lifted bodily and sent sprawling on the bracken.

"Eleanor!" Duncan burst from his hiding place just as the unicorn fled with the same rolls of thunder with which it had arrived.

She was curled on her side, coughing and gasping for breath. He left his longbow and sword behind and crouched by her, gingerly touching her arm and fearing how broken she might be.

"Eleanor, speak. Where are you hurt? Tell me." He touched her face, ran his hand to her neck and felt a rapid pulse.

"I'm all right," she said, wheezing, brushing his hands away and trying to sit up. "Lost my breath is all."

His hand went to her side to help her up, and she cried out and flinched away. Her breathing started to come in panicked gasps.

"Sit back. Breathe slow. Good." He helped her lay back against a tree and prodded her side. The pain came mostly in her ribs. Cracked, he wagered. She wasn't coughing blood, she could feel all her limbs. She'd come away lucky.

He made camp there and fetched a bucket of water from a cold stream. He came to where she lay curled up, favoring her injury.

"Strip," he said. "I'll have to wrap those ribs."

"What?"

"Take off your dress."

She blushed, crossing her hands over her chest. Then, a half-smile dawning on her lips, she gave him a look that made *him* blush.

"Yes, sir," she said and began unlacing her gown.

He pointedly did not stare at her breasts as he bandaged her torso. When had she gotten breasts? They weren't much, just large enough to fill a man's hand, and yet—he was not staring.

"What was that thing?" she asked, gritting her teeth as he pulled the cloth tight. "It didn't even notice me."

"A legend among legends. An old brute of a unicorn. Filled with rage and jaded to the scent of virgins."

"Like you," she said, sitting half-naked before him.

He tied off the bandage, giving it an extra tug that made her squeak.

"It's been watching us for some time," he said. "Perhaps—perhaps it is time I quit this game."

He helped her settle by the fire to rest, and he cooked their supper. They ate in silence. He put away the dishes, saw to their horses, and brought back his bedroll.

Eleanor watched him across the fire.

"We could catch it," she said.

"You don't just catch a beast like that. It is a god among unicorns, and we've inspired its wrath."

"You're afraid."

He grunted a denial and looked away. Not afraid—he'd spent

more nights alone in wilderness most folk dared not travel in daylight than he had under roofs. He could buy any man, lord or commoner, that he chose. He made way for no one. He did not fear. But he was getting old, finding himself wishing for some of the roofs he had shunned. Perhaps that was nearly the same as fear.

Eleanor wouldn't understand, young imp that she was. Her eyes were bright, her face clean of wrinkles of age and worry. Her time in the wild had made her luminous.

"I think I can tempt an old brute of a unicorn."

"A beast like that sees nothing but its own fury."

She moved to his side of the fire, wincing and pressing her hand to the bandage as she crawled. She sat close to him; they had not been so close since he carried her before him on his saddle.

She touched his face. Not pressing, she held her palm lightly against his cheek, just enough to brush the edge of his beard. She was trembling a little, unsure of the gesture. Her brow furrowed, her expression anxious and waiting. Then, she kissed him.

Her lips felt as soft and clean as she looked. Her breath brushed his cheek, sending warmth across his face, through all his blood.

He dared not move, lest he frighten the creature away.

When he did not react, she ran her hand up his cheek, tangled her fingers in his hair, and kissed him more firmly. She was clumsy, her nose jutting into his, her balance on her knees wavering.

He took her face in both his hands and taught her how to kiss properly.

He almost gave in, and she almost let him, but his hand went from her breast to clutch her bandaged side and she gasped and flinched away. Giggling, she curled up in his arms, head resting on his chest.

"See? I can tempt an old brute."

He brushed his fingers through her fine hair, touching her as he went, ear, neck, shoulder.

"I never intended to make a whore of you," he said softly.

She pulled away and looked at him. "You've done it from the first, using me to make your money, haven't you?"

He chuckled sadly. She was right, after all. "You've become too worldly for this hunt."

"Not yet. We have one more unicorn to catch."

It would be best to leave it. But even if he never entered another forest for the rest of his days, that old beast would haunt him. That prize, that challenge, the three foot horn—that was how he should end his hunting days. And the time was now: Eleanor had reached the peak of her maidenhood, unsurpassed beauty, her innocence still intact but ready to burst, a rose at the height of her bloom. Perhaps the old beast wouldn't be able to resist her. After all, five years of nothing but pure thoughts notwithstanding, only a cracked rib made him resist.

"Why do you want to do this?" he asked.

"The usual reasons: money, fame. Because it is the profession to which I was apprenticed and I have no choice."

"Then I set you free. Here and now, I have no hold over you, and moreover I will give you half of what we have earned these past years. I will not ask you to act as bait for the old one. So, will you leave?"

"No. I will hunt the old one."

"Why?"

She hesitated before answering, pursing her lips and looking around at trees and sky. "The power," she said finally. "The power I have over them. A girl like me—there's no other power I could have, is there?"

Heart pounding, he thought, *There is another power you have.*

They waited for Eleanor's ribs to heal before searching out the old one. They left their horses behind, took a minimum of gear, and traveled deeper into the northern woods than they ever had before.

Tracking unicorns, it was no good looking for hoof prints or broken twigs for signs of their passing. They left no prints. One searched for other evidence: a pool of water that should have been brackish, but was clear and fresh; a patch of grass greener than the foliage around it, where one of them had slept. Then, catching unicorns was more like fishing than hunting. Once a place they frequented was found, there was nothing to do but set the bait and wait.

They caught a glimpse of it after they had been looking for a week. Eleanor—watched by Duncan, who perched in a tree a hundred paces away—sat alone in a sunny clearing, brushing her hair. The beast, a fierce buck as large and thick as an oak tree, moved toward her, silently for all its bulk. Its thick mane and tail rippled, its coat shone like silver.

Duncan watched it pass to the edge of the clearing, but it did not enter. It circled, watching Eleanor. She looked up only when she heard its breath snort. When she did, it turned and galloped away.

Eleanor didn't eat much at supper that evening. "I think I'm afraid of it," she said, not meeting Duncan's gaze. "It sees into my heart, sees I'm proud. I can't fool it."

"Do you want to leave off?"

"No. Fear will pass."

The next day, clouds covered the sky. The day after, a drizzle set in, a long cold rain promising to last for days. They wrapped their cloaks tight around them and found sheltered hillocks in which to spend the nights. Eleanor said she caught glimpses of the old one twice, watching them through trees from far away.

"Who's hunting who, I wonder?" Duncan said, frowning.

A week later, at twilight, when the rain-damp sky was a breath away from falling to darkness, Eleanor stopped Duncan with a hand on his chest.

"Let me go on ahead," she said. "Circle 'round to that thicket, watch from there."

"You think he's there?"

"I think he's waiting for me."

He grabbed her hand and kissed her fingers before striking off.

A clearing lay where she had pointed him. He saw nothing, but crouched hidden, bow strung and arrow ready, and waited.

A moment later, Eleanor approached. She had left behind her

pack, cloak, and boots, and unbound her hair. Her linen dress was quickly becoming soaked, clinging to her until every part of her slim frame showed: the line of her waist, slope of hip, the matched curves of her breasts. Her hair, darker when wet, dripped down her shoulders and back, framing her face, slick with rain.

Wandering into the glade, she seemed like a creature of mist, a nymph from a tale, one of the watery maids who pulled men under lakes to their deaths. Being soaking wet did not detract from her grace; she stepped lightly, lifting her skirt away from her feet, and stood tall. She looked up at the sky and smiled.

A snorting breath, loud as a roar, preceded the old unicorn's charge into the clearing. He ran at her, legs pumping, head lowered so its horn aimed for her heart. Duncan almost let fly his arrow, knowing he could never hit it as it ran but fearing for Eleanor.

She stood her ground. She didn't move. Just smiled a little and waited.

A mere stride away from her, the unicorn slid to an abrupt stop, hind end gathered underneath it, front legs lifted, and shook its head, brandishing the horn.

Eleanor crouched, lowering herself on bent knees, and raised her arm to the beast, offering her hand. She showed herself submissive, the lesser of the two.

The unicorn shook his head, his obsidian eyes flashing. He seemed torn, straining forward even as he resisted, as if pressing against a barrier. The beast stepped back, pranced in place, then spun away. He did not flee, but trotted a circle around her. She circled with him, her hand outstretched, fingers splayed, waiting for a chance when he might brush against them. While he came close—drifting in tighter and tighter circles, then suddenly leaping out to the edge of the clearing again, like a child playing around a bonfire—he never let her touch him.

All the while, Eleanor smiled a soft, wondering smile.

It was a game, this teasing and dodging. They must have played it for an hour. Sometimes the unicorn stopped and seemed ready to step toward her, head bowed, tamed. Then he reared and jumped away, and Eleanor laughed. At this, his ears pricked forward, his neck arced, and he seemed pleased to hear her.

Duncan watched from the thicket, his cold hands gripping his bow and notched arrow, his face flushed.

The unicorn moved toward her, hot breaths coming in clouds of mist. His back stood a good deal taller than Eleanor; his head towered above her. He came close enough for his breath to wash over her lifted face, but he still would not cross the last stride to her arms.

So she played the tease, and backed away from him.

"I'm pure as starlight, dear one. Touch me."

She pulled at the laces closing the neck of her gown. She separated the front edges, enough to show breast but not nipple. She stretched her arms back, so that at any moment the gown might fall off her shoulders completely, but it didn't, and she shook back her hair. The unicorn stretched his neck toward her, but she stayed just out of reach.

Duncan bit his lip. He dared not shift, though he was hard, pressed painfully against his breeches. Blood pounded through his crotch. He willed his hands to remain steady.

Her feet and legs were caked with mud, the hem of her gown black with the stuff, even though she held it off the ground. She was wet as a drowned kitten, but smiling and shining, moving a slow dance like she was born to this damp world—as innocent as the rain. Rain which gave life, and which flooded and drowned. This, he thought, was why men paid more for virgins.

The old unicorn was also aroused.

She had him then. She got to her knees, as she had done instinctively that first time, and offered him her cupped hands. With deliberate steps he came to her, lowered his head until his whiskers brushed her fingers, and licked her palms with a thick pink tongue.

Duncan loosed his arrow.

Pierced through the throat, the unicorn screamed. He reared, becoming a tower of a beast, as tall as some of the trees. Duncan jumped from his blind and shot again and again. One arrow hit his chest, another his shoulder, but still the beast kept to his feet. Duncan thought the monster would turn and run, and he would have to track him until he dropped. But the unicorn stayed, kicking and rearing, pawing over and over again the ground where Eleanor had been.

She'd ducked away, crouching at the edge of the clearing; Duncan saw enough to know she was safe. He got one more shot away before the unicorn charged him. He drew his sword and managed a slice at him as he passed. The edge nicked his chest, drawing a little blood, but the unicorn didn't slow. He turned on his haunches, throwing a rain of mud behind him, and attacked. Neck arched, horn aimed, the unicorn ran at him. Duncan stumbled back and raised his sword to block.

He couldn't hold his own against the sheer force of the beast's movement. The unicorn pressed forward, his body a battering ram with his horn at the fore, and Duncan could only rush to escape, making token parries with his sword.

The unicorn got beside him and with a swipe of his head knocked Duncan over. He sprawled in the mud, and as he got to his knees the unicorn charged again, striking him as he turned away. The blow wrenched his shoulder and spun him around. Setting his will, he got to his feet and looked for the next attack—the unicorn was coming at him again, making a running start, ready to impale him on that prized, impossible horn.

He opened his hands—his sword was gone. He'd lost his bow as well.

He waited until the last moment to dodge, to keep the unicorn from swerving to stab him anyway, and again the beast's bulk shoved him over. With the wind knocked out of him, he was slower to rise this time. He heard the thunder of hot breaths coming closer.

Eleanor screamed. "Here I am! It's me you want!" She stood in the middle of the clearing, arms at her sides.

The unicorn stopped in a stride and turned to Eleanor, his betrayer. With a satisfied snort, he trotted at her, neck arced, horn ready.

"Eleanor, no," Duncan would have said, if he'd had the breath for it.

She got to her knees—putting herself too low for the beast to stab her comfortably. He'd have had to bring his nose nearly to his chest. So he had to crush her with his hooves. Duncan stumbled in the mud, hoping to get to her in time.

The unicorn reared, preparing to bring all his weight and anger down on Eleanor.

In a heartbeat, she stepped underneath him and raised Duncan's sword, which she'd hidden beside her.

She held it in place underneath his heart, and he came down on the point. For a split second he hung there, and it looked like she was holding him up with the sword. Blood rained down on her from the wound. Then he fell straight onto her, and they crumpled together.

Finally, too late, Duncan found his feet. The unicorn was dead. Its body lay on its side, a mound in the center of the clearing.

"Eleanor," he panted with each breath. He approached its back, his heart pounding in his throat. Blood streamed from the body, filling in puddles and footprints. He saw no movement, heard no cries.

He went around the great unicorn's head, twisted up from its neck, the horn half-buried in mud.

And there was Eleanor, streaked with blood and dirt, extricating herself from the unicorn's bent legs.

"Eleanor!" He slid into the mud beside her and touched her hair, her shoulders, her arms. He helped her wipe the grime from her face. "Are you hurt? Are you well?"

"I got away. I'm only a little bruised. But you—" She did the same, pawing him all over for signs of injury. His twisted shoulder hurt to move, but he could move it. All his limbs worked. He could draw breath. He would live. They both sighed.

Smiling, she took his hands.

"No more unicorns, Duncan. If you want me, I'm yours. And if you won't have me, I'll leave and find someone who will."

He swallowed her with kisses until she laughed. Then he took her, there in the rain and the mud, against the carcass of the unicorn.

SUN, STONE, SPEAR

Elu and I travel up the coast, keeping to the hills so we won't stumble on some unfriendly settlement. It's hard going, slow. We will wear out the leather on our slippers—the laces are already splitting. We journey toward the great tomb at Behru. The astronomers there will take us in, I hope. Anyplace between here and there will capture us for slaves, if not kill us outright and throw us in a bog. Until we get there, we are without a home to guard us.

Wind drives a misting rain, and we hold our hoods tight under our chins and bend our shoulders against the cold. Our leathers cling wetly to our backs and legs. This weather isn't dangerous, but it's annoying. We hatched this plan under sunshine, two silly girls spinning tales before they've happened.

"Are we doing the right thing?" Elu asks. The sky has lightened—the sun is overhead, but rain still falls. We've traveled most of this first day in silence—has it taken her so long to question herself?

"Funny to be asking that now," I mutter.

"Yes, it really is." She manages to sound bright, as if she is thinking out loud. "So, are we, Mahra?"

"I don't believe we are doing the *wrong* thing."

We walk another dozen steps. I lead; she is a pace or two behind and to my left, out of the way of my spear, which I carry parallel to the ground. She has a staff she uses as a walking stick; it has no spearhead, no sharpened point.

"We could go back, I suppose," she says.

"No, we couldn't."

We left Inscroe for flimsy, selfish reasons. Elu wants more than anything to be a chief astronomer someday. She'll do it, too. She knows enough already to mark the seasons, predict storms, and read the stories in the patterns of stars. But she won't ever be chief in Inscroe, with four apprentice astronomers ahead of her. Ours had become a crowded village.

I could argue that my ambition is worse: I want an adventure. The kind that folk tell tales about and write in patterns in the stars. And that isn't going to happen in a village with four apprentice astronomers and boundaries marked out by strips of planted barley.

I don't remember whose idea this was, mine or Elu's. We talked about leaving for years, so much that we had to either do it or stop talking about it at all. Then Elu's mother died. We saw her burned, her ashes put in the tomb with our ancestors, a spiral carved in the rock to mark her passage from this world, and found that nothing else was holding us there. So here we are.

"What's the worst that can happen?" she asks a little while later.

I say without hesitation, "Bandits will capture us, rob us, kill us, and throw us in a bog."

She rolls her eyes at me, rain streaming from the edge of her hood, and we crest a hill, descending to a slope strewn with jagged, storm-gray boulders. The last of the heather is blooming, a ruddy fuzz on the landscape.

"Or the gods will turn their backs on us," she says.

The words fall like stones. We walk on, our steps shushing through heather.

Late the next day we hear distant voices, male. A call, an answering bark of laughter rising up from the valley below. I make Elu get down; we lie in a cleft between hillocks, my spear flat beside me. Hardly breathing, we wait. Soon their footsteps brush through grass, coming closer. Elu and I are too well hidden to see what is happening; instead, we stare at the earth that shelters us, eyes wide.

There are three of them, speaking of rabbits and how well their snares worked. I imagine them carrying a dozen of the beasts, tied on rope and slung over their shoulders. My stomach rumbles, thinking of cooked meat. Maybe I should try for a rabbit tonight. That would warm us.

The footsteps move away, the voices fade. The hunters come within the distance of a thrown stone and don't see us.

We wait until there is only the sound of blowing wind and the cry of a jackdaw. I nod, Elu nods back. We unkink our muscles and move on, across the hill, away from the path of the hunters.

That night a storm comes in. The wind howls, rain drives, making yesterday's weather seem pleasant. We're sheltered under a thicket of hawthorn. I've used some of the precious dried turf I've brought along to give us heat. In this autumn season everything is damp—hard to start fires, but we manage a little sputtering thing, small so as to keep the smoke from giving us away.

I hear voices on the wind, more laughter like that of the hunters. My own fears reflected, or maybe something riding the storm. I make silent prayers, stroke the stone of my spear head, the sinews binding it, and check its edge. Sharp enough to slice skin. We are invisible to the world above and below; we will stay safe.

The wild is filled with every kind of demon and spirit. Elu is right, the bog may not be the worst that can happen to us. I am wearing every talisman I own, every one I learned to make, from the satchel of heather around my neck to the spiral painted in the juice of ground-up oak gall around my bicep. We are beset on all sides, both human and spirit. I watch the hillside for glowing eyes, in pairs—or worse, a single glowing orb. A carved stone clasped between her hands, Elu crouches with her head bent and her eyes closed. Her lips move silently.

We have days of this ahead of us.

*

The next day we enter a forest of oak along a dull gray lake. Across the water are more towering mountains. We won't have to cross these. They lie to the west, and we go north. I decide we will stay here an afternoon to rest. Elu has learned to be watchful, looking outward constantly, every moment expecting figures to appear. She hasn't asked again if we're doing the right thing, but I have been thinking it.

I find a likely place, wait patiently, and spear that rabbit I dreamed about last night. I butcher and spit the thing over our fire while Elu lays out items from her pouch. Organizing, taking a survey, enacting some ritual, I can't say which. There are stones etched with spirals and shaded squares, twisted lengths of leather, and a precious clay spindle whorl. They all have meaning, but she puts them in a certain order and regards them with a focus that eludes me.

She holds her staff to the night sky, sighting along the carved notch at its head. Holds out her arm—measuring a set of stars against the risen moon not quite full. This tells her something about the turning of the year, and the direction we travel. I rely on stories and the pictures in my mind.

I call her over to eat when the meat is ready. She's collected some berries and wild onions on the trek. It's not a bad meal, and for a moment I think we could live like this forever, rootless.

"Mahra. Do you know where we are?"

"Yes. We are north."

"And where is Behru from here?"

"North," I say. "If we reach the river Buss we've gone too far. We'll turn inland, then south toward the tomb."

"I've spent so much time looking at the sky I can't find my way around a meadow," she says.

"That's why I'm here." I know the stories, the names of all the hills and rivers between every coast and great court at Tawra. This is why I am taking care of Elu. I am the hunter, earthbound. "Between the two of us we'll manage."

"I'm not worried. I know we'll reach Behru safely."

"You are too confident."

Elu wears a thin strip of beaten gold woven in her hair, a mark of status and of pride—her old place at Inscroe, as her mother's daughter and a chieftain's granddaughter. I am just her friend. The ornament may save us if we are captured. We can demand ransom, buy our freedom. Or our would-be captors might simply cut it from her hair. Then kill us and throw us in a bog.

I am perhaps obsessed with that particular outcome of this journey. But until we reach our destination we are prey.

"You think we made a mistake."

This is a difficult road. Staying behind would have been easier in some ways. But not in others. "We made a choice, that's all."

"If you think we did wrong you can say it," she says.

I glare. "If I thought we did wrong, I would."

She pouts and turns away, drawing out her talismans again, lining them, shifting them. I wonder if she is cursing me.

Travel like this is usually done on well-known byways in sight of the ocean, in a trading party or war band with enough members to stand watch and to dissuade attacks from raiders and demons. We are far from the usual byways. The howling on the wind seems to grow louder. Or I am hearing it better the longer I spend in the wild.

I need sleep more than I need to stand watch. We both will rest lightly, and I have my spear. I know ways to keep out the night. Saying a prayer to the spirits of earth, I cut sprigs of hawthorn and twist them into spirals. At the four cardinal corners around our camp, I bury them in the earth and hope it will be enough.

"Will that help?" Elu asks. Her prayers all go to the sky, but those gods aren't the ones who will help us here.

"It won't hurt."

"True, I suppose. But the voices are still there."

"You hear them too?"

She looks up, around, studying her stars, the patterns she sees there. "Yes."

"Are they gods or demons?"

"Who can tell?"

You should, you're the astronomer, I want to tell her. Why else study the stars and sun and moon unless you can tell how they move the spirits on earth?

"If I see them, I'll ask them," she finishes.

Well, that would certainly make for that adventure I want so badly.

A couple of days later Elu falls and twists her ankle. It isn't bad, and though she tries to hide it I can tell walking on it hurts, so I find a place to camp. Kill another rabbit. We need to keep up our strength. I wrap her ankle with a strip of leather while she mutters about being clumsy and ruining our journey.

"You aren't clumsy," I say. "But you do watch the sky instead of the ground sometimes." She huffs, and smiles, because this is not an insult to her. But I think: she hasn't walked the miles I have, she hasn't stalked deer or lived off the land. Maybe this was a mistake, but I don't say it.

After dark I go to bury the rabbit's offal, and on the far side of a cleft of stone I see those glowing eyes I've been keeping watch for. Deep amber with the light of coals and shaped like leaves of ash. The bulk of the rest of it moves; I can't make it out against the shadow of stone and shrub.

I lower my spear and draw out a spiral-knotted piece of hawthorn from my belt pouch. The thing is watching me, I know it. If I take a step it will strike me. I think it might have wings, hawk feathers coming off its shoulders, and the mouth of a lizard.

The spear will do me no good here. I hope the hawthorn will. I hold it in front of me like a shield, though it's no bigger than my palm. It wouldn't shelter a fly. I back away, hoping this will interrupt the demon's gaze, that it will be entranced by the spiral and not by me.

I don't blink; I couldn't have blinked, my eyes feel so wide and stiff. But when I have gone a dozen paces back from it, the eyes are gone, the light is out, and the world is only shadows again.

I return to camp, where Elu is using a chisel to carve something into a river stone cupped in her hand. She's humming, and in the orange glow of the fire she looks unreal. I don't tell her about the demon, and that I think we're being hunted.

The world is large, dark and crowded.

"What is *that*?" Elu stops and stares. We both do.

We have entered a broad valley, which we will try to cross quickly. Squinting, I see in the distance cleared spaces of woodland, cultivated fields, and smoke from a fire. Ragged dirty sheep cluster on the green plain. Far across the plain is a great sloping hill, like the belly of a fat giant lying prone. At the top is a black structure, flat and round, one of Elu's river rocks made large. A house made of stone. A monument that must have broken a thousand backs to erect. I have never seen it myself, but I know the stories. On the one hand, the sight of it tells me we are on the right path and have another week or so of travel left. On the other, it tells me we are in dangerous territory. Even more dangerous.

"It's Brean's fort," I say.

"Brean—the chieftain?"

"I think he calls himself high king."

"Every king thinks he's high king," she huffs. "What is he, really?"

"He's gotten enough other people to call him high king to get them to build that fort for him."

Inscroe has done much building in its time, over generations. There is the great tomb passage where the winter burials are made—my grandmother told stories of carrying stones from the river to build it. It's never really finished—new standing stones are carved, more earth is packed onto the cairn, the hill grows as ashes of the dead crowd inside. A half dozen smaller cairns have been built, with standing stones to mark them. The folk of Inscroe, led by their chieftains and astronomers, build such things because they can, so that travelers will know that land is theirs, that their dead watch over them and are powerful.

A thing like this, so obviously built on top of the land and not a part of it, is entrancing. We stare at it for a long time, leaning on our staves, a nervous gnawing in our gut.

Elu says, "He picked the highest point and built it so all who see it will know whose eye watches them, and cannot travel without feeling his presence."

"Everyone in this valley lives in his shadow," I murmur. "Let's move quickly, Elu."

"Yes."

We don't stop until we are out of sight of Brean's fort, which means we are traveling until dark. I pick a glade to make our camp, but then I find a set of spiral-woven hawthorn talismans on the ground, four of them laid out in a row. They've been dug up, still have grime stuck in the cracks and whorls. They are mine, from an earlier camp; I recognize the knots and coils.

"Pack up, we've moving on."

Elu looks up; she's taken off her hood and is digging in her pouch. I grab my spear, settling my own hood back on my head.

"What is it?"

I collect the talismans, shove them in my pouch even though they're demon tainted. I don't want them lying around where anything can get hold of them.

"We've got to keep going."

"Mahra, it's dark, we can't—"

I walk on, leaving it up to her to follow me.

It's started raining again.

"It's like the whole sky wants us to go back," Elu says. We're huddled together in a sheltered stand of rocks, under our hoods, trying to keep warm. I couldn't get a fire lit. Me, the mighty hunter.

"No, the sky wants to make sure we really, really want to continue on," I answer.

"I haven't seen stars in days. If I can't see the sun, the moon, the stars, what am I then?"

"The skies will clear, they always do." When did I become the optimist between us?

"How many more days to Behru?"

I'm suddenly not sure if I'll know it when I see it. I know the stories, I know to look for standing stones on a hill, and a wall of white quartz gleaming in the sun. But what if I walk past it? "Four. I think."

She looks at me sidelong.

"We've made it this far, haven't we?"

"Maybe we should go back," she whispers.

"Elu!" I yell, and she cringes. I'm the one with the spear after all, and I wonder—does she think I'd use it, if I got angry enough? I wouldn't. I'm pretty sure I wouldn't.

A pause. The rain on stones sounds like a rushing stream. She says, "We're being watched."

"We're being followed," I answer. *Hunted*, I think.

"You can make more talismans, yes?"

"As long as you keep saying prayers."

I make the talismans. Elu traces spirals in the air, in the hopes that unseen spirits will turn away. I hear howling in the dark.

We can't see each other anymore, but she sings in a low droning voice, like distant thunder rolling in the night.

"'Storms rise, night comes, the cold is falling. Where are my spears, where are the hunters to bring in food for the winter? Deer, eagle, barley, berry, the light will fade. The dead press close, to cry on the wind, to tell us where we are going.'"

An autumn song, for dark nights and sputtering fires. If Behru does not take us in, we will not survive the winter.

*

We *are* being followed. Tracked.

Oddly, I smell them first: the ashen, sour smell of an old cooking fire long burned out, soot and grease smeared over the ground. Nothing wild has that smell. I sense a hint of it as I stop to crane my neck and look around, but there is no column of smoke in any direction. Something is there that should not be. My skin itches.

"Let's move this way," I say, changing our track to head further into the rolling hills, where a forest provides many chances to hide. Many chances to be ambushed as well, but I don't like being on the plain by the river, where the whole sky can see us.

Elu follows. "Do you know where we're going or not?"

She'll only be upset if I tell her I think we're being hunted. Either upset because we're being hunted, or because she thinks I'm trying to scare her.

"Patience," I mutter back. "Aren't you astronomers supposed to be good at that?"

"We're also good at being right. If we misplaced one marker a whole cairn would have to be rebuilt."

"I know where we're going."

The sour-ashy smell doesn't go away. It gets thicker, as if the forest is burning up ahead. I look through the trees, study shadows to see what is there—a single hunter, a whole pack of men, or something else entirely? Among the shadows between the trees, a flash glints that might be light reflecting off a spear point, or might be the glee-filled eyes of some demon. I pull a stone from my pouch that I can throw.

"What are you looking for, Mahra?" Elu's voice has gone low; she already knows.

"Stick close," I say. "Be ready to run."

She grips her staff two-handed. It's a tool with many uses.

Dusk has fallen, and that's when I see the first one, a shadow breaking off from the trees, hooting a signal across the way to a figure up ahead. I veer; Elu is right with me, I don't have to worry. We move fast without running, because I expect at any moment I'll need to turn and fight.

I can't see how many there are. Dozens, I assume. They might be merely men—bad enough. But demons also have arms and legs, wear coats of fur and carry spears. Until I see their eyes I won't know for certain.

The light is failing, the world is gray. Up ahead the trees break, revealing a hill of rocks—a natural outcrop, not a cairn, though I'm not sure until we reach it and see the tumbled edges and cracked breaks between stones.

"Up!" I call to Elu, because the outcrop is defensible. With a running start, she scrambles up the side. I turn, spear out, to defend her.

I still don't know how many there are, but a javelin flies from the trees and strikes granite by my head.

"Mahra!" Elu calls, reaching for me. I retrieve the fallen javelin first and take Elu's hand.

We are on the rocks, and there are three of them, wild men in rough furs, taunting us—I don't understand their language, which means they must come from some far-off land even more wild than this. Another world, maybe. In the lowering dark, with their hulking furs, they stop being men and start being large stoats or small bears, or both together. Creatures of fur that speak words. I look for glints of red in their eyes.

They will be up the rocks in moments unless I stop them. But as Elu said, patience and accuracy will always win out, so I pause, take a deep breath, and throw the rock I've been holding.

My target howls and falls back. Next, I thrust my spear down at another one of them; the sharpened point catches fur, digs in. He grunts but doesn't fall. I pull back, slash forward—and throw the borrowed javelin in my other hand while he is distracted. It strikes him. He falls but isn't dead. What will it take to kill them? I have to kill them, if we're going to get off this rock and escape.

I turn to check on Elu—she's gasping for breath, but she is safe behind me on the pinnacle of the outcrop. She looks over my shoulder; the third has bided his time.

A hand grabs my ankle, another stabs at me—a stone sharpened to a blade. I can't yank away fast enough but manage to hold back a scream as the edge slices through my naked calf.

Elu skids along the rock beside me and jabs with her staff, cracking my attacker in the face with its oaken head. Bone crunches. I know that sound from killing rabbits.

The fallen figure is nothing more than a furry lump on the ground.

I set my jaw, resettle my spear in my hands. I am not angry, I am calm. I have my task: to stop them, so we can move on. The first two come again. Blood pouring from my leg has made the rock slippery so I have to brace carefully. I kick, stab, slash—they fall back again, and I scramble up the rock to a higher purchase. Elu hands me two good solid stones she has found, broken pieces from the cracks in the outcrop. I throw, throw again. I'm good with stones. Our attackers lie there, senseless.

My leg throbs. Nothing left of it but flowing red, it feels like.

"Oh Mahra, Mahra!" Elu cries. She's cut a strip of leather from one of her pouches and moves to bind the wound.

"We don't have time, we have to run before they come at us again."

"You can't run!"

"I will, you'll help." I let her wrap the strip of leather around my leg because that seems prudent. The pressure of the bandage at least cuts down the throbbing pain.

Gripping each other's arms for balance and reassurance, we climb to the other side of the outcrop, slide down, and run. I stumble at first—the pain jabbing up my leg surprises me. But then I ignore it, and we run more sure. If I am confident, Elu won't stop.

Eventually, we leave that sour-ashen smell behind. I decide it wasn't the smell of old campfires at all but the smell of hungry demons.

We have to camp yet again. We will never reach Behru.

Elu fusses over my wound. The skin hangs loose from the muscle. In the morning light we both look at it, ugly and scabbed over with clotted blood. Horrified, I might faint at its mangled shape, so I look at the trees in the glade we've sheltered in. I think Elu might scream, but she finds water, washes the wound, and then binds it all back together with strips of leather.

"We should move in case they come back," I say.

"I've put charms every half a foot around this place, they won't find us. Heal. I command it."

I start to say I don't trust our charms anymore. But my leg is on fire, and what else are we going to do? I trust Elu.

She chatters brightly to distract me. It's like the day we started out. "You were magnificent. I'll make a song of how you fought."

"If I'd been faster my leg wouldn't be hurt."

"You know what? We'll tell folk we fought off wolves. A pack of wolves, and you drove them all off with nothing but your spear and your battle cries."

I have to smile. She commands it. "Demons. They were terrible demons."

"Demon wolves," she adds. "Worst kind."

They might as well have been. It makes a good story.

My leg hurts, but in two days we walk on. I'm too restless not to, but I have to limp along using my spear as a crutch.

The clouds break the next day, bringing sun. My skin stings with the heat, and it feels marvelous to push back my hood and rub the itch out of my hair. Elu smiles, squinting into the sky. It's like she's found the gods again.

Near dusk, we find stones. It isn't Behru—Behru is a whole complex, tombs surrounded by rings of stones and altars, with a village nearby to oversee it. This is three simple stones in a clearing surrounded by oak groves. They are our height, small enough around to hug, in a straight line. Grass has grown up around their bases, but there are no lichens growing on them. They might have been here a decade, or a hundred years. Not longer than that.

"It's a summer line," Elu says, looking at the sky, sighting along her staff. "It aligns to the solstice."

Even in autumn, when the sun has moved low, she can see this.

"Abandoned?" I ask.

"Nothing is ever really abandoned," she says. "*Something* lives here, no doubt." Her brow furrows; she presses her palm to the stone as if she feels a heartbeat. "They buried a bad harvest here, and plague. This is a tomb for ill fortune."

I want to run, then. "We should go. We must be close to Behru."

Turning to march away, I trip. My injured leg gives way, my foot catching on a tuft of clover, a dry stick, something, and I fall. I never fall. I'm not like Elu, looking up when I should be watching the earth. I know before I hit the ground that we are captured. My foot is stuck to the ground, my wound screams in pain, my hands are bound, I cannot see by what. My spear has fallen. It's the bog for us, then.

Elu stands over me now, putting herself between me and ... something. She is looking right at a thing that I cannot see and shouting curses, holding the stone she has been carving out straight-armed, like a shield, as if it will protect us.

A long moment passes, and I only hear her heavy breathing, and mine. Hand shaking, she reaches for me. I can raise my hand now, and I do so. When she grabs hold the weight comes off me, I can move again, though the throbbing pain keeps me on the ground. I retrieve my spear; even seated on the ground I hold it defensively. Elu stands over me with her staff, waiting.

A woman is sitting on the ground with her back against the center stone.

I know she is a goddess because she is too beautiful to look at. I turn away, my eyes watering, and sneak glances. She is a hunter, a shaggy gray hound at her side. Her spear tip gleams bronze—a rare and holy thing. She is like me but better. My better self, what I aspire to be but will never reach in all my striving, in all the silent vows I've made to bring Elu safe to Behru. She is Canna the Hunter.

"Oh my dears," the goddess says. "I have been watching you."

"You have been harrying us!" Elu says, much more sharply than she should. She bows her head in a late apology.

"Elu, no," I murmur, putting a hand on her thigh, the only part of her I can reach. Canna is not her goddess, she wouldn't understand. Her gods live in the sky and the stones. Mine walk upon the earth, among living things. Elu can be angry, but I can only weep.

Canna looks at Elu, back at me. Her face is young; her eyes are like a grandmother's, full of scolding wisdom.

"Do you know it was me?" Canna says. "The world is full of gods and spirits."

What can we say? The words of Elu's song pass through my mind.

"Command me," I say, struggling to get on my knees. I cannot speak for Elu, who stands at my side as if she will protect me.

"Answer me a riddle," the goddess says. "Are you running to, or away?"

That is not the real question: Are you brave, or are you a coward? Are you ambitious or merely discontent? I do not want to answer; I cannot trust my own honesty.

"We are not running at all," Elu says. "We travel carefully."

Canna laughs, and I don't know if that's good or bad. She looks at me. "And your answer?"

"Yes," I breathe. "I think the answer is, yes."

The goddess's smile is kind.

"Do we pass your test?" Elu asks, because we both know that is what gods do, they test you and punish you. "Or is this some lesson of how we ought to be satisfied with our places and not go questing for better?"

"Oh, dear, no. I wouldn't try to teach such a lesson. You simply crossed into my territory. I deserve to have a look at you." She scratches the hound's ears, and its tail thumps the ground. "You answered my question so nicely, though—do you have a question for me?"

This is an even worse test. Elu looks at me—Canna is my goddess, I should be the one to ask. But my mind is blank, and I can't think of a question, only wishes and reassurances. I look back at Elu and nod.

She says, "Are we doing the right thing?"

"Well," Canna says. "We won't know that until it's all done, will we? Come, Di, let's be off. It's almost dark. You girls should find a camp somewhere. There are spirits about."

She stands—she is clothed in leather that blazes white, leggings and tunic and hood, all of it from the purest doe that ever lived. Her smile is brighter. The dog walks at her side, as tall as her hip. They move off, vanishing behind one of the standing stones.

The world is suddenly dark and silent.

"Mahra?" Elu asks finally. I can't answer because I'm weeping. She touches my shoulder with a fist—still holding her spiral-carved stone.

I get to my feet—easily, feeling no more pain. When I unpeel the bandages, there's a thick scar there, well healed.

We move off. A full moon lights our way, and we are able to travel far from the standing stones before we stop and put talismans around our camp.

We first see the tomb a half a day's walk away—gleaming, it rises from its hill like a full moon. The village at the base of the hill is large—smoke from dozens of fires visible, part of a forest recently cleared, and all surrounded by the stubble of harvested fields. This time, we can't avoid the well-worn path that leads to the heart of the village. People watch us; I am careful to keep my spear lowered.

There isn't just the one tomb but a whole circle of altars, stone rings, barrows. The people here have started a new tomb. It's why we've come, Elu and I know the stories. The work is still for now—the autumn harvest has taken away most of the workers. But great stones lie on beds of logs and rope, ready to move, and a circling trench has been freshly dug.

All around the site, marker stakes made of stripped oak saplings stand driven into the ground around a new chamber of stone—the stakes, weathered and mossy, track the passage of the sun across their world. It takes years to get the map needed to build a tomb like this, aligned to the light of winter or summer. Elu studies the work, putting a light hand on each stake and sighting down its shadow to see what it marks. That brings the flustered gray-bearded chief astronomer rushing toward us, the woolen sleeves of his tunic flapping as he waves his arms.

We offer reassurances and are asked for our story. We tell them of days of travel, storms and cold, the forts and cairns we saw and the ghosts that haunted them. The bandits we avoided, the demons we didn't, and the otherworldly songs we'd heard chanted in the night. Eyes in the dark, talismans left behind, our own strength of stubbornness, if not will. We met a goddess, we told them, and she did not smite us, though I couldn't say why.

All in all, it's a pretty good story.

"Mahra has the favor of Canna herself," Elu tells them, sounding outrageous, but I can't say she is lying. Because she says it and not me it's not bragging and people believe her. They ask to see the scar on my leg. They are impressed; we are admired.

But Behru does not need us. They won't take us in, and the refusal feels like punishment for being brave.

Then the flustered old astronomer says, "A tomb is being built at Nowa, only a few hours' walk away. The chief astronomer there needs a young apprentice to carry on the building after her death." He smiles.

The gold in Elu's hair does not glint as brightly as her smile at this news.

The solstice sun has illuminated the standing stones at Nowa many times since then.

Now Elu is old, with apprentices of her own, and she has used her life to build a circle of stones and a tomb that will not be finished when she dies. "The Earth was not built by one soul in one life," she says. "It takes a dozen gods and all their children too."

I have children, and they have children, and Nowa has become ours. I still hunt, and my grandchildren tell the story of how I speared a charging boar and saved a chieftain. Sometimes in the evenings, after food and fire and song, Elu and I sit together over a smoldering piece of turf and tell a different set of stories, Remember whens? and Oh, we were so young. And yes, some cold dark nights when there is no moon and an interminable rain falls, we still ask, "Did we do the right thing?"

It should be a question with a firm answer, here at the end of our lives, but I think sometimes of all that could have happened, all that could have gone wrong, and I feel a terrible chill at all we would have lost. Not lost—all we never would have had. And I think the gods must have wanted us to be here.

Ambition drove us, but here at the end, when I know how it all turns out, I know our true purpose: to bury good fortune in our tombs, under our stones.

CROWS

Tull awakened under someone else's shield, his legs tangled around his own poleax. He'd fallen–tripped, not struck down. Clumsy. The ground still rumbled with the hoof-falls of a thousand charging horses. The clash of armies still echoed, though distantly. The battle had moved on, sunlight still shone, and he was still alive.

He started to rise, but the shield wouldn't move. Pulling himself with his arms, he slithered out from under it.

The shield was still strapped to his lord's arm. Lord Berold Whiteford, cousin to the King himself, lay on his side, his shield arm flung out, twisted and broken, his sword arm resting over a bleeding gash in his side where the fastening on his breastplate had ripped. His horse, a smoke-gray stallion, lay nearby, a spear imbedded in its chest.

Tull remembered them falling. He'd gone to help. Then he'd woken up.

He was within arm's reach of the knight. With a gloved hand, he touched the visor of Berold's helm. He lifted it, to show the face beneath.

"My lord?"

Lord Berold was twenty years old, Tull's own age, and handsome: golden hair, a straight nose, fine-boned face.

"My lord Berold?"

Lifeless blue eyes stared past Tull.

Tull closed the visor. Hoping to stop the ringing in his ears, he pulled off his open-faced helm. He wiped a hand through his hair, which was crusted with sweat and grime. He rubbed finger against thumb; they were slick with blood.

The line where the armies met pressed farther away. They'd left behind a field of dead horses and men, twisted together, spears rising from the ground like a forest of thin trees. Tull listened for the groans of the injured and dying.

Instead, he heard laughter, guttural and harsh. Or was it crying, the tears of maids weeping for the King's army?

Above, black specks swarmed, circling. The specks drifted closer, swooping on wings edged with broad feathers.

The crows were coming.

Tull found Berold's sword dropped nearby. He put the sword on Berold's chest, forced his hands to grip it, and lay the shield against the body so that he looked like a stone effigy on a tomb, armed in honor.

He would guard Lord Berold until the King came for him. The King would want Lord Berold protected. While crows landed on the bodies all around him, clawing at the flesh of horses' muzzles, perching on the chests of men and pecking at their eyes with quick, criminal jabs, like back-alley knife-fighters, Tull chased them off Berold. A crow landed on the ground nearby, danced forward on its claws, wings half-open, eyeing the pool of blood at Berold's side, as if it thought Tull wouldn't notice. Roaring, Tull thrust his poleax at the bird, which flew off, squawking and offended.

Tull kept watch in all directions, including above him, since they swooped from the sky. He rested his hand on Berold's chest. He'd made a circle of quiet around the knight. Everywhere else, the screaming crows fed. The birds studied him with eyes like cabochons of onyx. The circle inched closer, shrinking as the crows pressed toward him, until he shouted at them and swung his poleax, scattering them in a flurry of caws and feathers. Again and again they tested his defense, creeping closer. He drove them back throughout the afternoon.

They surely didn't have the courage to attack a living man.

The dogs might. A feral pack wandering the field found enough spoils elsewhere that Tull only had to shout to chase them away. They preferred easier scavenging.

The sun dropped westward. When would the King come looking for Berold?

When he saw movement on Berold's chest, Tull thought that he'd been wrong, that the lord had shifted his fingers, that he was alive. But the movement was only flies creeping in the blood. Tull swatted them away.

Flies crawled in through the visor of Berold's helmet. Tull opened the visor and slapped flies away from his eyes, pulled them out of his nose and mouth. He closed the visor and filled in the slots with fabric cut from his tunic.

Tull's mouth was dry, as dry as Berold's. His face was sticky with sweat and blood. His head throbbed with heat, though he could have sworn it was winter.

The sun moved low. The crows, thousands of them, gorged themselves. The flies swarmed; Tull felt them on his face, but he couldn't see them.

If the King lost the battle, he might never come looking for Berold.

Tull remembered Berold riding tall on his gray charger, smiling at those in his company, mounted knights and foot soldiers alike, who cheered to follow such a lord. That very morning, he'd ridden past their campfires to rouse them, lifting his mace in his gauntleted hand, the picture of a hero.

Berold had worn a lady's favor, a silk scarf of forest green on his belt under his breastplate. Tull shifted the breastplate, lifting it by its edge, feeling with his hand. Under the steel, amid the leather straps and wool padding, he felt a slippery bit of fabric, something fine and delicate, a lady's scarf. The knight wore the favor still. The lady would want him to keep it. No one would take it from him.

At twilight, they would light the torches in camp. Tull would stand watch with his fellows, and Lord Berold would order a cask of ale tapped, to warm the guards on the cold winter night.

Balancing with his poleax, Tull crouched on one knee by the body of Lord Berold Whiteford and kept watch.

The people did not carry torches. Hunched black forms, they were shadows only in the deepening twilight.

Like the crows, they settled on the bodies of men and horses alike. They pulled at the trappings of the horses, digging in the saddlebags. They picked at the armor of the fallen warriors, searching for pouches, coins and jewels.

When they came near, Tull swung the poleax, shouting and swearing as he did in battle. They crept away, leaving a space around him and Berold, as the crows had.

His shoulders ached from lifting the weapon. He couldn't feel his hands; they seemed as if they had melted into his gloves, which were cracked and stiff. His breath scratched in his throat. He sounded like the crows, squawking when he meant to curse.

The moon rose three quarters full.

If the King lost the battle, Tull might never know. No one would come to raise a mound for the bodies. No one would carry Berold to the tomb of his fathers, and Tull's watch would be in vain. But he stayed. Someone would come and tell him if the King had won or lost. Soon, someone had to come.

The woman had black hair.

It was stringy, dirty, hanging like cords around her face, which was round, with sunken cheeks. She watched Tull with wide, shining eyes. She moved toward him on all fours, like an animal.

"Get back!" He rose and lunged at her, thrusting with his poleax.

She hissed and backed away, but did not flee. She circled to Berold's horse, but Tull wouldn't let her have that either.

"Get away," he said, his voice almost a growl.

Out of reach, she crouched, tucked in between her bent legs, and watched him. Tull stood between her and Berold.

Methodically, the looters moved across the field, from one body to the next, collecting whatever little prizes they found, swords they could sell, pieces of armor light enough to carry. They were worse than the crows, who acted according to their natures when they feasted on the dead. The looters chose to profit from death. Tull might have attacked them all, swinging his weapon at their unprotected heads, smashing their bellies as easily as crushing eggs. Let them have a taste of true battle.

But if he left Berold, the woman would have him.

His head ached. He touched his temple and rubbed down his cheek to still the throbbing. He dared not close his eyes for more than a blink.

The looters moved on to another part of the battlefield.

The woman stayed, perched like a crow, watching.

"Why don't you leave with the others?" he said to her.

"I smell his blood. Royal kin. Rich blood." Her voice was low, muffled, as if she could not draw enough air to speak.

"You can't have him."

"Perhaps not now. But you cannot guard him forever. I will wait."

He glared at her, denying her. He could wait here forever. He was already dead, and this was the afterlife his spirit faced: to guard his liege lord for eternity. It was not hell; it was an honor. The crows would not have him.

She craned her neck and arched her back, stretching for a moment, then settled to her place again, arms bent, elbows resting on her knees.

After a time, he could not focus on her. She sat so still, and the shadows on her face bent so strangely in the moonlight, he was no longer sure what he was looking at. She had long teeth and shining black eyes, hard as stone. Her hair grew down her back, so long it touched the earth. It seemed the crows had returned, but this time they were large, people-sized, and spoke with words to taunt him.

Spirits of the dead. They could not have Berold.

The world contracted until it could only hold the pain between his temples. The ax slipped from his hand. He was not dead, he would not hurt so much if he were dead. But he could sleep, and it would be like dying, and the pain would stop.

The shadow with the hard black eyes crept forward, smooth as air, and reached out a hand bent like a claw.

The claw filled Tull's vision and he gasped, woke, grabbed up his weapon again, and thrust it between her and the body. The claw drew back.

"What are you?" he shouted. His own voice rasped in his sand-dry mouth.

She tilted her head, bird like. "Scavenger."

"Why won't you leave?" Tull said to her.

"Why won't you?"

With a throat-tearing battle-cry, he ran at the woman and swung the poleax over his head, straight down. He aimed the hammer end of it at her head, at the roots of her unwashed, mouse-nest hair. He meant to smash her to pieces.

She squealed and ran away with the speed and litheness of one used to moving in shadows. The steel thudded into soft earth.

Again, Tull stood alone with the bodies. A few crows lingered, but even they were sated. Now, he could hear the buzzing of flies.

He should have saved Lord Berold. He should have cried out when he saw the spear fly. Or perhaps he had cried out, and his voice hadn't reached over the storm of battle. He stood and his lord did not. He had failed.

Then he could not fail in this. The Whiteford tomb would see Lord Berold safe inside.

If the King won the battle, he would need time before he could return this way to collect the dead. Even now, he might be gathering prisoners for ransom. He'd be parlaying terms of surrender, having his wounds tended under a makeshift pavilion made of a tattered scrap of canvas. If the King had won the battle, surely he was exhausted, and must rest before he came searching for his cousin's body. Tull would be here, waiting.

Tull hadn't slept the night before the battle. He didn't sleep this night, either.

If the King won or lost. If the King won or lost. The battle had gone very far away. Tull hadn't heard the clanging of steel weapons beating armor since the afternoon.

Dawn hurt his eyes.

He shaded them and scraped away the blood that had dried on his face.

The land shimmered, heat rising from the dead earth. His vision wavered. He could not trust it. He listened and heard hoof-beats, and the rattle of tack and armor, as if the battle returned. He hefted his poleax in stiff hands.

Men came, a dozen of them, from all sides. They walked with confidence, like soldiers, not like looters.

"Stay back!" Tull cried, brandishing his poleax. "Get away from him!"

They did not listen. They were faceless men, hiding behind helms and armor. Without a word, they circled him, like damned spirits. Or messengers from the land of death. They'd come to fetch Berold, but they couldn't have him.

Tull swung his poleax at the one before him. His arms were heavy; the blow fell short. The figure merely had to step out of the way. Then the ones behind Tull grabbed him. They wrenched his arms back, and his stiff muscles ripped with pain. Screaming, he dropped the poleax, then reached desperately for it because he needed it to guard Berold.

"Let me go! Let me go! You can't have him! You can't take him!"

Two figures held his arm and pulled him to the ground until he was kneeling, tipped back, unable to struggle.

"You can't have him," he repeated, gasping for breath. He squinted through tears.

A row of horsemen stood before him, beyond his captors. The riders wore scarves over their noses and mouths.

"Is he one of ours?" said the leader, who rode a white charger, covered with dust.

"I think so, Sire."

"That knight, there. The one he guards. I know the colors of his shield. Rafe, lift his visor."

One of the footmen went to Berold. Tull kicked out, struggling, but his captors held him easily. He was weak as a child.

The visor scraped up.

The man on the white horse said, "It is Berold, my cousin."

King Ethelsten, Third of the Name, nudged his mount closer. "You are one of Berold's armsmen, I think. Tell me—do you serve Lord Berold?"

The horseman loomed over him, and Tull wondered if now he must die at last.

"I'm guarding him for the King. The crows won't have him."

"Indeed, they won't. Rafe, Gavin, bring a litter for Lord Berold."

Nodding at Tull, Rafe said, "Sire, what about him?"

"He must come with us, of course."

"But he's mad. He won't stop fighting us."

The white rider dismounted and approached. Tull saw how fine his armor was. Polished, even after battle. Afraid, Tull pulled back, into the grips of his captors.

The King pulled his scarf down from his face and said, "Will you continue to guard him, as we carry him to the tomb of his fathers?"

Guard him to the tomb of his fathers. Tull could still see Lord Berold, mace raised in his hand. They would bury him with his sword.

Tull stared hard at the man before him. "I will. I will guard him."

"Very good," the man said, squeezing his shoulder.

Tull's captors released him. He slumped forward, his arms limp, his head throbbing. They had placed Lord Berold on a litter with his sword and shield. They would carry him to the Whiteford tomb.

The King climbed onto his mount. "Get him some water. We march now."

Another rider said, "That wound on his scalp is festering. I do not think he will survive the journey."

The King said, "Then we will bury him, and the crows will not have him."

SALVAGE

"You two ready?" I ask.

"Yes, ma'am," Gert says with forced brightness, and Rally nods quickly, a shake of motion behind her helmet's faceplate. She's nervous, but she always seems to be a little nervous, so I'm not too worried.

We wait in *Iris's* airlock for the air to hiss out around us. It's a dangerous, thrilling sensation. I can almost feel air rushing over the fabric of my suit, hear a bit of wind through the helmet, until I can't hear anything. Then comes the eerie moment when we open the door to the unknown.

I know the captain isn't supposed to take part in these operations. I'm supposed to stay on the bridge, safe and sound, and not expose myself to unnecessary risk. Stick around to take the blame if something goes horribly wrong. But if I think that much risk is involved in boarding the *Radigund*, I wouldn't send any of my people aboard. We'd do an automated sensor sweep, mark the site for salvage, and let someone with more personnel and big guns do the work. *Radigund* is dead in space. No life signs, no energy readings, nothing. We have no reason to believe anything is there.

So we board, to better investigate and make a full report. Recover bodies, if any are there to recover. *Radigund* is—was—a small survey ship, like us, plying the edges of known spaceways, tracking routes and charting what we find. Trade Guild diverted our mission to look for her. It took us a month to find her, she'd drifted so far off course.

Using the mechanical override, we force open *Radigund's* hatch into the opposite airlock. I enter first, Gert and Rally follow, slipping soundlessly behind me. It's dark. My lamp panning across the space before me disorients rather than illuminates. I have to piece together a flash of wall, the viewport on the opposite hatch, a warning label above a control panel.

Gert closes the hatch behind us.

Sealed in the other airlock now, we have to pull off an access panel and open the interior hatch manually. *Radigund* has no power. No air, either, which gives a clue as to what happened. The door grinds open, gears stiff. I can't wait to get my hands on the log and the black box, to learn what happened. Assuming we can get enough power to the computer to download anything. No power also means no artificial gravity. We float through, pushing ourselves along the corridor walls.

"God, I hate this," Rally says, her voice thin over the comm. "I feel like something's going to jump out at us."

Gert chuckles. "You've been watching too many films."

We continue on to the bridge. Nothing unusual so far, besides the lack of power. The lack of life.

A second channel on my comm clicks on. It's Matthews, from *Iris's* bridge. "Captain, I've finished the second hull survey. Not so much as a pinhole."

Hull breach could have shut down the ship in a hurry. That had been my first thought. Matthews closes that possibility.

"Thank you," I say. Voices murmur in the background. The whole crew is on the *Iris* bridge, watching our progress on our suit cameras and monitors. Like it's one of Rally's films.

"What was that!" Rally says suddenly, and we all swing around, bumping against the walls and each other.

Her light shines on a blanket floating halfway through the hatchway leading to crew quarters.

"You really are losing it," Gert says, unkindly.

"Focus, you two," I say. I'm beginning to regret my decision to bring these two in particular. But Rally knows the computers; Gert knows the power system. And they mix like oil and water.

They're good people. Good crew. But sometimes, I'm tempted to lock them in a room together and watch the fireworks.

Our progress is slow, slower than I like. Because of the shadows, I think. Rally's monsters hiding in them. Venting, tubing, ladders, open hatches, all of them are shadows, foreshortened and flickering in our helmet lamps. We're hesitating, holding back. Expecting an unnamable thing that we don't want to find. My breathing grows loud, sealed with it against my ears as I am. A ship shouldn't be so quiet.

Gert's hand clutches my shoulder, hard enough to feel through my suit's padding, but I've seen what he's seen in the same moment. Breath and heart both stop, no doubt prompting spikes in biometric readouts on *Iris* that stop hearts among the crew there. Rally stifles a whimper.

It's a face glaring out from a doorway, all teeth and eyes, arms reaching.

We freeze, and all three helmet lamps focus on it.

It's a photograph, printed large and hung on the door. A person in a blue Trade Guild uniform. Male. He's grinning, throwing his hands up to guard against the camera, to prevent this picture from even happening. But it's all in good fun. Someone has drawn a party hat on the man's head and garland of flowers around his neck, and written in large, enthusiastic letters, *Happy Birthday, Captain.* I could guess the joke behind it: the Captain had declared he didn't want a party for his birthday. No celebration, just another day. And someone on the crew had taken revenge. *Radigund* must have been that kind of ship, where the crew could play a small joke on the captain, and he wouldn't mind.

Frost curls the edges of the paper.

"Geez," Gert breathes.

We climb the ladder to the bridge, following the circles of our flashlights. We find bodies there. Navigator, pilot, comm officer. Captain. Even frozen and dead, rimed with frost, I recognize my counterpart from the picture. There ought to be six more, somewhere on the ship. Crew cabins, engineering, and medical are where I expect to find them.

Captain and pilot are strapped to their seats, stiff arms raised a few inches above armrests. Weightlessness had set in before the freezing cold. The other two are curled up near the floor. All are wearing oxygen masks. They knew this was coming, that something was wrong. An open plate on the deck, cabling exposed, shows an attempt at repairs.

Ice crystals frost hair and skin, open eyes. They're all in their twenties and thirties, our age. Far too young to be so still. I don't know them. Didn't go to the Academy with any of them. But I might have. Close to home.

But there are bodies. I'm almost relieved. How much stranger, to come aboard and find nothing. To wonder if they all stepped out of the airlock twenty light years back, with no explanation. Sweat trickles down the back of my neck. My heart rate still feels too fast, but *Iris* hasn't said anything about it yet. The air inside my suit smells too much like me.

"Matthews," I say to my own comm officer. "Is this coming through?"

"Yes, ma'am," he says softly.

"Gert, start on the power. See if we can get the computers up. I want to see the log."

Rally's bulky glove touches Gert's padded shoulder. He can't possibly feel the contact. "Can I help?"

He glances at her awkwardly, sideways, through the helmet plate. "Yeah. We're going to take those panels off."

I work on retrieving the black box. The battery-driven recorder is stored in a protected safe in the back of the bridge. *Iris* has one just like it. I find it, pull it out, send it back through the airlock to *Iris* so Matthews and Clancy can look at it. Gert and Rally are still working. Over the comm, I can hear them arguing the whole time.

"We shouldn't let the captain wander off by herself," Rally says. As if I can't hear.

"She's fine. What do you expect is going to happen?"

"That's just it, I don't know. But this is weird. What happened here?"

Four frozen sets of eyes are staring at her. She has every right to be uncomfortable. Gert hides his own discomfort by mocking hers.

"You're paranoid."

"It's always the captain who dies first in these stories. Know why? Because it leaves everyone else feeling directionless, guilty, grief-stricken—"

"Rally! Please! Are you going to help me with this or not?"

A few moments of quiet, then, "There's nothing wrong with these circuits. I think the problem's in engineering."

A long pause, then Gert's gruff admission. "Okay. We'll check there. Captain?"

"I'll meet you," I say.

We find the engineer floating before his station, bundled in a suit. He'd survived the freeze, but asphyxiated when his suit oxygen ran out. He'd been working on the engine right up to the end.

I touch both Gert and Rally, patting the fabric of their suits. "You two work. I'm going to check for the rest of them."

I find them in crew quarters like I thought I would. We'll have to make recordings. ID, photos. Then we'll jettison them into the next star. Traditional burial in space. There'd never be a question about what happened to them.

I'm almost back to engineering when Gert and Rally start in again. But it's different this time.

"Rally, don't start. Not in your suit. Do you know what a pain in the ass—"

Rally sniffs. Tears thicken her voice. "I can't help it. I keep thinking—what if it was us? It could have been us."

"No, it couldn't. *Iris* is a good ship, this wouldn't happen. Captain wouldn't let it happen."

His earnestness surprises me. I'd have expected more mocking. I approach quietly—as quietly as I can, in a suit, bouncing against walls to control my momentum.

Rally and Gert are helmet to helmet, faces pressed as close together as they can, holding each other's arms. I can see their profiles in the halo of their helmet lamps. Gert is talking, Rally nods.

"You going to be okay?" Gert says.

"Yeah. Sorry. I just let it get to me. I'm okay now. I'm okay."

"Good. I need your help. I need you."

They gaze at each other. I back away and leave them alone. Head to the airlock, where Horace comes aboard to help me with the bodies.

We've been here two days, working in shifts, when Gert reports.

"I can't get power online, Captain. Not with what we have here. She's cooked."

That was always a possibility, and we have a plan for this. We mark the *Radigund's* position, place a beacon tagging Trade Guild property, though I doubt any other ship looking for salvage will find it. A cruiser with the power to tow the ship will have to retrieve it. Unless Trade Guild decides to junk her and let her float out here, a dead shell, forever.

We undock and leave, taking a course to the nearest star system for the burial. *Radigund* is a dark hulk in space. Her stories, the thousand little mundane events that happen every day aboard any ship, are her own. Gone, now.

Matthews heads the briefing around the galley table. Scenes like this play out thousands of times, on hundreds of ships. A thousand little events. Gert and Rally are sitting next to each other, and I can't remember that ever happening before. They're side by side, shoulders brushing, on the bench attached to the wall.

"Engine failure due to a corruption in the fuel cell line," he said. "There was a cascading failure in all systems after that. They were working on getting the engine back online when power to life support cut off. It was the compression system. Air pressure went fast." Air pressure went, temperature dropped, and the portable oxygen only lasted so long.

"Clancy, take a look at our fuel lines. Just in case," I say. "Thank you, all of you. Your professionalism has helped make a difficult situation go smoothly and is noted." Commendations go into the log, into personnel files, and they all know it. Maybe it'll help.

I start to walk out, to give them the space to vent or complain or laugh or cry without their captain looking on. Rally reaches out when I walk past her and takes my hand. A quick warm squeeze and a smile of comfort. It's enough to make my own eyes sting.

I squeeze her hand back and continue out of the galley.

DRAW THY BREATH IN PAIN

The man who walked through the entrance gazed up and around as if he'd never seen a theater before: thatched roof framing an "O" of sky, row upon row of seats in the gallery, empty now but echoing with the throng and cheers of past performances.

"There's no play 'til tomorrow, sir," Tom called from the stage, where he and a few others of the company were making repairs.

"I—I am not here for a play," the man said, showing himself foreign by his accent, from the north of the Continent perhaps. "I'm looking for—for Master Shakespeare."

"You a creditor?"

"No, indeed no. I would like to speak to him about—about a commission."

"Well, that's different. Will!" Tom shouted back to the tiring house, behind the stage.

"What!" A shape moved by the curtained doorway and emerged. He was in his thirties, with neck-length brown hair, a close-trimmed beard, and ink stains on his hands.

"Money for you." Tom nodded to the stranger.

The foreigner approached the stage like he might a wild dog. "You—you are the writer of plays?"

Will Shakespeare brushed off his shirt and smiled. "Yes, I am."

"I am told you are—quite good."

Will, Tom, and a couple of the other players exchanged glances.

Someone chuckled. The foreigner bit his lip and clutched his belt with nervous hands.

"I like to think I am." Will moved past his fellows and sat on the edge of the stage, putting himself more at a level with the stranger. "You are looking to commission a play?"

The man nodded, sighing. "I have a story. I would like—I would like you to write a play of it."

"Can you pay?" The man jingled a purse at his belt. "Right, then. What kind of story? Comedy? Love story?"

The man shook his head, his face puckered as he struggled for the word.

"Tragedy?" Will prompted.

The man's eyes lit. "Yes, yes it is a tragedy."

"Romantic tragedy, historical tragedy, revenge—"

"Revenge. Yes, revenge."

Will smiled broadly. "Ah, a revenge play. Very fashionable. Is this to be a play for your private pleasure or will my company have the benefit of performing it for the public?"

"Oh, yes! I mean, you *must* perform it. That is the purpose." The man had a haunted, desperate look when he said this. Shadows darkened his eyes, and his features were drawn.

"Why don't we go to a place I know where we can have a drink, and you'll tell me your story."

"*His* story. It's *his* story." The man gasped, his breath wheezing.

Will paused a moment, raising a brow. "His story. Yes. Well then."

He snapped his fingers at Tom, who threw him a hat and jacket that were lying by one of the stage's columns. He hopped down while shrugging these on. His movements were easy, agile; he was well at home on the stage. He walked, gesturing to guide the stranger along to the door of the Globe. "By the by, sir, what is your name?"

"I am Horatio."

*

Not wishing to startle the foreign gentleman, Will took him to the least noxious tavern he could think of in Southwark. The Dog and Firearm was a working man's inn, unfrequented by whores and pickpockets, who knew better than to target men with little coin to spare past a mug of ale in the evening. Still some hours 'til supper, the place was nearly empty. Will dodged chairs and timbers, escorting his patron across the sawdust covered floor to a table in the farthest corner.

Ale loosened tongues. Will put a large mug of it in front of Horatio and bade him drink.

Horatio wrapped his hands around the mug and opened his mouth. He might have wanted to say 'thank you,' tongue against teeth, breath drawn to speak the word, but he stopped. He inhaled, paused again, looking as if he might physically spit out the word. Will braced in sympathetic anxiety. Was the man a stutterer? He hadn't seemed so.

Then he said all at once, like air hissing from a bellows, "There was a king who died, a prince whose throne was usurped." He paused to catch his breath.

Will raised a hand. "Hold there. That's no good way to begin a story."

"But that is what happened—"

"Yes of course, and we'll come to that. But it must begin in darkness. A dark street, nighttime, two men argue—"

"This happened at a castle."

"Then we start with two guards on the battlements."

"But that is not how it happened."

"You will tell me what happened and I will make a play of it."

"Then let me tell it!" Horatio flushed, his breath came in gasps and he gripped the mug with trembling fingers. Startled at his vehemence, Will sat back and closed his mouth.

"I must tell it. There was a king who died, a prince whose throne was usurped—"

And he told the story in a desperate rush of words, delivered with much feeling and little style. The longer he spoke, the less agitated he became. It was like watching a man released from the tension of the rack. He became loquacious as the pressure from some unseen torture faded. Will would have attributed this change to the ale, but Horatio hadn't yet had a sip.

Sweat broke out on Horatio's brow and dampened his hair. He wasn't an old man, perhaps Will's own age of thirty-five. He had blond hair and a moustache, both rather shaggy, a thin face and grim set to jaw and brow. By the end of the telling, he looked exhausted but content, as if he had just run from Marathon to Athens, knew he was going to die but did not care because he had done his duty.

When he finished, he sighed in relief and took a long draw from his ale. The torture had ended, but the haunted look remained. He stared at a distant, unseen point. The tale had everything, beginning with a ghost and ending with a stack of bodies. It needed just a few revisions to make it a good revenge play.

Yet there was more to it, more he wasn't mentioning.

Will tapped his chin. "He cursed you, didn't he? 'Tell my story.' You're compelled to tell it."

"God. Oh God, he did, didn't he?" He leaned on the table, hunching over his drink. Will waited, but Horatio said no more. So much for the loosening effects of drink.

The man's story was already crafting itself in Will's mind. In such stark images, Will saw vividly the scenes he must write: the ghost appears on the battlements, the lover and brother wrestle over the dead girl's grave, a man with a skull stares eye to eye at mortality. With knives and swords, man is the only creature able to bring about his own end . . .

Will's hands itched for pen and paper. When he began writing, the words would flow.

But the other story—

"What happened after? Between then and now. Between the end of the story and you arriving here."

For a moment, Will wasn't sure Horatio understood what he had asked. The foreigner narrowed his eyes, furrowing his brow. The playwright was going to repeat the question, when Horatio shook his head.

That haunted look darkened his eyes, his voice fell to a pained whisper. "I cannot tell."

What had it been like, standing among the corpses after that last duel, the one charged to explain to the survivors?

"Why not? Are you hiding a dark secret?"

"Oh no, nothing like that. But I have told the one story for so long, I'm not sure how to begin another."

Will imagined more scenes: Horatio must have spent hours by his friend's grave, near the king's no doubt, grieving. Despairing. He seemed a brooding type.

"'Tell my story,' he said. It is my duty. But I am not a storyteller. I walk into a place like this and I cannot speak, not even the words to call for a drink, until I say, 'There was a king who died, a prince whose throne was usurped.' I cannot speak at all until I tell the story. But I am no storyteller. I seat myself in a tavern or market and begin, and I speak only a few lines before my audience turns away, uninterested. 'There was a king who died, a prince whose throne was usurped,' I say, and they shake their heads and talk over my voice. And still I hear him, 'Tell my story.' I resist until it hurts to breathe. But I must tell."

Will conjured this other story, the one Horatio could not tell: that castle was a haunted place. Horatio should not have been surprised when he looked across the flat marble of the prince's tomb and saw the figure standing there, as he had stood in life: pale skin and light hair showing stark against black garments, thin-lipped frown, slim hand—a scholar's hand, not a warrior's like his father's had been—pressed over his heart. He was not real—the outline of a granite column showed through the folds of the black cloak. The spirit's chin dipped as it nodded its head in a familiar greeting. The ghost reminded him of his duty. Horatio would have tried to tell the ghost—*I can't, I can't*. But like his father's ghost before him, the prince demanded, *swear*. What choice did he have, when a friend begged him from beyond the grave?

He'd have traveled long winter roads, and if he tried to rest or be silent, the voice drove him, *tell my story*, until he could not open his mouth except to speak those words.

"The power of his dying words is too much for me to bear alone. A company of players could carry it, perhaps. I hope that you may tell his story well enough to hold an audience."

Tell my story.

A sigh whispered through the tavern. Horatio slumped under the weight of his burden, so palpable Will could almost see it. It seemed as if a man stood just behind him, constantly speaking into his ear: a young man with pale hair, huddled in a black cloak, shivering from the frosts of hell. Enough of the dead man lingered in the world to ensure that his last request was fulfilled.

His own ale forgotten, Will sat rigid. He could feel the hairs on his neck. The murmur of conversation within and travelers on the street outside faded to nothing. A sudden noise would shatter him.

The ghost lifted a brimstone gaze, bright eyes above hollow cheeks, and looked at Will over Horatio's shoulder. The playwright exhaled, and the air caught in his throat, as if fish hooks were trying to pull words from him.

He shook his head, took a long drink, and the sunlight returned to the tavern, and the blood stopped pounding in his ears. Slowly, he took a breath, and felt no pain.

Too lightly Will said, "Why me? Why did you pick me—why a play? Why not hire some printer who could set your words in type and publish them for all posterity?"

"So that only those who are able to read might know the story? That is not enough. And—he liked plays. He loved watching them, writing them, speaking with players. A company of players delighted him when nothing else could. If he had not been a prince, he would have become a player and playwright. He had a way with words. When I asked, I was told you are the best."

Will murmured, too softly for any to hear, "Only because Kit Marlowe is dead."

"You see, the play must be good, the best you have ever written, so that people will want to see it again and again, so his story will be told and will spread, and I can rest."

The shade slipped from behind Horatio's chair to stand between them. Will dared not shift his eyes to follow its movement; that would make it real. Forcing a smile to play on his lips, he stared at Horatio.

"What, sir, do you mean to curse me as well? Demanding my best work? That's sure to get my worst."

"I—I am sorry. You have not even accepted the commission. Sir, will you write this play?"

Oh, it was far too late to ask that question. The damage had already been done. This was no longer Horatio's commission to give. This commission came from across the sea, from beyond the old Greek river of the dead. The shade would drive him, and peace would be the payment.

He did not think Horatio realized what had happened. The foreigner huddled at the table, stiff and weary, like a fox who only had a moment's rest before the cries of baying hounds reached him once more. He had carried his weight for so long, he could not feel when it lifted. His breath wheezed through clenched teeth.

"I will write this play," Will said. He shivered against a sudden draft and coughed.

Will wrote. Pages spilled across his table. Words, characters, scenes. These people, what must they have thought? What had they wanted when they stumbled through these actions? What words would fit them best?

Tell my story.

"I am," he told the ghost. "Better, I will let you tell your own story. You'll have more words than any of the others, I promise."

If he stopped writing, he stopped breathing.

Though the rare English sun shone directly through the window, the room felt dark. The sooner he finished this—

He set down the quill, closed his eyes, and sighed. He was going mad. *What do you read, my lord? Words, words, words.*

He wrote because he had to, and trusted to God whether or not the matter would be of any merit. He was watched by a shadow in the corner, the lurking shade of a brooding prince.

"I have Dick Burbage in mind to play you. He's an imposing man with a rich voice. A soliloquizing voice. Folk won't soon forget him."

Footsteps sounded on the wooden stairs to the little room above the tiring house where Will had hidden away. A moment later the man appeared, Richard Burbage himself. Already heroic in stature and bearing, Dick had spent so much time on stage, he posed constantly. He stood in the doorway, hands on hips, chin lifted.

"Will? Who're you talking to?"

Will twirled the quill between his fingers. "No one. Just trying out lines."

"The new play! Excellent, excellent." Without invitation, he picked up pages from the table, quickly shuffling through them. He frowned. "What's this? You're meant to be writing a comedy, aren't you?"

God, he'd forgotten all about it. But how could he write a comedy in this state of mind? He could feel his lungs, he had to think to draw breath, the air itself hurt him—

"Sorry. A new tale distracted me. How'd you like to play a prince?"

"A prince? Hm. Could do. What's the story?"

Will opened his mouth to speak and set the scene for him. His throat closed. He swallowed, swallowed again, and tried to start. "The story . . . the story. There—there was a king who died, a prince whose throne was usurped—"

"That's no way to start a story."

"I know!" He held his head, pulling his hair and grimacing. "I'm sorry. I haven't been myself recently."

"Hmph. Can't have that." He leafed through the papers and his reading slowed. He began to linger over each page. He took more from the table. "This—my God, how many bodies do you have here? Will this top *Titus*?"

"Nearly. Though in this one only the worms eat anyone. Dick, could you please leave me alone?"

Dick continued reading.

As much as he had written, as many of his plays he had seen produced on various stages, Will still held his breath when his work was read for the first time. Of course it wasn't finished yet, wouldn't be even after rehearsals and performances began. But this was the first.

When Dick finished what was there, he asked for more.

The story made no sense, that was the problem.

Any other person in his right mind would have killed the usurper in a vengeful rage and been done with it. But this prince had not. Somehow, some way, Will had to explain this indecision. God, if he were writing this of his own choice, under no compulsion—there'd have been armies, rival gangs sweeping across the stage as the whole country became embroiled in a civil war, a nation burning in the flames of one man's revenge.

But the ghost darkened his room. And Will stopped writing. His chest tightened, clenched in a vise.

"If you want me to write this, help me understand. Can you speak? It would have been better if you had told your own story. Why not haunt your castle and tell the story to shocked and impressed visiting dignitaries? Why must you hound your friend like this? Why must you hound *me*?"

He set down his quill. He'd worn the nib down just from tapping it on the table. Enough of this. He hadn't taken the foreigner's money, he did not have to write. He stood and went toward the door.

If he'd been allowed to walk free, Will might have convinced himself the ghost was a product of his own weary imagination. But the figure stood before the doorway and would not move. It raised its arm, pointed, and Will's throat tightened. He had to think about moving his lungs. The damned ghost would not let him breathe.

"Why don't you speak?" Will gasped. "You are a coward. That is one explanation for your refusal to act. Would you like me to write the play that way?"

The ghost pointed at the table, pages, ink and quill.

"I can't."

Fishhooks again, pulling the words from his throat. "There was a king who died, a prince whose throne—"

If he did not write, would he find himself wandering from town to town, sitting before indifferent audiences in seedy taverns, unable to tell this story? He was an actor; he ought to do better.

The shadow grew to fill the room, the ghost pressing close to him, *tell my story, tell my story*—

Will covered his face with his arms, fending off demons.

"Will? Where are you? God man, what are you doing there in the corner? Get up!"

Dick Burbage stood before him, hands on his shoulders, holding him upright. Will couldn't recall passing out and collapsing in the corner of the room, but that must have been what had happened. The ghost had been suffocating him.

"Will, what the bloody hell's the matter with you?"

He tried to meet Dick's gaze, but his nerves were weak and shuddering, his eyes weighted down by shadows. He must have looked like Horatio had.

"It's too much," he said with a sigh.

"The play?" Dick's enthusiasm was undiminished. The man showed no sympathy. "Then finish it! You always feel better once you've finished."

He propped Will against the wall and stalked out.

The bugger was right, of course.

Draw thy breath in pain to tell my story.

Will had never before had a character stand before him demanding that his story be told one way and not another. It was—disconcerting.

And what of this character? He had been a man existing in a world that failed to live up to his ideals.

Will returned to his chair and found another quill. The facts and motivations didn't matter. It was a story. A play did not have to be real, it only had to seem real. No—it did not even have to seem real, it only had to seem true.

Will wrote.

"This is quite a favor I'm doing for you. I'm not simply telling your story, you know. I'm explaining your actions to the world. You had best be a grateful spirit when I am through."

Any man might have given free rein to his vengeance. But not a scholar, a man who thought too much, introspected himself into corners again and again, until he stood frozen. Until he couldn't write another word.

"Just write it and be done with it. Don't make it real, just make it true."

To be or not to be . . . .

Horatio came to the theater to watch a rehearsal. He sat in the gallery off to the left, hands clenched on his lap, rapt.

Will didn't have much time to speak with him. He was busy marking changes in the prompt book, running back and forth to check entrances, staging, trapdoors and such, arguing with Dick over meter, and wondering if he could possibly work in a cannon.

In truth he was a little afraid of what Horatio would say—what was it like, to see one's self painted on stage? Would he weep at the recreation? Would he rant that the details were all wrong and the work must be rewritten? He watched the stage, the mock-Elsinore where his prince would die every week until the audiences grew tired of it, and his eyes remained dry.

There was a shadow near Horatio that Will tried not to look at too closely.

The rehearsal ended, the players dispersed, Will pretended to compromise with Dick over a turn of phrase, and at last he met with Horatio. Will held his breath.

The foreigner shook his head wonderingly. He even smiled a little, lighting his eyes. "It's marvelous. It's here, it's real—the story will live again and again. He would not wish for better. You work miracles, Master Shakespeare."

Will brushed the praise away, but his heart glowed. A play good enough to send a ghost back to hell—there was a wonder. He breathed easy.

"I have one problem," Horatio said.

"Oh?"

"You made me a character."

"Well, yes."

"You can't. I'm only a messenger. A fair scholar, a poor courtier. Not a character in a play."

"But a tragedy must have a messenger. It's a difficult part, most people underestimate it. But it is not easy standing on stage, surrounded by the bodies of the dead, saddled with the duty of telling your audience that there is no happy ending. The play would fall apart without that character, trust me."

"It is his story, not mine."

"You're right. But he is not here to tell it. He gave that task to you. So you must be part of it." Will thought, what a terrible curse to impose on one who had been a best friend. Will didn't think much of this prince.

"It—it is done. I will pay you well for this."

"You will not pay me at all, friend." Will squeezed the man's shoulder. "The story pays for itself."

Horatio thanked Will with a smile, bowed his head, and turned to leave through the main gate. His steps were slow, even though the shadow around him had lightened and almost disappeared. The whispering was gone. The story was told.

The next afternoon, Will received word from an excitable stable-boy that the foreign gentleman who had taken lodgings in his master's inn had been found dead in his room, stabbed through the heart with his own dagger, his hand clutching the hilt.

Will was not surprised. When Horatio had spoken of rest that first day in the tavern, he had given the word a finality that meant more than rest after a job well ended. Will imagined him spread out over the tomb of his prince, a dagger in his heart, blood spilling over white marble. *Draw thy breath in pain.* . . . He had probably wanted to take that course of action since the moment he found himself with the royal court spread dead around him. Only the prince's dying words kept him alive. And when those words fell still? *The rest is silence.*

THE GIRL WITH THE PRE-RAPHAELITE HAIR

Esther had a recurring dream in which her throat was cut.

She hangs back over the edge of the bed, arms flung out, crucifix-like. Blood from the gash across her neck pours into her hair, long, red, flowing like water. Rich and luxurious, her hair streams red, drips red, moves in a draft, alive. It is hair a man could bury his hands in, his face in, or grab and pull, jerking her around like a doll.

"That's her?"

"Yes. We brought her in an hour ago. You're lucky she wasn't killed in the firefight."

She didn't know if she'd woken up. Her eyes had opened, she thought, but the figures on the other side of the bars seemed indistinct. She couldn't see their minds, which bothered her. She should have been able to tell what they were thinking.

"She's drugged?" The man in the overcoat said this.

"As you instructed." The other man wore a beige uniform and a gun on his belt.

Esther could still hear the guns firing. They'd come from everywhere. She'd tried to warn Ike, tried to tell him when she felt the minds of two dozen police officers converging on the warehouse where he'd set up the deal. They'd catch him this time, with fifty kilos of dust on his hands. But the buyers had already arrived, the deal had progressed too far to call it off. She begged him, tried to pull him away. The buyer had drawn her gun first at the sign of Esther's panic.

Esther had ducked under the table, arms clasped over her head.

She could still hear the guns. Ike's blood still stained her shirt.

The man in the overcoat, the inquisitive one, looked her in the eye. She stared back. Maybe he noticed her staring at him. She couldn't get the taste of gunpowder out of her mouth. Ike had died before he hit the floor. She could still feel it, the light behind his eyes going out, a flash and then darkness. She couldn't feel much of anything else.

"Her parents signed the release?"

"They don't have to. She just turned eighteen."

"But I don't want them asking questions when she disappears."

"Don't worry, they won't. Not with this sort of kid."

"Right. My orderlies have our van around back. Thanks for your help, officer."

"Pleasure doing business with you, Doctor Grant."

They pulled Esther's long, thick hair when they carried her to the white van. She tried to tell them to be careful of it, her one vanity, her only pride. She tried to warn them.

Doctor Grant—that's what they called the slim man in the overcoat—stood nearby and spoke to her. "Be still. No one will hurt you."

The words lifted a weight from her. "You're here to save me? You'll help me?" Her voice sounded weak, tinny. She couldn't remember what she'd just said.

"She's really doped, isn't she?" Someone laughed.

"She'd better be," Grant's calm voice said. "Esther, what am I thinking?"

She ought to know. She would have told him. But she just shook her head. She could barely see his face, let alone his thoughts.

When he spoke again, he sounded pleased. "Well then. What are you thinking?"

No one had ever asked her that before.

He sounded confident, a man who could protect her. Protect her from—she couldn't remember. He stood very close to her.

"I want you to run your hands through my hair."

The same someone laughed again. Doctor Grant disappeared.

The blood from her throat flowed into her hair. She floated in a river of blood, her hair streaming out around her.

Saint Hilda's School for Profligate Girls had been closed for many decades now. Its last students had been guilty of such crimes as smoking in the alley behind the drug store, and had mooned over magazine cut-outs of Rudolph Valentino. Situated upstate, deep in a forest on a thousand acre nature preserve, it had been an ideal place to which to remove girls from the influences of unfeminine vices and Hollywood. It sat on a hill, commanding a view of the river valley below. The building itself, before being donated for the creation of the girls' school, had been the summer mansion of a steel baron. It exhibited all the multistoried, multilayered, ornamented decadence the Victorian gothic revival could produce. Multiple bay windows, a clock tower with a weathervane, gabled roofs, several porches, sashed windows, stained glass windows, round windows, cathedral windows. Gargoyles leered over the porticos.

Inside Saint Hilda's, there were mirrors: at the ends of corridors, along the walls of parlors, in the great dining hall that ran the length of one side of the building, in the study, and in the bedrooms. An observant person might note that the interior floor space of the mansion seemed a good deal smaller than was suggested by the exterior façade.

Esther knew who was there, behind the mirrors. And he knew, as he looked out of his duckblinds and saw her looking back, that Esther was the reason he'd begun this grand project of his in the first place, at this remote and rotting building that he'd turned into his laboratory. In her, he found a Vessel.

She still could not be sure she'd woken up. The sedative had worn off; she could hear them thinking again. But this place, however solid the floor beneath her feet, the walls under her hands, seemed dream-like, so unlike any place that had ever been real to her, like basements and gutters.

They treated her politely, here at Saint Hilda's. A collection of men and women in white lab coats escorted her from room to room. She ate meals in the kitchen. She slept in her own bedroom, with a real four-poster bed and feather pillows. She got new clothes, starched white shirts and prim dark slacks—a uniform, really, like the girls may have worn decades ago, when this was still a school. She walked outside sometimes, when the handlers let her. She'd never seen water as blue as that of the river.

Most days she spent in a bare room, charming almost with its scuffed hardwood floor and chipped plaster walls, where they showed her the backs of cards and made her tell the shapes on the fronts, asked her endless questions with cryptic psychological values, gave her tests, pasted electrodes to her temples and tracked the patterns her brain made, administered a polygraph—she'd had that one before. All the while, Grant watched from behind the mirrors. She passed all his tests, and she knew he smiled.

She wished he would come out from behind the mirrors. She could hear his thoughts, yes—his pleased, ambitious thoughts—but she wanted to see him react to her. To see what he would do when he had a chance to put his hand on her body. She could make him want to do that, if she tried—it had nothing to do with his mind, or hers. She'd done it before, with Ike. It was how she stayed safe. They didn't hurt her when they wanted her.

She saw him at last the day the minions brought her to the basement of Saint Hilda's for the first time. The brick and plaster room was the only one in the mansion that looked like a laboratory, with banks of computers and medical equipment, a long table full of monitors and needle-etched printouts, and a hospital bed, where they made Esther lie and strapped down her hands and feet.

While they attached her to various machines with wires and electrodes, she saw Grant, his tall, slim body wrapped in a labcoat. His brown hair was precisely trimmed, his face perfectly shaven. He looked younger than she thought he should be—his mind seemed older. He moved more slowly than his minions, surveying the proceedings, checking a reading, pointing his instructions. She followed him with her gaze, but his glance only passed over her briefly. She was just another piece of equipment.

She could read minds. Grant had been looking for one like her for years. She knew his plans, skimmed all his research off the surface of his thoughts—such thoughts were always on his mind. He had a computer, a Mental Interfacing Machine Intelligence, he called it. She'd known what he intended. But it hadn't seemed real, it hadn't seemed feasible until this moment when she lay here, wired to this computer.

"How are her vital signs?" Grant asked. If only he would look at her, really look at her. She clenched her fists.

"Good," someone answered, checking off on a clipboard. "Heartbeat elevated slightly, but within safe parameters."

"The MIMI?"

"Ready."

A case, gray plastic and smooth, the size of a table, lurked in its corner, staring with a steady green light.

"I'll start the flow myself."

Doctor Grant opened the floodgate.

You are mine.

The machine had no perception of itself. Esther tried to anchor the intruding thought to an image, a consciousness, but all she found was an amorphous intelligence that grasped the complexity and chaos of the universe. Expansive and overwhelming, it had only one need, which it expressed, driving to her marrow: it needed a tool.

Esther flinched, a startled convulsion which made her pull against the nylon bindings.

"Hold her down!"

"What's happening?"

Something clicked, and the room was silent. Esther tried to look at the ceiling, its beams and boards, the grain of the wood. She couldn't open her eyes.

"Interface complete."

"Esther, look at me," Grant said.

Something else looked out of her eyes.

Grant stood very close to her, looking down at her, just as she'd wanted. He touched her, his hand cupped around the side of her face, holding open her eyelid with his thumb.

"MIMI?"

Esther opened her mouth to say something, to say no, to ask what was happening. She felt so crowded, her mind filled to bursting. She winced because it hurt. Her voice creaked like rusted metal. She looked at him, tried to beg with her eyes. But he didn't see her. He'd never seen her.

"I am here," she said at last. "I am Esther."

No, that wasn't her. She couldn't find the thing that used her voice and name, not even to argue with it. Again, her limbs jerked against their bindings—then went limp. Nothing she thought made them move.

The machine began to see, feel, smell, hear, taste with refined human senses, an infinitely better interface with the world than any lens or microphone yet devised. It began to collect data.

And at last, Grant smiled at her.

The machine tried to erase the line between them.

They set her loose on the estate of Saint Hilda's with this beast staring out of her eyes. Esther was a puppet, screaming at the end of her strings. Screaming, with her mouth closed. The internal noise, her small will, kept the boundary of herself intact.

Once the MIMI knew it could not erase the line—after all, the purpose was to keep the Vessel intact, to learn from it—it tried to push the line back.

It made her touch a hot stove, to feel what it meant to be burned. It cut her, to discover what bleeding meant. It never did serious damage—nothing to scar. Esther became so tired of *feeling*.

Grant watched openly, without the mirrors now. He and an orderly followed her from room to room, across the lawn of the mansion or to the woods. Esther wanted to cry to him, save me, help me. He looked at her so tenderly sometimes.

A week after the invasion, she stripped, quickly, before the MIMI could intervene. Her guard neglected her when she was in her bedroom. Naked, with no clothes to brush and tingle against her skin, she made earplugs from wadded up toilet paper. She went to her small, dark closet, tied a knee sock around her eyes as a blindfold, wrapped herself in a smooth cotton sheet, and closed the door. She curled up in a corner of the closet and didn't move, didn't feel. Nothing to hear, see or taste in the darkness.

How do you like that?

The MIMI had discovered that it often could learn so much more if, instead of exerting control on the Vessel, it simply watched, to see what unexpected thing she'd do next. The MIMI could have made her open the door and release herself. Esther was trying to pick a fight.

I'll be no good to you. I'll gouge out my eyes before you can stop me. I'll cut out my tongue. What would you do then?

The MIMI didn't answer. It wanted to see how long she would lie there, immobile.

Grant came calling for her six hours later. "Esther? Esther, where are you?"

His voice sounded muffled through the paper in her ears. She felt the vibration of his footsteps on the floor and sensed the tremors of his mind. He was worried.

She'd vowed not to move, not to speak for anything. They'd have to drag her out, or the MIMI would have to take control. She wanted to see how long the MIMI would let her lie here.

She bit her lip and whimpered.

The closet door opened; a haze of light shined around the edges of her blindfold.

"Esther, what happened?"

Grant knelt by her, pulling the sheet and blindfold away. She looked at him, squinting, crying. Her muscles ached; she held the sheet to her chest.

Grant put his arms around her. "What did you do?"

"I don't understand it. I don't understand!" She clutched at him and sobbed, pressing her face to his arm.

Awkwardly, he held her, murmured things to her, and told her not to cry. He stroked her hair.

That calmed her. It always did, a touch against her scalp, along her hair, her shoulder, her back. She was lying naked in Grant's arms. Of all the strangeness, she never would have come to this without the MIMI.

She straightened, pulling herself up to look in his eyes. She held his arms, moved his hands so they rested at her hips, on her thighs. She kissed him.

He didn't pull away. The situation surprised him as much as it did her. But he didn't pull away.

"This isn't right," he murmured.

Anxious to learn, the machine—machine—intervened and encouraged.

"Propriety is irrelevant. Continue." Its words, not hers. She'd never speak like that.

But her words, the words she'd might have said—to Ike, say—wouldn't have encouraged him to move his hands up her back, beyond the sheet, to press her bare skin.

No! He's mine! Esther couldn't push back the line; she only retained control because the MIMI didn't know what to do next.

You are mine. Continue.

Esther clung to Grant like a drowning woman.

His thoughts about her had changed, from night to day, winter to summer, since their first meeting in the prison cell. His hands on her shoulders were heavy, protective. He was in love with her, she could see it in his thoughts.

Just as she could see that when he looked at her, he saw the MIMI. When he put his arms around her, she thought she wouldn't mind. She had him, he was hers. When they kissed, she thrilled. The exchange was fair, she thought—Grant's love as payment for servicing the MIMI-monkey on her back.

Every day, every hour, she was the MIMI's tool by which it learned, a conduit through which it impressed Grant and his scientists by its ability to learn. Beyond the interpretation of senses, of movement in a three dimensional world, it began to identify and express understanding of jealousy, confrontation, negotiation, compromise, trickery, rebellion, loyalty, friendship. Love, perhaps.

Esther became somewhat claustrophobic. Not that she had the chance to display phobias, but she felt more comfortable when the MIMI chose to spend its time outside. The MIMI learned that its Vessel was more compliant outdoors, with the breeze on their face, the sky in their sight. Esther became calm when she could look over the lawn to the river in the valley below. The MIMI didn't have to struggle so much to make its observations.

Doctor Grant kept guards around the facility. Esther understood that what he was doing here was illegal, perhaps a different illegal than the kinds of things Ike had done. But then, perhaps not. The guards—former soldiers mostly, distinctively paramilitary—walked the grounds with guns and dogs.

A gun misfired nearby, when one of them near the house was checking his ammunition. The noise should have sent Esther under a table or chair. But the MIMI wanted to watch. The man who'd been operating the weapon had blown off his hand.

He bit back screams while his partner tied off a tourniquet. Blood and bits of flesh had flown everywhere. Esther, unwilling, quailing, screaming internally, stood up and walked toward the injured man. Others came running. Saint Hilda's had doctors and a clinic. They bundled him inside, where he'd get surgery and shots for the pain.

Esther found a bit of finger lying in the grass. The MIMI picked it up, studying the feel of wet blood and dead flesh.

Grant came running, and Esther guiltily dropped the man's finger and wiped her hand on her shirt.

"Are you all right?" he asked, breathless.

Wonderingly, Esther looked at the blood on her shirt, dried in the cracks of her skin. She'd had Ike's blood on her hands. The MIMI had done it. She'd never have done it on her own. Now, the MIMI retreated to see how she would react.

She dropped to her knees and vomited, coughing out every last drop of bile while Grant watched.

"And what will she learn from that? Weakness?" Grant said, suddenly angry.

She? Esther hadn't noticed when the MIMI had become she and not it. She thought of it as the beast. She wasn't teaching it anything, only enduring it.

She ran her tongue over her teeth and spit. "It's not learning weakness. It's a machine. It's using me."

"It is you."

Esther struggled to collect herself, to read his cues. She'd shifted her behavior—so he shifted his, as he did whenever he was reminded that she was not his machine, his creation, but a delinquent, a drug dealer's slut. She saw the judgment in his mind.

She looked at him, shaking her head to toss her hair from her face. "Fuck you."

His expression fully transformed from its initial concern to taut-jawed resentment. "She's more important than you. Never forget."

"It doesn't love you, Grant."

Frowning, he turned and left her on the bloody lawn.

The MIMI stayed distant to observe. It collected the data generated between Grant and Esther as it analyzed the relationships it, as a computer, was asked to survey: between atoms, between planets, between nations, between corporations.

To it, Esther was only so much information. It let her loose only when she might generate useful data.

They were in bed together. He breathed a sigh of satisfaction into her hair. Then, she spoke. Words rushed from her during the times it let her speak.

"Do you remember the first time we met? In the jail? You asked me what I was thinking. Why don't you ask me that now?"

His thoughts turned to frost when he was reminded of the unmentionable, that she was not the MIMI, not really.

"Be quiet."

"Do you know what I'm thinking right now? I'm closer to it than you are. I'm closer to it than you'll ever be, no matter how hard you fuck me."

He grabbed her hair, winding his fist in it and yanking her to him, so he could pin her with his body. He laid his forearm across her neck and pressed.

The MIMI observed, intrigued by the sensation of fear, of heavy male body compressing her lungs, preventing them from expanding. Naked flesh against naked, angry flesh.

Esther gasped out a laugh. "The bitch of it is," she choked at him, "how much you really need me, isn't it?"

Grimacing, he released her, with a last painful wrench to her hair. Esther's scalp tingled for a week.

Grant's minions debated whether or not the machine was learning love. The MIMI smiled at Grant and kissed him with Esther's lips. But Esther would have done those things anyway.

From Esther, it learned sight and sound. It also learned amusement, anger, fear, despair. And pride. It would watch Esther through her eyes as she sat before the mirror, brushing her shining hair, like a vision from a Dante Gabriel Rossetti painting.

Esther and Grant sat at a table, eating. She still had to eat, despite it all. Her sensory interface might have been superior, but the scientists couldn't plug her into a wall. The MIMI didn't care for eating, once it had surveyed the usual range of tastes. It left Esther to her own self.

"When will you let me go?" she asked, setting down her utensils. She wasn't hungry.

Grant paused, mid-bite. He liked to pretend sometimes that they were all normal here. This was just a house, he was just a man, and she was the woman he sat down to dinner with every night. Esther didn't like to let him pretend.

She heard the answer in his thoughts, a flat refusal, an uncompromising never. Grant usually didn't voice his thoughts, however.

"You don't know how lucky you are to be here. To be the first in an experiment like this."

Indeed, she did not.

"Do you love me, Grant?"

Again, she knew the answer. He was confused; he didn't know who was speaking, Esther or the MIMI.

"I love you," she said. "Do you know who I am?"

He stood up, scraping the chair on the floor. Trembling, he bit his lip, a repressed snarl. He wanted to hurt her. He imagined himself lunging across the table to strangle her. Amazement registered in his expression—he was not a violent man. But the feelings she aroused in him—violence, anger. Irrational, all of it. She was an experiment. A tool. Peripheral to the object, true artificial human intelligence. When had he stopped seeing her as a tool?

He looked helpless, standing with his impotent fists. She laughed at him. At this his face flushed red. He stalked from the table in the dining room.

Esther rested her elbows on the table, pressed her face to her hands, and bodily held the tears inside.

The MIMI watched, weaving its silicon cogitations.

I hate you, Esther told it.

It understood hate, taunting and laughter. Even when it didn't speak, Esther could read its moods. It enjoyed her helplessness. Nothing she could think at the beast changed that. That didn't keep her from trying.

What would it take to make him kill me?

Counterproductive. Your death is undesirable.

Then, she thought, *what would it take to make him love me?*

He already does.

In a manner of speaking. Esther didn't feel up to arguing the point. *What would it take to make him hate you?*

Also counterproductive.

Do you care?

His emotional stability is desirable.

They debated about whether or not the machine was learning love.

Steak had been the meal tonight—Grant was fond of his small luxuries. Esther's hand found the steak knife by her plate. She did not think of cutting herself—the MIMI would have intervened as soon as the thought formed. In the meantime, the MIMI would let her go, to see how far she'd run.

I will cut my hair.

Your hair is your one pride. You will not go so far.

She grabbed her hair, the whole lot of it, in her fist and began to slice, at the level of her neck.

Like fire, the MIMI grabbed her mind, her limbs. Esther whimpered as her fingers stretched open against her will. Her hands fell. She held a lock of red hair. That was all she'd been able to cut, before the MIMI stopped her.

So her hair was her pride. It had become the MIMI's too.

They trod a fine line that week, Esther and the MIMI. The MIMI teased, letting Esther's words flow, letting her taunt and provoke Grant. Letting her find and conceal knives and scissors, letting her get so close, then pulling up the strings at the last. The game, the thrill, was something new to the beast. Anticipation, risk, triumph. It risked more each time.

Grant could tell something was afoot. The transitions between the two personae came so quickly, so violently sometimes, as when the word "Grant" wrenched out around Esther's clenched teeth. He began to tell the two of them apart, something he'd never bothered learning before. Sometimes, after only a word or two, "Grant" spoken in a certain self-assured tone of voice, he knew his lover had returned.

He loved her, he slept. Esther raised herself on an elbow and looked at him, spoke a word to test herself, thought angry, teasing thoughts at him, so the MIMI wouldn't guess.

"Grant." She nudged him awake. She retrieved the latest kitchen knife she'd smuggled and hidden under the mattress. The MIMI watched closely to see how far she could go.

Very carefully, she adjusted the tone of her voice, so he could not tell. She'd heard the MIMI often enough. She could mimic it. Slowly, he woke. He watched her; her body was tense.

She put the knife in his hand, pressing his fingers closed around it. "Grant. Cut Esther's hair. I tire of it."

She hadn't been sure how he would react, if he would refuse, if he would ask questions. As it was, he couldn't have done better if she had guided his hand herself. He took the whole of her hair in his fist and cut at the neck, sawing at it, before the MIMI could make her move, before it could stop him with a word. All his anger at her—at Esther—surged out in the cut, as though the innocuous action would sever the girl from the computer, separate the two forever.

Esther pulled back with a laugh; her hair ripped away.

Then, the MIMI learned disbelief. Then uncertainty, embarrassment, loss—even fear, that Esther had the ability to win the little game, which raised the concern of what else she might do. So many emotions one upon the other.

It was only hair. Only a small loss, a temporary loss. This Esther knew; the computer hadn't learned yet. It hadn't ever lost, or dealt with the accompanying grief. But Esther—she had a world of experience with the emotions of loss and fear. These experiences, these memories, she flung at the MIMI. It wanted to learn. It wanted to feel. So let it.

Ike's face. She couldn't see his face. Because it was covered with blood. She reached out from her hiding place under the table, touched his face, tried to wipe away the blood. And no—she couldn't touch his face because it wasn't there. She didn't stop screaming until they sedated her.

Ironically, Ike had been the one to clean her up. She'd been kicked out of the house—she didn't remember why. Or had she run away? She couldn't recall much about that time; she'd been high all the time. It was the only way to shut out the voices of the world. But Ike believed her, when she said what she could do. He cleaned her up and used her. She owed him a lot.

She could smell the blood, his blood, mixed with the smell of burning. Voices. Spotlights. They wanted to kill her, the police. They all wanted to, but she wasn't holding a gun, so they couldn't. She lay curled up by Ike, screaming.

Her throat slit, her blood flowing, creeping over her cheek to her scalp. The dream had become more and more vivid over the years. The MIMI had dreamed with her, it understood dreams. But not how real they could seem in the face of such terror.

It screamed against the flood of horrors with which Esther filled her senses. A synapse in its network misfired. Or something. Perhaps a silicon stroke. The minions never learned exactly what.

The green light on the box in the basement winked out.

Esther sat silent, tangled in sheets, frozen in her own moment of disbelief. Her mind opened, a sky blown clear after a storm. The beast had fled.

Grant knelt on the bed, naked and primitive, hefting the knife in one hand and the dead mass of her red hair in the other, like murdered prey.

Esther's head was suddenly weightless, like air, like a balloon lifting off her shoulders, with a tickling fringe of hair brushing her chilled neck. She shook her head; clear, all clear and free.

"I killed it!" She grinned at Grant. "It's dead, and you can't love it anymore!"

Grant stared for a moment, gripping the knife so the tendons showed white on his hands. Then he threw her hair at her and went off for his clothes, to go to the basement to see if she was right.

Esther found a robe, wrapped herself up. She had to run. She had nowhere to run. She didn't care. Finally, she felt light enough to run.

Grant only needed a second to confirm what Esther had declared in such a loud, joyous voice.

"No. No, no!" His voice grew louder as he flew up the stairs.

He caught her in the dining room. He only wore pants. His bare chest, pale and smooth, heaved.

She ran through a set of French doors which opened onto a tiny balcony. Five feet from the ground and surrounded by holly shrubs, it was the kind of balcony where in another century a woman in a silk gown might have leaned over the iron railing to say farewell to her beloved. The railing, crafted to shape decorative ivy tendrils, trapped Esther.

She leaned back against the railing as Grant came at her. He still held the knife clutched in his hand.

Her hair was cut, a ragged fringe at her neck. It tossed in the air instead of drifting, graceful. Now, where would the blood flow?

GAME OF CHANCE

Once, they'd tried using sex to bring down a target. It had seemed a likely plan: throw an affair in the man's path, guide events to a compromising situation, and momentum did the rest. That was the theory—a simple thing, not acting against the person directly, but slantwise. But it turned out it *was* too direct, almost an attack, touching on such vulnerable sensibilities. They'd lost Benton, who had nudged a certain woman into the path of a certain Republic Loyalist Party councilman and died because of it. He'd been so sure it would work.

Gerald had proposed trying this strategy again to discredit the RLP candidate in the next executive election. The man couldn't be allowed to take power if Gerald's own favored allies hoped to maintain any influence. But there was the problem of directness. His cohort considered ideas of how to subtly convince a man to ruin his life with sex. The problem remained: there were no truly subtle ways to accomplish this. They risked Benton's fate with no guaranteed outcome. Gathering before the chalkboard in their warehouse lair, mismatched chairs drawn together, they plotted.

Clare, sitting in back with Major, turned her head to whisper, "I like it better when we stop assassinations rather than instigate them."

"It's like chess," Major said. "Sometimes you protect a piece, sometimes you sacrifice one."

"It's a bit arrogant, isn't it, treating the world like our personal chess board?"

Major gave a lopsided smile. "Maybe, a bit."

"I think I have an idea," Clare said.

Gerald glanced their way and frowned.

Much more of this and he'd start accusing them of insubordination. She nudged Major and made a gesture with her hand: *Wait. We'll tell him later.* They sat back and waited, while Gerald held court and entertained opinions, from planting illegal pornography to obtaining compromising photographs. All of it too crass, too mundane. Not credible. Gerald sent them away with orders to "come up with something." Determined to brood, he turned his back as the others trailed to the corner of the warehouse that served as a parlor to scratch on blank pages and study books.

Clare and Major remained, seated, watching, until Gerald looked back at them and scowled.

"Clare has a different proposal," Major said, nodding for her to tell.

Clare ducked her gaze, shy, but knew she was right. "You can't use sex without acting on him, and that won't work. So don't act on him. Act on everything around him. A dozen tiny decisions a day can make a man fall."

Gerald was their leader because he could see the future. Well, almost. He could see paths, likely directions of events that fell one way instead of another. He used this knowledge and the talents of those he recruited to steer the course of history. Major liked the chess metaphor, but Gerald worked on the canvas of epic battles, of history itself. He scowled at Clare like she was speaking nonsense.

"Tiny decisions. Like whether he wears a red or blue tie? Like whether he forgets to brush his teeth? You mean to change the world by this?"

Major, who knew her so well, who knew her thoughts before she did, smiled his hunting smile. "How is the man's heart?"

"Yes. Exactly," she said.

"It'll take time," Major explained to a still frowning Gerald. "The actions will have to be lined up just so."

"All right," he said, because Major had proven himself. His voice held a weight that Clare's didn't. "But I want contingencies."

"Let the others make contingencies," Major said, and that made them all scowl.

Gerald left Clare and Major to work together, which was how she liked it best.

She'd never worked so hard on a plan. She searched for opportunities, studied all the ways they might encourage the target to harm himself. She found many ways, as it happened. The task left Clare drained, but happy, because it was working. Gerald would see. He'd be pleased. He'd start to listen to her, and she wouldn't need Major to speak for her.

"I don't mind speaking for you," Major said when she confided in him. "It's habit that makes him look right through you like he does. It's hard to get around that. He has to be the leader, the protector. He needs someone to be the weakest, and so doesn't see you. And the others only see what he sees."

"Why don't you?"

He shrugged. "I like to see things differently."

"Maybe there's a spell we could work to change him."

He smiled at that. The spells didn't work on them, because they were outside the whole system. Their spells put them outside. Gerald said they could change the world by living outside it like this. Clare kept thinking of it as gambling, and she never had liked games.

They worked: the target chose the greasiest, unhealthiest meals, always ate dessert, and took a coach everywhere—there always seemed to be one conveniently at hand. Some days, he forgot his medication, the little pills that kept his heart steady—the bottle was not in its place and he couldn't be bothered to look for it. Nothing to notice from day to day. But one night, in bed with his wife—no lurid affair necessary—their RLP candidate's weak heart gave out. A physician was summoned quickly enough, but to no avail. And that, Clare observed, was how one brought down a man with sex.

Gerald called it true. The man's death threw the election into chaos, and his beloved Populist Tradition Party was able to hold its seats in the Council.

Clare glowed with pride because her theory had worked. A dozen little changes, so indirect as to be unnoticeable. The perfect expression of their abilities.

But Gerald scowled. "It's not very impressive, in the main," he said and walked away.

"What's that supposed to mean?" Clare whispered.

"He's angry he didn't think of it himself," Major said.

"So it wasn't fireworks. I thought that was the point."

"I think you damaged his sensibilities," he said, and dropped a kind kiss on her forehead.

She had been a normal, everyday girl, though prone to day-dreaming, according to her governess. She was brought up in proper drawing rooms, learning how to embroider, supervise servants, and orchestrate dinner parties. Often, though, she had to be reminded of her duties, of the fact that she would one day marry a fine gentleman, perhaps in the army or in government, and be the envy of society ladies everywhere. Otherwise she might sit in the large wingback arm-chair all day long, staring at the light coming in through the window, or at sparks in the fireplace, or at the tongue of flame dancing on the wick of the nearest lamp. "What can you possibly be thinking about?" her governess would ask. She'd learned to say, "Nothing." When she was young, she'd said things like, "I'm wondering, what if fire were alive? What if it traveled, and is all flame part of the same flame? Is a flame like a river, traveling and changing every moment?" This had alarmed the adults around her.

By the time she was eighteen, she'd learned to make herself presentable in fine gowns, and to arrange the curls of her hair to excite men's interest, and she'd already had three offers. She hadn't given any of them answer, but thought to accept the one her father most liked so at least somebody would be happy.

Then one day she'd stepped out of the house, parasol over her shoulder, intending a short walk to remind herself of her duty before that evening's dinner party, and there Gerald and Major had stood at the foot of the stairs, two dashing figures from an adventure tale.

"What do you think about, when you look at the flame of a candle?" Gerald had asked.

She stared, parasol clutched in gloved hands, mind tumbling into an honest answer despite her learned poise. "I think of birds playing in sunlight. I wonder if the sun and the fire are the same. I think of how time slows down when you watch the hands of a clock move."

Major, the younger and handsomer of the pair, gave her a sly grin and offered his hand. "You're wasted here. Come with us."

At that moment she knew she'd never been in love before, because she lost her heart to Major. She set her parasol against the railing on the stairs, stepped forward, and took his hand. Gerald pulled the theatrical black cape he'd been wearing off his shoulders, turned it with a twist of his wrists, and swept it around himself, Major, and Clare. A second of cold followed, along with a feeling of drowning. Clare shut her eyes and covered her face. When Major murmured a word of comfort, she finally looked around her and saw the warehouse. Gerald introduced himself and the rest of his cohort, and explained that they were masters of the world, which they could manipulate however they liked. It seemed a very fine thing.

Thus she vanished from her old life as cleanly as if she had never existed. Part of her would always see Gerald and Major as her saviors.

Gerald's company, his band of unseen activists, waited in their warehouse headquarters until their next project, which would only happen when Gerald traced lines of influence to the next target. The next chess piece. Clare looked forward to the leisure time until she was in the middle of it, when she just wanted to go out and *do* something.

Maybe it was just that she'd realized a long time ago that she wasn't any good at the wild version of poker the others played to pass time. She sat the games out, tried to read a book, or daydreamed. Watched dust motes and candle flames.

The other four were the fighters. The competitive ones. She'd joined this company by accident.

Cards snicked as Major dealt them out. Clean-shaven, with short cropped hair, he was dashing, military. He wore a dark blue uniform jacket without insignia; a white shirt, unbuttoned at the collar; boots that needed polishing, but that only showed how active he was. Always in the thick of it. Clare could watch him deal cards all day.

"Wait a minute. Are we on Tuesday rules or Wednesday?" Ildie asked.

Fred looked up from his hand, blinking in a moment of confusion. "Today's Thursday, isn't it?"

"Tuesday rules on Thursday. That's the fun of it," Marco said, voice flat, attention on the cards.

"I hate you all," Ildie said, scowling. They chuckled, because she always said that.

Ildie dressed like a man, in an oxford shirt, leather pants, and high boots. This sometimes still shocked Clare, who hadn't given up long skirts and braided hair when she'd left a proper parlor for this. Ildie had already been a rebel when she joined. At least Clare had learned not to tell Ildie how much nicer she'd look if she grew her hair out. Fred had sideburns, wore a loosened cravat, and out of all of them might be presentable in society with a little polish. Marco never would be. Stubble shadowed his face, and he always wore his duster to hide the pistols on his belt.

A pair of hurricane lamps on tables lit the scene. The warehouse was lived-in, the walls lined with shelves, which were piled with books, rolled up charts, atlases, sextants, hourglasses, a couple of dusty globes. They'd pushed together chairs and coffee tables for a parlor, and the far corner was curtained off into rooms with cots and washbasins. In the parlor, a freestanding chalkboard was covered with writing and charts, and more sheets of paper lay strewn on the floor, abandoned when the equations scrawled on them went wrong. When they went right, the sheets were pinned to the walls and shelves and became the next plan. At the moment, nothing was pinned up.

Clare considered: was it a matter of tracing lines of influence to objects rather than personalities? Difficult, when influence was a matter of motivation, which was not possible with inanimate objects. So many times their tasks would have been easier if they could change someone's *mind*. But that was like bringing a sledgehammer down on delicate glasswork. So you changed the thing that would change someone's mind. How small a change could generate the greatest outcome? That was her challenge: could removing a bottle of ink from a room change the world? She believed it could. If it was the right bottle of ink, the right room. Then perhaps a letter wouldn't be written, an order of execution wouldn't be signed.

But the risk—that was Gerald's argument. The risk of failure was too great. You might take a bolt from the wheel of a cannon, but if it was the wrong bolt, the wrong cannon . . . The variables became massive. Better to exert the most influence you could without being noticed. That didn't stop Clare from weaving her thought experiments. For want of a nail . . .

"I raise," Major said, and Clare looked up at the change in his voice. He had a plan; he was about to spring a trap. After the hundreds of games those four had played, couldn't they see it?

"You don't have anything." Marco looked at his hand, at the cards lying face up on the table, back again. Major gave him a "try me" look.

"He's bluffing." Ildie wore a thin smile, confident because Major had bluffed before. Just enough to keep them guessing. He did it on purpose, they very well knew, and he challenged them to outwit him. They thought they could—that was why they kept falling into his traps. But even Major had a tell, and Clare could see it if no one else could. Easy for her to say, though, sitting outside the game.

"Fine. Bet's raised. I see it," Fred countered.

Then they saw it coming, because that was part of Major's plan. Draw them in, spring the trap. He tapped a finger, the air popped, a tiny sound like an insect hitting a window, that was how small the spell was, but they all recognized the working of it, the way the world shifted just a bit, as one of them outside of it nudged a little. Major laid out his cards, which were all exactly the cards he needed, a perfect hand, against unlikely—but not impossible—odds.

Marco groaned, Ildie threw her cards, Fred laughed. "I should have known."

"Tuesday rules," Major said, spreading his hands in mock apology.

Major glanced at Clare, smiled. She smiled back. No, she didn't ever want to play this game against Major.

Marco gathered up the cards. "Again."

"Persistent," Major said.

"Have to be. Thursday rules this time. The way it's *meant* to be." They dealt the next hand.

Gerald came in from the curtained area that was his study, his wild eyes red and sleepless, a driven set to his jaw. They all knew what it meant.

"I have the next plot," he said.

Helping the cause sometimes meant working at cross-purposes with the real world. A PTP splinter group, frustrated and militant, had a plan, too, and Gerald wanted to stop it because it would do more harm than good.

Easier said than done, on such a scale. Clare preferred the games where they put a man's pills out of the way.

She and Major hunched in a doorway as the Council office building fell, brought down by cheap explosives. A wall of dust scoured the streets. People coated in the gray stuff wandered like ghosts. Clare and Major hardly noticed.

"We couldn't stop it," Clare murmured, speaking through a handkerchief.

Major stared at a playing card, a jack of diamonds. "We've done all we can."

"What? What did we do? We didn't stop it!" They were supposed to stop the explosion, stop the destruction. She had wanted so much to stop it, not for Gerald's sake, but for the sake of doing good.

Major looked hard at her. "Twenty-nine bureaucrats meant to be in that building overslept this morning. Eighteen stayed home sick. Another ten stayed home with hangovers from overindulging last night. Twenty-four more ran late because either their pets or children were sick. The horses of five coaches came up lame, preventing another fifteen from arriving. That's ninety-six people who weren't in that building. We did what we could." His glare held amazing conviction.

She said, "We're losing, aren't we? Gerald will never get what he wants."

So many of Gerald's plans had gone just like this. They counted victories in lives, like picking up spilled grains of rice. They were changing lives, but not the world.

"Come on," he ordered. "We've got a door."

He threw the card at the wall of the alley where they'd hidden. It stuck, glowed blue, and grew. Through the blue glare a gaping hole showed. Holding hands, they dove into it, and it collapsed behind them.

"Lame coach horses? Hangovers?" Gerald said, pacing back and forth along one of the bookshelves. "We're trying to save civilization."

"What is civilization but the people who live within it?" Clare said softly. It was how she said anything around Gerald.

"Ninety-six lives saved," Major said. "What did anyone else accomplish?" Silent gazes, filled with visions of destruction, looked back at him. The rest of them: Fred, Ildie, and Marco. Their jackets were ruffled, their faces weary, but they weren't covered with dust and ragged like Clare and Major were. They hadn't gotten that close.

Gerald paced. "In the end, what does it mean? For us?" The question was rhetorical because no answer would satisfy him. Though Clare thought, it means whatever we want it to mean.

*

Clare and Major never bothered hiding their attachment from the others. What could the company say to disapprove? Not even Gerald could stop them, though Ildie often looked at her askance, with a scowl, as if Clare had betrayed her. Major assured her that the other woman had never held a claim on him. Clare wondered if she might have fallen in love with any of the men—Fred, Benton, or even Marco—if any of them had stood by Gerald to recruit her instead of Major. But no, she felt her fate was to be with Major. She didn't feel small with him.

Hand in hand, careless, they'd leave the others and retreat to the closet in an unused corner of the warehouse's second floor, where they'd built a pallet just for them. A nest, Clare thought of it. Here, she had Major all to herself, and he seemed happy enough to be hers. She'd lay across his naked chest and he'd play with her hair. Bliss.

"Why did you follow Gerald when he came for you?" she asked after the disaster with the exploded building.

"He offered adventure."

"Not for the politics, then? Not because you believe in his party?"

"I imagine it's all one and the same in the long run."

The deep philosophy of this would have impressed her a few years ago. Now, it seemed like dodging the question. She propped herself on an elbow to study him. She was thinking out loud.

"Then why do you still follow him? You could find adventure without him, now that he's shown you the way."

He grinned sleepily and gathered her closer. "I'd wander aimlessly. His adventures are more interesting. It's a game."

"Oh."

"And why do you still follow him? Why did you take my hand the day we met?"

"You were more interesting than what I left behind."

"But I ask you the same question, now. I know you don't believe in his politics. So why do you still follow him?"

"I don't follow him. I follow you."

His expression turned serious, frowning almost. His hand moved from her hair to her cheek, tracing the line of her jaw as if she were fragile glass. "We're a silly pair, aren't we? No belief, no faith."

"Nothing wrong with that. Major—if neither of us is here for Gerald, we should leave. Let's go away from this, be our own cohort." Saying it felt like rebellion, even greater than the rebellion of leaving home in the first place.

His voice went soft, almost a whisper. "Could we really? How far would we get before we started missing this and came back?"

"I wouldn't miss the others," she said, jaw clenched.

"No, not them," he said. "But the game."

Gerald could fervently agitate for the opposite party, and Major would play the game with as much glee. She could understand and still not agree.

"You think we need Gerald, to do what we do?"

He shook his head, a questioning gesture rather than a denial. "I'm happy here. Aren't you?"

She could nod and not lie because here, at this small moment with him, she was happy.

One *could* change the world by nudging chances, Clare believed. Sometimes, she went off by herself to study chances the others wouldn't care about.

At a table in the corner of a café—the simple, homelike kind that students frequented, with worn armchairs, and chess boards and pieces stored in boxes under end tables with old lamps on them—Clare drew a pattern in a bit of tea that dripped from her saucer. Swirled the shape into two circles, forever linked. In front of the counter, a boy dropped a napkin. The girl behind him picked it up. Their hands brushed. He saw that she had a book of sonnets, which he never would have noticed if he hadn't dropped the napkin. She saw that he had a book of philosophy. They were students, maybe, or odd enthusiasts. One asked the other, are you a student? The answer didn't matter because the deed was done. In this world, in this moment, despite all the unhappiness, this small thing went right.

This whole thing started because Gerald saw patterns. She wondered later: Did he see the pattern, identify them because of it, and bring them together? Was that his talent? Or did he cause the pattern to happen? If not for Gerald, would she have gone on, free and ignorant, happily living her life with no knowledge of what she could do? Or was she always destined to follow this path, use this talent with or without the others? Might she have spent her time keeping kittens from running into busy streets or children from falling into rivers? And perhaps one of those children would grow up to be the leader Gerald sought, the one who would change the world.

All that had happened, all their work, and she still could not decide if she believed in destiny.

She wouldn't change how any of it had happened because of Major. The others marveled over Gerald's stern, Cossack determination. But she fell in love with Major, with his shining eyes.

"We have to do better, think harder, more creatively. Look how much we've done already, never forget how much we've done."

After almost a decade of this, only six of the original ten were left. The die-hards, as mad as Gerald. Even Major looked on him with that calculating light in his eyes. Did Gerald even realize that Major's passion was for tactics rather than outcome?

"Opportunities abound, if we have the courage to see them. The potential for good, great good, manifests everywhere. We must have the courage to see it."

Rallying the troops. Clare sighed. How many times had Gerald given variations of this speech in this dingy warehouse, hidden by spells and out of the world? They all sounded the same. She'd stopped being able to see the large patterns a long time ago and could only see the little things now. A dropped napkin in a café. She could only change the course of a few small lives.

"There's an assassination," said Gerald. "It will tip the balance into a hundred years of chaos. Do you see it?"

Fred smiled. "We can stop it. Maybe jam a rifle."

"A distraction, to throw off the assassin's aim."

"Or give him a hangover," Major said. "We've had great success with hangovers and oversleeping." He glanced at Clare with his starry smile. She beamed back. Fred rolled his eyes.

"Quaint," Gerald said, frowning.

The game was afoot. So many ways to change a pattern. Maybe Clare's problem was she saw them as people, not patterns. And maybe she was the one holding the rest back. Thinking too small. She wasn't part of *their* pattern anymore.

This rally was the largest Clare had ever seen. Her generation had grown up hearing grandparents' stories of protest and clashes (civil war, everyone knew, but the official history said clashes, which sounded temporary and isolated). While their parents grew up in a country that was tired and sedate, where they were content to consolidate their little lives and barricade themselves against the world, the children wondered what it must have been like to believe in idealism.

Gerald's target this time was the strongest candidate the PTP had ever put forward for Premiere. The younger generation flocked to Jonathan Smith. People adored him—unless they supported the RLP. Rallies like this were the result. Great crowds of hope and belief, unafraid. And the crowds who opposed them.

Gerald said that Jonathan Smith was going to be assassinated. Here, today, at the rally, in front of thousands. All the portents pointed to this. But it would not result in martyrdom and change, because the assassin would be one of his own and people would think, *our parents were right,* and go home.

Clare and Major stood in the crowd like islands, unmoving, unfeeling, not able to be caught up in the exhilarating speech, the roaring response. She felt alien. These were her people, they were all human, but never had she felt so far removed. She might have felt godlike, if she believed in a god who took such close interest in creation as to move around it like this. God didn't have to, because there were people like Gerald and Major.

"It's nice to be saving someone," Clare said. "I've always liked that better."

"It only has to be a little thing," Major said. "Someone in the front row falls and breaks a bone. The commotion stalls the attack when Smith goes to help the victim. Because he's like that."

"We want to avoid having a victim at all, don't we?"

"Maybe it'll rain."

"We change coach horses, not the weather." But not so well that they couldn't keep an anarchist bomb from arriving at its destination. They weren't omnipotent. They weren't gods. If they were, they could control the weather.

She had tried sending a message about the government building behind Gerald's back. He would have called the action too direct, but she'd taken the risk. She'd called the police, the newspapers, everyone, with all the details they'd conjured. Her information went into official records, was filed for the appropriate authorities, all of which moved too slowly to be of any good. It wasn't too direct after all.

Inexorable. This path of history had the same feeling of being inexorable. Official channels here would welcome an assassination. The police would not believe her. They only had to save one life.

She wished for rain. The sky above was clear.

They walked among the crowd, and it was grand. She rested her hand in the crook of Major's elbow; he held it there. He wore a happy, silly smile on his face. They might have been in a park, strolling along a gentle river in a painting.

"There's change here," he said, gazing over the angry young crowd and their vitriolic signs.

She squeezed his arm and smiled back.

The ground they walked on was ancient cobblestone. This historic square had witnessed rallies like this for a thousand years. In such times of change, gallows had stood here, or hooded men with axes. How much blood had soaked between these cobbles?

That was where she nudged. From the edges of the crowd, they were able to move with the flow of people surging. They could linger at the edges with relative freedom of movement, so she spotted a bit of pavement before the steps climbing to the platform where the demagogue would speak. A toe caught on a broken cobblestone would delay him. Just for a second. Sometimes that was enough to change the pattern.

"Here," she said, squeezing Major's arm to anchor him. He nodded, pulled her to the wall of a town house, and waited.

While she focused on the platform, on the path that Jonathan Smith would take—on the victim—Major turned his attention to the crowd, looking for the barrel of a gun, the glint of sunlight off a spyglass, counter-stream movement in the enthusiastic surge. The assassin.

Someone else looking for suspicious movement in a crowd like this would find *them*, Clare thought. Though somehow no one ever did find them.

Sometimes, all they could do was wait. Sometimes, they waited and nothing happened. Sometimes they were too late or early, or one of the others had already nudged one thing or another.

"There," Major said, the same time that Clare gripped his arm and whispered, "There."

She was looking to the front where the iconic man, so different than the bodyguards around him, emerged and waved at the crowd. There, the cobblestone—she drew from her pocket a cube of sugar that had been soaked in amaretto, crumbled it, let the grains fall, then licked her fingers. The sweet, heady flavor stung her tongue.

Major lunged away from her. "No!"

The stone lifted, and the great Jonathan Smith tripped. A universal gasp went up.

Major wasn't looking to the front with everyone else. He was looking at a man in the crowd, twenty feet away, dissolute. A trouble-maker. Hair ragged, shirt soiled, faded trousers, and a canvas jacket a size too large. Boots made for kicking. He held something in his right fist, in a white-knuckled grip.

This was it, the source, the gun—the locus, everything. This was where they learned if they nudged enough, and correctly. But the assassin didn't raise a straight arm to aim. He cocked back to throw. He didn't carry a gun, he held a grenade.

Gerald and the others had planned for a bullet. They hadn't planned for this.

Major put his shoulder to the man's chest and shoved. The would-be assassin stumbled, surprised, clutched the grenade to his chest—it wasn't active, he hadn't lit the fuse. Major stopped him. Stopped the explosive, stopped the assassin, and that was good. Except it wasn't, and he didn't.

Smith recovered from his near-fall. He mounted the platform. The bodyguard behind him drew his handgun, pointed at the back of Smith's head, and fired. The shot echoed and everyone saw it and spent a moment in frozen astonishment. Even the man with the grenade. Everyone but Major, who was on the ground, doubled over, shivering as if every nerve burned.

Clare fell on top of him, crying, clutching at him. His eyes rolled back enough to look at her, enough for her to see the fear in them. If she could have held onto him, carried him with her, saved him, she would have. But he'd put himself back into the world. He'd acted, plunged back into a time and place he wasn't part of anymore, and now it tore him to pieces. The skin of his face cracked under her hands, and the blood and flesh underneath was black and crumbling to dust.

She couldn't sob hard enough to save him.

Clare was lost in chaos. Then Gerald was there with his cloak. So theatrical, Major always said. Gerald used the cloak like Major used the jack of diamonds. He swept it around the three of them, shoving them through a doorway.

But only Clare and Gerald emerged on the other side.

*

The first lesson they learned, that Major forgot for only a second, the wrong second: they could only build steps, not leap. They couldn't act directly, they couldn't be part of the history they made.

So Jonathan Smith died, and the military coup that followed ruined everything.

Five of them remained.

The problem was she could not imagine a world different from the burned-out husk that resulted from the war fought over the course of the next year. Gerald's plan might have worked, bringing forth a lush Eden where everyone drank nectar and played hopscotch with angelic children, and she still would have felt empty.

Gerald's goal had always been utopia. Clare no longer believed it was possible.

The others were very kind to her, in the way anyone was kind to a child they pitied. *Poor dear, but she should have known better.* Clare accepted the blanket Ildie put over her shoulders and the cup of hot tea Fred pressed into her hands.

"Be strong, Clare," Ildie said, and Clare thought, easy for her to say.

"What next, what next." Gerard paced the warehouse, head bent, snarling almost, his frown was so energetic.

"Corruption scandal?" Marco offered.

"Too direct."

"A single line of accounting, the wrong number in the right place, to discredit the regime," Ildie said.

Gerald stopped pacing. "Maybe."

Another meeting. As if nothing had happened. As if they could still go on.

"Major was the best of us," Clare murmured.

"We'll just have to be more careful," Ildie murmured back.

"He made a mistake. An elementary mistake," Gerald said, and never spoke of Major again.

The village a mile outside the city had once been greater, a way station and market town. Now, it was a skeleton. The war had crushed it, burned it, until only hovels remained, the scorched frames of buildings standing like trees in a forest. Brick walls had fallen and lay strewn, crumbling, decaying. Rough canvas stretched over alcoves provided shelter. Cooking fires burned under tripods and pots beaten out of other objects. What had been the cobbled town square still had the atmosphere of an open-air market, people shouting and milling, bartering fiercely, trading. The noise made a language all its own, and a dozen different scents mingled.

Despite the war and bombing, some of the people hadn't fled, but they hadn't tried to rebuild. Instead, they seemed to have crawled underground when the bombardment began, and when it ended they reemerged, continued their lives where they left off as best they could, with the materials they had at hand. Cockroaches, Clare thought, and shook the thought away.

At the end of the main street, where the twisted, naked foundations gave way and only shattered cobblestones remained, a group of men were digging a well into an old aquifer, part of the water system of the dying village. They were looking for water. Really, though, at this point they weren't digging, but observing the amount of dirt they'd already removed and arguing. They were about to give up and try again somewhere else. A whole day's work wasted, a day they could little afford when they had children to feed and material to scavenge.

Clare helped. Spit on her hands, put them on the dusty earth, then rubbed them together and drew patterns in the dust. Pressed her hands to the ground again. The aquifer that they had missed by just a few feet seeped into the ditch they'd dug. The well filled. The men cheered.

Wiping her hands on her skirt, Clare walked away. She was late for another meeting.

"What is the pattern?" Gerald asked. And no one answered. They were down to four.

Ildie had tried to cause a scandal by prompting a divorce between the RLP Premiere and his popular wife. No matter how similar attempts had failed before. "This is different, it's not causing an affair, it's destroying one. I can do this," she had insisted, desperate to prove herself. But the targets couldn't be forced. She might as well have tried to cause an affair after all. Once again, too direct. Clare could have told her it wouldn't work. Clare recognized when people were in love. Even Republic Loyalists fell in love.

"What will change this path? We must make this better!"

She stared. "I just built a well."

Marco smirked. "What's the use of that?"

Fred tried to summon enthusiasm. They all missed Major even if she was the only one who admitted it. "It's on the army now, not the government. We remove the high command, destroy their headquarters perhaps—"

Marco said, "What, you think we can make earthquakes?"

"No, we create cracks in the foundation, then simply shift them—"

Clare shook her head. "I was never able to think so big. I wish—"

Fred sighed. "Clare, it's been two years, can you please—"

"It feels like yesterday," she said, and couldn't be sure that it *hadn't* been just yesterday, according to the clock her body kept. But she couldn't trust that instinct. She'd lost hours that felt like minutes, studying dust motes.

"Clare—" Gerald said, admonishing, a guru unhappy with a disciple. The thought made her smile, which he took badly, because she wasn't looking at him but at something in the middle distance, unseen.

He shook his head, disappointment plain. The others stared at her with something like fascination or horror.

"You've been tired. Not up to this pressure," he explained kindly. "It's all right if you want to rest."

She didn't hear the rest of the planning. That was all right; she wasn't asked to take part.

She took a piece of charcoal from an abandoned campfire. This settlement was smaller than it had been. Twenty fires had once burned here, with iron pots and bubbling stews over them all.

Eight remained. Families ranged farther and farther to find food. Often young boys never came back. They were taken by the army. The well had gone bad. They collected rainwater in dirty tubs now.

And yet. Even here. She drew a pattern on a slab of broken wood. Watched a young man drop a brick of peat for the fire. Watched a young woman pick it up for him and look into his eyes. He smiled.

Now if only she knew the pattern that would ensure that they survived.

When they launched the next plan—collapse the army high command's headquarters, crippling the RLP and allowing the PTP to fill the vacuum, or so Gerald insisted—she had no part to play. She was not talented enough, Gerald didn't say, but she understood it. She could only play with detritus from a kitchen table. She could never think big enough for them. Major hadn't cared.

She did a little thing, though: scattered birdseed on a pool of soapy water, to send a tremor through the air and warn the pigeons, rats and such that they ought to flee. And maybe that ruined the plan for the others. She'd nudged the pattern too far out of alignment for their pattern to work. The building didn't collapse, but the clock tower across the square from which Fred and Marco were watching did. As if they had planted explosives and been caught in the blast.

Too direct, of course.

*

She left. Escaped, rather, as she thought. She didn't want Gerald to find her. Didn't want to look him in the eye. She would either laugh at him or accuse him of killing Major and everyone else. Then she would strangle him, and since they were both equally out of history she just might be able to do it. It couldn't possibly be too direct, and the rest of the world couldn't possibly notice.

Very tempting, in those terms.

But she found her place, her niche, her purpose. Her little village on the edge of everything was starting to build itself into something bigger. She'd worried about it, but just last year the number of babies born exceeded the number of people who died of disease, age, and accident. A few more cook fires had been added. She watched, pleased.

But Gerald found her, eventually, because that was one of his talents: finding people who had the ability to move outside the world. She might as well have set out a lantern.

She didn't look up when he arrived. She was gathering mint leaves that she'd set out to dry, putting them in the tin box where she stored them. A spoonful of an earlier harvest was brewing in a cup of water over her little fire. Her small realm was tucked under the overhang formed by three walls that had fallen together. The witch's cave, she called it. It looked over the village so she could always watch her people.

Gerald stood at the edge of her cave for a long time, watching. He seemed deflated, his cloak worn, his skin pale. But his eyes still burned. With desperation this time, maybe, instead of ambition.

When he spoke, he sounded appalled. "Clare. What are you doing here? Why are you living in this . . . this pit?"

"Because it's my pit. Leave me alone, I'm working."

"Clare. Come away. Get out of there. Come with me."

She raised a brow at him. "No."

"You're not doing any good here."

She still did not give him more than a passing glance. The village below was full of the evening's activities: farmers returning from fields, groups bustling around cook fires. Someone was singing, another laughing, a third crying.

She pointed. "Maybe that little girl right there is the one who will grow up and turn this all around. Maybe I can keep her safe until she does."

He shook his head. "Not likely. You can't point to a random child and make such a claim. She'll be dead of influenza before she reaches maturity."

"It's the little things, you're always saying. But you don't think small enough," she said.

"Now what are you talking about?"

"Nails," she murmured.

"You have a talent," he said, desperately. "You see what other people overlook. Things other people take for granted. There are revolutions in little things. I understand that now. I didn't—"

"Why can't you let the revolutions take care of themselves?"

He stared at her, astonished. Might as well tell him to stop breathing. He didn't know how to do anything else. And no one had ever spoken to him like this.

"You can't go back," he said as if it was a threat. "You can't go back to being alive in the world."

"Does it look like I'm trying?" He couldn't answer, of course, because she only looked like she was making tea. "You're only here because there's no one left to help you. And you're *blind*."

Some days when she was in a very low mood she imagined Major here with her, and imagined that he'd be happy, even without the games.

"Clare. You shouldn't be alone. You can't leave me. Not after everything."

"I never did this for you. I never did this for history. There's no great sweep to any of this. Major saw a man with a weapon and acted on instinct. The grenade might have gone off and he'd have died just the same. It could have happened to anyone. I just wanted to help people. To try to make the world a little better. I like to think that if I weren't doing this I'd be working in a soup kitchen somewhere. In fact maybe I'd have done more good if I'd worked in a soup kitchen."

"You can't do any good alone, Clare."

"I think you're the one who can't do any good alone," she said. She looked at him. "I have saved four hundred and thirty-two people who would have died because they did not have clean water. Because of me, forty-three people walked a different way home and didn't get mugged or pressed into the army. Thirty-eight kitchen fires *didn't* reach the cooking oil. Thirty-one fishermen did *not* drown when they fell overboard. I have helped two dozen people fall in love."

His chuckle was bitter. "You were never very ambitious."

"Ambitious enough," she said.

"I won't come for you again. I won't try to save you again."

"Thank you," she said.

She did not watch Gerald walk away and vanish in the swoop of his cloak.

Later, looking over the village, she reached for her tin box and drew out a sugar cube that had been soaked in brandy. Crumbling it and licking her fingers, she lifted a bit of earth, which made a small girl trip harmlessly four steps before she would have stumbled and fallen into a cook fire. Years later, after the girl had grown up to be the kind of revolutionary leader who saves the world, she would say she had a guardian angel.

ROARING TWENTIES

The good thing about Blue Moon is that it's invisible, so it never gets raided. Bad thing is, being invisible makes it hard to find for the rest of us. You have to have a little magic of your own, which Madame M does, and finding places that aren't there is never much of a problem for her.

Madame M has the car drop us off at the corner of Fifth and Pine, and she sends the driver away. I follow her down a damp sidewalk along brick buildings. It's early enough that the streets are crowded, cars and people jammed up on their way to somewhere else, no one much looking around. A few wheezing horns honk, and the orange from the streetlights make polished steel and frowning faces seem like they're lit with embers. I shrug my mink more firmly over my shoulders. Madame M's has slipped down to her elbows, showing off the smooth skin of her back. We look like sisters, walking side by side, in step.

The alley she turns down looks like any other alley, and that passage leads to another, until we're alone with the trash cans and a yowling cat, under iron fire escapes and a sky threatening rain. She knocks on a solid brick wall, blocks from any door or window, and I'm not surprised when a slot opens at head-height. She leans into whisper a word, and the door opens. Either a door painted to look like bricks, or the wall itself swinging out; I can't tell and it doesn't really matter.

The music of a three piece combo playing jazz drifts in from down the hall, and it sounds like heaven.

The doorman, a gorilla of a guy in a brown suit that must be tailored to fit those shoulders, looks us over and nods his approval. He's got a little something else, extra fur around the collar, on his hands and tufting off his ears. When he smiles, he shows fang, and his eyes glint golden. He's some kind of thing, far be it from me to guess what. I walk on by without meeting his gaze. A coat check girl who seems normal enough, but who knows, takes our furs, and I tip her well. A clean-cut, scrubbed and polished waiter guides us into the club proper. There's a table just opened up, of course, a table always opens up for Madame M. I order soda water for us both, and the waiter looks at me funny, because why come to a place like this if you're not into booze? The booze here is good, top shelf, smuggled in, not cooked up in some unsavory backwoods tub. Maybe later, I tell him, and he scurries off.

We're near the dance floor, in the middle of everything, and the place is full. The band is a white guy on piano, and two black guys on bass and drums, and a microphone stand means someone might sing later, but for now they're playing something with a bit of a kick, and couples are dancing on a tiny floor down front. At first glance it's a normal crowd on a normal night, flappers and fine women in evening gowns, men in suits and even a few tuxes. Looking closer I see the odd fang and claw, the glimmer of a fae wing, a bit of horn under slicked-back hair, other bits and pieces I might guess at, but I'd likely be wrong. These folk aren't drawing attention to themselves, so I won't either, because then they might start looking too closely at me and Madame M.

Doorways lead to back rooms where you can find cards and craps whatever else you might fancy. One doorway is covered by a shimmering beaded curtain, and through them and the cigarette smoke haze beyond I can just make out a grand lady holding court at a sofa and coffee table, surrounded by men in suits and women dolled up like paintings. The scene is vague, like I'm seeing it through etched glass.

Madame M wants to talk to Gigi, the woman behind the beaded curtain, who runs the place, and I think it's a bad idea, but I'm not going to argue because M's smarter about these things than I am. The back-and-forth and the deals, the secrets and the swindles. The things I'm smart about: watching her back and seeing trouble a minute before it happens.

It's just the two of us in a den where the gamblers and bootleggers are the least of it. There are people here who'll drink your blood dry if you let them, others who'll tear out your throat, and a few who'll buy your soul, even knowing how little some souls around here are worth. M and I do all right, her tricks and my eyes keeping us safe. A couple of molls out on the town, that's what we look like, in our colored silk and fringe, bare shoulders and knees, dresses that swish and show off our hips when we kick our heels and shimmy our legs. Sequins and feathers over bobbed hair. They think we're easy prey, and they'll be wrong.

The drinks arrive more quickly than I expect, because I think the waiter is on the other side of the room taking someone else's order. But no, he's right here, polished as ever, smiling as he transfers glasses from tray to table. The music plays on, and M sips.

"Something bad's coming," she murmurs.

I'm looking out. A card game's going in the corner. Nearby, a gangster's foot soldier is trying to impress his girl, both of them leaning over their tiny round table while he shows her the gold band on his watch. Her lips are smiling, but her eyes are hungry. She's trying to get something out of him. A dozen small intrigues are brewing. Mostly, though, people are here to have a good time, to drink some good booze and revel in the feeling of getting away with something bad.

"Raid?" I answer. "A takeover? Is Rocco finally moving in on Margolis?" Anthony Margolis is the one presiding over the card game. He's here playing to show he isn't worried about Rocco or anyone else.

"No, this is bigger. Everything goes to hell."

With her I can't tell if that's a metaphor. "This one of your dreams?"

"Visions," she said. Takes a sip, leaves a print of red lipstick on the glass.

"The future?"

"It is."

"What do you want me to do?"

"Same as always: Keep your eyes open and invest in liquor."

She's thinking out loud, and it makes me nervous. More nervous. I nod to the beaded curtain. "She's gotta know you're here."

"She's going to make me ask," M says.

"That's what we're here for, yeah?"

"Let's just pretend like we're here for a good time." She leans, stretching through her back, and puts one arm behind my chair. I draw a cigarette out of my clutch, light it, offer it to her. Her gloved and jeweled hand takes it, she draws a long breath from it and lets out a cloud of smoke, her mouth open and lazy. Her foot taps along with the music.

Her pretending to have a good time looks like the real thing. She could make a living doing anything she put her mind to, but she's ended up in a place like this for a reason. So have I.

The place smells of alcohol and sawdust. Nothing is off in the rhythm, waiters and drinks flowing from bar to tables and back, a cigarette girl making the rounds. The card game in the corner is accompanied by a lot of nervous laughter, men pretending like the grand they just lost doesn't matter while sweat drips onto their collars. If any trouble is going to happen, it'll come from them, one of the jokers taking issue with another, then tipping over the table and starting a fist fight. The gorilla by the door would have made them leave their guns, so that's one thing I don't have to worry about. M and I can take cover easy enough from a fist fight. Bullets, not so much. Being invisible can't always save you from getting shot in a crossfire.

Third song in, halfway through my drink, a guy stumbles in from outside, gaping like a fish out of water, which he is, and I wonder what he said to get past the gorilla. He must have something, a charm or an aura, first to find the place and another to make himself look like he belongs. Now he stands at the entrance, gazing around, eyes wide like he didn't expect it to work, and now that it has he doesn't quite know what to do. He wears a nondescript brown suit, belatedly takes off his fedora. He's clean cut and square jawed, and he has a gun in a shoulder holster under the jacket. He must have had a spell to hide that, too, because the gorilla should have spotted it.

Everything in Blue Moon pauses for a half a breath, because some kind of balance has shifted and everyone feels it. The piano muffs a cord, and a string on the bass twangs. The guy looks back at all the eyes on him before straightening an extra inch and scowling.

Then it all goes back to what it had been a second ago as if nothing happened.

I watch the band, keep the new guy in view out of the corner of my eye, and lean into M like I'm telling a joke. "I think we've got ourselves a Fed."

She's too polite to turn and stare but does raise an eyebrow. "How'd he get in?"

"I don't know. He's armed."

"Maybe he's just here to have a good time, like everyone else."

The Fed looks like a hunter who's found himself a prize. Casual-like, he leans on the bar. Doesn't flag the bartender, doesn't ask for anything, just watches, staring hungrily at all that bootlegged liquor sitting on the shelf, wondering how big a raid this would really be, if he could pull off a raid. The bartender ignores him, wiping down the counter cool as ice and pretending he doesn't have a Fed breathing down his neck. A minute later, the Fed flags the waiter who shows him to a table in back, and my neck itches, because I can't see him anymore but I feel him staring straight at me.

Guy knew enough to get in here, he'll figure out soon enough who the people with the power are, and the problem of getting M out of here in one piece when trouble starts gets a lot more complicated.

M puts a hand on my arm, pats it once. A signal to calm down. I listen to the music, watch the dancers on the floor, and try to remember that we're supposed to look like we're having fun.

The cigarette girl walks past our table for the fourth time, eyeing me and M but not saying a word. Cute kid in satin shorts and a bustier, dark hair done up under a little hat. She's one of those girls with legs up to here and too much makeup painted on, but that's the style and she knows how to wear it. She slinks deftly between the tables, maneuvering her box in front of her, counting out change and never missing a beat, like she's been doing this a while. Still manages to smile.

The fifth time she walks past, not offering cigarettes but still catching my eye, I raise my hand for her to stop. She seems grateful when she does, a bit of a sigh expanding the spangles of her neckline.

"Pack of cigarettes," I say. "There's something else you want to ask, isn't there?"

She looks back and forth between us, which tells me she knows us by reputation, but doesn't know which of us is Madame M, and which of us is just that sidekick Pauline. I nod at M, indicating that she's the one the girl ought to talk to.

"What's the problem, dear?" M asks. "Quickly."

I pretend to dig in my clutch for an elusive bill, making her wait, giving her as much time as she needs.

She screws up her expression and says, "I'm stuck. I mean, we're both stuck. I mean—" She lowers her voice to the barest whisper. I can barely hear, but M doesn't even have to lean forward. "—I mean, I gotta get out of here, and I gotta take my guy with me."

"Your guy?"

"One of Anthony's boys." Her eyes dart to the card game in the corner, and I spot her guy right off, one of the heavies standing guard, medium-size and baby-faced, in a cheap suit. He's got his hands deep in his trouser pockets and he's sweating harder than any of them. He keeps glancing over here, lips trembling like he wants to say something.

"We've saved up the money to get to California, to go straight. But we don't need Anthony or . . . or her coming after us." She doesn't have to gesture to the woman behind the beaded curtain. "I . . . we . . .

we can pay you." She looks worried, like she knows exactly what she's really saying, what the price of M's help might really be.

M regards her, a sly smile on her face. I've got my hand on a bill; I can only keep digging around in my clutch for so long.

"Your bosses don't approve, I take it? Of you kids ditching your gainful employment—your *families*—to run off? Regular Romeo and Juliet story?"

The cigarette girl bites her lip. It shouldn't be too tough a problem, not the kind of problem a person would usually bring to M. But she knows Anthony, and even more than that she knows Gigi, and the problem isn't so simple as all that. I watch M; even I don't know what she's going to say.

She stubs out her last cigarette and takes another from the pack I just bought. "I think we can manage something. But pay attention— you won't get a second chance."

The girl nods quickly. "And how much—"

"I'll ask for something, when I think of the right thing. But for now . . . Pauline?"

My hand already in the bag, I scrounge around a second and find the empty matchbox I know she's asking for.

M says, "I need a hair from you and a hair from him. It'll help me keep track of you. Can you do that?"

She already has, it turns out, reaching into the back of her white glove and drawing out the two thin strands, twined together. M seems impressed that she's come prepared—she knows exactly what she's asking for.

I offer the girl the dollar bill I've dug out of my clutch, which hides her slipping the hairs to me. I put the hair in the box and hand the box to M. Transaction complete, the girl dons her professional cherry-lipped smile again and bounces off.

"You going to ask for their first born?" I say to M, raising a brow. She grimaces. "What would I do with a kid?"

So now I have to look out for the girl and her beau, and wonder what it is exactly M has planned for them. Should be fun to watch.

M will decide when she makes a move, and all I can do is wait for her to give the sign.

The combo takes a break, comes back, and a singer, a beautiful round black woman in a rose sequined gown, her hair twisted up and pinned with a silk magnolia, steps on stage and adjusts the microphone stand.

M pushes her tumbler away and stands from the table.

"I'm going to be brazen. I'm going to get a message to Gigi," she says, nodding at the bartender.

I glance at the bartender, who hasn't looked up, who's been pouring drinks and sodas all night, shaking cocktails and dropping cherries into tumblers like clockwork. When no one's around he just wipes down the surface, over and over.

"Think it'll work?"

"Maybe if I look desperate, Gigi'll talk to me."

I don't say that M already looks a little bit desperate. "I'll hold down the fort."

She tosses me a grin. I watch her slink to the bar, hips sashaying under her dress, causing the beads and sequins to flash. Her brown hair in a perfect bob, not a strand out of place, her skin that perfect flawless ivory. People assume she keeps up her looks with magic, but she doesn't. It's all her, just her. She isn't so vain that she'd waste her magic on something as trite as looking good.

The woman at the microphone sings, her voice as rich and sweet as I knew it would be, the kind of jazz too hot for the clubs you can just walk into off the street. I sit back in my chair, sip my soda water, and pay attention. Watch the people who are watching M, wondering what angle she's working.

Behind the beaded curtain, the smoke and shadows haven't changed. Gigi must know we're here, but she must not care.

Back to the card game. The poor young goon keeps glancing toward the worried cigarette girl, who circulates and does good business, smiling enough that most people don't notice the crease in her brow. She's smarter than her beau, because she doesn't dare look back at him.

The boy doesn't give himself away, because anyone can forgive him for staring at a long-legged girl all night. I try to think of how M will make good on her promise to help them out. She might just send them a couple of train tickets and a bit of a spell to make them invisible, or at least make it so no one sees them. That'd be the simple thing.

On the other hand, I bet there's a way to do the whole thing without magic. If there is, that's what M will do, just to show that it can be done, to show that she doesn't rely too much on the tricks she's known for. To keep people guessing. A distraction, and a threat. That's all she'd need to get those kids out of town. And I hope once they get where they're going, they settle down for good and have kids and all the rest, and realize forever how lucky they are.

The back of my neck is still itching, where the Fed's been watching me this whole time. Me, not M, or he would have wandered over to the bar where she's leaning in to talk to the bartender. I can't see the Fed, but I'm not surprised when he arrives at our table, pulls out M's chair, and sits. I don't even flinch.

"Mind if I join you?"

I smirk at him. The pack of cigarettes we bought from the girl is still there, so I pick it up and hold it out. "Cigarette?"

The Fed takes one and keeps his gaze on me. I strike a match and offer a light, because it's only polite. Then I wait for him to say something. He seems content to watch, and my job is to let him. I can wait all night, as long as that beauty at the microphone keeps singing.

"I know who you are," he says finally.

"Oh?"

"I think we can help each other." He leans back, acting cool, and turns his gaze to the singer. "Say I wanted to move in, and I wanted a partner—"

"I give you the key to the place, you make sure I don't get swept up in the raid, maybe slip me something under the table, especially if you keep me in your pocket?"

Right up till that moment, he thought he had me fooled. "Well. That's putting it bluntly."

"I thought I'd save time."

"This place is going down one way or another, but having help will make it easier, and you look like a woman who knows what's what."

He's talking to the wrong woman, he's gotta know that. Maybe he thinks I want to move up, that I'm tired of being hired help. Which tells me something about how he sees the world.

"Flatterer," I say, my eyes half-lidded.

"It's a sweet little setup here, I have to admit," the Fed says. He scans the room, the players and dancers, and I'm pretty sure he doesn't see the horns tucked under feathered headbands or the tails curled under trousers. He pauses a moment at the card game in the corner before landing back on the singer. He never seems to notice the beaded curtain. "To think it's been slipping past us all this time." He snubs out his cigarette.

"Can I ask you a question?" I say, studying him with honest curiosity. He waves a hand for me to continue. "How'd you get in here? Guy like you, with such a clean suit and clean hands, shouldn't have been able to find the door, but here you are."

"Give me a little credit. We've had our eye on this place for a long time."

He's bluffing. He got himself a few tricks and trinkets, maybe strong-armed some low-level fortune teller into helping him out. Or maybe, heaven help him, he found a book of spells and worked it out on his own. Like handing a guy a loaded gun without showing him how it works.

I can't write him off because nothing in Blue Moon will keep the bullets in that gun from killing if he decides to shoot.

"What exactly are you looking for from me, Mr. Clean Suit?"

"How about you just keep quiet for now, and not warn anyone I'm here?" he says. Like I'd have to warn anyone. "If you have anything else for me, we could work out a deal."

"I'll think it over, let you know."

"Thanks for the cigarette," he says, and leaves my table to return to his own, and I get the feeling he thinks I might really help him, if he just sticks around long enough.

M leans on the bar for a respectable few minutes before returning, a sway in her hips, her smile wry. She's brought a couple of fresh sodas.

"You made a friend," she says.

"I believe we have ourselves a crusader with a stick of dynamite and no idea what to do with it," I say. "We might think about being on our way. Take care of our Romeo and Juliet, then wander out while we can. Give the word, I can start a diversion—"

"No, I still have to talk to Gigi."

I know that's what she'd say. "So what did the bartender say?"

"Not a damn thing. He's a zombie."

Gigi's got herself a zombie bartender? I chuckle. "Cute. So a shot of whiskey's a shot of whiskey, nothing skimmed off the top and nothing extra for the band." I glance over, and sure enough, the bartender's standing in the same place, wiping down the surface, back and forth, over and over. His skin is gray, his expression slack.

"She'll talk to me, I just have to wait her out."

"Not a thing you can do about it, if she doesn't want to talk to you."

She's got her chin in her hands and is looking hard at the beaded curtain. We wait, and I have to resist an urge to look over my shoulder at the Fed, who's still sitting there, watching, waiting.

The singer's finished her latest song, a slow sad piece about how he done her wrong, and she keeps coming back, like the girls always seem to do in these songs. People listen to the songs and think they'd never do that, they'd never go back to a guy who treated them bad. Then they do, because they're different. Their love is different, like it is for everybody, and it's hard to stay away when you're in love, and you're sure he'll change, so you keep going back. Unless you have someone in your life who sits you down and says, "Don't." Like M did for me.

A rare thing, having someone like that in your life.

Gigi's not going to talk to M, I'm sure of it, and we're going to sit here all night, and I'm sure now the Fed's going to do something stupid because if he'd been smart he'd have cased the joint then left to make a plan to come back with more muscle. He's painted a target on himself. I can get M out through a back door. You need a little magic to get into Blue Moon, and it helps to have a little magic to get out, but I'll charge straight out if I have to. Lack of subtlety, that's how you beat magic.

"He's got you worked up," M says.

My back is stiff, and I keep glancing over my shoulder out of the corner of my eye. Not doing a good job of pretending to have a good time.

She continues, "He's harmless. He's got no trap to spring, and he's too proud to leave without a trophy."

"I'm worried about what happens when he pulls out that gun."

"Pauline, relax. I'm more worried about Gigi than I am about some guy in a government suit."

The scene behind the beaded curtain hasn't changed. Gigi is back there, holding court, not paying any attention to M at all. I ought to trust Madame M. She's so rarely wrong. But she's not seeing the big picture right now.

I think I have a plan for getting rid of the Fed.

"You trust me?" I say to M, who furrows her brow at me.

"Sure. What are you thinking of?"

"It'll just take a minute."

"That's not what I asked."

But I'm already gone. Looking around casual like, dodging past that fast-moving waiter, my gaze falls on the Fed. I look thoughtful, interested. He's been watching me like I'd hoped, and I give him a sweet smile. There's a chair at the table, tilted out, just waiting for me. Let him think he made the invitation and planned the whole thing himself.

"Mind if I sit?"

He gestures to the chair and I fold myself into it, demurely crossing my ankles. I reach into my clutch for a pack of cigarettes, but not the pack we bought from the girl—another one that I save for emergencies.

"Another cigarette?" I offer, and he takes one, and I helpfully light a match for him.

He takes a long, slow drag, and what he blows out doesn't smell quite like tobacco, but he doesn't notice. "You look like you have something to say."

"Just some advice," I say. "The thing is, you're talking to the wrong woman if you think you'll get anything from me or my friend."

His expression turns skeptical, his brow furrowed. He thought he had the place figured out. "I know who you two are. Madame M and Pauline, the two dames who aren't what they seem. You think you're out of the way, but you've left fingerprints on a lot of business in this town."

"Fingerprints don't mean we're holding the bag. We leave that to the fancy people." We don't have a place like Blue Moon of our own, or a gang like Anthony's, for a reason. We keep moving because it makes us a harder target to hit.

"Then what fancy people should I be talking to?"

"The deal still stands? I help you, you'll let me know when I should get out, before anything happens?" I even bat my eyes at him.

He taps off the ash and takes another long drag. "Of course. I'll keep you out of it for sure."

Doesn't even matter if I believe him. "You really want to know what's going on here and who you need to deal with, you gotta talk to her." I nod to the stage.

He frowns. "The singer?"

"That's right. Quite a front, huh? She stands up there, keeps an eye on the whole place, and no one ever realizes she isn't just working for tips."

"That's very interesting."

"You bet it is."

I'm about to stand and leave, when he leans in close. His breath smells of what he's been smoking, sweet and sour and just a bit wrong. "Can I get you a drink? Show my appreciation?"

"Thanks, but I've got my drink. Soda water. I'm a law-abiding citizen, just like you."

"Well then. You keep your nose clean, hear?"

I can't punch him, not yet. If this works, I won't have to.

Heading back to my table I pause, because the scene has shifted. Not paying attention, I missed the moment the cigarette girl disappeared. The cigarette girl's beau is sweating buckets, and his boss is going to notice, especially when the lunk can't stop looking at the door and is fidgeting like he wants to run out. M is over by the door talking to the gorilla and trying to catch my eye. Her frown shows it's serious, and I've missed her cue. She raises an annoyed eyebrow. Past time for that distraction. I understand her plan, the need for a long fuse and a slow burn. That means I probably still have time to get started.

I put on a smile and walk on over to the card game.

Anthony sees me. He's likely been watching both M and me just as hard as we've been watching him. Maybe not *just* as hard. But I doubt he'll have any idea what we're up to. What we're *really* up to, I mean. We're those two crazy witches, and who knows what a broad's looking for when she starts scheming, right?

I touch the shoulder of the player across from Anthony. The guy shivers and licks his lips, and he won't be good for anything for the rest of the game. I focus on Anthony.

"Got room for one more, Mr. Margolis?" I ask, sweetly as I know how.

"Pauline. Doll," Anthony says, opening his arms, a gesture of false generosity. "How much would it take to hire you away from that broad?"

He thinks he's being clever. He thinks he's putting me in my place, and M too, for all that. I know what he sees, what he thinks he sees.

"Oh honey, you know you can't afford me," I say, as if I'm really sorry.

"But Madame over there can?"

"You gotta understand, we're like sisters."

He shakes his head like he thinks it's a pity. "Harry, deal the lady in, why don't you?" He makes a sign and the men at the table shift their places, and the cigarette girl's beau brings over an extra chair. I know what the stake is, two grand, and I draw the bundle of bills out of my clutch and put it on the table. The players pretend not to be surprised.

The one called Harry, who's got a thin moustache and a suit so blue it's almost purple, deals me in, and we play cards. Harry's a local guy who's completely honest because if he wasn't nobody would play in Anthony's game. People play in Anthony's games because they think they can get rich off him, but the secret is that Anthony's actually a pretty good player. He doesn't play with his pride is the thing and can fold when he has to.

The dealer deals, I sweep up my hand, and play. I've done this enough it's reflex, habit. The cards are going to do what they do, I just have to keep up the rhythm.

First order of business is to break even, because two G's is worth something no matter what you have. And it's a matter of saving face, and making sure the boys don't think they pulled one over on the doll. So we play poker, and I earn back what I put in, and after that I'm not playing to lose, but I'm not exactly playing to win, either. I'm playing to bide time, watching Anthony watch me, because he thinks I'm up to something, while I'm also watching the kid, M, and the Fed. And the beaded curtain, just in case. M's about to mess up her pretty club, surely Gigi will notice and put her foot down.

M is by the bar again, looking more relaxed than she did a minute ago, so maybe I'm not too late with this. Maybe it'll all work out and we won't have to run out in a rain of bullets. People might wonder why M's not surrounded by men hoping to make time with the beautiful doll who's all on her own. I think maybe she's decided not to let them see her.

Two of the guys at the card game know about M and know, therefore, that they can't discount me. But two of the guys figure I'm the rube. They have a very bad time of it, but stick it out because of pride. Who's the rube, then?

I lose a hand, win a hand, and the players chalk it up to luck because it's easier than admitting a woman can actually play. I don't win too much, so they don't get angry. They start bantering again, not forgetting I'm there so much as not taking me seriously.

"Tommy, you okay there?" Anthony studies his young heavy, who's been tugging at his collar. He's going to blow the whole thing if he's not careful, and I realize why the girl needed help to pull this off. All I can do at the moment is glance at him with a bit of sympathy, then study my cards.

Tommy looks back, rabbit-eyed. "It's a little warm in here, sir."

"You're not feeling faint, are you? Tell me you're not feeling faint."

"No, no sir!"

"Good."

And now Anthony's on edge, and this could all fall to pieces. It isn't too late to walk away, if I can warn M . . .

The Fed, still smoking the cigarette I gave him, is looking green around the gills, and in a fit of agitation pushes away from the table and squares his gaze on the card game. On *me*. Like he knows I lied, or that the cigarette I gave him isn't really tobacco. He starts toward the table, and he's got to know better than to approach Anthony. Or maybe he doesn't, after all that smoking . . .

I have to stay cool and not jump up in a panic, which isn't easy. I just have to look like I don't have a clue.

"What's this clown want?" Anthony grumbles, and all his boys go stiff, perking up like hunting dogs at a duck pond.

And just then the singer hits a high note, crazy high, rattling the glasses on the tables and setting my heart pounding. We all can't help but look on in admiration as she holds that note with full lungs, arms wide, eyes closed and head tipped back, like she's singing the world into being.

The Fed stops, listens, drifts to a table close to the stage, sinks into the chair like he's caught in quicksand. The singer's voice falls back into the chorus and she smiles sweetly at her brand-new greatest admirer.

I catch M winking at the singer. Yeah, M always knows what she's doing.

The game continues. Anthony's boys relax a notch, except for the cigarette girl's guy, who's still watching the door, and Anthony just shakes his head. Not too much longer after that, M touches her earring, adjusts her headband, and strokes the plume across her hair. Time to light the fuse. So I slip a couple of extra aces into my hand. Which I fold. When the hand ends, the dealer sweeps up the cards, shuffles, and deals them out again.

No one ever thinks to accuse me of palming cards, because where the hell would I hide them in this outfit, with all this bare skin?

"Boys," I say, gathering the rest of my winnings, arranging them neatly, fastidiously. "I want to thank you for a lovely time of it, but I've got to go. I hope you're not offended." I blush and bat my eyes, and they can't argue because I haven't done anything to offend them. I haven't cleaned them out. I haven't damaged their pride too terribly much.

"Pauline. Darling. You are welcome at my table any time." Anthony spreads his arms like he always does. I lean in and kiss his cheek, and his compatriots at the table glare bullets at him. Smiling sweetly over my shoulder, I return to Madame M.

"Well, I was starting to wonder if we could pull this off," she says.

I scowl. "Whatever do you mean?"

"Doesn't matter, we're both on the same page now."

"You'll thank me for putting the whammy on the Fed, just wait."

She nods at the card game. "About five minutes, before they figure it out?"

"About."

"I'm going to go powder my nose. Hold down the fort?"

"I always do."

In about five minutes, right when we called it, the first of the players shouts, "Hey, what are you trying to pull?" Loud enough that everyone in Blue Moon looks over.

"What do you mean, what am I trying to pull, what are *you* trying to pull?"

"You can't have three aces, because I have three aces!"

"Boys, boys!" Anthony hollers, but it's too late. Anthony follows the rules, so they've left their guns outside, but that doesn't stop one of the players from tipping over the table when another guy takes a swing at him. Cards and chips and bills go flying, then skitter across the floor. The bodyguards and hangers-on rush in, trying to protect Anthony, who's already taken one on the jaw.

All except Tommy, who's smarter than he looks because he's gotten out of the way. M moves to his side and whispers in his ear. He follows her to the front of the club, and I might have been the only one to see them go.

I move to the back of the club and try to be invisible, but I'm not as good at it as M is. A dancer screams as the fight spills onto the floor, and the band is back, playing in an only partially effective distraction. A couple of guys look on eagerly, crack their knuckles and smile wide enough to show inhuman fangs. They'd enjoy a fight, and they'd win, oh yes.

I know better than to ask for trouble, so I sit on the bar, out of the way. But I have to move when the zombie bartender starts wiping down the surface around me.

M joins me, and we're watching the proceedings, along with a few other creatures of the night. I've got a bottle in hand, an empty that the zombie bartender missed, just in case.

"Everything cool?" I ask M, and she smiles, and I imagine the cigarette girl and Tommy are on a bus for the coast. Good luck to them.

"Nice bit of entertainment," she observes, and I beam.

The Fed only has eyes for the singer and doesn't seem to notice the whole place falling into an uproar around him. The singer has moved to sit at the edge of his table, still crooning, and twining a strand of his hair around her finger. She's somehow gotten a drink in her hand and offers it to the Fed, who takes a grateful, enamored sip. We won't have to worry about him for the rest of the evening.

"You know she's a siren, yeah?" M says, watching this play out.

"I sure do," I say.

She grins. "And that I wouldn't trust that drink as far as I could spit it?"

"Oh, I know." The Fed's sipping down his bootleg whiskey like he's in heaven, and thinking the siren's singing just for him.

"He wasn't going to cause any trouble, you know," she says. "Not tonight, anyway."

"No, I didn't know." She just shakes her head.

One of the heavies slams up against the bar, and I crack the bottle over his head, because it's a classic move and I can't resist. The bottle breaks, pieces of glass rain down like bells, and the lunk of a guy slides to the floor, unconscious. Very satisfying.

There's a wrestling mob in the middle of Blue Moon now, accompanied by otherworldly growls, and a few more people seem to be sporting fur than did before, and some of those fangs might be dripping blood now, and it's a bit more than I'd anticipated, and I'm thinking it's time to get M out of here.

Then, a glass chiming like the sound of icicles rings over it all. The sound should be subtle, but it's rattling, and the whole place pauses, time stopping. The fistfights cease, the punches stop landing, chairs are raised over heads but don't come down, and everyone turns to the beaded curtain. A woman stands there, pushing back the strings of beads with an ebony cigarette holder, studying the place through long lashes. She's wearing a red silk dress like second skin, her hip cocked out, arms crossed, and she's got a thing about her, like once you see her you can't look past her. And once she sees you, you're trapped, because she knows everything about you and there's nothing you can do about it.

And everyone, even the singer, even Anthony, even me, looks away, chagrined, knowing we've stepped out of bounds. Everyone looks away but the Fed, who's put his face down on the table and seems to be weeping, and M, who looks right back at her.

It's all over. At some signal, the gorilla bouncer and a couple of his buddies wade in and start throwing people out, including Anthony and his boys. The gangster is shouting that he doesn't know what happened and he had nothing to do with it, but it doesn't matter. He never even notices his kid Tommy is gone. When he does notice, he might even figure out that me and M had something to do with it. But he won't be able to do a thing about it. Besides, there's a hundred kids where Tommy came from and revenge isn't good for business.

Once the trouble is gone, the waiters rush in to sweep up glass and set tables upright, and I realize why I've had such a hard time keeping track—there are three, identical triplets or something else. They move in a coordinated routine without speaking, like they can read other's minds, zipping through the place, so efficient because they can do triple the work. How do you like that?

Across the tables and past the waiters cleaning up broken glasses and spilled drinks, the woman in red meets M's gaze, and a long moment passes. I hold my breath and wait, heart thudding, because I don't know what's going to happen, how this is going to play out, who's going to look away first and what it'll mean. All M wants to know: will Gigi talk to her? Gigi isn't giving anything away.

Gigi looks behind her to a handful of people who troop out of the back room as she holds the curtain aside. Men in suits, but none of them are goons, they're all fine businessmen in tailored jackets, expensive handkerchiefs peeping out of front pockets, rosebuds nestled on lapels. On their arms walk beautiful women with perfectly painted faces, flappers in short dresses and ropes of pearls, walking on high heels, looking bored and superior. Kept, I think, not hired, because they cling a little too desperately to their beaus' arms, as if they might fall off if they're not careful. And this, I think, is why M is self-employed.

We're not kept. We work for our place, and we do not have to cling.

Then, the woman in red, Gigi, nods, and M nods back, and at the same time they turn away, the one retreating back behind the curtain, M looking around for her chair. Right around us, the chairs and tables are knocked over, and we stand there like a couple of rowboats gone adrift. I wave to a waiter, who runs over and sets a table and a couple of chairs upright, wipes them down, and even finds a little vase of silk flowers to put in the middle of it.

We sink down into the chairs at our table and lean close to talk.

"What's it mean?" I say.

"I don't know."

"She going to talk to you or not?"

"I don't know." She says it calmly, like it doesn't matter, and maybe it doesn't. This was a long shot to start with.

"She's playing with you, making you wait. She thinks she's better than you, and this is how she proves it."

"If she has to prove it, she knows she ain't."

"How long are we waiting?" I'm impatient. We've been here too long already, and I have this vision of Anthony and his boys, or his remaining boys rather, waiting outside for us, to give us one of those little talks. M's got her tricks and we'll walk away, but Anthony's got his tricks too, and I worry that one of these days M's won't be enough. I have to see that day before it comes, and I worry that I won't.

"A little while longer," she says. "I thought you liked her." She nods at the singer, who's back, and M is right, the woman is beautiful and her voice is ringing, and couples are back to dancing on the floor like nothing's wrong, because fights break out all the time in a place like this, it's part of the reason people come here. I also notice: the Fed is gone, probably thrown out with the rest of the mob. I hope he's too trashed to remember Blue Moon or any of the rest of us.

We've been here too long.

"It's just one beautiful girl on one night," I say. "I'm worried about you."

"I'm fine." She frowns, and I raise my brow at her. "I thought I was looking after you," she says.

"That's right, you are."

A waiter comes over. Either the first or one of his brothers, I can't guess. I don't know if it's a trick, if there's a reason for it, some con Gigi runs where she needs a set of identical triplets waiting tables, but it wouldn't surprise me. I spend a few minutes thinking about it, and what I would do with identical triplets working for me. M would have some ideas, if I ask her about it.

But the waiter is talking to M, and I cock my ear to listen.

"She'll see you now, in the back, if you'll come with me."

M turns to give me a look like I told you so and moves to push back from the table. I pick up my clutch and do likewise, when the waiter says, wincing apologetically, "I am sorry, it's only Madame who may come with me."

How do you like that? I try to plan out the next few moments, because there's no way I'm letting M walk into that room without me.

"Pauline is my best friend in the world," M says, clearly shocked and offended. "We don't go anywhere apart. We're like sisters!"

Not much like, I think, but that's too long a story to tell. But M doesn't have to tell the story because she's batting her eyes at the guy, who's clearly ready to fold. "Please, it won't hurt a thing, I just know it."

The poor kid sighs. He knows he's being duped, but what can he do? "All right, all right. Both of you, come with me."

We pass through the beaded curtain, bits of glass chiming around us, bending the soft light into colors. The music outside is suddenly distant, like we're in a whole other building, or a whole other world.

Gigi lies back on a red velvet sofa, her smooth legs tucked up next to her. She frowns. "I only wish to speak to Madame." Her tone is light, observational, but the waiter wilts.

M launches in, "Oh, let Pauline stay, I promise you she won't hurt a fly." And butter wouldn't melt in her mouth, I swear to God.

Arching a skeptical brow, Gigi taps ash off the cigarette in the end of the holder. "Peas in a pod, you are. Fine. Let them both in."

She has no bodyguards, no goons to watch for hidden guns or break up fights before they start. Rather, she doesn't have the usual kind, apart from the gorilla at the door. Here in her sanctum, she doesn't need the men in suits with shoulder holsters tucked under their jackets. She's got other eyes looking out for her. I don't know what exactly would happen to someone who tried something back here, but I'm not going to be the one who tests it.

Gigi turns the cigarette holder to a straight-backed padded chair across from a little round table in front of her, an arrangement designed for serious meetings, for two people staring at each other, reading each other while they make deals. M folds into this chair like a pro, crossing her ankles, leaning forward like she's about to tell a secret. I put myself in a sofa tucked off to the side and pretend to study my nails.

The room is set up like a parlor, with the chairs and sofas collected around the table, cabinets against the walls holding cut crystal decanters, sparkling with amber liquids. Tiffany lamps give off soft yellow light, so that the dark brocade wallpaper seems painted with shadows. Looking into this room from outside, the place is shrouded, the beaded curtain and cigarette smoke fogging the view. Looking out, though, the bar, tables, dance floor and band are all clear. I can see straight back to the entryway and the main door and the gorilla standing guard. Doesn't seem like I should be able to, it doesn't seem quite right, but there it is and I try not to question it too much. The mist in the air might be as exotic as opium, but I'm pretty sure it's only tobacco. She might try to dope her associates, but never herself.

The woman in red starts, which is only right because it's her place. "Well, my dear, how are we going to do this little dance?"

"You know what's coming," M says, to the point, not playing the game or doing the dance, and I can't tell if Gigi is surprised by this. She doesn't twitch a muscle, not even to blink, and the cigarette holder never trembles. Smoke flows straight up from its end to the ceiling.

A moment passes; we wait for Gigi to agree or disagree. She doesn't. "And?"

"I'm aiming to circle the wagons. Safety in numbers. We're stronger together than we are apart, we always have been."

"What's it in for me?" she asks. The cliché is beneath her. I can't help but think, she's gone soft. Not soft, not in the way she treats people or runs her business. But soft in that she's comfortable. She knows what she's got and she's keeping hold of it. She's not thinking ahead because she thinks that she's got it as good as it can get. M isn't going to get the answer she wants at the end of the meeting.

"Safety," M says without hesitation. "Longevity. Peace."

"Those are very abstract words."

M says, "We can pool resources, double protections around us and ours, and the vultures—like Anthony Margolis and that Fed—won't be able to touch us. How'd that Fed even get in here tonight, hm? It isn't like you, Gigi, to let a crack open up in your armor."

Gigi tries not to fidget, but her legs straighten and re-cross, and she looks on M with such contempt. "He's nothing. Didn't take much to take care of him, did it?" She looks at me, her smile cruel.

How hard it is to keep quiet. I bite my tongue and try to watch every square inch of the room for the thing that will leap out and bite us.

There's a phonograph in the corner, sitting on a little mahogany table. Its scalloped bell is turned out to the room, like it should be, but there's no record on the platter, and no needle on the arm, which means it's doing something else than playing records. The skin on my neck crawls a bit, thinking of what else it might be doing.

"This thing that's coming," M says, trying one more time. "It's not magical. It's not the vampires or the sirens or anything. It's economic. It's the businessmen, the bankers and stockbrokers and money people who'll bring it all down. People like you, who think you're safe, and that nothing's ever going to change. What'll you do, Gigi, when everything changes?"

"Why are you so worried about me?" Gigi says, as if amazed.

"Why not?"

"I can take care of myself. You should take care of *yourself*, instead of worrying about people who don't need your help." She takes another drag on the cigarette, lets it out in a cloud through round mouth.

Just like M might do. M studies the woman in red for a long moment, and Gigi won't notice the sadness there, because she isn't looking. She leans over to tap off her ashes into a glass dish.

Then suddenly she looks up, concerned for no reason that I can see. M hasn't done anything different, and I haven't moved an inch. But she's looking over M's shoulder, through the beaded curtain to the dining room, which is silent. The band's stopped playing, voices have stopped humming, not even glasses clink against each other, and now I'm worried too. I don't need any extra sense to tell that the whole pattern of the place has changed, and it's got to be worse than I think for Gigi to be looking like that.

There's a gunshot, a body falling to the floor with a thud.

M rushes to the curtain to see, and I follow, ready to push her back into safety. It should be me walking first into the trouble and why does she always have to see what's happening? Gigi pauses a moment to pull back the slit panel of her skirt and retrieve the pistol held in a garter, and that's when I know it's bad, worse than bad.

M pushes back the curtains and we all see the tableau as it happens, the five or ten guys in suits and fedoras pulled low over their heads storming into the place, all armed and ready for battle like soldiers in the Great War. Some with tommy guns, some with shotguns, one guy with a revolver. All led by him, the arrogant Fed who's got his raid, just like he promised. Must have sobered up after he got thrown out—and he remembered, too bad. Must have stuck wax in his ears to get past the siren, and sure enough, I see them all with cotton sticking out of their ears. Had to hand it to the guy, he may not have held all the cards but he was figuring out the game all the same. But he should have waited until he had the whole thing figured out, and not just part of it. Footsteps pound, a woman screams.

The gorilla manning the door is lying dead on the floor, and the Fed must be using silver bullets to be able to kill him. That's why no one's taken him out.

"Everybody freeze!" the Fed hollers.

It's like some scene out of a moving picture, and I imagine everyone getting shot and dying, reaching up, trembling dramatically as the bullets hit them, collapsing in ways that no one ever does in life but people in the pictures must think looks good. Can't see the blood splatter in the pictures, or maybe they just haven't figured out how to fake that yet.

I grab M's arm to pull her out of the way just as Gigi pushes past us, maybe to get a better look. I don't care if she gets shot, but I have to get M out of here.

Everyone's staring, frozen just like the Fed asked, Gigi and all her people all stare, the band and singer, and even the zombie bartender, because this isn't supposed to happen, Blue Moon is supposed to be safe, and if Feds can raid the place that's supposed to be invisible, then what else can they do? It's like a little bit of magic going out of the world.

M puts her hand over mine, smiles at me with an unspoken command: wait. She's crazy, or she's got a plan, and because it's M it's got to be a plan, so I wait.

"Everybody, down on the floor! Flat on the floor! This is a raid!" He sounds so pleased, like he's won a battle. His men spread out through the room.

From across the room, the Fed looks right at me like I've done him some specific wrong. He's too far away for me to reach, for me to do anything but frown at him. I've got all kinds of thoughts, though, about snatching that gun right out of his hand and maybe kicking in his kneecaps. I clench my hands and glare, for all the good it does.

M leans close to Gigi and says, "Didn't see this coming, did you?"

"Did you?" Gigi spits back.

M looks at me, and I smile.

She walks past Gigi, onto the dance floor. Now all gazes fall on her, she has drawn every last bit of attention just by moving, and I want to scream, because here and now attention isn't a good thing—every Fed in the place turns his gun to her, and fingers move to triggers. But she knows what she's doing, she always knows.

Raising her arm, she makes a gesture, fingers bent in a pattern that looks simple but no one could ever replicate. Looking right at the Fed, she waves her other arm to encompass them all, and it's like the air goes thin and sound fails. There's a pop in my ears, like sinuses clearing after a bad cold, and the Fed's rage-filled snarl freezes. Trigger fingers are still, the gunmen stand still, and no one even blinks. They are more still than stone, because the stillness of stone is natural, and this is something else.

The others in the room, the band and singer, the waiters and patrons and gangsters look at each other as if confirming this is a dream, and brush themselves off like they've been in a storm. They start moving around, studying the gunmen, who are nothing more than obliging statues.

"I'm just doing what the guy asked." M brushes her hands like she's wiping off dust, but I know they're spotless. The Fed can't do a damn thing now, when she walks up to him and starts patting down his jacket and trouser pockets. I can almost see the protest in his watering eyes, though.

It's the jacket's inside pocket where she finds the spell book, a drab little thing with a red cover, worn edges and a broken spine, like it's been sitting in some attic for a century or two, just like you'd expect an old lost spell book to look. M scans the first couple of pages, smirks.

"That's what I thought," she says. "You had talent to get this far. You could have made something of yourself. But you thought you could pick this up and aim it like a gun. Well, it doesn't work like that. Pauline?"

I step forward at her call. She hands me the book, and I put it in my clutch. We'll get rid of it later.

"You can clean this up?" Madame M asks Gigi.

Gigi purses her lips. She might be thinking a million things and won't say any of them. She might be shocked at what M could do on Gigi's own territory, but she won't show it. Even after this Gigi still doesn't know how much power M really has. She so rarely shows off.

"Yeah. Sure. I'll clean 'em up and throw 'em out." She nods, and the triplet waiters go around to all the goons, depriving them of their weapons. However much we all might want to make the whole crowd of them disappear, most likely Gigi will just obfuscate their memories and throw them in some far off alley where they can't bother her anymore. She'll find a new guard for the door.

"Remember what I said," M adds. "Call me if you change your mind."

Gigi wears her sneer like a mask. "I'll do that."

M's got on a sad look and might stand there all night, but I touch her arm and point her to the door. I don't know what to think about Gigi, except maybe to feel sorry for her. To have someone like M around wanting to help and to snub her like that.

Gigi calls after us, one last time. "M. Don't get in too much trouble."

"You too, Gigi."

And that's that. I take one last look over my shoulder to the beautiful singer, who's singing again, trying to get back to normal, crooning about how wonderful it is to dance in the arms of your man. It's got to be near dawn, closing time. She's singing to a near empty room, the only ones still around are the waiters and the zombie bartender, who's still got that rag in his hand, wiping.

We retrieve our furs from the coat check girl, a new guard—also thick as a barrel, with odd fur around his ears—opens the door to let us outside, and we're back on the street, next to a dirty brick wall, and the glow from a distant streetlight makes our shadows long. She keeps walking. The car ought to be around here somewhere. It'll find us when she wants it to find us. Meanwhile, she's in a mood to walk, and I stay at her side.

"You got a bottle of whiskey in that thing?" M asks, nodding at my clutch.

"Probably. Might have to go digging around for it." The clutch is no bigger than my two hands put together, but it's got everything in it, because that's what it's designed for. Cigarettes, cash and poker chips, a pretty little Derringer for emergencies that no one will ever find unless I want them to, a handful of bus tokens, an extra pair of stockings, a spool of thread, and a lipstick. And now an odd little book of spells. Maybe I can find a bottle of whiskey.

"Never mind." She gives a deep sigh. "I knew it was a long shot. Oh well."

"She doesn't know what she's doing," I say.

"Not our problem. Not anymore."

We walk for maybe half a mile, and I might be tough and M might be magic, but my shoes aren't built for this and I'm getting sore. But I'll stay right with her. The sky is gray, the sun's coming up.

We pause when we hear singing, gruff and out of tune. It's around the next corner, and I can't help it, I have to go look. And there he is: the Fed's lying in the gutter, no jacket, his shirt torn open. His shoulder holster is hanging lopsided, and he's got a revolver in hand, waving it around in what might be despair. Gigi took their guns—but he must have had one hidden, under a trouser leg maybe. So the Fed's standing here, gun in his hand, lost as a puppy and trying to figure out where his life went, and who to blame.

I put myself in front of M like I always do in my imagination in this scenario. This isn't too rough. We can get away, get out of his sight before he even knows we're here, and I press back against M, urging her to turn around.

Too late, though, because the Fed sees us, and his arm suddenly becomes steady, and scrambling to his feet, he levels the weapon.

He's got us in sight and the gun is real. No back door to escape out of. I can hear M breathing hard behind me, and I don't know if she has any tricks for this.

"What—what *happened* in there?" He's gesturing with the gun, like it's an extension of his arm.

I can feel sweat freezing on my skin under the silk of my dress. "I don't even know what you think you saw."

"Yes, you do, you saw everything, you saw it all! I don't even remember! What am I supposed to tell the director?"

He can shoot me and say it was my fault. Sure, he can. Can't come back from his raid empty handed, and I think how silly, that it all comes down to this, getting held up in a back alley by some drunk-ass Fed.

I step forward and grab the gun out of his hand, all in one smooth movement that he doesn't see coming. The weapon comes loose from his hand like a plucked flower, and he collapses into a sob, leaking tears and snot, hands over his face. He slumps to the sidewalk.

We stand looking down at him. I'm holding this weapon I don't want. But I'm relieved, M is safe, and all is well. Sprawled on the concrete, he starts singing his mashed-up song again, and this time I can hear what it is, or what it's supposed to be: the one the siren at Blue Moon sang, about the guy who done her wrong.

I empty the bullets from the chamber into my clutch and drop the gun on the sidewalk. I say, "You think we should help him? Call the cops or something?"

"He's not going anywhere. They'll find him soon enough. Come on, Pauline."

She loops her arm around mine and we walk away. The car pulls up to the curb ahead of us, right on schedule, and the driver gets out to open the door for us. Time to go home, wash the paint off my face and roll into bed.

"I wonder sometimes how it all could have come out different," M says. "With Gigi, I mean."

"I don't think you could have said anything—"

"Not here, not now," she says, turning inward, thoughtful, and I can't guess what webs she's spinning, what plans she's making, or past plans she's picking apart for the flaws. "I'm talking ten, twenty years ago. Did all this happen because I took her doll, or because she stole my licorice? Or because Mama loved her best, or me best. I don't know who Mama loved best, or if she loved either of us at all. Probably doesn't matter one little bit."

I don't say anything, because what can I say? I've never gotten the whole story about M and Gigi's mama, probably because I haven't asked. And I won't. I don't want or need to know, because it wouldn't change a thing.

"I imagine it doesn't," I say. "You and your sister have done most of this your own damn selves."

M smiles, squeezes my arm. "I'm a lucky woman, to have you walking by my side."

"Oh, I don't know about that. I thought I was lucky that you put up with me at all."

"The two of us make the best damn gang in this city, you know that? No matter what comes, we'll be okay." She doesn't sound certain.

"Yes, ma'am," I say firmly. "We will."

A RIDDLE
IN NINE SYLLABLES

After the attack, my team brought me straight to the med lab at base camp. They must have commed ahead, because as soon as the stretcher went through the door seals, Dr. Traynor was yelling orders.

"That table there! Bring her over. Ready, one, two, three, lift!" My view of the room shifted as I went from stretcher to examining table. "Get the scanner up! Where's the entry point? Dr. Casey—Meg—can you hear me?"

I lay face down on the table. I lifted my head and tried to make an affirmative noise, but a hand pushed me back down.

"Casey, can you feel that?"

"Feel what?" I mumbled into the table's padding.

"Dammit!" Traynor continued. "What am I looking at here?"

He was just muttering. He knew what he was looking at: a six-inch slash down the back of my environmental suit and the thing that got inside. It hit me from behind. I never saw it.

A whole crowd seemed to surround me: Traynor, his assistant Yons, my own assistant Harima. I didn't know how many. I couldn't see them, just hear their voices traveling around me, over me. I felt stupid lying there, unable to answer my colleague's questions.

Traynor's words were intent, pointed. I could trust him to solve a problem presented to him. "Has it broken skin?"

Harima stood to the side. I could picture her wringing her hands. "Yes. It burrowed."

"Is burrowing," Yons said in a hushed tone.

"By the Light!"

"What happened?" A new voice, harsh and demanding, entered the med lab. Captain Alvarez. Alvarez headed the Tiga 32-A survey mission of which I was Chief Xeno-ecologist. Every world was a new conquest to him, a recruit to be tamed and disciplined to the service of the greater galaxy.

He came to the head of the table and caught my eye while Traynor spouted.

"Dr. Casey was hit. Unknown lifeform. Possibly parasitic. Hand me those forceps!"

I remembered the attack. Something slammed into me like a cannonball. I fell forward to the ground and screamed as a burst of pain lit up my spine. Then I went completely numb. I was paralyzed and staring when my team members packed me up to bring me here.

"I know, never turn your back on the enemy," I mumbled at Alvarez, giving him a wan smile. Good advice to be sure, but hard when the planet itself was the enemy and I was on the surface. Alvarez looked stern, his weathered face set in hard lines.

"We have to get this thing out of there," Yons said. "It's insinuating itself in the spinal column."

"We can't, not until we know the extent of its invasion into her system."

"Did you say spinal column?" Alvarez said, his voice admirably calm.

Traynor ignored the Captain. "We'll start slow. Yons, hypo. Five cc's of halcyoncine."

"For her or the thing?"

"I just want to try something . . . there . . . dammit!"

Everything went black.

I woke up on a bed instead of the examining table, wearing a thin hospital gown. My neck was cold.

I moved an arm, shifted to prop myself up and turn over, then stopped. There was nothing to turn over. I couldn't feel a thing below my waist. I looked; the shapes of two legs and a set of spreading hips showed under the sheet. I willed my right leg to move and swing over the edge of the cot. Nothing happened.

"Doctor Traynor!" I raised my voice to as much of a shout as I could manage, but my lungs were tired, as though I'd been swimming. I started coughing, slumped back to the pillow with my arms tucked under my head, and waited.

"Casey? You're awake?" He stood behind me, so I couldn't properly glare at him. "How do you feel?"

Tired, cranky. At least that's how the parts of me that could feel felt. Scared, that I was missing so much of what I ought to be feeling.

"I don't," I said evenly. "If I wasn't looking at them I'd tell you I have no legs. What happened?" I was a scientist. I could be rational about this. I waited for his report.

Traynor pulled a chair over and sat at my eye level. He was older, long faced and earnest, his blond hair cut close to disguise its thinning. His background was primarily in research, and it showed when he looked at me, teeth kneading his lower lip. In research, one seldom had to look one's patient in the eye and give a prognosis.

"We couldn't remove the lifeform. Within half an hour it had extended through most of your lower spine, anchoring itself to vertebrae. From there, it's absorbing nearly every neural signal traveling down your spine to your lower body. We're not sure how, but we think it's feeding off those neural impulses. Harima took your team out to try and collect live samples so that we can pinpoint what we're dealing with, then find a way to make it release naturally so we don't rip out your whole spinal column trying to remove it." He dispensed with sensitivity as his explanation progressed and shrugged apologetically.

An alien organism inside my body couldn't be good. Could the majority of the organism be removed, then perhaps the remaining attached portions would die off on their own? Could I live without a spine? The academic problems of the situation kept a wall between myself and panic.

"Show me the scan image." I couldn't twist at the right angle to see that part of my back. I wasn't sure I wanted to. My nerves couldn't tell me if the creature had made a bloody gash or an elegant little hole, how much of the thing still protruded from my body, or if it was solely interior. Images from elementary biology texts filled my mind: ticks, heads buried in the skin of a dog; wasps injecting their eggs into the paralyzed bodies of spiders; mistletoe crawling up the trunk of an oak, strangling branches one by one.

Traynor hesitated, working at his lips again. "I'm not sure that's a good idea."

"Just show it to me."

Nodding curtly, lips pressed grimly together, Traynor went to a desk at the other side of the lab. He brought back a portable terminal with a large screen for graphics viewing. Sitting again, he tilted the screen in my direction. The image of my body jumped out in holographic imaging.

I quickly mapped out parts. The fuzzy purple lines running down the center were the track of nerves of the spinal cord. The defined, gray series of linked shapes surrounding the purple was the backbone. Ribs showed gray, various organs nestled in their correct places, defined in coded colors. The heart showed as a still red fist in the static image. The whole image was laced with red vines of the circulatory system. I could pretend the scan belonged to another body.

The lower half of the spine was shrouded in a brown cloud, from which thin tendrils shot up and down in a straight line along the backbone from a fist-sized mass situated around the third and fourth lumbar. The thing was almost vegetable in form, sending a runner to a spot of bone, where it grabbed hold, then sent off another runner. Its form reminded me of what we had misnamed trees in our unconscious effort to impose our own order on this alien world. One of the first species we investigated when our survey began two weeks ago was a lifeform that grew in colonies. They were the general size of trees, immobile and tree-like with columnar trunks grouped together in copses. However, they were glass smooth and bright blue, and their branches curved back to the ground where they started a new set of roots and sent up a new trunk. We found single organisms that spread in this manner for over five hundred kilometers.

The parasite was doing the same thing on my spine. This was a static image; it may have grown since being taken.

Traynor watched me watching the terminal. We'd worked together on other missions before Tiga. We did well as a team because we never stepped on each other's toes—I supervised field work, delivered the samples to him in the lab, where my jurisdiction ended. Our skills—his determination, my systematic curiosity—complemented each other.

Becoming the object of his scientific scrutiny was disconcerting. I was about to tell him so, when he announced, with a tired smile, "We thought we'd name it Neuroparasite Megcasius, with your permission."

I reached over to shut the terminal off. "I guess I'm here for the duration, until you find a way to wheedle it out of there." He nodded. I returned a curt, military nod. "Then I'm heading up the research on this thing. Get me a terminal I can use from the bed as soon as possible. And if you can find a way for me to move around—"

"Meg—Dr. Casey—I don't really think you should exert yourself."

If I spent the hours lying around doing nothing, I really would start to feel, out of sheer imagination, the thing inching its way up my spine.

"Dr. Traynor, I have Ph.Ds in biology from Cambridge and xeno-ecology from New Home University. I'm still Chief Xeno-ecologist on this survey, and I'm working on this problem."

We glared at one another for several moments, irresistible force and immovable—or in my case immobile—object, until Traynor looked away. He probably felt sorry for me. We'd had radiation burns, xeno-poisonings and allergic reactions, equipment accidents, all sorts of sudden, traumatic injuries in his tenure as head physician. In most of those cases he either saved the victim or he didn't, and he knew the outcome within moments. Seldom did he ever have to face a patient and not know if she would be alive in a week.

"I'll show you everything we've been able to find so far," he said and scrolled up a different file on the terminal before handing it over to me.

For four days, I studied the thing buried in my back. Neuroparasite Megcasius. Good name. I lay on my side in a cot in the lab's work space, medical scanners and analyzers on one side of me, terminals and databases on the other. Except for the paralysis, I felt fine. Good, even. Very aware and watchful. I'd slept maybe two hours since I woke up from Traynor's halcyoncine injection, which affected me through his treatment of the parasite.

"You need to get some rest, Doctor," Traynor said, finishing the analysis of the most recent scan. We took scans of Megcasius every three hours. It had stopped expanding and was consolidating its position, its limbs growing thicker. I should have been able to feel it.

"I'm not tired."

"That's because it's flooding your system with something that looks suspiciously like an amphetamine compound. It's keeping your neural activity at as high a level as possible."

"So it's pumping me high on speed. There's no reason not to take advantage of little side effects," I said with a grin.

"If this keeps up for too long, it'll kill you. Your brain will burn out."

"Would it really kill its host that quickly?"

"If this is part of its life cycle, and it reaches the end of this stage, yes."

We needed a live sample, to see how Megcasius interacted with native hosts. I scrubbed my hand over my face once to clear my thoughts. I'd been looking at strings and rings of carbon and hydrogen for too long. The biochemistry involved was appalling.

"This critter is lucky your systems are so compatible," Traynor murmured at the jumble of compounds drawn out on the terminal.

"You got it backwards." I brought the image to a higher magnification, until the scan showed fine tendrils of individual nerve cells reaching out to one another. "It's adapting itself to my system. It's started manufacturing human acetylcholine. Compare this to its native enzyme from the tissue sample you took when we first brought it in."

More compounds and molecules modeled themselves in three dimensions on the terminal. Acetylcholine facilitates the transfer of ions between neural cells and is crucial to transmission of signals throughout the nervous system. Looking at the scan, at the molecular analysis, Megcasius' system was becoming indistinguishable from my own. Its brown nerves melded fluidly into my purple ones. Signals traveled smoothly between the two.

"It's like I'm growing an extra brain at the base of my spine."

Yes.

Instinct spoke to me. A second voice, a sixth sense. I don't know. I couldn't trust my own brain anymore, not with what was happening to me. If I heard a voice, it was my drugged imagination.

Life.

I closed my eyes. As I did every hour, or half hour, or fifteen minutes, depending on how busy I was digesting data, I checked my body. Twitched a toe, clenched a thigh. Nothing. I was only feeding the thing more ions.

More.

I could almost feel it, a weight on my backbone. A little creature curled above my hips, drinking from my spine. I didn't know how much of that was imagination and how much was truth.

Truth?

What are you? I asked it.

Life.

Traynor was right. I needed sleep.

"Traynor!" The com unit in the med lab hissed to life and shouted in Harima's voice. "Doctor, we've got a live one! Bringing it in, ETA fifteen minutes."

Traynor was out for the moment, but I relayed the message, pouncing on the internal com unit I kept on hand in case of emergency—i.e., sudden change in my condition. I'd give Traynor a coronary by using it.

"Traynor, live one's coming in, get your butt over here!"

Both Traynor and Alvarez were in the lab in under a minute. They cleared two of our sealed habitats, just in time for Harima's team to rush in, with close to the same state of panic as when they'd brought me in. They carried two portable sealed habitats. In the rush of people and shouts, I didn't get a good look until Traynor had the samples installed in two different cages and got everyone calmed down and herded out. Yons and Alvarez stayed in the lab.

Tiga 32-A had an Earth-type, oxygen atmosphere, but the temperatures on the surface averaged upward of 130 Fahrenheit. The habitats we'd rigged for live samples kept the temperature at that searing level, allowing us to work in our more comfortable climate.

Yons explained the captures. "We lucked out. They seem to be solitary by nature, but we found two of them together, adult and pre-adult. They strike from behind, which is why Casey never saw it coming."

He said they found two, but the samples looked nothing alike. One I recognized. It was a small specimen of six-legged herd animal that seemed ubiquitous on Tiga. A black, bleeding patch on its epidermis where the lower end of its central nervous system was located told me everything I needed to know about why Harima brought it in. I had one of those wounds on my own back, which suffered through Traynor's cleaning it twice a day. I was tired of him telling me to thank the Light of Existence I had no feeling in that part of my body. The curved beast, slumped over and half-paralyzed, moaned plaintively.

"You found a native host for Megcasius," I said.

The second was much smaller, rabbit-sized, spherical and covered with lumpy nodules. It was dark, dull, and lifeless.

"From what little I could tell from field observation, this is a larvae colony for what develops into the adult parasite." Yons gestured to the oversized golf ball. "This is strictly speculation, but an adult lays one of these, which sits around waiting for a herd of one of those"—he nodded at the grazer—"to come along, then ejects the smaller pods which drill through the epidermis to attach themselves to the hosts' nervous systems. They mature and separate when the host dies, then go off and produce another colony. Elegant, textbook life cycle," he said smugly.

"The host always dies?" I asked.

Yons blanched. "We found several dead grazers. The epidermis was ripped open, nerve columns exposed."

I looked at the grazer. It seemed like a young one. If it had eyes, we would have exchanged a sympathetic look.

Kin.

"What?" I said softly, barely recognizing that I'd spoken aloud.

"Dr. Casey, I know this is difficult." Traynor came at me with raised, calming hands.

"No, I'm okay. We figured that's what would happen. I just thought I heard something." I must have looked curious, because the three men stared at me, full of concern. My own face was twisted in concentration, listening for phantom voices.

"Maybe you should rest," Traynor said. "You can look at the reports once we've finished the initial investigation."

Leaning back into the pillow, I sighed. Traynor was probably tired of me glaring over his shoulder. "Yeah. Fine."

"Chin up, Casey." Alvarez gave me my daily pat on the shoulder before leaving.

Yons looked earnest. "Doctor, we'll find a way to get it out. Having the samples is two thirds the battle."

Kin! Kin!

By the Light, what was happening to me?

When I was about twenty, I had a dream I was raising a child, and that the child was me. I walked hand in hand with a little girl, who looked just like me in old holos. I hadn't tried to interpret it; I didn't want to. It was just a dream, an odd expression of a repressed maternal urge. It was such a strange image, though, I never forgot it.

Now, twenty years later, I dreamed again.

I dreamed I was pregnant, and that the baby spoke to me. We carried on conversations. Philosophical, emotional, academic conversations, like I hadn't had since I was twenty and thought I knew everything.

Who are you?

I'm Meg.

Kin?

I suppose.

Who am I?

A pause as I considered.

You're you. Yourself.

Self?

It's who you are. You, no one else. Individual. Self.

It could not vocalize its lack of understanding, but I felt it, a wash of confusion.

Do you have a name?

What's a name?

Your parents give it to you, then you're stuck with it until you reach majority age and can change it.

Parents?

They're the ones who name you.

Name me.

Neuroparasite Megcasius.

I woke up, sweating.

The grazer died three days after Harima's team brought it in. It had plenty of sand to eat, lots of heat. Traynor dissected it and pronounced "neural overstimulation" as cause of death. A brown, spidery organism that moved in rapid twitches emerged from the body shortly after the grazer's death, extruded a spherical egg colony a day later, then promptly died itself.

"That's one way to get rid of it," I said sardonically. Traynor and Yons didn't appreciate the joke.

The conversations with my invented child continued after I woke up from my dreams. They became more detailed, more mature, as though the child were growing up in minutes instead of years.

Sad? Happy?

Neither. You?

Content. You feel?

Why do you want to know?

Curious.

I feel helpless.

Why?

I'm dying.

Oh.

A long pause, and I questioned.

You still there?

Yes. But now I feel sad.

Another long pause. I could feel its sadness, a sympathetic reaction, heavy and depressing.

Who are you? I asked, noticing the change from 'what' to 'who' only after I asked.

Neuroparasite Megcasius. Good name.

I had to consider.

"Traynor. Any chance Megcasius could be intelligent?"

"What?" He stood from his latest experiment. He'd introduced another lifeform to the first egg colony's habitat. For one lifeform, one nodule erupted and attacked. Megcasius had no preference. All the sample species we brought in—grazers, climbers, lopers, and hunters—were fair game. It was extraordinarily adaptable, little more than protoplasm looking for a nervous system to fuel it.

"Any intelligence at all? Higher brainwave functions, advanced communication, something other than the usual artifact evidences?"

We had found no sign of advanced intelligence on Tiga 32-A. No structures, tools, domesticated animals, advanced forms of communication. But the bounds of scientific ignorance in these matters never ceased to amaze me.

"Not a single one. What are you thinking?"

"I want to try a different kind of scan."

I waited patiently for the hour it took the med scanners to go over my torso and brain with an electronic fine-toothed comb.

"This is strange," Traynor said, examining the first batches of data. If I'd been able to move more than my arms, I would have tackled him.

"What?"

"It's not just absorbing neural impulses anymore. It's emitting them. When did this start?"

Four days after the attack, when I asked 'what are you' and received an answer: life.

"It's adapting itself to me, mimicking my system, right? I think it's configuring itself for functions of higher intelligence."

"Meg, that's crazy," Traynor said, running a hand over his short cropped hair and looking tired. I still felt wired, too awake and eager. In the last few days, however, my hands had begun shaking uncontrollably. I hid them under the sheets when I could to keep Traynor from seeing.

"Traynor, it's talking to me. I'm hearing voices in my head."

He hesitated, gnawing his lip before answering. "Are you sure that isn't some other side effect? You said it yourself. If it's adapting itself to you, it's probably reflecting some of your own neural impulses. You're talking to yourself."

I crossed my arms, clamping my hands under my elbows. All this nervous energy and no place to put it. "It's inside my head. I don't . . . I don't think it's anything else." I sounded unsure, even to my own ears.

"I think you should rest." His most often repeated phrase this last week.

"I can't!" I shouted. I squeezed my eyes shut and felt tears starting. "I'm sorry, Pete," I said, forcing my voice to a whisper.

His hand touched my shoulder and gave a quick squeeze before he moved off.

Now you're scared.

How can you tell?

You're shaking.

It's your fault, you know.

Why?

You're the reason I'm dying. You're making my nervous system work too hard so you can feed off the excess impulses, and it's killing me. I'll die, then you'll go off and reproduce. That's what your kind does.

Oh.

I didn't know if it understood. It seemed to relish these conversations, but it didn't seem to understand that it was living off me, a parasite. It didn't seem to understand that we were different and incompatible, not simply two ganglions locked in mutual discourse.

Almost two weeks had passed since we first encountered Megcasius. I wasn't working on research anymore. My hands were no longer reliable. All I could do was lie in bed, reading reports the others produced, think, and talk with my eponymous parasite. The questions never ended.

I want to help.

Then leave. Just get your nerves out of my nerves and leave.

It didn't answer. Its new-found sentience couldn't overcome instinct.

I'm sorry, Meg.

I'd seen the scans of the impulses. It was throwing my own thought patterns back at me. I couldn't tell if its sentiments were its own, or my reflected anxieties.

I'm sorry, I'm sorry.

Despair and love. It was a strange feeling, not originating from myself, yet so close I just had to shut my eyes to feel it. And shut my eyes against stinging tears. It wasn't its fault. I was the one who'd given it intelligence, the ability to feel the pain it inflicted on me. But then it wasn't my fault either. I never wanted to have a child.

I thought I was dead. Megcasius wasn't talking to me anymore. I heard Traynor and Yons moving around the bed.

"Easy there," Traynor was saying. "Gently, expose her back, good. Now onto the stretcher. Get her prepped quick. We don't have much time." If they moved me, I couldn't feel it.

Meg, wake up! Wake up!

Urgency shot up my spine and jolted me awake. Probably a shot of epinephrine to boot, produced by Megcasius.

I was on a stretcher being shifted to the operating theater when I spasmed and tried to sit up.

"Meg! Doctor, easy there." Traynor stood at my side, pushing me back down.

"What's happening?" I asked, my voice cottony and weak. The paralysis had spread. I couldn't feel my arms, and could only move them with effort.

"We've got an antidote. We spent all morning testing it, one hundred percent success rate. You'll be fine in just a bit," he explained rapidly as he continued guiding the stretcher.

"How?"

"It's an agent that inhibits cholinesterase. We can inject the parasite, disable it, and separate it from your system before the compound affects you."

Cholinesterase reacts to break down acetylcholine. While acetylcholine is instrumental to the transmission of neural impulses, a build up of it eventually impedes transmission, like someone holding down the button of a telegraph transmitter instead of tapping it. When cholinesterase is inhibited, the production of acetylcholine is unrestricted and overwhelms the nervous system, eventually resulting in seizures, catanonia . . .

"That'll kill Megcasius." I tried to wake myself up.

"Of course," Traynor said.

"You're going to kill Megcasius!" I think I shouted.

"Meg, you're one step away from a coma. We won't be able to pull you out. It's your last chance."

"No. It's alive. It's sentient." It thinks I'm its mother.

"It's killing you, Meg."

"Then find another way, one that'll let it live."

"Meg, you'll see this more clearly later," he said evenly. His calm was maddening.

"Just when did I lose the Doctor in front of my name?" All this yelling was making me lightheaded.

"Captain?"

I didn't see Alvarez, but he was standing nearby, overseeing the proceedings.

"Captain," I called before Traynor could continue. "It's sentient. It's communicating with me. You can't let him kill it!"

"It's either you or it," Alvarez said curtly.

"No! I'm responsible for it! I can't let you!" I didn't know what I was thinking, arguing with them while sprawled on a stretcher, three-quarters paralyzed.

"Doctor Casey," Alvarez said, instituting his most severe voice. The inarguable voice. "You are relieved of duty due to unstable mental state and critical medical condition. I'm ordering Dr. Traynor to remove that parasite from your system. That is final."

"Bastards!" I had a thing alive inside of me, and they were going to kill it.

Megcasius?

Meg, you're scared.

Yes.

It'll be okay. Everything'll be okay.

It tried to comfort me. It was trying to comfort me, clumsily, ineffectually, like a child. I could have cried. I think I did, screaming and incoherent, until Yons stuck me with a hypo and I went under.

*

I needed a week to recover from the nerve agent Traynor used, which did in fact affect my system. Traynor told me that I'd had a bad reaction during the surgery. They almost lost me due to severe shock, and the parasite almost didn't let go, even after the poisoning. I was glad I didn't remember any of it.

As soon as I could I was walking again, at least a little. Across the med lab and back. I could feel my back now, where Megcasius had burrowed, and it hurt. Like someone had ripped my spine out. Early on, I made a small, unambitious trek from my bed to the specimen hood.

Traynor had two Megcasius specimens dissected and laid out behind the transparent plastic shield. The first, from the grazer Harima's team brought in. The second, from me. My Megcasius.

I stared through the transparency at it, a gelatinous brown mess the size of my hand, its tendrils spread out in a star, eventually tapering off to microscopic neurons.

"We found something," Traynor said. I didn't hear him come up behind me. He moved softly, spoke softly around me. They all did, Yons, Alvarez and the rest.

He punched a key on the terminal beside the hood, bringing up two diagrams.

"This is the nerve structure of a normal parasite, the one we took from the grazer. You see it's primitive, a completely linear circuit." He lectured, and I followed the line he traced on the screen. Nerves radiated from the center of the thing in simple blue lines, one after the other.

"Here's the structure of the other parasite. The one we took from you." He pointed.

The picture was completely different. A rough circuit still existed, but along it lay starbursts, clouds of neurons in three-dimensional arrays, complicated patterns that led nowhere and everywhere. My mouth hung open. Traynor took a deep breath. "Neural networking. Almost identical to that of the human cerebral cortex."

"Intelligence," I said flatly.

He ducked his head. "We don't know that. It was mimicking your system. It wasn't . . . originating intelligence."

That thing spent two weeks inside my body, growing and thinking. I asked questions to the place it used to live, now a palpable emptiness.

"I don't know what else to say," Traynor said quietly.

I must have looked stricken. I shook my head and the apology away. "It's okay, Pete. I'll be okay. I just need time to get my brain chemistry back to normal."

How much time that would take, I didn't know. The scientist in me argued that I was being irrational. I should have been questioning whether or not it had even happened, acknowledging that any sentience had been a quirk of the parasite's biology. I should have been writing papers on it, not mourning it.

But that wasn't what the mother in me felt.

1977

Have another one," the guy said, and Megan did because she was thirsty, though a martini was probably not what she should be drinking. She was too far gone to question.

She downed the drink in three swallows while the guy laughed. Craig. Conner. Whatever his name was. The music changed, and her eyes got wide. She shoved the glass at the bar, knocking something over, but was already turning to the dance floor.

"This is my favorite!"

Whatshisname laughed. "Baby, you say that every other song!"

So? she thought. Every other one was her favorite.

She'd popped something a little while ago and it was starting to kick in. Everything went away but the music, the lights, and her. Her body became ethereal, and she loved the feeling. She didn't have to think about moving, she just did, like the music came from her. She danced like she was part of it.

The guy joined her, gluing himself to her, his hand on her thigh, sliding over the silky fabric of her dress. From where he stood, he could see straight down the low-cut neck. Not that she discouraged him. He was a good dancer, and she'd probably go back to his place. Keep the movement going as long as she could.

He pulled her against him like he owned her, a slim little doll in a knee-length lavender dress and white strappy heels. Her brown hair feathered around her cheeks, bouncing as she moved her head in time with the music, becoming damp with sweat. She laid her arms across his shoulders and let him guide her. She was on tonight, and her energy fed his. In moments a space formed around them as people stopped to watch. He took her hand, spun her out, spun her back. She faced out now, snugged close in his arms. Reveling, she looked up as multicolored lights flowed around her.

She was going to be so sick tomorrow, hung over and sore, and she wasn't going to remember his name, and she didn't want to see the sun ever again. Two months since she caught Rod in bed with her sister and walked out on him. She ought to be getting over it. She ought to find a job, a place to live that wasn't somebody's couch. She ought to ought to ought to. She ought to care, but she didn't. She only wanted this moment, forever.

People cheered them on, and it became just another layer of the music. She and her partner moved in harmony, like it was all planned, but it wasn't. She looked him in the eyes and challenged him: *keep up with me if you can.* She looked at a lot of guys like that, and many walked away.

He dipped her, and she curled her leg around his and arced her body toward him. Like she was going to jump him right here in the middle of the club. That got a cheer. It was all part of the dance. She gave him a sultry, half-lidded smile.

"Oh my God you are so hot," he breathed at her.

She traced a line from his throat down the open collar of his shirt to the first button, somewhere below his sternum. Dark hairs peeked out.

"Let's get out of here," he said, and she shook her head.

"Not until it's over." She always stayed until the music fell silent.

He tried to hide his disappointment. Megan only smiled. He wouldn't be the first guy she'd danced into the ground. The song changed. Her skin burned, her head throbbed, and tomorrow didn't exist.

"This is my favorite," she breathed.

At some moment the lights shifted—out of synch with the music, she noticed, annoyed. They'd all turned to yellow on the off beat, then grew brighter. They'd done something funky—the sparklers disappeared, along with the reds and blues. Everything was yellow and so piercing she had to close her eyes. Her partner had spun her out again, and she was alone, face upturned, watching the back of her eyelids turn red in the lights.

Then the floor disappeared.

This was it. She'd finally done it. Too much booze, too many pills, it had all caught up with her and she was going to die of an overdose right here on the lit-up dance floor. Perfect, she thought, smiling vaguely. This was exactly how she wanted to die. This moment really would last forever. It didn't even hurt.

For a moment, her body felt weightless. She was leaving it, her mind was flying, and there was a tunnel of light just like the crackpots said.

But she was still standing when the fierce light faded to normal lit-room brightness. She looked at her feet, her pink painted toenails peeking out of the white plastic sandals. She stood on a textured yellow floor. Not the club's dance floor with its lighted tiles. She looked at her hands, which were shaking. She was going to throw up.

"Hey! It worked!" a voice called.

She looked up to find a guy in a white leisure suit staring at her, bug-eyed. He had dark hair and trimmed sideburns, a couple of gold chains, and too many rings. He looked like someone who was trying way too hard. The club never would have let him in.

But they weren't in the club.

The ceiling was too low, and the walls were too round. The walls were round, Megan observed, blinking. Everything was a buttery yellow. She might have said this was a living room. Around the edges were armchairs and a sofa, a coffee table, all expensive looking and vaguely attractive with soft lines and warm colors. Lava lamps occupied a couple of nooks and they were lit and morphing in an ideal way that seldom happened in real life. In real life they tended to gum up. On the other side of the room, a pair of bucket seats sat before a complicated-looking instrument panel—a sound board times a million—and a cockpit window. The window looked out over black sky and a few pure stars that didn't twinkle.

She put her hand on her head. "Fuck, I've never been this drunk."

The guy stepped toward her. He wasn't Whatshisname. There wasn't anyone here but the two of them. She stepped back.

"Um . . . can I get you something?" he said. "Water maybe?"

"Yeah. Water. Sure." She was still looking around, off balance. Even the ceiling curved a bit. At least the floor was flat. "Can I sit down?"

"Yeah, anywhere," he said from a cabinet in the back where he was pouring something that looked like water.

The sofa was the most comfortable seat she'd ever had. The stuffing sank, but not too much. It curved around her, supporting her, but still felt soft as goose down. She could curl up and go to sleep right here.

The guy brought her a glass of water. In his other hand he held out a little white pill. "Take this," he said.

She shook her head, which made the room spin. "No. No more."

"It'll clear out your whole system. Instant sobriety."

Too good to be true. Did she trust him? Well, it wouldn't be the first time she'd taken a strange pill from a strange guy.

She popped the pill and downed half the water before she felt ready to ask "What. . .where . . .?" She closed her eyes, took a breath, started over. "I don't remember you."

"No reason you should. We've never met."

"Then what am I doing here?"

He smiled. "You're from 1977."

She shook her head. "I'm from Glendale."

"No, I mean I found you in 1977 and brought you here. To the future. Your future, I mean. This is my ship, the *Travolta*. We're in orbit just outside the Asteroid Belt."

It wasn't the craziest pick-up line she'd ever heard. He wasn't claiming to be an alien from Venus. He hadn't asked her what her sign was. "Why?"

He looked eager. No—he looked crazy, with this fire in his eyes. His hands beseeched. "I want you to teach me to dance."

She looked over to what for some reason she thought of as the front of the room, and through the window to what might have been night sky. Or outer space.

"You couldn't find someone . . . local to help you?"

He sat next to her, and she resisted an urge to scoot away. He wasn't a bad-looking guy. Looked like he had muscles under the shirt. He was taller than she'd thought at first. And he had an earnest smile.

"Here's the thing. In your time, disco's got another two years of life in it, tops. After that, it's all kitsch. Sure, lots of people say they like it, there are lots of movies out there that show how it was done. But it's all missing something. Nobody takes it seriously. So I want to learn from someone who was there. Who understands what it really means."

"I'm not sure I know what it really means. It's music, you know? That's all." She thought about what he'd said: two years, and the music would all change? She wasn't sure she could imagine that. She wasn't sure she'd be alive then anyway.

"You can tell me what it was really like. You can show me. Ever since I heard the Bee Gees in music history class I've loved that whole period, that whole style, everything about it. But it's so hard to find good information, much less anything with any kind of emotion."

"You learned about disco in music history?"

"Sort of. We only spent about ten minutes on it. But I've become a bit of . . . how would you put it? A fan."

Her brain felt clearer, like the pill was actually doing what he said it would do. Or it might have been the water. Or both. She suddenly had to go to the bathroom, and this still didn't make any sense.

She squinted. "Why couldn't you just go back? You like it so much and if you really do have a . . . a time machine, you could go back to the middle of it."

He gave a shrug. "You know how it is. Everyone loves romanticizing the past, but who'd really want to live there? You probably don't even realize how dangerous it is. All the wars, no antibiotics, no—

"1977 has antibiotics," she said.

"It does?" He looked perplexed for a moment, gaze turned inward, maybe to a distant history class. "Twentieth Century America . . . you're right on the edge, aren't you?"

She put her head in her hands. "This isn't happening."

He hovered near her, but he didn't touch her, for which she was grateful. "I know this wasn't really fair of me to yank you out of your life like this. But I can put you back—same exact time and place, no problem."

Like she would want to go back. She hiccupped a laugh and looked at him. His returning gaze was so profoundly hopeful. So clear. No booze, drugs, or sex. He just wanted to dance.

"What's your name?" he said.

"Megan."

"I'm Oz."

She hiccupped again. "You sure are. Do you have a restroom?"

"Through the door."

She hadn't seen the door until he pointed. A panel that had been flush with the wall near the closet that was, she supposed now, a kitchen of sorts, slid open to reveal a fully appointed restroom.

She fled.

The fixtures were recognizable enough that she could do what she needed to do. As happy as she was that she didn't have to ask how to use anything, she was a little disappointed that humanity hadn't advanced to space-age super-sonic bathrooms, or whatever they were supposed to have. This couldn't be the future. It was so . . . ordinary. This was some game; she could play along.

There wasn't a mirror to check how badly her mascara had smeared or to touch up her lip gloss. Not that she had any lip gloss with her. Maybe it was for the best that she couldn't check. She ran her fingers through her hair and smoothed her dress out as best she could, adjusting the thin chains around her neck so they lay straight. But she didn't know why she had to be presentable when she was going crazy.

The door slid open when she merely stood in front of it hopefully. Nice effect, but it didn't make it the future. Taking a deep breath, she returned to the main cabin.

Oz handed her a thing about the size of a paperback but thin, like a piece of corrugated cardboard. It had a screen on it, and a row of glowing letters. Song titles.

"This is all the music I have on file," he said. "Here, scroll down by touching that button there."

She did. He had hundreds of songs. All the music, he said. Sure looked that way. She spotted a Bee Gees title she didn't recognize. Something that hadn't been released yet? If this was the future . . .

"Can I play this one?" When she touched the title on the screen, it highlighted. She squinted at it.

"Push the play button, there." He pointed to a little arrow on the screen. Just like the play key on a tape recorder. She did.

Sound flowed from everywhere. She couldn't see any speakers. It was like the whole room was a speaker. It enveloped her like a warm blanket, and she didn't care anymore if it was the future or not. Maybe she really had died and this was heaven.

There it came, Barry Gibb's voice, rich and sweet, and a beat to die for. And if this really was the future, she was hearing this song before anyone else in the world. Before the Bee Gees even. At least, before anyone in 1977. What a nice idea.

"I thought maybe you'd teach me some steps before we started with the music. The classes I've taken before usually start that way."

She shook her head. "You have to learn to feel the music before you learn any steps. The steps don't mean anything if you can't feel it."

And she felt it. The steps came naturally, without her thinking, because she'd been doing them for so long. But the important part was still the music and how it ran through you. It didn't matter where or when you were.

She'd been kidnapped, she thought absently. Didn't matter who Oz claimed to be, or what. She ought to be screaming. Breaking down the door. She ought to be too scared to dance, but she wasn't.

She just closed her eyes and she was back at the club.

"I have a little piece of 1977 right here on my ship. I think I'm going to cry."

She looked at him; he was watching her with an intensity—an appreciation—she wasn't used to. She had to interrupt that look.

"Come on, you try it." She took his hand and led him to the middle of the floor.

She expected him to be clumsy. Something about his enthusiasm didn't inspire confidence in his abilities. If he'd been good at this, he wouldn't have needed to kidnap her. But he wasn't clumsy. Restrained, maybe. Nervous, self conscious. Most people were, and hung out on the edges of the dance floor, eyeing the crowd like they wanted to make sure no one was actually watching them. Frowning instead of smiling, pursing or biting their lips in concentration. And they didn't really move. They might do the steps and pump their arms, but they didn't flow.

He swayed from foot to foot but seemed most interested in watching her. He had a nice smile, she realized. And the kind of hair you wanted to run your fingers through. Soft and thick. She took his hand and tried a spin. He didn't have to do anything but hold her hand and let her wind herself in and out of his arms. But he would feel like he was part of something. His smile brightened, becoming less about wonder and more about happiness.

Part of her rhythm and joy of movement flowed into him. She found a different song on his list. "Let's try this one—it's got real easy steps."

"The Hustle" started playing. The thing about that one was the basic steps were easy, but you could build on them and make the dance more complex as you went along, as you got better. She added a couple of spins, and Oz said, "See, that's what I'm talking about, they don't show that kind of thing on any of the vids!" So she had to do it again, then show it to him, and they did it together.

Then she faced him, putting his hands on her hips and resting hers on his shoulders.

His smile quirked. "I haven't been able to practice anything like this," he said, giving a shy little shrug. "Can't find anyone who's interested in dancing with me."

"Well then. This is your big chance."

They danced. He held back at first, but she was brazen, spinning into him so they were only inches apart, daring him not to back off. She fell and made him catch her in a dip, and he did, and the music pulsed, the singers going on about love and loss and forgetting about it all while you danced.

He righted her from another dip and held her shoulders. "You could stay here," he said suddenly. "I—I don't have to send you back."

If she'd wanted an escape, this was the ultimate. She stared at him, breathing a little hard from the dancing, wondering at the song playing. It was another one she'd never heard before but nonetheless sounded familiar. Like this whole place. Like him. Never going back sounded like the best thing in the world.

A crash sounded, and an alarm blared through the room.

"Shit!" Oz ran to the cockpit, leaving her standing alone. Absently, she smoothed out her skirt and rearranged her necklace.

While he was doing who knew what, the lights flickered, then a space of air brightened, like a light bulb the second before it burns out. There was a pop, a puff of breeze, and two people appeared from nowhere, standing before her.

They were cops. Even if the uniforms were unfamiliar, their attitudes weren't. They both wore black boots, trousers, and padded jackets with some kind of insignia, and they both had crew cuts and sunglasses. The short one was a woman.

The man read from a handheld screen. "Osric Nu? We detected the unauthorized use of a temporal transducer along your route at approximately 0341. We'd like to ask you a few questions."

Oz faced them from the cockpit. "This is an illegal search! I'll call my lawyer! Where are your idents?"

The man sighed, like he'd expected this sort of outburst. "I'm Officer Brady, this is Officer Jellicle, of the Temporal Authority. And we have a warrant." He showed Oz the screen he held.

Megan hoped they didn't notice her. If they did, she had to hope she wasn't important, that they didn't have anything they could pin on her. This was like any other bust, right? Just stay out of the way.

The woman, Officer Jellicle, said, "This isn't a petty violation, Nu. You're not going to talk your way out of it."

"What? Using a transducer isn't illegal. I haven't done anything wrong."

Both officers looked at him, then looked at Megan.

Jellicle looked her up and down. "What is that, 1977? '78?"

She shrugged. "Yeah, I guess."

Brady tipped his head at Jellicle and said, "You still got it." She gave him a thin smile.

Oz rushed to stand between Megan and the officers. She resisted an urge to hang on him, begging to know what was going on.

"I was going to put her back—"

Except that he'd asked her to stay. And she wanted to say yes. She should tell him yes.

Jellicle winced and cocked her head to listen. "What is that? The ship's engines—did you program them for a rhythm?" They all listened for a moment.

"'Disco Inferno,'" Megan said. "I noticed it awhile ago."

"This is your second offense, Nu," Brady said, scowling.

"So to speak," Jellicle added.

Megan looked at Oz. "What did you bring back the first time?"

"Disco ball," he said, pointing to the one on the ceiling. "That's the copy. I put the original back." He glared at the officers.

"We're going to have to confiscate your transducer," Brady said.

"And send back the girl," Jellicle said.

Megan grabbed Oz's arm. "I want to stay. You said I could stay."

He met her gaze, and for a moment music played, even though the song had cut out a long time ago. She imagined it—flying through space with Oz, dancing. Bliss.

Jellicle glared at the ceiling and gave a long suffering sigh. Her partner just shook his head.

"Ma'am," he said, "That isn't going to be possible."

She didn't know anything about the rules here, but she should have guessed. The minute it looked like she was getting a break, that something amazing was happening to her and she could dream again, it disappeared. Swallowed up by life. She was afraid she was going to start crying, but she only frowned and looked away.

Oz said, "There has to be a way. An exemption—museums get exemptions all the time.

"That's just the thing," Jellicle said, pulling Oz away. Brady joined them for a huddled conference a few paces away. Nonetheless, Megan listened closely and heard them. The room had great acoustics. "Museums get exemptions for objects that were destroyed in history. Things that don't have any further significance. We stopped you because we tracked *her*. She's important, she has kids, she makes a difference. If she was one of those girls who ended up with her brain fried and drowned in her own vomit, I'd say yeah, let her stay. But she wasn't, and she can't. She has to go back. Now."

Oz looked back at her with an expression of frank longing. She couldn't feel her own face to tell what she gave back to him. She was going to wake up from all this like it was a dream. It was all going to fade, and she hated that.

But then Jellicle's words hit her. She was talking about their past—and her future. Like she had a future. They were going to send her back because she had a future.

Amazing. Here was an epiphany to top all the others of the last couple of hours.

Her voice cracked. "I have kids?"

They all looked at her. Jellicle said, "Uh. Yeah. You're not supposed to know that."

Megan only nodded, lips pressed in a line. What she didn't say was, *I have a future.*

Oz returned to her. "Megan, I'm sorry. I—it was wrong. I didn't have the right to take you. I'm sorry. But—I had a great time."

"No—don't be sorry. I had a great time too. Thanks." She put her hand behind his neck and kissed his cheek. They spent another moment giving each other goofy smiles.

"Stand back, Nu," Brady said.

Oz did, then he opened his mouth to say something, but Megan never heard it. Jellicle pointed some device at her—a box with an egg beater thing sticking out the side—and the disco lights times a million surrounded her, filling her up, drowning out sight and sound, and the floor gave way, and she was falling.

Then she was standing in the middle of the club, a hundred bodies dancing around her, arms raised, hips swaying, feet stepping, beat throbbing. Whatshisname was dancing with someone else now, and Megan was sort of relieved. Except for that, she was right back where she started. But clear this time. She could see the people, the lights, the speakers, the bar, the drinks. Everything was so clear.

She could see the future.

Raising her arms straight up, she laughed, thinking, *I will survive.*

DANAË AT SEA

Thems that tells what's right and wrong to the rest of us decided I'd done wrong, more or less. How else is a girl like me s'posed to make a living? I shouted at them as they drug me out of Old Bailey. Then it was to Newgate, then to the docks, then away. Seven years transport was my sentence. They might as well have killed me. Seven years, they said, but it was really death. Who'd ever heard of someone coming back from transport?

I knowed they done it to a thousand others. But when the others went away it was easy enough to think 'em dead. I'd never see 'em again. Guess I would now. It was like dying, that last glimpse of the docks before they shoved me down into the hold with the rest of the convicts and closed the lid on us. That smell of London air, the wet shit and coal smoke smell, I breathed deep, so deep, because it was London and I was dying.

They shut out the light, leaving me in a damp, dark room with a hundred other women—whores, thieves, and swindlers all of us. How else were girls like us meant to make our way in the world, when our men beat us and the Queen herself couldn't think of anything better for us than to ship us to God-forsaken Australia?

I'd heard a story like this. An old story, one that I saw on a broadsheet or that some gent told me when he was all drunk and spent. A girl's father thought she was a whore, all on account that she wasn't married and she had a baby. He couldn't kill her—not right, killing your own daughter, even the worst of 'em knows that, usually—but

he didn't want her 'round to shame him, not at all. So he put her to
sea in a sealed box. Nailed the lid down tight over her and her baby
both. How the babe must have cried, was all I could think. How they
both must have cried. But since this was a story and just the start of
it, no less, they lived. They washed up on a distant shore and a kind
fisherman saved them, married her, adopted the baby boy as his own.
I hoped he was handsome, or at the very least good to her, since she
obviously hadn't much choice 'bout marrying him or no. Man saves
your life, what else are you meant to do? The boy grew to be a hero.
Killed monsters, saved a princess, went back to the start and killed
his grandfather, the one that put him and his mum in the coffin. It's a
story and revenge always comes 'round at the end.

I never knew my father.

The first two weeks, most of us was sick as dogs. The few that
weren't—lucky girls born with sea-legs, who didn't mind the swaying
and rolling, the way the floor and your stomach never stayed still—
took care of us that were. Poured water down our throats, no matter
how much we puked it back up again. Soaked bread and made us eat.
Molly, she's the one looked after me, and how I loved her for it. She
said if any of us were to get through this alive, we'd have to help each
other. Weren't no such thing as crime or hate down here, she said. Just
keeping each other alive. I believed her, and I'd have done anything
she asked after that.

Couldn't count how many of the girls got here by whoring.
Couldn't count how many kept whoring after they got here. Wasn't
this all meant to cure us of it, then? But it was an easy way to get an
extra piece of bread or salt pork, or even a mug of ale. Couldn't put a
hundred women on a boat with a hundred men and expect them to
keep apart.

Molly never told me what she'd done to get here. We all told our
stories to each other, and happy to, to pass the time, but not her. She
must have done something awful. Murdered someone or the like. She

might have been a murderer, even though she seemed right peaceful. My guess was she wasn't a whore, because she kept me from it on the boat. I almost did, then she asked me if it was what I wanted, if it made me happy. It didn't, though I'd never thought of it like that before. It was what my mother'd done, it was what I'd done. A job, like working in a factory. No pleasure to be had. So she says to me, don't. Simple as that. Don't. When one of the sailors turned his eye to me and made noises like he could help me—an extra hour up top in the fresh air, a boiled egg—I told him off. He didn't like that, saying he figured that once a girl was a whore she was always a whore and for sale. I screamed and hit him. I might have gotten lashes for that, but my screaming drew notice and he left me, shamed.

Didn't matter, when my belly grew. I counted back and yes, there was that guard at Newgate. Couldn't say no, then. Counting the time on the ship, I'd be so far along with a baby.

At least I knew who the father was.

There was the girl in her coffin, adrift at sea, crying and crying. I cried and cried, but there was nothing to be done for it but muddle on. A baby should be born on land, where things were dry and still, not rotten and moldy like our bread and our hammocks. I counted forward. I might get there in time.

I'd only ever gone to church when they promised a meal at the end of the service. They did that, some of the fine folk, bribed us to religion with food we were desperate for. They didn't realize we were so hungry the words drifted 'round us like a fog, we barely heard the difference between gospel and hymnal. But I sang their songs and thought the glass in the windows was pretty. Sparkled like rainbows. I'd not prayed much then, but I prayed now. Lord God, wash me up on land safely. I'm turning a new leaf just like they said I should. I heard talk from the girls that the land we were heading for was filled with men who'd gotten rich with sheep and gold mines, all of them desperate for wives since women were scarce. The girls talked like this with stars in their eyes, and it kept 'em hopeful. They could live through the night and wake in the morning, if only they kept sight of those stars.

No man'll marry a whore with a bastard in her arms.

We were all getting so thin, even me with a baby in my belly. Molly was giving me half her bread—for the baby, she said—and I screamed at her, cried at her, worried her. She was getting so thin, and I couldn't do without her. But she wouldn't argue, she wouldn't take back her ration, and if I didn't eat it, it would have gone to waste or been taken by rats. I couldn't let that happen. Not with the baby.

Strange how I should want the thing to live so badly, when most like it'll have a life like mine—hard, hungry, with a long, drawn-out death at the end of it. But maybe it'll do better. It'll have schooling, learn figures, apprentice with some fine master, live in a pretty house with a garden. If it's a boy. If it's a girl—she could be a maid. A maid to some fine lady.

There were no such fine ladies in Australia, of course. A land of convicts. She'll turn out just like me, only they won't have no place to ship her off to when they decide she's done wrong.

A fever came over the ship. Some of us died. The men wrapped the bodies in old sailcloth and took them up top, pitched 'em over the side. Buried at sea and they weren't even sailors, how d'you like that?

My turn to take care of Molly when she caught it. I told her she couldn't die. How'd I ever get along without her? She only smiled, said she didn't mean to die, but if she did she thought I'd do fine. She was cracked. I hated this place and so many times I'd gone to sleep hoping I'd never wake up, wishing I'd died back in England. Heaven or hell, either would be better than this. Drifting, a girl in a coffin, with nothing to do but sit in her box and pray.

Now I knew why Molly took such good care of me at the start: she knew I'd have to return the favor. Obligation. A couple of the girls came aboard hating everyone and cursing everything. They died alone, no one to sit with them, no one to cry for them. That hell was worse than the one I lived in. The littlest kindnesses kept us together and kept this hell from being worse.

When Molly was asleep, I told her of a little dream I'd been making up, a bit of a plan which I'd never think of trying in an old, cold place like London. I told her, we could make our own work, that if Australia really was a place filled with men and the dust of deserts thousands of miles wide, there's bound to be laundry needing done. I could do washing—or I could learn quickly, and Molly could help, I knew she could because she was smart. When our terms were up we could pay our own way, be our own masters. I'd never have had the courage to tell this to Molly when she was awake, being afraid she'd laugh at me and my silliness. So I told her when she slept, when I was afraid she'd die no matter how hard I prayed. I told her, whispering in the dark, my voice muffled by the sound of waves slapping the sides of the boat.

When they lifted the lid to the hold, I could barely climb the ladder, as big as I was. Not as big as I should have been, and I was afraid this was all for nothing and I wouldn't have a baby to show for it. But the babe was kicking. Weeks now, I'd felt kicking, tiny but strong.

Molly helped, coming up behind me with her hand on my back.

A week before the ship docked, she told me an idea she had, that we could pay our own way, be our own masters, by taking in the laundry of the hordes of men crawling over the continent, who were bound to need desert dust washed from their shirts. She said it with a smile, and I blushed, but we shook on it, and it gave me more hope than I deserved.

When I came up top, the sun was the brightest sun I'd ever seen. It hurt my eyes and made me dumb with its strangeness. The sky was big, clear of coal smoke, and the land went on and on.

I had washed up on shore with my baby, ready to slay monsters.

FOR FEAR OF DRAGONS

In a certain kingdom, very young women—still girls—commonly had babies. It proved they were not virgins, and so their names would not go into the lottery that was held every year to choose a sacrifice for the dragon.

Jeannette had asked her mother once why only girls were made to be sacrifices, why her brothers had not faced the lottery.

Her mother, who had been quite young when she bore Jeannette and was still fresh-faced, smiled sadly. "The dragon would probably take a boy virgin as well as a girl. But there's no way to tell with boys, and the priests won't take a chance of making a mistake."

"That isn't fair."

"No, it isn't," her mother said. "But women go through childbirth while the men sit back happy as you please, and that isn't fair either."

The year came when soldiers rode to Jeanette's family's holding. Their captain announced that from the sea to the mountains, Jeanette was the only woman over the age of ten known to be a virgin. Only one possible name could be drawn in the lottery.

Jeanette's mother sobbed, and the soldiers had to tie her father to keep him from doing violence. They held her three brothers off with crossbows. Her family had urged her time and again to marry someone, anyone, a young whelp, an old widower on his deathbed. They had even begged her to find a likely boy to love her for a night and give her a child. But Jeanette had refused, because she knew that this day would come, that one day she would be chosen, and she knew her destiny.

Before the soldiers led her away, Jeanette held her mother's face in her hands. "It's all right. I have a plan, I know what to do."

She kissed her mother's cheeks, smoothed away the tears, smiled at her father and her brothers, and rode away, seated behind the captain on his horse. She smuggled with her a homemade lock-pick and a dagger.

Jeanette sat by the fire, wrapped in a blanket, eating the bread and dried meat the soldiers had given her. One of the soldiers sat a little ways off, cleaning the sweat from girths and saddles. He watched her with a gaze that burned like molten iron in the firelight.

"You're a pretty girl. I could help you."

She ignored him and his hands rubbing the leather with a soiled cloth. She stared at the fire, but felt his gaze on her, heavy, like a calloused fist.

The captain walked past and cuffed the soldier's head. "Keep your eyes on your work."

The captain sat between him and Jeanette to finish his own meal. She suspected his job was to protect her, to ensure she reached her destination safely and intact, as much as it was to take her prisoner and ensure she fulfilled her obligation.

"Perhaps this is best for her. She can't be normal, a virgin at her age."

Whispering and staring, hundreds lined the road where Jeannette walked, flanked by guards and led by priests. The people believed in destiny as Jeanette did, but the one they believed was different. They looked on her with curiosity and pity.

The procession was something out of a story, happening just the way the stories had told it for generations. Beautiful, in a way. Garbed in white, white flowers woven in her dark hair, she looked ahead at the back of the brown cloak of the priest who walked in front of her, and tried to be calm. She'd had her chance to avoid this. She could have accepted the soldier's offer, let him lead her into the dark and raise her skirt for him. The captain and priests might have punished her, but she probably wouldn't have died. She'd have been sent home in disgrace, perhaps. But alive.

She had known this day would come. She had looked forward to it, because she had a plan. It was all right. It was going to be all right.

"The girls usually cry."

"She doesn't even look frightened. It isn't natural."

The dragon lived in a corner of the arid plain in the northern part of the kingdom. Dry brush sprouted on the dusty land, which became more rocky the farther north one traveled on the narrow road. Ravines cut across the plains, crumbling spires of granite rose from windswept outcroppings, and ridges held caves and channels that delved into the earth.

A path led from the road to one of these caves. The mouth of the cave was a dark slit in the rock, a depthless shadow, empty and featureless even in the midday sun. Outside the cave, a platform of rock stood exposed. A tall iron pole had been driven into the granite. A cold wind rattled a set of chains dangling from the pole. Jeanette brushed a strand of hair from her face.

The priests led her to the pole. The soldiers stood near, guarding her in case she panicked and tried to run, as some girls had done in other years, or so Jeanette had heard. Four manacles dangled from chains, two at the base of the pole and two in the middle. The master of the priests guided her to the pole and fastened the bindings himself, one on each wrist, one on each ankle.

The priests recited a blessing, a plea, begging their nemesis to accept the offering, to keep the peace for another year. They lauded the value of virgins, who were most pure. Jeanette knew the truth, though, that no one prized virgins. If virginity were valuable as anything other than a bribe for dragons, why did all the girls want to lose it so quickly?

She wondered how one small virgin could satisfy a dragon for a whole year.

"Go to your fate in peace, child."

The master priest was an old man who had sent dozens of girls on this final journey, had probably given them all this final command.

"I'll be fine," she told the priest, keeping any tremor out of her voice.

The priest met her gaze suddenly, like he hadn't meant to. He'd kept his face downcast until that moment. Now he looked at her with a watery, wavering gaze. Jeanette smiled, and he quickly turned away.

The priests and soldiers departed, and the crowd that had come to watch followed them quickly, before the dragon appeared. Jeanette was left alone, tied hand and foot to a post at the mouth of the cave to await her fate.

She didn't know how much time she had before the dragon emerged from the cave. She waited until the procession had gone away and she couldn't hear them anymore, so no one could stop her. She hoped she had time. She only needed a few moments.

The chains weren't meant to restrict her movement, only to keep her from leaving. She was lucky in that. By leaning down and reaching up, she retrieved the lock-pick she'd woven among the flowers in her hair.

She had been afraid the priests would find her tools and take them away. She'd kept them hidden among her clothes while she changed into the ceremonial gown and a priestess washed and braided her hair. Her guardians turned their backs for a moment, and she slipped the pick into her hair and tied the dagger to her leg. They didn't expect such behavior from a pure young girl, so they weren't looking for rebellion.

For months, she'd practiced picking locks. She'd practiced with all sorts of variations: hands chained above her head, behind her back, on many different kinds of locks, by feel, with her eyes closed, and she'd practiced for speed.

These shackles were difficult because they were stiff with rust and grime.

Stay calm. She kept her breathing steady. Even so, she let out a sigh when the first shackle around her wrist snapped open.

This was taking too long. She hadn't yet heard a dragon's roar or the crunch of massive footfalls on the rocky ground. She didn't know what she would hear first. The beast must have been near.

Working methodically, keeping her hands steady—she dared not drop the pick—she finally sprang the second lock. She crouched and started work on the bindings around her ankles.

That was when she heard the scrape of claws against stone, felt the ground tremble as some monstrous beast stepped closer. A few pebbles tumbled from the hill above her.

The grime caked into the keyholes and cracks of the shackles was old blood, of course.

The dragon seemed to take forever to climb from its den, along the passage to the mouth of the cave. Jeanette fumbled, cut her hand and dropped the pick. Drawing a sharp breath, she found it and tried again. The scraping footsteps crept closer.

Finally the last shackle snapped open, and with a yelp she clawed it away and sprang from the pole. She climbed the rocks, scrambling to get above the cave entrance. She found a sheltered perch behind a jagged boulder.

It wasn't enough just to escape. Without its sacrifice, the dragon would break the peace and ravage the countryside. Another girl would be brought here, and the sacrifices would continue. Jeanette had to find a way to destroy the dragon.

She retrieved her dagger. It was a fool's hope. Perhaps she'd be lucky.

At last the dragon slipped out of the cave and into the light.

It raised itself on a boulder and looked around, snout lifted to the air, nostrils flaring. It was perhaps twice the size of a horse, broad of back, with a long, writhing neck and sinewy limbs.

It was also thin. Its ribs showed above a hollow belly. Its scales were brown, dull. Many were missing; scattered spots of flaking pink skin showed along its length. Its yellow eyes squinted. It pulled back its lips to reveal broken teeth.

When it turned to make a circuit of its realm, it limped, one of its forelegs stumbling under its weight. It stepped, slumped, picked itself up and lurched forward again, making agonizing progress over the rocks. Tattered membranes hung between its forelegs and body, the remnants of wings.

The dragon was old, its skin cracked, its scales stained, its body wasted. It might once have been a terror, but not for many years. It might once have flown over the countryside, devouring every living thing in its path. Now, it might be able to do battle with a young girl. But only if she were tied to a post.

This dragon couldn't ravage the countryside. A few men on horseback with spears—the soldiers who had brought her from her family's farm, for instance—could put it out of its misery. Jeanette wondered when was the last time anyone had seen the dragon, or if the priests and soldiers had simply been abandoning the girls to the rocks without a backward glance all these years.

The task before her became much less difficult, though she almost felt sorry for the beast.

If she did nothing, it would probably starve. It looked as if it was barely surviving on its one virgin a year. But if she wanted to return home and ensure that no other girls were bound here and left to die, she had to do more. She couldn't leave the beast alone.

It hadn't seen her yet. It was sniffing around the rocks, searching slowly and carefully. Perhaps it couldn't see at all.

Still crouched on an outcropping above it, she inched toward the edge, gripping her knife, preparing herself. It was just a creature, after all, though it may have lived a thousand years and devoured a million men.

She had hunted rabbits and helped slaughter pigs. She knew how to kill beasts. She could not be afraid.

She jumped.

Landing on the dragon's back, she sprawled and almost slipped, tumbling off the animal. Desperate, she scraped her hands against the scales, hoping to reach a handhold. She found a grip on the ridged spine with one hand while supporting herself with the knuckles of the hand that held the knife, which she couldn't drop or she was lost. A living heat rose off the creature, smelling of peat and dying embers.

The dragon shrieked, a choking, wheezing sound. Not so much as a puff of smoke emerged from its mouth. At least Jeanette didn't have to worry about fire. The beast lurched, but not very quickly. She kept hold of her perch. She could imagine the dragon at the peak of its strength, its great body pulsing with power, flinging itself one way and another in the blink of an eye, its fierce head whipping around to snap at her with dagger-like fangs.

But its head turned slowly on a neck stiff with age. It hissed, and its chest heaved with labored breathing.

It was almost dead already.

Gripping the ridges where its backbone protruded, she crawled up its back, then up its neck, which collapsed under her weight, smashing against the rock. The dragon squealed, snapping uselessly as it tried to reach back for her. The tail lashed against the rock, knocking loose pebbles which clattered around them.

Slumped on its neck, pinning it to the ground, she reached over its head. Its body rolled as it tried to free itself, and the joints along its spine cracked.

She placed her hand between the curled spines that grew out the back of its head, and balancing herself, she drove her knife into its right eye, using her body to force the weapon as far as it would go, until her shoulder rested on the bone of the socket, and the knife lodged deep in its brain.

The dragon shuddered, its death rippling along its entire body. Jeanette held on tightly, closing her eyes and hoping it would end soon.

She lay stretched along the dragon's neck, her head pillowed on its brow, her arm resting in the wetness of the burst eye socket. The blood was growing cold and thick. It smelled sweet and rotten, much worse than slaughtered pigs. The bones along its neck dug through the fabric of her gown, making an uncomfortable bed.

She scraped the brain and gore off her arm as well as she could, wiping her hands on the hem of her gown. The silky fabric wasn't much use for that.

She could go home. Though if she wanted them to believe that the dragon was dead, she had to bring back proof. She'd show the priests, and they wouldn't hold any more lotteries.

She couldn't carry back the head, as impressive as it would be to see it hanging on a wall. In the end, she cut off a toe and its claw, unmistakably the black, curved claw of a dragon. Once it might have been as sharp as a sword, but now it was dull with age. She left the dragon sprawled among the heaps of stone. Within half an hour of walking, she looked back, and the dragon's body was only another shadow among the crevices.

A flock of ravens circled overhead.

One would think, having slain a dragon, she could face anything.

She did not find shelter by nightfall, so she lay down in a sandy depression on the lee side of a boulder, hugged herself, and tried to sleep. She also had not found any water, and her throat was swollen, her mouth sticky. Her gown and skin were grimy, itchy.

The desert was painfully cold at night, even in summer. Too cold to let her sleep. She clutched the dragon's claw and longed for morning, for light. She had killed a dragon, she had the proof here in her hands. She would not let the night kill her.

She'd held the claw for so long, so tightly, that it was warm to the touch. Hot, even. As if it still had life, despite the scabbed stump. The toe still had muscles, it still flexed. It hadn't stiffened in death.

It gave her warmth, a small and odd companion in the lonely darkness.

They will not thank you for killing me.

The voice came as a whisper, like wind through desert scrub.

She must have fallen asleep; her mind was thick with dreaming, and she couldn't open her eyes. She imagined that she held the dragon in her hands, she held its life in her hands.

They will fear and curse you.

"No, they won't. They will thank me. I've saved them."

You have destroyed a tradition that has lasted for centuries. But I must thank you. Dragons cannot die, they can only be killed. I waited a long time.

"You could have been killed anytime, you could have found a warrior anywhere and let him kill you."

Its chuckle rumbled through the earth. *Don't you think I tried that?*

Jeannette curled tighter to herself, shivering, and whimpering.

Hush there. You're probably right. They'll cheer for you and throw flowers in your path, and you'll be safe. Sleep now. Don't be afraid.

She nestled into what felt like the warm embrace of a friend and fell asleep.

On the second day she found a pool and slow-running stream, enough water to wash and to keep herself from dying of thirst.

On the third day, disheveled and exhausted, she arrived at the door of the abbey at the first town beyond the northern waste, where she had been washed and dressed for the sacrifice.

People stared at her as she passed by. Her white gown, no matter how stained and tattered, made clear who she was, or who she was supposed to be—the sacrifice to the dragon. By the time she reached the abbey, a crowd had gathered to watch what the priests would say about her return.

She pulled the chain at the door of the abbey. It opened, and the priest who appeared there looked at her, eyes wide.

"I killed the dragon," she said and showed him the claw.

Stammering, he called back into the abbey. Jeanette stayed at the door, unsure of what would happen, of what she expected to happen when she came here. She thought they would be happy. The crowd remained, whispering among themselves and hemming her in.

The dragon's claw, as long as her forearm, lay in her hands, still warm, as if it were still attached to the dragon's foot and ready to spring to life. The scales were dull. She ran her finger along the claw. It was smooth, hard as iron.

She wanted to go home.

The priest returned with several of his fellows. They grabbed her, surrounded her, pulled her inside, shut the door behind her. It happened quickly, and they did not seem surprised, or glad, or impressed that she had returned. Instead, they seemed worried, which made her afraid.

In moments, they'd brought her to the room where she'd been prepared as a sacrifice, a bare stone antechamber with a fireplace and washbasin, where a week ago she had been cleaned and anointed. She stood in the middle of the room, a ring of priests surrounding her. The master priest stood before her.

"What have you done?" he said.

"I killed the dragon." She cradled the claw to her chest.

"Why have you done this?" Horror filled his voice. Inexplicable horror. Was there something about the dragon Jeanette didn't know?

They will not thank you.

"I didn't want to die. I thought—I believed I could do this thing." She hoped she might, eventually, by chance, say the thing that would make this right. "It was old, crippled. Anyone could have done it. I picked the locks on the shackles. I planned it. I—I didn't understand why no one had done it before. Someone should have killed it a long time ago."

Harshly, the priest said, "Whether or not the dragon could be killed, whether or not it should have been killed, is not important. The sacrifice is important. The sacrifice is why you were chosen, why the choice is made every year."

Very quietly she said, "I don't understand."

"Fear," the old priest said, his voice shaking. "We sacrifice so that we will not have to fear. Without the dragon, how will we banish our fear? What will we sacrifice, so that we do not have to be afraid?"

"Nothing," Jeanette said without thinking. "We can choose not to fear."

One of the other priests said, "How does a girl kill a dragon?"

"It isn't natural," said another.

"It isn't possible."

"Not without suspicion."

"Suspicion of witchcraft."

Jeanette looked around as the priests talked. She began to understand, and began to fear in a way she hadn't when she faced the dragon.

"We cannot tolerate a witch among us."

The old priest stepped toward her, the circle closed around her, and she had a vision of herself bound to another post, with knotted rope she couldn't escape from, and flames climbing around her, which she couldn't kill. They had found a new fear to make a sacrifice to; something else to kill, to comfort themselves.

The dragon's claw was dull, worn by age and use. But it still had a point on it, and this was the hand she had used to kill a dragon.

Don't be afraid. Some hunters believe they take the power of the creatures they kill. You have killed me. My power is yours.

Jeanette slashed the claw at the old priest, as the dragon might have slashed in its younger days. He fell back, and the priests shouted in panic. Half of them reached to help their master, half lunged to stop Jeanette.

She was young and quick and escaped them all, running out of the room. She didn't know if the crowd would still be gathered at the front door, so she escaped to the back of the building and found another door, another way out.

She couldn't go home; the priests would send soldiers after her. Instead, she traveled far away, to a desert land where a dragon might live.

There was a kingdom that held a lottery every year, to choose a virgin who would be sacrificed to the witch who lived in a cave at the edge of the northern desert. She was so powerful, it was said, that she knew the ancient language of dragons, which had not been spoken on earth in centuries.

The girls were chained to a rock near her cave and left to their fates. The witch used their pure white bones in her spells, and fed on their untainted flesh, to preserve and restore her own rotten body.

One year, the girl who was left on the rock had only just begun to grow the first curve of breast and to dream of dancing at the country fair. Now that the priests were gone and could no longer intimidate her to silence, she cried and struggled against the chains until her wrists bled.

When the witch appeared at the mouth of the cave, the girl screamed and thrashed like a wild thing, stupid with fear.

The witch was an old, old woman, with gray hair tied in a braid draped over her shoulder, coiled and tucked into her belt. She walked stooped, leaning on a cane of knobbed wood. And it was true what the stories said, that she had bound a dragon's claw, curved and polished black, to the head of the staff. She held a key in her hand.

"Hush, child, hush. I am too old to fight you."

Her voice was old and kind, like a grandmother's voice, which made the girl fall still and silent.

"There, that's a good girl," the witch said.

One by one, the witch unfastened the shackles with her key. The girl started trembling so hard her teeth chattered.

When she was free, the witch took her hand and helped her to her feet. Then she unfolded the cloak she'd held draped over one arm and put it around the girl's shoulders. "You can't travel in that flimsy gown they gave you, can you? And here."

The witch put a pouch filled with coins into the girl's hand.

Holding her other hand, the witch led her to the far side of the hill, opposite the mouth of her cave. She pointed to a path that led down the hill and away, far into the distance.

She said, "Take this path. In a day it will bring you to a country where girls are not sacrificed to anything. The family at the first farm will help you. Go now, and don't be afraid."

The girl stared at the witch a long time, deciding whether or not to be afraid, wondering if she should dare to believe that she would live. The witch smiled a grandmother's smile.

Impulsively, the girl hugged her, arms around the witch's shoulders, gently because the woman seemed frail. Then she drew away and ran down the path, clutching the cloak around her.

THE ART
OF HOMECOMING

This was not how I imagined my career ending. I'd
hoped for a blaze of glory, a fiery punctuation mark, starships
screaming through an atmosphere before crashing, hand-to-hand
battles with the robot minions of an evil empire. At the very least. Not
the most hideously uncomfortable meeting I'd ever been a part of.

We had already gone around in circles for twenty minutes. De-
scribing the incident, trying to predict inherently unpredictable out-
comes, avoiding veiled accusations. The Trade Guild liaison who'd been
assigned to clean up the mess, an Agent Parma, desperately wanted a
scapegoat, displaying a simmering need in her eyes that had me reaching for a blaster pistol that wasn't on my hip. The *Raja Ampat's* captain,
Song, was certain this would all blow over if we just ignored it. The
trouble was, I didn't know which of them was right. Because of my direct actions, the Trade Guild had been barred from Cancri Four. How
big a deal that was depended on who you asked. Somehow, Song had
to convince Parma to just go away, but Parma wasn't going.

A pause came in the conversation, and for several long moments,
none of us said a word. Captain Song watched me warily, no doubt
waiting for me to lose it. Parma hung back from the conference table
where Song and I had parked. All the cards were on the table. It only
remained to see who was going to do anything with them.

There was, I decided, a simple way to cut through this mess. "Sir,"
I said, standing, smoothing out the fabric of my uniform jumpsuit.
"I'd like to offer my resignation immediately—"

"Major Daring, you will not," he said, without even thinking.

But Parma's gaze lit up. The two of them engaged in a brief, silent contest of wills, and I realized they'd already discussed this possibility, just not in front of me. Parma had asked for my resignation, Song had already refused, and this was probably out of my hands one way or another.

After a moment of glaring at Song, Parma sighed. "Major Daring, that won't be necessary. You're far too valuable an asset and your experience will be appreciated moving forward."

Parma's vote of confidence was a political nicety. I was too valuable to let go but too much a liability to keep around. Did they think I was too naive to understand what was really being said here? I dug my heels in for a fight. The mention of resigning—the forced opportunity to just *go away* and do something else, suddenly seemed golden. "Sir, my resignation offers the best compromise—"

"You will not resign," Song said. "Major, truly. This isn't worth throwing away your career over. The Guild won't require such an extreme gesture." Parma frowned but didn't argue, so maybe he was right.

There didn't seem to be much of my career left to throw away. If I didn't resign, I'd be demoted, taken off the Diplomatic Corps, and who knew what else. I'd rather leave entirely.

Parma edged closer. "If I might perhaps suggest early retirement rather than resignation as a more respectable alternative."

Semantics. We were arguing semantics.

I knew that look on Song's face, the gritted teeth and the glare to cut steel. He was wishing he was on the *Raja Ampat* so he could just throw this woman off. But we weren't, we were on the Cancri transit station, and neither Trade Guild nor Mil Div had jurisdiction here. And that was the problem: my screw-up—which still hadn't been officially defined as a screw-up, or this would have been a much simpler process—happened on a joint mission, and now no one knew what to do with me. Which was why walking away was looking better and better.

"Agent Parma, would you excuse us for a moment?" Song said finally.

"Of course." Parma bowed herself out of the room in a gesture of precise politeness, hands together and eyes lowered. She wasn't enjoying this, I realized. She just wanted it all to go away so she could do her job——making Trade Guild look good. Small comfort.

"Sit," Song said after she'd gone, and I did, reflexively following command. But he didn't say anything else.

So I said, "Retirement isn't a bad idea. Looks better in the records than resignation, doesn't it? We can just say I'd lost my edge and it was time."

"Don't tell me you really want to retire. You have another twenty years of service in you. Thirty years. You won't retire, you don't have it in you."

I raised an eyebrow, because he made it sound like a challenge. "The Guild will never be allowed back in the Cancri system, not in any of our lifetimes. Not after what I did."

"So what? It's a nothing system. And this was Trade Guild's fault—they didn't do the proper intel, and now they're trying to pin the blame on us. Don't sacrifice yourself for them."

That *us* gave me an unexpected warm feeling. He had my back. "Anybody can do my job," I muttered. I commanded a Mil Div diplomatic security unit. A very experienced, very good unit. But at best I was a glorified bodyguard. And I'd destroyed the mission, this go around.

Song leaned back, steepled his hands, glared some more. "What would you say if I told you that blowing the drones was the right call? The Di didn't want us there, they were going to find a way to sabotage the meeting at some point, you were just the first one to see it and beat them to the punch."

"I'd say it's a little more complicated than that," I answered, deadpan.

"Good thing I'm making the report to the Guild and not you, then. Forget about Parma, I'll handle her. Here's what I want you to do: take a leave of absence. Just a month or two. Let this blow over, let the next scandal distract everyone, and you can get your head on straight and come back and do your job, no demotions. Where's home for you?"

I hated when people asked that. "I don't really have one."

"Family? You must have family somewhere."

I did. Zelda, Mim, Tom, on Ariana. I'd already thought of them, in that moment when retirement sounded like the best plan in the universe. But Ariana was their home, not mine. Could I make it mine?

"Go visit them. Sit still and do nothing for a month and see how you feel about retirement then."

"Sir, Captain Song, I appreciate that, but I really think it would be better for everyone—for the ship, for the Guild, if I left—"

"You're not thinking straight. Get out of here and clear your head so you can listen to yourself. Maybe you're right, maybe you're ready to retire. But try it first before you give up on the *Raja Ampat* and Mil Div."

This was the real compromise Song had already worked out for himself—get me away for a little while so he could clean up, then welcome me back, no harm done. What the captain didn't understand was how serious I was about the retirement. I already had a standing offer for another life. Maybe it was time to give it a try.

Nobody in the arrival lounge was wearing a uniform, which I expected, so it shouldn't have bothered me. But I was wearing mine, dark blue with pale-green piping, silver rank tabs glaring obvious on the collar. After the last three years on the *Raja Ampat*, surrounded by uniforms, being planetside among civilians felt weird. I should have changed clothes—if I'd had anything more appropriate to change into. Gym shorts, maybe. People were looking at me, but not with anything more than casual interest. Not many Mil Div officers came through here, that was all. They were interested, not accusing. I was the one who was uncomfortable. Zelda would loan me some more casual clothes until I could get some outfits of my own.

Officially, this was a holiday, but I couldn't stop worrying. About my clothes, about seeing Zelda after almost a decade apart. About whether I'd even be going back to the *Raja Ampat,* or staying. Captain Song, Agent Parma, no one else was going to make the decision. No one wanted to be the one to boot out the decorated Major Daring. So it was up to me to decide, and I was too tired to think straight.

Reaching immigration and customs, seeing the agents in their gray jumpsuits, badges on their shoulders, was something of a relief. Fellow officers, people who understood the stiffness in my posture and seriousness in my gaze. But no, the guy still gave me that curious, mildly awestruck *look* that the civilians were giving me. I offered my wrist and its implant for the agent to scan. His answering smile was broad and welcoming, like something out of a tourism advert.

"Here on holiday, Major Daring?" Was it worse, that the smile seemed genuine and not a put on?

"Maybe, unless I decided to stay." My accent was foreign here, too flat and atonal next to his lilting, rolling voice.

"Wouldn't that be something?" he said, clicking his scanner until a light went green. "Have a marvelous time, Major."

The rank didn't feel right anymore and made me twitch. "Wendy. Just Wendy, here," I murmured.

People mostly came to Ariana on holiday, but the planet attracted a larger than usual number of immigrants. The habitable continents remained intentionally pastoral; the whole economy was based on agriculture, agricultural support, and tourism. People who came here to live were expected to work hard, but for the right people, the reward was paradise. Zelda, Mim, and Tom had come here eight standard years ago, took every crash course in artisanal farming they could, homesteaded, and became Arianan. Even their accents had shifted, as I'd noted in their vid messages over the years. My own sister sounded foreign, now. Like I'd told the captain—I didn't really have a home.

I finally escaped immigration and went through sliding doors to an outdoor courtyard.

Here was sunshine filtered through an oxygenated planetary atmosphere, which didn't feel like any other kind of light in the universe. I stopped, put my hand up to shade my eyes. How long had it been since I'd stood under open sky? Was the sudden bought of vertigo real, or did I only think I ought to be feeling this dizzy? I smelled unfiltered air, scented with trees and flowers and something roasting on a food cart somewhere. The courtyard opened to a street with pedicabs and a moving sidewalk, and kiosks offered guided tours of the capital city, Sage. I'd need more than a month to take all this in, surely.

And there was Zelda, waving and yelling. "Wendy! Wendy Wendy Wendy!"

My sister looked like some kind of elf from a story, in loose white shirt and knee-length pants, red hair pulled back from her face and falling loose past her shoulders, face dappled with freckles, arms taut with muscles. And that smile.

Behind her, sitting in an open-canopied gray ground car, were Mim and Tom, twin brother and sister. Mim had short dark hair, mahogany skin, a bright blue dress, and a necklace of beads, as pastoral and otherworldly as Zelda. Sitting at the steering column, Tom wore a tunic and pants, and his eyes crinkled when he smiled. Wry and welcoming, he hadn't changed at all since the last time I'd seen him. I didn't know why I'd been worried.

Zelda ran up and caught me in a tackling, rib-crushing hug. I was almost too stunned to respond.

"I missed you so much!" Zelda exclaimed, laughing.

That wave of dizziness again, overwhelming. To finally be here with Zelda, to see them all again in the flesh, no video delay, no recording. Zelda hadn't changed, everything had changed.

"Careful," I said, pulling away to regain my balance. "I'm a bit wobbly. Still feels like I'm on the rocket." Zelda nodded as if she understood and hugged me again, gently.

When Song said take time off, I supposed I could have gone to any one of a thousand planets with sun-drenched beaches, powder-covered mountains, gorgeous vistas, or luxurious resorts. I'd been given a generous allowance and an enviable stretch of time with which to decide my future. But I came here, and this was why.

Zelda and Mim married young, twenty-three and twenty-four standard, far too young most of us thought, even more so when they came up with their outrageous plan to move to Ariana and raise goats. The plan didn't surprise me—it was Zelda all over, romantic and impossible, full of dreams, lacking details. I was more worried for Mim and what would happen to the relationship when they got halfway there and Zelda lost interest. But she didn't lose interest. Moreover, they invited Tom to come with them, and he did. They worked out a business plan, entered the lottery for a land grant, won, and the future opened up for all three of them.

They invited me to come with them, too. Well, Tom did, really. But I'd just landed my position in the Diplomatic Security Corps and my career had too much momentum to turn away from it for anything. Especially goat farming. Hard, right at the moment, to remember what that had felt like, willing to give up everything for the corps. The galaxy had seemed very big, then. Right now, I thought I might be just competent enough to handle a goat farm and not much else.

Over the last eight years I'd been present during first contact protocols for six different alien civilizations, become certified to provide security during summits with twelve more, and had briefed countless system governing bodies on security concerns and xeno relations. I had the kind of life people wrote stories about.

But Zelda did, too. In a technology-drenched galaxy, she had brought to life an ancient time. Their farm targeted the luxury foods market with goat cheese and home-grown herbs, which they exported off planet, entered in competitions and won awards, and sold to wholesalers years in advance. One time, I saw cheese from Daring-Patel Farms in a pricey food boutique on a transit station twenty light years away from Ariana. I couldn't afford it. But I'd get to try the cheese now.

*

Originally, I'd planned on hiring an aircab to take me out to the farm. Zelda wouldn't hear of it. She insisted they'd be in town picking up some things anyway, and that the best way to see Ariana's countryside was by ground, so they absolutely had to come to the spaceport to pick me up.

I had to admit now that taking the ground car was a brilliant idea.

Transit usually wasn't so physical for me. In space, in warp, I entered the metal shell of my ship, the quantum processes of interstellar travel worked their magic, and I hardly even felt it except as a twinge, a moment of dizziness, like going into a room and not remembering why I wanted to be there. I left my cabin, and the ship was in a different part of the galaxy. Transit meant nothing.

Here, I couldn't deny the movement. Rubber-padded wheels on a packed dirt road, an open canopy, landscape passing by—and wind, the very air moving around me, playing with my short-cropped hair, making my scalp itch. It should have felt like standing in a compartment that had just opened to vacuum, but it didn't. This was . . . organic, for lack of a better word. I could have closed my eyes and still known that I was under open sky and not in a wind tunnel.

Once we left the capital, I smelled the endless rolling fields passing by, hot living grasses, a musty organic scent that somehow managed to smell green. I could taste the vegetation on the back of my tongue, as if I were chewing one of those blades of grass between my teeth. My stomach rumbled, full of appetite. The tires' humming vibrations massaged my muscles, rattling loose the last months—years—of stress.

I'd fought in battles to protect worlds like this. Made the battles seem worthwhile, though they didn't often seem so while I was in the middle of them. I liked it better when all the sides stayed at the negotiating table, or pillar, or cloud drift, or wherever, and all I had to do was stand there looking official. Captain Song pulled this vacation on me because he thought I'd get bored. That was going to backfire. I could retire to this. I could stay here forever, under the sun.

The agoraphobia—the blank shock at having so much open sky around me, miles and miles to the nearest wall—came and went. I did okay as long as I was gripping the door handle. I never once told Tom he was driving too fast. He would have made a joke about the speed of spaceflight and laughed at me.

Zelda planned a picnic on a hill, part of a vast public parkland near the farm, a rolling meadow of grasses kept short by wandering sheep. The sheep weren't here at the moment, and we spread a blanket in the shade of a tree overlooking a field of green. So much green. We had a view of a whole valley: the grid of farmland stretching out, with furrowed acres and rows of olive trees and vineyards. This part of Ariana might have been built to order, its beauty was so heart-stopping. Probably had been designed, just so.

Then came the food. All of it fresh from the farm's kitchen. Tom carried the wicker basket from the car, Mim arranged wooden plates and cloth napkins, sliced cheese and broke bread, filled little bowls with plump red grapes and blackberries she'd picked that morning. It was crazy, unbelievably decadent to my eyes. It must have cost a fortune, except they'd grown most of it themselves, so no. I'd be eating up a day or two of profit, that was all.

I picked up a slice of firm, yellowish cheese, and a beeping rang, accompanied by a vocal warning in my audio bug. I'd turned off all the official channels when I left the *Raja Ampat*, but this was a medical alert, which I couldn't shut down: *These consumables have not passed Mil Div testing standards. Non pasteurized, non sterilized—*

"What's that?" Zelda said. The beeping had been loud enough for everyone to hear.

I gave a subvocal command to my transponder implant—also a rudimentary scanner, meant to ensure that I didn't eat something incompatible or outright poisonous to my system while I was on an alien world. So really, the device was doing exactly what it was supposed to be doing, and I was pretty sure such rich food would play havoc with my digestive system for the next few days. I'd brought medication to avert the worst of it. Zelda and the others didn't have to know the details.

A bit chagrined, I said, "My transponder. I can't shut off all the functions. I'm sorry, it shouldn't bother us again."

"They're not calling you back to work, are they?"

I was hoping to avoid talking too much about work while I was here. I *wouldn't* be called back, not unless the Cancri mess cleared up a whole lot faster than I expected it to. Another possibility: Mil Div might call me back if they were very, very desperate. Naturally, the scenarios spun out in my mind, because I was often thinking about such scenarios. It was habit, or pathological maybe. I could think of at least three xenopolitical situations that would render my recent disaster moot and require me returning to the ship immediately, and all of them involved some kind of invasion or multi-system armed conflict. Even Ariana would be affected. I wished I was sure something like that couldn't possibly happen.

I had to pull myself back to the current idyll.

"No, no, I've got a whole month, they won't call me unless there's a disaster, and that kind of disaster would mean we had bigger problems." Again, they didn't need to know the details.

Zelda's smile returned full force. Carefree and happy, and I hoped she'd stay that way the whole visit. Mim distributed food, and Tom gave me a look, like he suspected what was going on under the surface.

"Wendy, eat, eat!" Zelda insisted, and I finally tried the bite I'd been holding.

The food was so fresh it lit up my tongue. Mil Div nutritionists insisted nobody could tell the difference between fresh or vat-grown and preserved, dirt-grown or hydroponics. I could tell. There was wine. I hadn't had a drink in weeks—alcohol and warp travel made my stomach do things that didn't make the pleasure worthwhile. This went straight to my head and felt divine.

"Tell us stories, Wendy," Zelda said. They'd started a second bottle of wine and were sprawled out on the blanket, watching shapes in the clouds, and shadowed surfaces of the two moons hanging near the horizon.

"I don't know any stories."

"Where you were last, then? What was the last planet you went to and what happened? What did you do? I know you always say it's boring, but I want to hear about it anyway. It's only boring to you."

The last mission? Oh, what the hell. They wouldn't have actually heard of the place and I could gloss over the worst of it. "All right, then. My last stop: 55 Cancri. The fourth planet."

Tom stared. "Cancri Four? Where that riot happened? Where the Trade Guild was booted out? You were there for that?"

So they had heard of it. Oops. "Yeah, I was there."

"Oh my gosh, you weren't actually *there*, were you? On the planet, I mean?" Mim said, eyes round, horrified.

"No, I was in orbit." And that wasn't a lie, as far as it went. My *drone* had been on the planet, and I'd been interfaced with my drone, which was almost just like being there. The whole team had gone down in drones, because the planet was a gas giant, it was the only way we could meet with the Di hydrogen breathers. But my team hadn't quite been able to explain to the Di that the drones were machines, not suits, and when the Di started wrenching open the metal shells looking for weapons, I'd ended up pulling the pin on the drones' destruct sequences. Destroyed the Trade Guild contingent and did quite a bit of damage to the Di in the process. The Di cried foul and refused to send another delegation. Riot was a strong word for the ensuing chaos as the Di forced all Trade Guild personal off the planet and out of orbit.

The incident was still under review when I'd left. Truth be told, I agreed with Captain Song: my destroying the drones had been the right call, based on my suspicion that what the Di really wanted was to confiscate the technology, not negotiate. From an economic and political standpoint, it should have been a minor incident. The Trade Guild had mining rights at plenty of gas giants and Cancri Four wasn't an essential trading partner. But the event had been enough of a disaster that it had made news. Not the kind of news that was actually news, like the stellar-political balance of power shifting, war and famine and failures of technology and the rest that would actually make a difference, but the kind of freak-show news that drew crowds of gawkers because people couldn't look away. My name had never come into it, except as "the unnamed Military Division officer who allegedly instigated the riot." Which wasn't accurate or reassuring.

"Really, it was embarrassing more than anything. You'd be surprised how often stuff like this happens." I winced; now they'd be even more worried.

"I don't want to know," Mim said, holding her hand flat in a "stop" gesture, her eyes shut. "I don't want to think about anyone blowing you up."

"I told you, I wasn't even there. My *drone* got blown up. We use drones where we can't handle the atmosphere or gravity. It's safer." Or in case the host species decided to attack us, for example . . .

"The worst thing you'll face around here is goats shitting on you," Tom said.

"I think I would rather have my drone blown up by aliens," I said, and they laughed like they were supposed to, and ate more food, and talked about the weather.

We'd started packing up when Zelda, Mim, and Tom exchanged looks in a silent conversation. They wanted to say something, but was it good or bad? Curious, patient, I waited.

"We have news," Zelda said finally, and her whole face lit up. I was ashamed that my heart sank a little. This was the look my sister had had when she announced that she and Mim were getting married. It was her Big Plan Look, that meant she was going to turn her world upside down chasing a dream. What exactly was so enticing that she'd give up all this?

"Can you guess?" Zelda said. "You have to guess."

"Look at that, Zel, she's scared to death. Drop the suspense and tell her," Mim chided.

"You tell her, I can't even get the words out."

"She's *your* sister!"

Zelda bit her lip, as if to keep her smile from getting any bigger. "Okay okay okay. Well. The news is—we've got a baby started."

The three of them looked at me expectantly, and I didn't know what to say.

I didn't know how I *felt*. First, relieved, that Zelda seemed well and truly settled, happy and confident enough to take on something like a baby. Second—how had my little sister grown up enough to have a *baby?*

"Wow," was all I could say.

Zelda babbled. "She's a little girl, three months along. We must have spent months talking about how to do it, whose DNA and how and if we wanted to go natural, but then which one of us would carry her, but then we decided neither of us could take the time off from the farm and this is safer anyway, and then this was Mim's idea, since she and Tom are so much alike anyway, we just had them pop his sperm and my egg in a test tube, no extra expense for genetic manipulation, apart from basic screening and so on, and there we go, baby! Anyway she's incubating at the pre-natal center in Sage, and I can't wait until we can bring her home."

I covered my mouth with my hand to hide the disbelieving smile, and my eyes were stinging. I had to say something before I started leaking.

"And that's why we're so glad you could come visit," Zelda went on. "I mean it would have been better in a few months after she's born and you could meet her, but you can come back, and this way I could tell you in person. I really wanted to tell you in person."

"Oh, Zelda I'm so happy for you all," I said finally, opening my arms to take my sister in for another fierce hug. A minute later Tom and Mim and joined us. One big group hug, one big happy family, and I wondered at my luck to ever be a part of it. I was going to be an aunt. At least, if I stayed I would be. Or I could go back to Mil Div and be the distant, mysterious aunt who had adventures and was never around.

*

Zelda and I had grown up in a city, on a planet that was all city, even the polar ice caps, which housed cold-weather research and manufacturing. We'd been born into a collective, with eleven adults operating in an accounting firm and six children growing up together. Our four collective-siblings continued on in the business, but we'd always been different. None of us had paid much attention to which adults were whose parents—it wasn't supposed to matter, when you operated a family like a business—but I understood that we shared a biological mother, Eva, and that she'd been different, too. She took the auditing cases, traveled, and was sought after by corporations looking to track down embezzlement and other internal problems. Eva was an accounting hit man, and she loved adventure. That was the word in the family, that Eva loved adventure, and she'd passed that trait to her daughters. We had her red hair, too.

So while the other siblings certified as accountants, Zelda went to a college where she could try everything, from art to science to solar sail racing, looking for inspiration. She'd found Mim. By then, I'd graduated from the planet's Mil Div academy. I hadn't known what I wanted any more than Zelda had, only that I wanted to go *away*. Away from the planet that was a city, away to something completely different, to some wide open spaces, and you couldn't get more wide open than space. Same impulse as Zelda, opposite direction. Once at the academy, I discovered an aptitude for security. From there, the Diplomatic Corps beckoned because of the prestige. They were the best, they saw the real action. Almost a thousand space-faring species populated the galaxy, and I wanted to meet them all. I wanted to keep moving. In the years since then, I'd never been bored.

People sometimes said there was nothing new in the universe, but there was. Mil Div was finding new civilizations all the time. Trillions of sentient beings in the universe, and the thing that made them all alike was that they made choices. Each choice that each life made was new to that life.

Nobody could say that Zelda and I had picked wrong. We'd each picked our direction and kept running full tilt. Something to be admired in that.

I still wasn't bored with the job, with Mil Div or the Diplomatic Corps. I still had a good nine hundred species to encounter. So I hadn't come to Ariana because I'd gotten bored. I'd come because I was tired. For the first time, I'd come to a fork, and not known which way to go.

I fell asleep on the last few miles of driving to the farm, and even though I protested that I was fine, Zelda diagnosed rocket lag and put me to bed. My own bed, in a wide room that would have fit four cabins on the *Raja Ampat*, with wood-paneled walls and gauze curtains. A room with a window. It was novel.

Zelda hung a blanket over the window to cut out the sunlight, and I slept for twelve standard hours.

After waking up, I wandered into the kitchen wrapped in a soft cotton robe Zelda had left for me. I ran my hands along the wood-paneled walls. Real wood, which seemed extravagant to eyes used to sleek metal and plastiform. The texture of it intrigued me, and Mim found me in the living room, hands pressed to the walls, caressing them.

"You okay?" she asked, and I blinked back to wakefulness. I was fine.

Mim stuffed food and coffee into me—fresh coffee, grown on another continent on Ariana, was a revelation. My medical alert had reset itself overnight and went off again, ranting about excessive addictive compounds and potential for systemic overload. That was the point, I muttered at it. I got dressed, wandered outside, and Tom and Zelda taught me how to milk goats. It was the most visceral, organic thing I'd ever done in my life, except for eating and sex.

The goats reminded me of at least a couple of species I'd dealt with. Their eyes with the warped pupils, their flopping accidental ears. Their tempers, expressed in the way they bounced on sharp hooves and bleated indignantly. Hell, I'd met ambassadors who sounded like that.

My visit didn't stop the others from work—work never let up on a farm, with goats and chickens to feed and garden plots to weed and the rest. I was happy enough to sit, watch, and not think about much of anything in particular.

I slept another ten hours, amazed that I hadn't noticed how tired I was. Ten missions on thirteen worlds in the last year alone—I should have noticed. No wonder Song wanted me to take time off.

I thought about calling Captain Song, or better yet the XO, Achebe, to find out if an initial report on the Cancri Four incident had been issued yet, and what it said about me. Had my abrupt disappearance started any rumors? I wasn't sure I cared, but it would be nice to know.

I finally had a chance to unpack and distribute the gifts I'd brought: a silk tunic-style shirt for Zelda, who tried it on immediately, then spun and admired the way the light played off the blue and yellow abstract pattern; a string of hand-made glass beads for Mim; and a bottle of scotch for Tom. Gifts quickly chosen from an import boutique at the Cancri transit station when I realized I'd be coming to visit. They seemed appreciative.

Then came another meal: potatoes, chicken, asparagus, more herbs, goat butter, and candied peaches for dessert. The rich fresh food did, in fact, upset my digestion, and the medical alert went off again, and I shut it down, again. The parameters were set too conservatively, which on a mission was fine, but on vacation? You were supposed to overindulge on vacation. I could imagine the *Raja Ampat's* physician downloading the record and raising an eyebrow at me. Assuming I ever went back. Never mind. A couple of pills took care of the problem. In that, at least, I'd come prepared. Alien world, indeed.

Over dinner, we talked about the baby. They were arguing names. Wendy was on the list, but I shot down the idea as too confusing. Eva, I liked.

After dinner, Zelda and Mim went out to check the barns, lock up the goats for the night, and turn on the perimeter fence. The original terraformers had imported coyotes to serve as the ecosystem's apex predators and as pest control for the inevitable rodent infestations, and they'd become a problem for farmers with livestock. The fence had motion-activated laser deterrents that singed without killing. Zelda didn't want to kill the predators. The canines had mostly learned to stay away.

I helped Tom clean up the kitchen. He was of average height, with broad shoulders, his brown skin burnished by sun and wind. A farmer's life seemed to suit him. Back in the day, when Zelda and Mim had first hooked up, we'd had a fling. Recreational and satisfying. Could have grown into more, maybe. I could have come with them to Ariana, but I'd picked Mil Div. One of those long-gone forks in the road.

He kept throwing sidelong glances at me, a wry smile on his lips. Finally I said, "Why don't you pour me a glass of wine and we can talk." So he did, and we sat across the kitchen table from one another.

He took a sip. "Zelda keeps thinking you'll be ready to retire soon and finally come stay with us. We could use the help."

I flushed, because as far as they were concerned, I was on vacation. I hadn't told them about the review, about my attempt to resign, or anything. How much did Tom guess? "I've thought about it," I said, quietly, cryptically.

"You didn't tell everything about what happened on Cancri Four, did you? What else happened?" His eyes widened. "They're not kicking you out, are they?"

"No, not yet," I said. "But I offered to take early retirement."

Was that a flash of hope in his gaze, and did my heart sink a little, seeing it?

"My offer was not initially accepted," I added. "I'm supposed to be here thinking it over."

"I'm glad you came," he said, heartfelt. It wasn't just Zelda who wanted me to stay.

My eyes stung, yet again. I was never usually this weepy. "I have a confession," I said, studying the ruby liquid in my glass. "I'm amazed you guys have made it this long. I'm amazed *you've* stuck it out this long. I love those two dearly but they drive me crazy sometimes."

Tom said, "I like it here. I want a family. This is a good family. Zelda and Mim are the right kind of crazy." He ducked, smiled. The love in the room was thick, apparent. "With the sprout on the way . . . we've decided on three. But I think we can talk the natal council into a couple more. We've got the space and savings for it."

"Five kids. You want five kids?"

"I want a *big* family. Can't get that on a starship." He held out the vision like bait.

Five little Zeldas running around . . . No, five Zeldas, Mims and Toms. With a herd of goats and fifty acres of farm, with blackberry brambles and apple trees. Like something out of a story. A myth.

"I'm in awe." My stare had become a bit glazed, thinking of five little Zeldas. I couldn't imagine it. It had never occurred to me to imagine it. It still didn't.

"You shouldn't be. This is what everyone used to do. But what you do . . ." He shook his head in vague explanation, as if he didn't even know what I did. Maybe he didn't. He continued, "If you decide you want a family, this is place for it. But I guess you kind of have a family already, with Mil Div and your ship and all." He glanced away, blushing in apology.

That gave me an unexpected pang, because as soon as he said it I thought of Captain Song, and Achebe, and my squad and even Sergeant Barrett who ran the mess hall. I could picture them all, perfectly. "I guess so," I said. "I don't have any regrets, Tom, if that's what you're asking."

"No, it's not what I'm asking. I just thought you might be ready for a change."

I couldn't have had this talk with Zelda, who wouldn't understand why I loved to travel at all, and would have become flustered trying. Nearly every message she sent me, she asked when I was coming home. But I'd always believed what I told Captain Song: I didn't have a home.

We finished our wine just as Zelda and Mim came in. I told Tom, "I'll think about it. I'm here to think about it."

Zelda stared. "You talked? Tom, did you talk to her? Wendy, what did you decide?"

"I decided to think about it," I said.

Zelda looked at the ceiling and groaned in frustration. "We'll just have to keep stuffing with you wine until you agree to stay."

Sounded like a good plan to me.

I got a bad sunburn my second week on Ariana. After the first week of napping and eating and more sleeping, I'd woken up and felt the need to do something, so Zelda took me to the coast and we'd gone for a hike on a trail overlooking ocean. Ocean was something I didn't see very often, and I must have spent an hour just staring out.

Zelda was very apologetic—they had sunblock lotion, but they all spent so much time outside they'd gotten tan enough that it didn't matter. They wore wide-brimmed hats outside to keep the sun off, and she hadn't thought to get a hat for me.

I assured her that I didn't mind. "It's just so nice feeling the warmth off a G-type main sequence star, it's worth a little burn." Really, the redness felt like carrying the sun inside with me, which made me smile.

Zelda had stared at me for a minute. Like I'd been speaking a different language, there. "Weird," she said finally, shaking her head.

Yeah.

They babied me with aloe for my face, the big fluffy bed and clean, sun-dried bedding, and lots and lots of food. I was gaining weight by the day, enough to throw off fuel calculations for a drop shuttle. I wasn't sure I deserved all the attention from Zelda and the others, however much they kept going on about their interstellar heroic sister and begging me for stories. They weren't really celebrating the Mil Div hero, of which there were hundreds; they were celebrating me because I was family. I was *their* Mil Div hero.

After that first week, I sent a short message to Achebe asking for news and the mood of the ship. Just out of curiosity.

We played card games by the fireplace in the evenings, Zelda and the others teaching me the ones they'd learned on Ariana, me teaching the ones I'd learned on my travels. Tom lit a fire, not because it was cold but because I was amazed that they actually burned organic materials with open flame. Oxygen-devouring open flame. They had air to burn, on a planet like this. Once I remembered to breathe, I could appreciate the fire's smoky warmth, the friendly crackling of the burning wood.

"Are you sure you're okay?" Mim asked. I must have been acting like a freak.

I always said yes.

I tried to imagine myself as part of the routine here. Milking goats, treading in gravity. Babysitting. Something attractive about that kind of life. It was something we talked about on the ship sometimes. Most Mil Div folk had this assumption that if we managed to survive, we would retire one day to plots of land on bucolic worlds like Ariana, with spouses and babies and green growing things. I'd send them pictures of the coast and cliffs, breaking waves, blossoms in the trees, and they'd sigh with envy. And then they'd all sign up for another tour.

A couple of times a week, supper was a production because Tom came back from the market in Sage with treasures, fresh foodstuffs they didn't grow themselves, sausages and vegetables that were specialties on other farms. Tom sold their own that didn't go to the wholesalers. Lots of bartering, which seemed to me to be just as exotic as the wood paneling and sunburns.

He and Mim cooked, Zelda cleaned house, and they wouldn't let me help, and I wondered if I'd ever be allowed to help. Or would I be their showpiece, their exotic space-faring sometime-sister. They'd throw parties and I'd tell stories about blasting my team's drones on Cancri, for entertainment.

Mim let me pour wine. We gathered around the table, and Tom brought out a wide platter and gave us each a serving.

My plate landed in front of me, and I choked, gagging on a sensation of horror. The center of the meal was a wide, round shining slab that might have been dense vegetable, marinated and roasted, or some kind of spineless fish. Its color was a deep, rich purple, almost black and pale, and it had been sliced lengthwise, skin side facing out, and garnished with greens, and some kind of cheese was dribbled and melted over it. I'd never seen any food like it. It was alien. Familiarly alien.

I couldn't possibly disguise my expression of open-mouthed shock. The others ceased their noises of delight at the feast and stared at me staring at my plate.

How could I explain? "I'm sorry, but . . . it looks like someone I know."

Zelda put her hand over her mouth to hide a smile.

"Wendy," Tom said. "It's eggplant. It's just eggplant."

And I knew that, of course I knew that, I'd been warned in all the briefings before the Heeban mission, that the Heeban delegates were gas-giant dwellers and had air bladders that allowed them to float at altitude, but also made them look like eggplants. Some of the negotiators had still expressed shock upon meeting the Heebans. It had been abstract to me, who had never seen an eggplant, and so wasn't bothered at all. And now, finally confronted with an eggplant, I discovered that the Heebans didn't look like eggplants; rather, eggplants looked like the Heebans. It was an intriguing cognitive difference that I'd have to talk to the linguistics and psych people about later.

"I know, and I'm sorry, I know how hard you worked making this. It's just food." Determined, I hefted my knife and fork, swallowed hard against a gag reflex, and tried to cut.

"These consumables have not passed Mil Div testing standards. Non pasteurized, non sterilized—"

I put down my utensils and rested my head on my hands. I just couldn't do it.

Zelda rolled her eyes. "Oh Wendy, you're so *weird.*"

It was something Zelda always said, ever since we were little, but the words had a different flavor this time. They'd never cut, before. I'd had never felt like I'd done something *wrong* before.

"I'm not trying to be." I should have kept quiet and eaten the damn thing.

No, I shouldn't have. I had a right to say no to what turned my stomach. Not to eat something that looked like a friend.

I said, "They're called the Heeban, and I was part of a team negotiating with them for hydrogen mining rights. They're about this big"—I showed a space with my hands the size of my head—"and they're made mostly of air bladders that let them swim in the dense atmosphere. And they're mostly really nice—"

It was even the right size for a Heeban, just bigger than my spread hand. The … eggplant, whatever … had the right sheen to its skin, and the same boneless, dense appearance as the gas giant-dwelling species I'd spent most of a year with, some four years ago now. The Heeban had a great appreciation for calm. I'd liked them, especially my security counterpart, who'd been about my relative age and had been amused by the proceedings. We'd traded jokes about our respective charges— one-liners about airbags and drifting conversations—that had actually translated, which didn't happen very often in the greater galaxy. I hadn't talked to ¡Fíver in almost a year. I owed my friend a message.

The others were staring again. Mim was already five bites into her meal, and she looked guiltily at the greenish flesh stabbed on her fork.

"I'm sorry," I said and pushed away from the table. "You all finish, I'll just take a walk."

I went up the grassy hill behind the farm to watch the sunset. A slow, planetary sunset, not the blazing flash of light I'd see in orbit. The heat of it stung my still toasted cheeks. Which sunset did I like better? I couldn't decide. The sky went on forever here, and I couldn't control it, and I realized, only two weeks on now, I missed the *Raja Ampat*. Captain Song had been right.

Zelda found me maybe half an hour later. Long enough to scarf down eggplant without me looking at them like they were murderers. She brought a blanket with her, and a thermos of hot cocoa with two cups. We sprawled out on the blanket, watched the last of the sunset, the moons glowing with its reflected light, and the first of the stars coming out. There were a lot of them. Ariana's star was coreward, so the sky was crowded, thick bands of stars, blues and whites and red, roiling in tangles. I looked up and saw a thousand civilizations, each vying for their little stake in the world. And I had to go back to the middle of it.

Zelda and the farm were on the outside, watching contently. They'd still be here, years or decades from now. I could look into any sky and think of them.

"You're not going to stay, are you?" Zelda said, after a long stretch of quiet.

"No."

"Is it because of the eggplant? Was it that totally offensive?"

"No," I said, chuckling. Everyone on the ship was going to laugh hysterically at the eggplant story.

"Are you happy?"

I turned to look at Zelda and said, unambiguously, so that my sister would not mistake the meaning for some otherworldly euphemism, "Yes."

"I don't understand you."

Likewise, I might have said, but didn't because it didn't matter. I playfully shoved my sister's shoulder and said, "And I will never, ever understand what you see in goats. They *stink*."

Zelda shrugged. "You have to put up with some shit to get the really great cheese."

I laughed because it was the most absurd and true thing I'd ever heard in my life.

"You'll come visit again, yeah?" Zelda said, in a small voice that made her sound like she was twelve once more, and we were back home in the city and wondering how we were going to get out of there.

We'd done it. We'd really done it, and when it came time for me to take a break, I didn't go back to the city and the collective that had raised me. I came here.

"Of course I will," I said. "This is home."

ASTROPHILIA

After five years of drought, the tiny, wool-producing household of Greentree was finished. First the pastures died off, then the sheep, and Stella and the others didn't have any wool to process and couldn't meet the household's quota, small though it was with only five of them working at the end. The holding just couldn't support a household and the regional committee couldn't keep putting credits into it, hoping that rains would come. They might never come, or the next year might be a flood. No one could tell, and that was the problem, wasn't it?

None of them argued when Az and Jude put in to dissolve Greentree. They could starve themselves to death with pride, but that would be a waste of resources. Stella was a good weaver and ought to have a chance somewhere else. That was the first reason they gave for the decision.

Because they dissolved voluntarily, the committee found places for them in other households, ones not on the verge of collapse. However, Az put in a special request and found Stella's new home herself. "I know the head of the place, Toma. He'll take good care of you, but more than that his place is prosperous. Rich enough for children, even. You could earn a baby there, Stella." Az's wrinkled hands gripped Stella's young ones in her own, and her eyes shone. Twenty-three years ago, Greentree had been prosperous enough to earn a baby: Stella. But those days were gone.

Stella began to have doubts. "Mama, I don't want to leave you and everyone—"

"We'll be fine. We'd have had to leave sooner or later, and this way we've got credits to take with us. Start new on a good footing, yes?"

"Yes, but—" She hesitated, because her fears were childish. "What if they don't like me?"

Az shook her head. "Winter market I gave Toma the shawl you made. You should have seen him, Stella, his mouth dropped. He said Barnard Croft would take you on the spot, credits or no."

But what if they don't like *me*, Stella wanted to whine. She wasn't worried about her weaving.

Az must have seen that she was about to cry. "Oh, dear, it'll be all right. We'll see each other at the markets, maybe more if there's trading to be done. You'll be happy, I know you will. Better things will come."

Because Az seemed so pleased for her, Stella stayed quiet, and hoped.

In the spring, Stella traveled to Barnard Croft, three hundred miles on the Long Road from Greentree, in the hills near the coast.

Rain poured on the last day of the journey, so the waystation driver used a pair of horses to draw the wagon, instead of the truck. Stella offered to wait until the storm passed and the solar batteries charged up, but he had a schedule to keep, and insisted that the horses needed the exercise.

Stella sat under the awning on the front seat of the wagon, wrapped in a blanket against the chill, feeling sorry for the hulking draft animals in front of her. They were soaked, brown coats dripping as they clomped step by step on the muddy road. It might have been faster, waiting for the clouds to break, for the sun to emerge and let them use the truck. But the driver said they'd be waiting for days in these spring rains.

She traveled through an alien world, wet and green. Stella had never seen so much water in her whole life, all of it pouring from the sky. A quarter of this amount of rain a couple of hundred miles east would have saved Greentree.

The road curved into the next green valley, to Barnard Croft. The wide meadow and its surrounding, rolling hills were green, lush with grass. A handful of alpaca grazed along a stream that ran frothing from the hills opposite. The animals didn't seem to mind the water, however matted and heavy their coats looked. There'd be some work, cleaning that mess for spinning. Actually, she looked forward to it. She wanted to make herself useful as soon as she could. To prove herself. If this didn't work, if she didn't fit in here and had to throw herself on the mercy of the regional committee to find some place prosperous enough to take her, that could use a decent weaver . . . no, this would work.

A half a dozen whitewashed cottages clustered together, along with sheds and shelters for animals, a couple of rabbit hutches, and squares of turned black soil with a barest sheen of green—garden plots and new growth. The largest cottage stood apart from the others. It had wide doors and many windows, shuttered now against the rain—the work house, she guessed. Under the shelter of the wide eaves sat wooden barrels for washing wool, and a pair of precious copper pots for dyeing. All comfortable, familiar sights.

The next largest cottage, near the garden plots, had a smoking chimney. Kitchen and common room, most likely. Which meant the others were sleeping quarters. She wondered which was hers, and who she'd be sharing with. A pair of windmills stood on the side of one hill; their trefoil blades were still.

At the top of the highest hill, across the meadow, was a small, unpainted shack. It couldn't have held more than a person or two standing upright. This, she did not recognize. Maybe it was a curing shed, though it seemed an unlikely spot, exposed as it was to every passing storm.

A turn-off took them from the road to the cottages, and by the time the driver pulled up the horses, eased the wagon to a stop, and set the brakes, a pair of men wrapped in cloaks emerged from the work house to greet them. Stella thanked the driver and jumped to the ground. Her boots splashed, her long woolen skirt tangled around her legs, and the rain pressed the blanket close around her. She felt sodden and bedraggled, but she wouldn't complain.

The elder of those who came to greet her was middle aged and worn, but he moved briskly and spread his arms wide. "Here she is! Didn't know if you would make it in this weather." This was Toma. Az's friend, Stella reminded herself. Nothing to worry about.

"Horses'll get through anything," the driver said, moving to the back of the wagon to unload her luggage.

"Well then," Toma said. "Let's get you inside and dried off."

"Thank you," Stella managed. "I just have a couple of bags. And a loom. Az let me take Greentree's loom."

"Well then, that is a treasure. Good."

The men clustered around the back of the wagon to help. The bags held her clothes, a few books and letters and trinkets. Her equipment: spindles and needles, carders, skeins of yarn, coils of roving. The loom took up most of the space—dismantled, legs and frames strapped together, mechanisms folded away in protective oilskin. It would take her most of a day to set up. She'd feel better when it was.

A third figure came running from the work house, shrouded by her wrap and hood like the others. The shape of her was female, young—maybe even Stella's age. She wore dark trousers and a pale tunic, like the others.

She came straight to the driver. "Anything for me?"

"Package from Griffith?" the driver answered.

"Oh, yes!"

The driver dug under an oil cloth and brought out a leather document case, stuffed full. The woman came forward to take it, revealing her face, sandstone-burnished skin and bright brown eyes.

Toma scowled at her, but the woman didn't seem to notice. She tucked the package under her arm and beamed like sunshine.

"At least be useful and take a bag," Toma said to her.

Taking up a bag with a free hand, the woman flashed a smile at

Stella, and turned to carry her load to the cottage.

Toma and other other man, Jorge, carried the loom to the work house. Hefting the rest of her luggage, Stella went to the main cottage, following the young woman at a distance. Behind her, the driver returned to his seat and got the horses moving again; their hooves splashed on the road.

Around dinner time, the clouds broke, belying the driver's prediction. Some sky and a last bit of sunlight peeked through.

They ate what seemed to her eyes a magnificent feast—meat, eggs, preserved fruits and vegetables, fresh bread. At Greentree, they'd barely got through the winter on stores, and until this meal Stella hadn't realized she'd been dimly hungry all the time, for weeks. Months. Greentree really had been dying.

The folk of the croft gathered around the hearth at night, just as they did back home at Greentree, just as folk did at dozens of households up and down the Long Road. She met everyone: Toma and Jorge, who'd helped with the loom. Elsta, Toma's partner, who ran the kitchen and garden. Nik and Wendy, Jon and Faren. Peri had a baby, which showed just how well off Barnard was, to be able to support a baby as well as a refugee like Stella. The first thing Peri did was put the baby—Bette—in Stella's arms, and Stella was stricken because she'd never held a wriggly baby before and was afraid of dropping her. But Peri arranged her arms just so and took the baby back after a few moments of cooing over them both. Stella had never thought of earning the right to have her implant removed, to have a baby—another mouth to feed at Greentree would have been a disaster.

Elsta was wearing the shawl Stella had made, the one Az had given Toma—her audition, really, to prove her worth. The shawl was an intricate weave made of finely spun merino. Stella had done everything—carded and spun the wool, dyed it the difficult smoky blue, and designed the pattern herself. Elsta didn't have to wear it, the croft could have traded it for credits. Stella felt a small spark of pride.

Wasn't just charity that brought her here.

Stella had brought her work basket, but Elsta tsked at her. "You've had a long trip, so rest now. Plenty of time to work later." So she sat on a blanket spread out on the floor and played with Bette.

Elsta picked apart a tangle of roving, preparing to draft into the spindle of her spinning wheel. Toma and Jorge had a folding table in front of them, and the tools to repair a set of hand carders. The others knit, crocheted, or mended. They no doubt made all their own clothing, from weaving the fabric to sewing, dark trousers, bright skirts, aprons, and tunics. Stella's hands itched to work—she was in the middle of knitting a pair of very bright yellow socks from the remnants of yarn from a weaving. They'd be ugly but warm—and the right kind of ugly had a charm of its own. But Elsta was probably right, and the baby was fascinating. Bette had a set of wooden blocks that she banged into each other; occasionally, very seriously, she handed them to Stella. Then demanded them back. The process must have had a logic to it.

The young woman wasn't with them. She'd skipped dinner as well. Stella was thinking of how to ask about her, when Elsta did it for her.

"Is Andi gone out to her study, then?"

Toma grumbled, "Of course she is." The words bit.

Her study—the shack on the hill? Stella listened close, wishing the baby would stop banging her blocks so loudly.

"Toma—"

"She should be here."

"She's done her work, let her be. The night's turned clear, you know how she gets."

"She should listen to me."

"The more you push, the angrier she'll get. Leave her be, dearest."

Elsta's wheel turned and purred, Peri hummed as she knit, and Bette's toys clacked. Toma frowned, never looking up from his work.

Her bags sat by one of the two beds in the smallest cottage, only half unpacked. The other bed, Andi's, remained empty. Stella washed, brushed out her short blond hair, changed into her nightdress, and curled up under the covers. Andi still hadn't returned.

The air smelled wrong, here. Wet, earthy, as if she could smell the grass growing outside the window. The shutters cracked open to let in a breeze. Stella was chilled; her nose wouldn't stop running. The desert always smelled dusty, dry—even at night, the heat of the sun rose up from the ground. There, her nose itched with dust.

She couldn't sleep. She kept waiting for Andi to come back.

Finally, she did. Stella started awake when the door opened with the smallest squeak—so she must have slept, at least a little. Cocooned under the covers, she clutched her pillow, blinking, uncertain for a moment where she was and what was happening. Everything felt wrong, but that was to be expected, so she lay still.

Andi didn't seem to notice that she was awake. She hung up her cloak on a peg by the door, sat on her bed while she peeled off shoes and clothes, which she left lying on the chest at the foot of her bed, and crawled under the covers without seeming to notice—or care—that Stella was there. The woman moved quickly—nervously, even? But when she pulled the covers over her, she lay still, asleep in moments. Stella had a suspicion that she'd had practice, falling asleep quickly in the last hours before dawn, before she'd be expected to rise and work.

Stella supposed she would get a chance to finally talk to her new roommate soon enough, but she had no idea what she was going to say to her.

The next day, the clouds had more than broken. No sign of them remained, and the sun blazed clear as it ever had in the desert, but on a world that was wet, green, and growing. The faint sprouts in the garden plots seem to have exploded into full growth, leaves uncurling. The angora in the hutches pressed twitching noses to the wire mesh of their cages, as if they could squeeze out to play in the meadow. Every shutter and window in the croft was opened to let in the sun.

The work house was wide, clean, whitewashed inside and out. It smelled of lanolin, fiber and work. Lint floated in beams of sunlight. Two—now three—looms and a pair of spinning wheels sat facing each other, so the weavers and spinners could talk. Days would pass quickly here. The first passed quickly enough, and Stella finished it feeling tired and satisfied.

Andi had spent the day at the wash tubs outside, cleaning a batch of wool, preparing it to card and spin in the next week or so. She'd still been asleep when Stella got up that morning, but must have woken up soon after. They still hadn't talked. Not even hello. They kept missing each other, being in different places. Continually out of rhythm, like a pattern that wove crooked because you hadn't counted the threads right. The more time passed without them speaking, the harder Stella found it to think of anything to say. She wanted to ask, *Are you avoiding me?*

Stella had finished putting away her work and was headed for the common room, when she noticed Andi following the footpath away from the cottages, around the meadow and up the hill to the lonely shack. Her study, Elsta had called it. She walked at a steady pace, not quite running, but not lingering.

After waiting until she was far enough ahead that she was not likely to look over her shoulder, Stella followed.

The trail up the hill was a hike, and even walking slowly Stella was soon gasping for breath. But slowly and steadily she made progress. The path made a couple of switchbacks, and finally reached the crest of the hill and the tiny weathered shack planted there.

As she suspected, the view was worth the climb. The whole of Barnard Croft's valley was visible, as well as the next one over. The neighboring croft's cottages were pale specks, and a thread of smoke climbed from one. The hills were soft, rounded, cut through with clefts like the folds in a length of fabric. Trees along the creek gave texture to the picture. The Long Road was a gray track painted around the green rise. The sky above stretched on, and on, blue touched by a faint haze. If she squinted, she thought she could see a line of gray on the far western horizon—the ocean, and the breeze in that direction had a touch of salt and wild. From this perspective, the croft rested in a shallow bowl that sat on the top of the world. She wondered how long it would take to walk around the entire valley, and decided she would like to try some sunny day.

The shed seemed even smaller when she was standing next to it. Strangely, part of the roof was missing, folded back on hinges, letting in light. The walls were too high to see over, and the door was closed. Stella hesitated; she shouldn't be here, she was invading. She had to share a room with this woman, she shouldn't intrude. Then again— she had to share a room with this woman. She only wanted to talk. And if Andi didn't like it, well . . .

Stella knocked on the door before she could change her mind. Three quick, woodpecker-like raps.

When the door swung out, she hopped back, managed not to fall over, and looked wide-eyed to see Andi glaring at her.

Then the expression softened, falling away to blank confusion. "Oh. Hi."

They stared at each other for a long moment. Andi leaned on the door, blocking the way; Stella still couldn't see what was inside.

"May I come in?" she finally asked, because Andi hadn't closed the door on her.

"Oh—sure." The woman seemed to shake herself out of a day-dream, and stepped back to open the door wide.

The bulk of the tiny room was taken up by a device mounted on a tripod as tall as she was. A metallic cylinder, wide as a bucket, pointed to the ceiling. A giant tin can almost, except the outer case was painted gray, and it had latches, dials, levers, all manner of protrusions connected to it. Stella moved around it, studying it, reminding herself not to touch, however much the object beckoned.

"It's a telescope, isn't it?" she asked, looking over to Andi. "An old one."

A smile dawned on Andi's face, lighting her mahogany eyes. "It is—twelve-inch reflector. Century or so old, probably. Pride and joy."

Her finger traced up the tripod, stroking it like it was a favorite pet.

Stella's chest clenched at that smile, and she was glad now that she'd followed Andi here. She kept her voice calm. "Where'd you get it? You couldn't have traded for it—"

"Oh no, you can't trade for something like this. What would you trade for it?" Meaning how many bales of wool, or bolts of cloth, or live alpacas, or cans full of fish from the coast was something like this worth? You couldn't put a price on it. Some people would just give it away, because it had no real use, no matter how rare it was. Andi continued, "It was Pan's, who ran the household before Toma. He was one of the ones who helped build up the network with the observatories, after the big fall. Then he left it all to me. He'd have left it to Toma, but he wasn't interested." She shrugged, as if unable to explain.

"Then it actually works?"

"Oh yes." That smile shone again, and Stella would stay and talk all night, to keep that smile lit up. "I mean, not now, we'll have to wait until dark, assuming the weather stays clear. With the roof open it's almost a real observatory. See how we've fixed the seams?" She pointed to the edges, where the roof met the walls. Besides the hinges and latches that closed the roof in place, the seams had oilskin weatherproofing, to keep rain from seeping through the cracks. The design was clever. The building, then, was shelter for the equipment. The telescope never moved—the bottom points of the tripod were anchored with bricks.

Beside the telescope there wasn't much here: a tiny desk, a shelf filled with books, a bin holding a stack of papers, and a wooden box holding pencils. The leather pouch Andi had received yesterday was open, and packets of paper spread over the desk.

"Is that what you got in the mail?"

She bustled to the desk and shuffled through the pages. "Assignment from Griffith. It's a whole new list of coordinates, now that summer's almost here. The whole sky changes—what we see changes, at least—so I make observations and send the whole thing back." The flush in her brown face deepened as she ducked away. "I know it doesn't sound very interesting, we mostly just write down numbers and trade them back and forth—"

"Oh no," Stella said, shaking her head to emphasize. "It's interesting. Unusual—"

"And useless, Toma says." The smile turned sad, and last night's discussion became clear to Stella.

"Nothing's useless," Stella said. "It's like you said—you can't just throw something like this away." This wasn't like a household that couldn't feed itself and had no choice but to break up.

Three sharp rings of a distant brass bell sounded across the valley. Stella looked out the door, confused.

"Elsta's supper bell," Andi explained. "She only uses it when we've all scattered." She quickly straightened her papers, returned them to their pouch, and latched the roof back in place. Too late, Stella thought to help, reaching up to hold the panel of wood after Andi had already secured the last latch. Oh well. Maybe next time.

Stella got a better look at Andi as they walked back to the croft. She was rough in the way of wind and rain, her dark hair curly, pulled back by a scrap of gray yarn that was unraveling. The collar of her shirt was untied, and her woven jacket had slipped off a shoulder. Stella resisted an urge to pull it back up, and to brush the lock of hair that had fallen out of the tie behind her ear.

"So you're really more of an astronomer than a weaver," Stella said. She'd tried to sound encouraging, but Andi frowned.

"Drives Toma crazy," Andi said. "If there was a household of astronomers, I'd join. But astronomy doesn't feed anyone, does it? Well, some of it does—meteorology, climatology, solar astronomy, maybe. But not what we're doing. We don't earn anyone a baby."

"What are you doing?"

"Astronomical observation. As much as we can, though it feels like reinventing the wheel sometimes. We're not learning anything that people didn't already know back in the day. We're just—well, it feels like filling in the gaps until we get back to where we were. Tracking asteroids, marking supernovae, that sort of thing. Maybe we can't do much with the data. But it might be useful someday."

"There, you see—it's planning ahead. There's use in that."

She sighed. "The committees mostly think it's a waste of time. They can't really complain, though, because we—those of us in the network—do our share and work extra to support the observatories. A bunch of us designate ration credits toward Griffith and Kitt Peak and Wilson—they've got the region's big scopes—to keep staff there maintaining the equipment, to keep the solar power and windmills running. Toma always complains, says if I put my extra credits toward the household we could have a second baby. He says it could even be mine. But they're my credits, and this is important. I earn the time I spend with the scope, and he can't argue." She said that as a declaration, then looked straight at Stella, who blushed. "They may have brought you here to make up for me."

Stella didn't know what to say to that. She was too grateful to have a place at all, to consider that she may have been wanted.

Awkwardly, Andi covered up the silence. "Well. I hope you like it here. That you don't get too homesick, I mean."

The words felt like a warm blanket, soft and wooly. "Thanks."

"We can be kind of rowdy sometimes. Bette gets colicky, and you haven't heard Wendy sing yet. Then there's Jorge and Jon—they share a bed as well as a cottage, see, and can get pretty loud, though if you tease them about it they'll deny it."

"I don't mind rowdy. But I did almost expect to find a clandestine still in that shed."

Andi laughed. "I think Toma'd like a still better, because at least you can drink from it. Elsta does make a really good cider, though. If she ever put enough together to trade it would make up for all the credits I waste on the observatories."

As they came off the hill and approached the cluster of cottages, Andi asked, "Did you know that Stella means star in Latin?"

"Yes, I did," she answered.

*

Work was work no matter where you were, and Stella settled into her work quickly. The folk of Barnard were nice, and Andi was easy to talk to. And cute. Stella found excuses to be in the same room with her, just to see that smile. She hadn't expected this, coming to a new household. But she didn't mind, not at all.

Many households along the Long Road kept sheep, but the folk at Barnard did most of the spinning and weaving for trade. All the wool came to them. Barnard also produced a small quantity of specialty fibers from the alpaca and angora rabbits they kept. They were known for the quality of all their work, the smoothness of their yarns, the evenness of their weaving. Their work was sought after not just along the Long Road, but up and down the coast.

Everyone spun, wove, and dyed. Everyone knew every step of working with wool. They either came here because they knew, or because they'd grown up here learning the trade, like Toma and Nik, like Bette would in her turn. As Andi had, as Stella found out. Andi was the baby that Toma and Elsta had earned together.

Stella and Andi were at the looms, talking as they worked. The spring rains seem to have broken for good, and everyone else had taken their work outside. Wendy sat in the fresh air with her spinning wheel. A new batch of wool had arrived, and Toma and Jorge worked cleaning it. So Stella had a chance to ask questions in private.

"Could you get a place at one of the observatories? How does that work?"

Andi shook her head. "It wouldn't work out. There's three people at Kitt and two each at Griffith and Wilson, and they pick their successors. I'm better use to them here, working to send them credits."

"And you have your telescope, I suppose."

"The astronomers love my telescope," she said. "They call my setup Barnard Observatory, as if it's actually important. Isn't it silly?"

"Of course it isn't."

Andi's hands flashed, passing the shuttle across. She glanced up every now and then. Stella, for her part, let her hands move by habit, and watched Andi more than her own work. Outside, Wendy sang as she spun, in rhythm with the clipping hum of her wheel. Her voice was light, dream-like.

The next time Andi glanced up, she exclaimed, "How do you *do* that? You're not even watching and it's coming out beautiful."

Stella blinked at her work—not much to judge by, she thought. A foot or two of fabric curling over the breast beam, only just starting to wind onto the cloth beam. "I don't know. It's what I'm good at. Like you and the telescope."

"Nice of you to say so. But here, look at this—I've missed a row." She sat back and started unpicking the last five minutes of her work. "I go too fast. My mind wanders."

"It happens to everyone," Stella said.

"Not you. I saw that shawl you did for Elsta."

"I've just gotten good at covering up the mistakes," Stella said, winking.

A week after her arrival, an agent from the regional committee came to visit. A stout, gray-haired, cheerful woman, she was the doctor who made regular rounds up and down the Long Road. She was scheduled to give Bette a round of vaccinations, but Stella suspected the woman was going to be checking on her as well, to make sure she was settling in and hadn't disrupted the household too much.

The doctor, Nance, sat with Bette on the floor, and the baby immediately started crying. Peri hovered, but Nance just smiled and cooed while lifting the baby's arms and checking her ears, not seeming at all bothered.

"How is the world treating you then, Toma?" Nance turned to Toma, who was sitting in his usual chair by the fire.

His brow was creased with worry, though there didn't seem to be anything wrong. "Fine, fine," he said brusquely.

Nance turned. "And Stella, are you doing well?"

"Yes, thank you," Stella said. She was winding yarn around Andi's outstretched hands, to make a skein. This didn't feel much like an inspection, but that only made her more nervous.

"Very good. My, you're a wiggler, aren't you?" Bette's crying had finally subsided to red-faced sniffling, but she continued to fling herself from Nance's arms in an attempt to escape. After a round with a stethoscope, Nance let her go, and the baby crawled away, back to Peri.

The doctor turned her full attention to Toma. "The committee wants to order more banners, they expect to award quite a few this summer. Will you have some ready?"

Toma seemed startled. "Really? Are they sure?"

Barnard supplied the red-and-green patterned cloth used to make the banners awarded to households who'd been approved to have a baby. One of the things Nance had asked about when she first arrived was if anyone had tried bribing him for a length of the cloth over the last year. One of the reasons Barnard had the task of producing the banners—they were prosperous enough not to be vulnerable to bribes. Such attempts happened rarely, but did happen. Households had been broken up over such crimes.

The banner the household had earned for Bette was pinned proudly to the wall above the mantel.

Nance shrugged. "The region's been stable for a couple of years. No quota arguments, most households supporting themselves, just enough surplus to get by without draining resources. We're a healthy region, Toma. If we can support more children, we ought to. And you—with all these healthy young women you have, you might think of putting in for another baby." The doctor beamed.

Stella and Andi looked at each other and blushed. Another baby so soon after the first? Scandalous.

Nance gathered up her kit. "Before I go, let me check all your birth control implants so we don't have any mishaps, eh?"

She started with Elsta and Toma and worked her way around the room.

"Not that I could have a mishap," Andi muttered to Stella. "They ought to make exceptions for someone like me who isn't likely to get in that kind of trouble. Because of her *preferences*, you know?"

"I know," Stella said, blushing very hard now. "I've had that thought myself."

They stared at each other for a very long moment. Stella's mouth had suddenly gone dry. She wanted to flee the room and stick her head in a bucket of cool water. Then again, she didn't.

When Nance came to her side to prod her arm, checking that the implant was in place, Stella hardly felt it.

"Looks like you're good and covered," Nance said. "For now, 'eh? Until you get that extra banner." She winked.

The doctor stayed for supper and still had enough daylight left to walk to the next waystation along the road. Elsta wrapped up a snack of fruit and cheese for her to take with her, and Nance thanked her very much. As soon as she was gone, Toma muttered.

"Too many mouths to feed—and what happens when the next flood hits? The next typhoon? We lose everything and then there isn't enough? We have enough as it is, more than enough. Wanting more, it's asking for trouble. Getting greedy is what brought the disasters in the first place. It's too much."

Everyone stayed quiet, letting him rant. This felt to Stella like an old argument, words repeated like the chorus of a song. Toma's philosophy, expounded by habit. He didn't need a response.

Stella finished winding the skein of yarn and quietly excused herself, putting her things away and saying goodnight to everyone.

Andi followed her out of the cottage soon after, and they walked together to their room.

"So, do you want one?" Stella asked her.

"A baby? I suppose I do. Someday. I mean, I assumed as well off as Barnard is I could have one if I wanted one. It's a little odd, thinking about who I'd pick for the father. That's the part I'm not sure about. What about you?"

Besides being secretly, massively pleased that Andi hadn't thought much about fathers . . . "I assumed I'd never get the chance. I don't think I'd miss it if I didn't."

"Enough other people who want 'em, right?"

"Something like that."

They reached their room, changed into their nightclothes, washed up for bed. Ended up sitting on their beds, facing each other and talking. That first uncomfortable night seemed far away now.

"Toma doesn't seem to like the idea of another baby," Stella prompted.

"Terrified, I think," she said. "Wanting too much gets people in trouble."

"But it only seems natural, to want as much as you can have."

Andi shook her head. "His grandparents remembered the old days. He heard stories from them about the disasters. All the people who died in the floods and plagues. He's that close to it—might as well have lived through it himself. He thinks we'll lose it all, that another great disaster will fall on us and destroy everything. It's part of why he hates my telescope so much. It's a sign of the old days when everything went rotten. But it won't happen, doesn't he see that?"

Stella shrugged. "Those days aren't so far gone, really. Look at what happened to Greentree."

"Oh—Stella, I'm sorry. I didn't mean that there's not anything to it, just that . . ." She shrugged, unable to finish the thought.

"It can't happen here. I know."

Andi's black hair fell around her face, framing her pensive expression. She stared into space. "I just wish he could see how good things are. We've earned a little extra, haven't we?"

Unexpected even to herself, Stella burst, "Can I kiss you?"

In half a heartbeat Andi fell at her, holding Stella's arms, and Stella clung back, and either her arms were hot or Andi's hands were, and they met, lips to lips.

One evening, Andi escaped the gathering in the common room, and brought Stella with her. They left as the sun had almost set, leaving just enough light to follow the path to the observatory. They took candles inside shaded lanterns for the trip back to their cottage. At dusk, the windmills were ghostly skeletons lurking on the hillside.

They waited for full dark, talking while Andi looked over her paperwork and prepared her notes. Andi asked about Greentree, and Stella explained that the aquifers had dried up in the drought. Households remained in the region because they'd always been there. Some survived, but they weren't particularly successful. She told Andi how the green of the valleys near the coast had almost blinded her when she first arrived, and how all the rain had seemed like a miracle.

Then it was time to unlatch the roof panels and look at the sky.

"Don't squint, just relax. Let the image come into focus," Andi said, bending close to give directions to Stella, who was peering through the scope's eyepiece. Truth be told, Stella was more aware of Andi's hand resting lightly on her shoulder. She shifted closer.

"You should be able to see it," Andi said, straightening to look at the sky.

"Okay . . . I think . . . oh! Is that it?" A disk had come into view, a pale, glowing light striped with orange, yellow, cream. Like someone had covered a very distant moon with melted butter.

"Jupiter," Andi said proudly.

"But it's just a star."

"Not up close it isn't."

Not a disk, then, but a sphere. Another planet. "Amazing."

"Isn't it? You ought to be able to see some of the moons as well—a couple of bright stars on either side?"

"I think . . . yes, there they are."

After an hour, Stella began shivering in the nighttime cold, and Andi put her arms around her, rubbing warmth into her back. In moments, they were kissing, and stumbled together to the desk by the shack's wall, where Andi pushed her back across the surface and made love to her. Jupiter had swung out of view by the time they closed up the roof and stumbled off the hill.

*

Another round of storms came, shrouding the nighttime sky, and they spent the evenings around the hearth with the others. Some of the light went out of Andi on those nights. She sat on a chair with a basket of mending at her feet, darning socks and shirts, head bent over her work. Lamplight turned her skin amber and made her hair shine like obsidian. But she didn't talk. That may have been because Elsta and Toma talked over everyone, or Peri exclaimed over something the baby did, then everyone had to admire Bette.

The day the latest round of rain broke and the heat of summer finally settled over the valley, Andi got another package from Griffith, and that light of discovery came back to her. Tonight, they'd rush off to the observatory after supper.

Stella almost missed the cue to escape, helping Elsta with the dishes. When she was finished and drying her hands, Andi was at the door. Stella rushed in behind her. Then Toma brought out a basket, one of the ones as big as an embrace that they used to store just-washed wool in, and set it by Andi's chair before the hearth. "Andi, get back here."

Her hand was on the door, one foot over the threshold, and Stella thought she might keep going, pretending that she hadn't heard. But her hand clenched on the door frame, and she turned around.

"We've got to get all this new wool processed, so you'll stay in tonight to help."

"I can do that tomorrow. I'll work double tomorrow—"

"Now, Andi."

Stella stepped forward, hands reaching for the basket. "Toma, I can do that."

"No, you're doing plenty already. Andi needs to do it."

"I'll be done with the mending in a minute and can finish that in no time at all. Really, it's all right."

He looked past her, to Andi. "You know the rules—household business first."

"The household business is *done*. This is makework!" she said. Toma held the basket out in reproof.

Stella tried again. "But I *like* carding." It sounded lame—no one liked carding.

But Andi had surrendered, coming away from the door, shuffling toward her chair. "Stella, it's all right. Not your argument."

"But—" The pleading in her gaze felt naked. She wanted to help, how could she help?

Andi slumped in the chair without looking up. All Stella could do was sit in her own chair, with her knitting. She jabbed herself with the needle three times, from glancing up at Andi every other stitch.

Toma sat before his workbench, looking pleased for nearly the first time since Stella had met him.

Well after dark, Stella lay in her bed, stomach in knots. Andi was in the other bed and hadn't said a word all evening.

"Andi? Are you all right?" she whispered. She stared across the room to the slope of the other woman, mounded under her blanket. The lump didn't move, but didn't look relaxed in sleep. But if she didn't want to talk, Stella wouldn't force her.

"I'm okay," Andi sighed, finally.

"Anything I can do?"

Another long pause, and Stella was sure she'd said too much. Then, "You're a good person, Stella. Anyone ever told you that?"

Stella crawled out from under her covers, crossed to Andi's bed, climbed in with her. Andi pulled the covers up over them both, and the women held each other.

Toma sent Andi on an errand, delivering a set of blankets to the next waystation and picking up messages to bring back. More make-work. The task could just as easily have been done by the next wagon messenger to pass by. Andi told him as much, standing outside the work house the next morning.

"Why wait when we can get the job done now?" Toma answered,

hefting the backpack, stuffed to bursting with newly woven woolens, toward her.

Stella was at her loom, and her hand on the shuttle paused as she listened. But Andi didn't say anything else. Only glared at Toma a good long minute before taking up the pack. She'd be gone most of the day, hiking there and back.

Which was the point, wasn't it?

Stella contrived to find jobs that kept Toma in sight, sorting and carding wool outside where he was working repairing a fence, when she should have been weaving. So she saw when Toma studied the hammer in his hand, looked up the hill, and started walking the path to Andi's observatory.

Stella dropped the basket of wool she was holding and ran.

He was merely walking. Stella overtook him easily, at first. But after fifty yards of running, she slowed, clutching at a stitch in her side. Gasping for breath with burning lungs, she kept on, step after step, hauling herself up the hill, desperate to get there first.

"Stella, go back, don't get in the middle of this."

Even if she could catch enough of her breath to speak, she didn't know what she would say. He lengthened his stride, gaining on her. She got to the shed a bare few steps before him.

The door didn't have a lock; it had never needed one. Stella pressed herself across it and faced out to Toma, marching closer. At least she had something to lean on for the moment.

"Move aside, Stella. She's got to grow up and get on with what's important," Toma said.

"This *is* important."

He stopped, studied her. He gripped the handle of hammer like it was a weapon. Her heart thudded. How angry was he?

Toma considered, then said, "Stella. You're here because I wanted to do Az a favor. I can change my mind. I can send a message to Nance and the committee that it just isn't working out. I can do that."

Panic brought sudden tears to her eyes. He wouldn't dare, he couldn't, she'd proven herself already in just a few weeks, hadn't she?

The committee wouldn't believe him, couldn't listen to him. But she couldn't be sure of that, could she?

Best thing to do would be to step aside. He was head of the household, it was his call. She ought to do as he said, because her place here *wasn't* secure. A month ago that might not have mattered, but now—she *wanted* to stay, she *had* to stay.

And if she stepped aside, leaving Toma free to enter the shed, what would she tell Andi afterward?

She swallowed the lump in her throat and found words. "I know disaster can still happen. I know the droughts and storms and plagues do still come and can take away everything. Better than anyone, I know. But we have to start building again sometime, yes? People like Andi have to start building, and we have to let them, even if it seems useless to the rest of us. Because it isn't useless, it—it's beautiful."

He stared at her for a long time. She thought maybe he was considering how to wrestle her away from the door. He was bigger than she was, and she wasn't strong. It wouldn't take much. But she'd fight.

"You're infatuated, that's all," he said.

Maybe, not that it mattered.

Then he said, "You're not going to move away, are you?"

Shaking her head, Stella flattened herself more firmly against the door.

Toma's grip on the hammer loosened, just a bit. "My grandparents—has Andi told you about my grandparents? They were children when the big fall came. They remembered what it was like. Mostly they talked about what they'd lost, all the things they had and didn't now. And I thought, all those things they missed, that they wanted back—that was what caused the fall in the first place, wasn't it? We don't need it, any of it."

"Andi needs it. And it's not hurting anything." What else could she say, she had to say something that would make it all right. "Better things will come, or what's the point?"

A weird crooked smile turned Toma's lips, and he shifted his grip on the hammer. Holding it by the head now, he let it dangle by his leg. "God, what a world," he muttered. Stella still couldn't tell if he was going to force her away from the door. She held her breath.

Toma said, "Don't tell Andi about this. All right?"

She nodded. "All right."

Toma turned and started down the trail, a calm and steady pace. Like a man who'd just gone out for a walk.

Stella slid to the ground and sat on the grass by the wall until the old man was out of sight. Finally, after scrubbing the tears from her face, she followed him down, returning to the cottages and her work.

Andi was home in time for supper, and the household ate together as usual. The woman was quiet and kept making quick glances at Toma, who avoided looking back at all. It was like she knew Toma had had a plan. Stella couldn't say anything until they were alone.

The night was clear, the moon was dark. Stella'd learned enough from Andi to know it was a good night for stargazing. As they were cleaning up after the meal, she touched Andi's hand. "Let's go to the observatory."

Andi glanced at Toma, and her lips pressed together, grim. "I don't think that's a good idea."

"I think it'll be okay."

Andi clearly didn't believe her, so Stella took her hand, and together they walked out of the cottage, then across the yard, past the work house, and to the trail that led up the hill to the observatory.

And it was all right.

BANNERLESS

Enid and Bert walked the ten miles from the way station because the weather was good, a beautiful spring day. Enid had never worked with the young man before, but he turned out to be good company: chatty without being oppressively extroverted. Young, built like a redwood, he looked the part of an investigator. They talked about home and the weather and trivialities—but not the case. She didn't like to dwell on the cases she was assigned to before getting a firsthand look at them. She had expected Bert to ask questions about it, but he was taking her lead.

On this stretch of the Coast Road, halfway between the way station and Southtown, ruins were visible in the distance, to the east. An old sprawling city from before the big fall. In her travels in her younger days, she'd gone into it a few times, to shout into the echoing artificial canyons and study overgrown asphalt roads and cracked walls with fallen roofs. She rarely saw people, but often saw old cook fires and cobbled together shantytowns that couldn't support the lives struggling within them. Scavengers and scattered folk still came out from them sometimes, then faded back to the concrete enclaves, surviving however they survived.

Bert caught her looking.

"You've been there?" Bert said, nodding toward the haze marking the swath of ruined city. No paths or roads ran that way anymore. She'd had to go overland when she'd done it.

"Yes, a long time ago."

"What was it like?"

The answer could either be very long or very short. The stories of what had happened before and during the fall were terrifying and intriguing, but the ruins no longer held any hint of those tales. They were bones, in the process of disappearing. "It was sad," she said finally.

"I'm still working through the histories," he said. "For training, right? There's a lot of diaries. Can be hard, reading how it was at the fall."

"Yes."

In isolation, any of the disasters that had struck would not have overwhelmed the old world. The floods alone would not have destroyed the cities. The vicious influenza epidemic—a mutated strain with no available vaccine that incapacitated victims in a matter of hours—by itself would have been survivable, eventually. But the floods, the disease, the rising ocean levels, the monster storms piling one on top of the other, an environment off balance that chipped away at infrastructure and made each recovery more difficult than the one before it, all of it left too many people with too little to survive on. Wealth meant nothing when there was simply nothing left. So, the world died. But people survived, here and there. They came together and saved what they could. They learned lessons.

The road curved into the next valley and they approached Southtown, the unimaginative name given to this district's main farming settlement. Windmills appeared first, clean towers with vertical blades spiraling gently in an unfelt breeze. Then came cisterns set on scaffolds, then plowed fields and orchards in the distance. The town was home to some thousand people scattered throughout the valley and surrounding farmlands. There was a grid of drained roads and whitewashed houses, solar and battery operated carts, some goats, chickens pecking in yards. All was orderly, pleasant. This was what rose up after the ruins fell, the home that their grandparents fled to as children.

"Will you let the local committee know we're here?" Bert asked.

"Oh, no. We don't want anyone to have warning we're here. We go straight to the household. Give them a shock."

"Makes sense."

"This is your first case, isn't it? Your first investigation?"

"It is. And . . . I guess I'm worried I might have to stop someone." Bert had a staff like hers but he knew how to use his for more than walking. He had a stunner and a pack of tranquilizer needles on his belt. All in plain view. If she did her job well enough he wouldn't need to do anything but stand behind her and look alert. A useful tool. He seemed to understand his role.

"I doubt you will. Our reputation will proceed us. It's why we have the reputation in the first place. Don't worry."

"I just need to act as terrifying as the reputation says I do."

She smiled. "Exactly—you know just how this works, then."

They wore brown tunics and trousers with gray sashes. Somber colors, cold like winter, probably designed to inspire a chill. Bert stood a head taller than she did and looked like he could break tree trunks. How sinister, to see the pair of them approach.

"And you—this is your last case, isn't it?"

That was what she'd told the regional committee, that it was time for her to go home, settle down, take up basket weaving or such like. "I've been doing this almost twenty years," she said. "It's time for me to pass the torch."

"Would you miss the travel? That's what I've been looking forward to, getting to see some of the region, you know?"

"Maybe," she said. "But I wouldn't miss the bull. You'll see what I mean."

They approached the settlement. Enid put her gaze on a young woman carrying a basket of eggs along the main road. She wore a skirt, tunic, apron, and a straw hat to keep off the sun.

"Excuse me," Enid said. The woman's hands clenched as if she was afraid she might drop the basket from fright. As she'd told Bert, their reputation preceded them. They were inspectors, and inspectors only appeared for terrible reasons. The woman's expression held shock and denial. Why would inspectors ever come to Southtown?

"Yes, how can I help you?" she said quickly, nervously.

"Can you tell us where to find Apricot Hill?" The household they'd been sent to investigate.

The woman's anxiety fell away and a light of understanding dawned. Ah, then people knew. Everyone likely knew *something* was wrong, without knowing exactly what. The whole town would know investigators were here within the hour. Enid's last case, and it was going to be all about sorting out gossip.

"Yes—take that path there, past the pair of windmills. They're on the south side of the duck pond. You'll see the clotheslines out front."

"Thank you," Enid said. The woman hurried away, hugging her basket to her chest.

Enid turned to Bert. "Ready for this?"

"Now I'm curious. Let's go."

Apricot Hill was on a nice acreage overlooking a pretty pond and a series of orchards beyond that. There was one large house, two stories with lots of windows, and an outbuilding with a pair of chimneys, a production building—Apricot Hill was centered on food processing, taking in produce from outlying farms and drying, canning, and preserving it for winter stores for the community. The holding overall was well lived in, a bit run down, cluttered, but that could mean they were busy. It was spring—nothing ready for canning yet. This should have been the season for cleaning up and making repairs.

A girl with a bundle of sheets over her arm, probably collected from the clothesline the woman had mentioned, saw them first. She peered up the hill at their arrival for a moment before dropping the sheets and running to the house. She was wispy and energetic—not the one mentioned in the report, then. Susan, and not Aren. The heads of the household were Frain and Felice.

"We are announced," Enid said wryly. Bert hooked a finger in his belt.

A whole crowd, maybe even all ten members of the household, came out of the house. A rough looking bunch, all together. Old clothes, frowning faces. This was an adequate household, but not a happy one.

An older man, slim and weather-worn, came forward and looked as though he wished he had a weapon. This would be Frain. Enid went to him, holding her hand out for shaking.

"Hello, I'm Enid, the investigator sent by the regional committee. This is my partner, Bert. This is Apricot Hill, isn't it? You must be Frain?"

"Yes," he said cautiously, already hesitant to give away any scrap of information.

"May we step inside to talk?"

She would look like a matron to them, maybe even head of a household somewhere, if they weren't sure she didn't have a household. Investigators didn't have households; they traveled constantly, avenging angels, or so the rumors said. Her dull brown hair was rolled into a bun, her soft face had seen years and weather. They'd wonder if she'd ever had children of her own, if she'd ever earned a banner. Her spreading middle-aged hips wouldn't give a clue.

Bert stood behind her, a wall of authority. Their questions about him would be simple: How well could he use that staff he carried?

"What is this about?" Frain demanded. He was afraid. He knew what she was here for—the implications—and he was afraid.

"I think we should go inside and sit down before we talk," Enid said patiently, knowing full well she sounded condescending and unpleasant. The lines on Frain's face deepened. "Is everyone here? Gather everyone in the household to your common room."

With a curt word Frain herded the rest of his household inside.

The common room on the house's ground floor was, like the rest of the household, functional without being particularly pleasant. No vase of flowers on the long dining table. Not a spot of color on the wall except for a single faded banner: the square of red and green woven cloth that represented the baby they'd earned some sixteen years ago. That would be Susan—the one with the laundry outside. Adults had come into the household since then, but that was their last baby.

Had they wanted another child badly enough that they didn't wait for their committee to award them a banner?

The house had ten members. Only nine sat around the table. Enid took her time studying them, looking into each face. Most of the gazes ducked away from her. Susan's didn't.

"We're missing someone, I think?" Enid said.

The silence was thick as oil. Bert stood easy and perfectly still behind her, hand on his belt. Oh, he was a natural at this. Enid waited a long time, until the people around the table squirmed.

"Aren," Felice said softly. "I'll go get her."

"No," Frain said. "She's sick. She can't come."

"Sick? Badly sick? Has a doctor seen her?" Enid said.

Again, the oily silence.

"Felice, if you could get her, thank you," Enid said.

A long stretch passed before Felice returned with the girl, and Enid was happy to watch while the group grew more and more uncomfortable. Susan was trembling; one of the men was hugging himself. This was as awful a gathering as she had ever seen, and her previous case had been a murder.

When Felice brought Aren into the room, Enid saw exactly what she expected to see: the older woman with her arm around a younger woman—age twenty or so—who wore a full skirt and a tunic three sizes too big that billowed in front of her. Aren moved slowly, and had to keep drawing her hands away from her belly.

She might have been able to hide the pregnancy for a time, but she was now six months along, and there was no hiding that swell and the ponderous hitch in her movement.

The anger and unhappiness in the room thickened even more, and it was no longer directed at Enid.

She waited while Felice guided the pregnant woman to a chair—by herself, apart from the others.

"This is what you're here for, isn't it?" Frain demanded, his teeth bared and fists clenched.

"It is," Enid agreed.

"Who told?" Frain hissed, looking around at them all. "Which one of you told?"

No one said anything. Aren cringed and ducked her head. Felice stared at her hands in her lap.

Frain turned to Enid. "Who sent the report? I've a right to know my accuser—the household's accuser."

"The report was anonymous, but credible." Part of her job here was to discover, if she could, who sent the tip of the bannerless pregnancy to the regional committee. Frain didn't need to know that. "I'll be asking all of you questions over the next couple of days. I expect honest answers. When I am satisfied that I know what happened here, I'm authorized to pass judgment. I will do so as quickly as possible, to spare you waiting. Frain, I'll start with you."

"It was an accident. An accident, I'm sure of it. The implant failed. Aren has a boy in town; they spend all their time together. We thought nothing of it because of the implant, but then it failed, and—we didn't say anything because we were scared. That's all. We should have told the committee as soon as we knew. I'm sorry—I know now that that was wrong. You'll take that into consideration?"

"When did you know? All of you, starting with Aren—when did you know of the pregnancy?"

The young woman's first words were halting, choked. Crying had thickened her throat. "Must . . . must have been . . . two months in, I think. I was sick. I just knew."

"Did you tell anyone?"

"No, no one. I was scared."

They were all terrified. That sounded true.

"And the rest of you?"

Murmurs answered. The men shook their heads, said they'd only known for a month or so, when she could no longer hide the new shape of her. They knew for sure the day that Frain ranted about it. "I didn't rant," the man said. "I was only surprised. I lost my temper, that was all."

Felice said, "I knew when she got sick. I've been pregnant—" Her gaze went to the banner on the wall. "I know the signs. I asked her, and she told."

"You didn't think to tell anyone?"

"Frain told me not to."

So Frain knew, at least as soon as she did. The man glared fire at Felice, who wouldn't lift her gaze.

"Aren, might I speak to you alone?"

The woman cringed, back curled, arms wrapped around her belly.

"I'll go you with you, dear," Felice whispered.

"Alone," Enid said. "Bert will wait here. We'll go outside. Just a short walk."

Trembling, Aren stood. Enid stood aside to let her walk out the door first. She caught Bert's gaze and nodded. He nodded back.

Enid guided her on the path around the house, to the garden patch and pond behind. She went slowly, letting Aren set the pace.

The physical state of a household carried information: whether rakes and shovels were hung up neat in a shed or closet, or piled haphazardly by the wall of an unpainted barn. Whether the herb garden thrived, if there were flowers in window boxes. If neat little water-smoothed stones edged the paths leading from one building to another, or if there were just dirt tracks worn into the grass. She didn't judge a household by whether or not it put a good face to the world—but she did judge them by whether or not the folk in a household worked to put on a good face for themselves. They had to live with it, look at it every single day.

This household did not have a good face. The garden patch was only just sprouting, even this far into spring. There were no flowers. The grass along the path was overgrown. There was a lack of care here that made Enid angry.

But the pond was pretty. Ducks paddled around a stand of cattails, muttering to themselves.

Enid had done this before, knew the questions to ask and what possible answers she might get to those questions. Every moment reduced the possible explanations. Heavens, she was tired of this.

Enid said, "Stop here. Roll up your sleeve."

Aren's overlarge tunic had wide sleeves that fell past her wrists. They'd be no good at all for working. The young woman stood frozen. Her lips were tightly pursed, to keep from crying.

"May I roll the sleeve up, then?" Enid asked carefully, reaching.

"No, I'll do it," she said, and clumsily pushed the fabric up to her left shoulder.

She revealed an angry scar, puckered pink, mostly healed. Doing the math, maybe seven or eight months old. The implant had been cut out, the wound not well treated, which meant she'd probably done it herself.

"Did you get anyone to stitch that up for you?" Enid asked.

"I bound it up and kept it clean." At least she didn't try to deny it. Enid guessed she would have, if Frain were there.

"Where did you put the implant after you took it out?"

"Buried it in the latrine."

Enid hoped she wouldn't have to go after it for evidence. "You did it yourself. No one forced you to, or did it to you?" That happened sometimes, someone with a skewed view of the world and what was theirs deciding they needed someone to bear a baby for them.

"It's me, it's just me. Nobody else. Just me."

"Does the father know?"

"No, I don't think . . . He didn't know I'd taken out the implant. I don't know if he knows about the baby."

Rumors had gotten out, Enid was sure, especially if Aren hadn't been seen around town in some time. The anonymous tip about the pregnancy might have come from anywhere.

"Can you tell me the father's name, so I can speak to him?"

"Don't drag him into this; tell me you won't drag him into this. It's just me. Just take me away and be done with it." Aren stopped, her eyes closed, her face pinched. "What are you going to do to me?"

"I'm not sure yet."

She was done with crying. Her face was locked with anger, resignation. "You'll take me to the center of town and rip the baby out, cut its throat, leave us both to bleed to death as a warning. That's it, isn't it? Just tell me that's what you're going to do and get it over with—"

Goodness, the stories people told. "No, we're not going to do that. We don't rip babies from mother's wombs—not unless we need to save the mother's life, or the baby's. There's surgery for that. Your baby will be born; you have my promise."

Quiet tears slipped down the girl's cheeks. Enid watched for a moment, this time not using the silence to pressure Aren but trying to decide what to say.

"You thought that was what would happen if you were caught, and you still cut out your implant to have a baby? You must have known you'd be caught."

"I don't remember anymore what I was thinking."

"Let's get you back to the kitchen for a drink of water, hmm?"

By the time they got back to the common room, Aren had stopped crying, and she even stood a little straighter. At least until Frain looked at her, then at Enid.

"What did you tell her? What did she say to you?"

"Felice, I think Aren needs a glass of water, or maybe some tea. Frain, will you come speak with me?"

The man stomped out of the room ahead of her.

"What happened?" Enid said simply.

"The implant. It must have failed."

"Do you think she, or someone, might have cut it out? Did you ever notice her wearing a bandage on her arm?"

He did not seem at all surprised at this suggestion. "I never did. I never noticed." He was going to plead ignorance. That was fine. "Does the local committee know you're here?" he said, turning the questioning on her.

"Not yet," she said lightly. "They will."

"What are you going to do? What will happen to Aren?"

Putting the blame on Aren, because he knew the whole household was under investigation. "I haven't decided yet."

"I'm going to protest to the committe about you questioning

Aren alone. You shouldn't have done that, it's too hard on her—" He was furious that he didn't know what Aren had said. That he couldn't make their stories match up.

"Submit your protest," Enid said. "That's fine."

She spoke to every one of them alone. Half of them said the exact same thing, in exactly the same way.

"The implant failed. It must have failed."

"Aren's got that boy of hers. He's the father."

"It was an accident."

"An accident." Felice breathed this line, her head bowed and hands clasped together.

So that was the story they'd agreed upon. The story Frain had told them to tell.

One of the young men—baffled, he didn't seem to understand what was happening—was the one to slip. "She brought this down on us, why do the rest of us have to put up with the mess when it's all her?"

Enid narrowed her gaze. "So you know she cut out her implant?"

He wouldn't say another word after that. He bit his lips and puffed out his cheeks, but wouldn't speak, as if someone held a knife to his throat and told him not to.

Enid wasn't above pressing hard at the young one, Susan, until the girl snapped.

"Did you ever notice Aren with a bandage on her arm?"

Susan's face turned red. "It's not my fault, it's not! It's just that Frain said if we got a banner next season I could have it, not Aren, and she was jealous! That's what it was; she did this to punish us!"

Banners were supposed to make things better. Give people something to work for, make them prove they could support a child, *earn* a child. It wasn't supposed to be something to fight over, to cheat over.

But people did cheat.

"Susan—did you send the anonymous report about Aren?"

Susan's eyes turned round and shocked. "No, of course not, I wouldn't do such a thing! Tell Frain I'd never do such a thing!"

"Thank you, Susan, for your honesty," Enid said, and Susan burst into tears.

What a stinking mess this was turning in to. To think, she could have retired after the murder investigation and avoided all this.

She needed to talk to more people.

By the time they returned to the common room, Felice had gotten tea out for everyone. She politely offered a cup to Enid, who accepted, much to everyone's dismay. Enid stayed for a good twenty minutes, sipping, watching them watch her, making small talk.

"Thank you very much for all of your time and patience," she said eventually. "I'll be at the committee house in town if any of you would like to speak with me further. I'll deliver my decision in a day or two, so I won't keep you waiting. Your community thanks you."

A million things could happen, but these people were so locked into their drama she didn't expect much. She wasn't worried that the situation was going to change overnight. If Aren was going to grab her boy and run she would have done it already. That wasn't what was happening here. This was a household imploding.

Time to check with the local committee.

"Did they talk while I was gone?" Enid asked.

"Not a word," Bert said. "I hate to say it but that was almost fun. What are they so scared of?"

"Us. The stories of what we'll do. Aren was sure we'd drag her in the street and cut out her baby."

Bert wrinkled his face and said softly, "That's awful."

"I hadn't heard that one before, I admit. Usually it's all locked cells and stealing the baby away as soon as it's born. I wonder if Frain told the story to her, said it was why they had to keep it secret."

"Frain knew?"

"I'm sure they all did. They're trying to save the household by convincing me it was an accident. Or that it was just Aren's fault and no one else's. When really, a household like that, if they're that unhappy they should all put in for transfers, no matter how many ration credits that'd cost. Frain's scared them out of it, I'm betting."

"So what will happen?"

"Technology fails sometimes. If it had been an accident, I'm authorized to award a banner retroactively if the household can handle it. But that's not what happened here. If the household colluded to bring on a bannerless baby, we'd have to break up the house. But if it was just Aren all on her own—punishment would fall on her."

"But this isn't any of those, is it?"

"You've got a good eye for this, Bert."

"Not sure that's a compliment. I like to expect the best from people, not the worst."

Enid chuckled.

"At least *you'll* be able to put this all behind you soon," he said. "Retire to some pleasant household somewhere. Not here."

A middle aged man, balding and flush, rushed toward them on the path as they returned to the town. His gray tunic identified him as a committee member, and he wore the same stark panic on his face that everyone did when they saw an investigator.

"You must be Trevor?" Enid asked him, when he was still a few paces away, too far to shake hands.

"We didn't know you were coming, you should have sent word. Why didn't you send word?"

"We didn't have time. We got an anonymous report and had to act quickly. It happens sometimes, I'm sure you understand."

"Report, on what? If it's serious, I'm sure I would have been told—"

"A bannerless pregnancy at the Apricot Hill household."

He took a moment to process, staring, uncertain. The look turned hard. This didn't just reflect on Aren or the household—it reflected on the entire settlement. On the committee that ran the settlement. They could all be dragged into this.

"Aren," the man breathed.

Enid wasn't surprised the man knew. She was starting to wonder how her office hadn't heard about the situation much sooner.

"What can you tell me about the household? How do they get along, how are they doing?"

"Is this an official interview?"

"Why not? Saves time."

"They get their work done. But they're a household, not a family. If you understand the difference."

"I do." A collection of people gathered for production, not one that bonded over love. It wasn't always a bad thing—a collection of people working toward shared purpose could be powerful. But love could make it a home.

"How close were they to earning a banner?" *Were.* Telling word, there.

"I can't say they were close. They have three healthy young women, but people came in and out of that house so often we couldn't call it 'stable.' They fell short on quotas. I know that's usually better than going over, but not with food processing—falling short there means food potentially wasted, if it goes bad before it gets stored. Frain—Frain is not the easiest man to get along with."

"Yes, I know."

"You've already been out there—I wish you would have talked to me; you should have come to see us before starting your investigation." Trevor was wringing his hands.

"So you could tell me how things really are?" Enid raised a brow and smiled. He glanced briefly at Bert and frowned. "Aren had a romantic partner in the settlement, I'm told. Do you know who this might be?"

"She wouldn't tell you—she trying to protect him?"

"He's not in any trouble."

"Jess. It's Jess. He works in the machine shop, with the Ironcroft household." He pointed the way.

"Thank you. We've had a long day of travel, can the committee house put us up for a night or two? We've got the credits to trade for it, we won't be a burden."

"Yes, of course, we have guest rooms in back, this way."

Trevor led them on to a comfortable stone house, committee offices and official guest rooms all together. People had gathered, drifting out of houses and stopping along the road to look, to bend heads and gossip. Everyone had that stare of trepidation.

"You don't make a lot of friends, working in investigations," Bert murmured to her.

"Not really, no."

A young man, an assistant to the committee, delivered a good meal of lentil stew and fresh bread, along with cider. It tasted like warmth embodied, a great comfort after the day she'd had.

"My household hang their banners on the common room wall like that," Bert said between mouthfuls. "They stitch the names of the babies into them. It's a whole history of the house laid out there."

"Many households do. It's a lovely tradition," Enid said.

"I've never met anyone born without a banner. It's odd, thinking Aren's baby won't have its name written anywhere."

"It's not the baby's fault, remember. But it does make it hard. They grow up thinking they have to work twice as hard to earn their place in the world. But it usually makes people very careful not to pass on that burden."

"Usually but not always."

She sighed, her solid inspector demeanor slipping. "We're getting better. The goal is making sure that every baby born will be provided for, will have a place, and won't overburden what we have. But babies are powerful things. We'll never be perfect."

The young assistant knocked on the door to the guest rooms early the next day.

"Ma'am, Enid? Someone's out front asking for the investigator."

"Is there a conference room where we can meet?"

"Yes, I'll show him in."

She and Bert quickly made themselves presentable—and put on their reputation—before meeting.

The potential informant was a lanky young man with calloused hands, a flop of brown hair and no beard. A worried expression. He kneaded a straw hat in his hands and stood from the table when Enid and Bert entered.

"You're Jess?"

He squeezed the hat harder. Ah, the appearance of omniscience was so very useful.

"Please, sit down," Enid said, and sat across from him by example. Bert stood by the wall.

"This is about Aren," the young man said. "You're here about Aren."

"Yes." He slumped, sighed—did he seemed relieved? "What do you need to tell me, Jess?"

"I haven't seen her in weeks; I haven't even gotten a message to her. No one will tell me what's wrong, and I know what everyone's been saying, but it can't be true—"

"That she's pregnant. She's bannerless."

He blinked. "But she's alive? She's safe?"

"She is. I saw her yesterday."

"Good, that's good."

Unlike everyone else she had talked to here, he seemed genuinely reassured. As if he had expected her to be dead or injured. The vectors of anxiety in the case pointed in so many different directions. "Did she tell you anything? Did you have any idea that something was wrong?"

"No . . . I mean, yes, but not that. It's complicated. What's going to happen to her?"

"That's what I'm here to decide. I promise you, she and the baby won't come to any harm. But I need to understand what's happened. Did you know she'd cut out her implant?"

He stared at the tabletop. "No, I didn't know that." If he had known, he could be implicated, so it behooved him to say that. But

Enid believed him.

"Jess, I want to understand why she did what she did. Her household is being difficult. They tell me she spent all her spare time with you." Enid couldn't tell if he was resistant to talking to her, or if he simply couldn't find the words. She prompted. "How long have you been together? How long have you been intimate?" A gentle way of putting it. He wasn't blushing; on the contrary, he'd gone even more pale.

"Not long," he said. "Not even a year. I think . . . I think I know what happened now, looking back."

"Can you tell me?"

"I think . . . I think she needed someone and she picked me. I'm almost glad she picked me. I love her, but . . . I didn't know."

She wanted a baby. She found a boy she liked, cut out her implant, and made sure she had a baby. It wasn't unheard of. Enid had looked into a couple of cases like it in the past. But then, the household reported it when the others found out, or she left the household. To go through that and then stay, with everyone also covering it up . . .

"Did she ever talk about earning a banner and having a baby with you? Was that a goal of hers?"

"She never did at all. We . . . it was just us. I just liked spending time with her. We'd go for walks."

"What else?"

"She—wouldn't let me touch her arm. The first time we . . . were intimate, she kept her shirt on. She'd hurt her arm, she said, and didn't want to get dirt on it—we were out by the mill creek that feeds into the pond. It's so beautiful there, with the noise of the water and all. I . . . I didn't think of it. I mean, she always seemed to be hurt somewhere. Bruises and things. She said it was just from working around the house. I was always a bit careful touching her, though, because of it. I had to be careful with her." Miserable now, he put the pieces together in his mind as Enid watched. "She didn't like to go back. I told myself—I fooled myself—that it was because she loved me. But it's more that she didn't want to go back."

"And she loves you. As you said, she picked you. But she had to go back."

"If she'd asked, she could have gone somewhere else."

But it would have cost credits she may not have had, the committee would have asked why, and it would have been a black mark on Frain's leadership, or worse. Frain had them cowed into staying. So Aren wanted to get out of there and decided a baby would help her.

Enid asked, "Did you send the tip to Investigations?"

"No. No, I didn't know. That is, I didn't want to believe. I would never do anything to get her in trouble. I . . . I'm not in trouble, am I?"

"No, Jess. Do you know who might have sent in the tip?"

"Someone on the local committee, maybe. They're the ones who'd start an investigation, aren't they?"

"Usually, but they didn't seem happy to see me. The message went directly to regional."

"The local committee doesn't want to think anything's wrong. Nobody wants to think anything's wrong."

"Yes, that seems to be the attitude. Thank you for your help, Jess."

"What will happen to Aren?" He was choking, struggling not to cry. Even Bert, standing at the wall, seemed discomfited.

"That's for me to worry about, Jess. Thank you for your time."

At the dismissal, he slipped out of the room.

She leaned back and sighed, wanting to get back to her own household—despite the rumors, investigators did belong to households—with its own orchards and common room full of love and safety.

Yes, maybe she should have retired before all this. Or maybe she wasn't meant to.

"Enid?" Bert asked softly.

"Let's go. Let's get this over with."

*

Back at Apricot Hill's common room, the household gathered,

and Enid didn't have to ask for Aren this time. She had started to worry, especially after talking to Jess. But they'd all waited this long, and her arrival didn't change anything except it had given them all the confirmation that they'd finally been caught. That they would always be caught. Good for the reputation, there.

Aren kept her face bowed, her hair over her cheek. Enid moved up to her, reached a hand to her, and the girl flinched. "Aren?" she said, and she still didn't look up until Enid touched her chin and made her lift her face. An irregular red bruise marked her cheek.

"Aren, did you send word about a bannerless pregnancy to the regional committee?"

Someone, Felice probably, gasped. A few of them shifted. Frain simmered. But Aren didn't deny it. She kept her face low.

"Aren?" Enid prompted, and the young woman nodded, ever so slightly.

"I hid. I waited for the weekly courier and slipped the letter in her bag, she didn't see me; no one saw. I didn't know if anyone would believe it, with no name on it, but I had to try. I wanted to get caught, but no one was noticing it; everyone was ignoring it." Her voice cracked to silence.

Enid put a gentle hand on Aren's shoulder. Then she went to Bert, and whispered, "Watch carefully."

She didn't know what would happen, what Frain in particular would do. She drew herself up, drew strength from the uniform she wore, and declaimed.

"I am the villain here," Enid said. "Understand that. I am happy to be the villain in your world. It's what I'm here for. Whatever happens, blame me.

"I will take custody of Aren and her child. When the rest of my business is done, I'll leave with her and she'll be cared for responsibly. Frain, I question your stewardship of this household and will submit a recommendation that Apricot Hill be dissolved entirely, its resources and credits distributed among its members as warranted, and its members transferred elsewhere throughout the region. I'll submit my recommendation to the regional committee, which will assist the local committee in carrying out my sentence."

"No," Felice hissed. "You can't do this, you can't force us out."

She had expected that line from Frain. She wondered at the deeper dynamic here, but not enough to try to suss it out.

"I can," she said, with a backward glance at Bert. "But I won't have to, because you're all secretly relieved. The household didn't work, and that's fine—it happens sometimes—but none of you had the guts to start over, the guts to give up your credits to request a transfer somewhere else. To pay for the change you wanted. To protect your own housemates from each other. But now it's done, and by someone else, so you can complain all you want and rail to the skies about your new poverty as you work your way out of the holes you've dug for yourselves. I'm the villain you can blame. But deep down you'll know the truth. And that's fine too, because I don't really care. Not about you lot."

No one argued. No one said a word.

"Aren," Enid said, and the woman flinched again. She might never stop flinching. "You can come with me now, or would you like time to say goodbye?"

She looked around the room, and Enid wasn't imagining it: The woman's hands were shaking, though she tried to hide it by pressing them under the roundness of her belly. Enid's breath caught, because even now it might go either way. Aren had been scared before; she might be too scared to leave. Enid schooled her expression to be still no matter what the answer was.

But Aren stood from the table and said, "I'll go with you now."

"Bert will go help you get your things—"

"I don't have any things. I want to go now."

"All right. Bert, will you escort Aren outside?"

The door closed behind them, and Enid took one last look around the room.

"That's it, then," Frain said.

"Oh no, that's not it at all," Enid said. "That's just it for now. The rest of you should get word of the disposition of the household in a couple of days." She walked out.

Aren stood outside, hugging herself. Bert was a polite few paces away, being non-threatening, staring at clouds. Enid urged them on, and they walked the path back toward town. Aren seemed to get a bit lighter as they went.

They probably had another day in Southtown before they could leave. Enid would keep Aren close, in the guest rooms, until then. She might have to requisition a solar car. In her condition, Aren probably shouldn't walk the ten miles to the next way station. And she might want to say goodbye to Jess. Or she might not, and Jess would have his heart broken even more. Poor thing.

Enid requisitioned a solar car from the local committee and was able to take to the Coast Road the next day. The bureaucratic machinery was in motion on all the rest of it. Committeeman Trevor revealed that a couple of the young men from Apricot Hill had preemptively put in household transfer requests. Too little, too late. She'd done her job; it was all in committee hands now.

Bert drove, and Enid sat in the back with Aren, who was bundled in a wool cloak and kept her hands around her belly. They opened windows to the spring sunshine, and the car bumped and swayed over the gravel road. Walking would have been more pleasant, but Aren needed the car. The tension in her shoulders had finally gone away. She looked up, around, and if she didn't smile, she also didn't frown. She talked, now, in a voice clear and free of tears.

"I came into the household when I was sixteen, to work prep in the canning house and to help with the garden and grounds and such. They needed the help, and I needed to get started on my life, you know? Frain—he expected more out of me. He expected me to be his."

She spoke as if being interrogated. Enid hadn't asked for her story, but listened carefully to the confession. It spilled out like a flood, like the young woman had been waiting.

"How far did it go, Aren?" Enid asked carefully. In the driver's seat, Bert frowned, like maybe he wanted to go back and have a word with the man.

"He never did more than hit me."

So straightforward. Enid made a note. The car rocked on for a ways.

"What will happen to her, without a banner?" Aren asked, glancing at her belly. She'd evidently decided the baby was a girl. She probably had a name picked out. Her baby, her savior.

"There are households who need babies to raise who'll be happy to take her."

"Her, but not me?"

"It's a complicated situation," Enid said. She didn't want to make Aren any promises until they could line up exactly which households they'd be going to.

Aren was smart. Scared, but smart. She must have thought things through, once she realized she wasn't going to die. "Will it go better, if I agree to give her up? The baby, I mean."

Enid said, "It would depend on how you define 'better.'"

"Better for the baby."

"There's a stigma on bannerless babies. Worse some places than others. And somehow people know, however you try to hide it. People will always know what you did and hold it against you. But the baby can get a fresh start on her own."

"All right. All right, then."

"You don't have to decide right now."

Eventually, they came to the place in the road where the ruins were visible, like a distant mirage, but unmistakable. A haunted place, with as many rumors about it as there were about investigators and what they did.

"Is that it?" Aren said, staring. "The old city? I've never seen it before."

Bert slowed the car, and they stared out for a moment.

"The stories about what it was like are so terrible. I know it's supposed to be better now, but . . ." The young woman dropped her gaze.

"Better for whom, you're wondering?" Enid said. "When they built our world, our great-grandparents saved what they could, what they thought was important, what they'd most need. They wanted a world that would let them survive not just longer but better. They aimed for utopia knowing they'd fall short. And for all their work, for all our work, we still find pregnant girls with bruises on their faces who don't know where to go for help."

"I don't regret it," Aren said. "At least, I don't think I do."

"You saved what you could," Enid said. It was all any of them could do.

The car started again, rolling on. Some miles later on, Aren fell asleep curled in the back seat, her head lolling. Bert gave her a sympathetic glance.

"Heartbreaking all around, isn't it? Quite the last case for you, though. Memorable."

"Or not," Enid said.

Going back to the way station, late afternoon, the sun was in Enid's face. She leaned back, closed her eyes, and let it warm her.

"What, not memorable?" Bert said.

"Or not the last," she said. "I may have a few more left in me."

AMARYLLIS

Inever knew my mother, and I never understood why she did what she did. I ought to be grateful that she was crazy enough to cut out her implant so she could get pregnant. But it also meant she was crazy enough to hide the pregnancy until termination wasn't an option, knowing the whole time that she'd never get to keep the baby. That she'd lose everything. That her household would lose everything because of her.

I never understood how she couldn't care. I wondered what her family thought when they learned what she'd done, when their committee split up the household, scattered them—broke them, because of her.

Did she think I was worth it?

It was all about quotas.

"They're using cages up north, I heard. Off shore, anchored," Nina said. "Fifty feet across—twice as much protein grown with half the resources, and we'd never have to touch the wild population again. We could double our quota."

I hadn't really been listening to her. We were resting, just for a moment; she sat with me on the railing at the prow of *Amaryllis* and talked about her big plans.

Wind pulled the sails taut and the fiberglass hull cut through waves without a sound, we sailed so smooth. Garrett and Sun hauled up the nets behind us, dragging in the catch. *Amaryllis* was elegant, a 30-foot sleek vessel with just enough cabin and cargo space—an antique but more than seaworthy. She was a good boat, with a good crew. The best.

"Marie—" Nina said, pleading.

I sighed and woke up. "We've been over this. We can't just double our quota."

"But if we got authorization—"

"Don't you think we're doing all right as it is?" We had a good crew—we were well fed and not exceeding our quotas; I thought we'd be best off not screwing all that up. Not making waves, so to speak.

Nina's big brown eyes filled with tears—I'd said the wrong thing, because I knew what she was really after, and the status quo wasn't it.

"That's just it," she said. "We've met our quotas and kept everyone healthy for years now. I really think we should try. We can at least ask, can't we?"

The truth was: No, I wasn't sure we deserved it. I wasn't sure that kind of responsibility would be worth it. I didn't want the prestige. Nina didn't even want the prestige—she just wanted the baby.

"It's out of our hands at any rate," I said, looking away because I couldn't bear the intensity of her expression.

Pushing herself off the rail, Nina stomped down *Amaryllis'* port side to join the rest of the crew hauling in the catch. She wasn't old enough to want a baby. She was lithe, fit, and golden, running barefoot on the deck, sun-bleached streaks gleaming in her brown hair. Actually, no, she *was* old enough. She'd been with the house for seven years—she was twenty, now. It hadn't seemed so long.

"Whoa!" Sun called. There was a splash and a thud as something in the net kicked against the hull. He leaned over the side, the muscles along his broad, coppery back flexing as he clung to a net that was about to slide back into the water. Nina, petite next to his strong frame, reached with him. I ran down and grabbed them by the waistbands of their trousers to hold them steady. The fourth of our crew, Garrett, latched a boat hook into the net. Together we hauled the catch onto the deck. We'd caught something big, heavy, and full of powerful muscles.

We had a couple of aggregators—large buoys made of scrap steel and wood—anchored fifty miles or so off the coast. Schooling fish were attracted to the aggregators, and we found the fish—mainly mackerel, sardines, sablefish, and whiting. An occasional shark or marlin found its way into the nets, but those we let go; they were rare and outside our quotas. That was what I expected to see—something unusually large thrashing among the slick silvery mass of smaller fish. This thing was large, yes, as big as Nina—no wonder it had almost pulled them over—but it wasn't the right shape. Sleek and stream-lined, a powerful swimmer. Silvery like the rest of the catch.

"What is it?" Nina asked.

"Tuna," I said, by process of elimination. I had never seen one in my life. "Bluefin, I think."

"No one's caught a bluefin in thirty years," Garrett said. Sweat was dripping onto his face despite the bandanna tying back his shaggy dark hair.

I was entranced, looking at all that protein. I pressed my hand to the fish's flank, feeling its muscles twitch. "Maybe they're back."

We'd been catching the tuna's food all along, after all. In the old days the aggregators attracted as many tuna as mackerel. But no one had seen one in so long, everyone assumed they were gone.

"Let's put him back," I said, and the others helped me lift the net to the side. It took all of us, and when we finally got the tuna to slide overboard, we lost half the net's catch with it, a wave of silvery scales glittering as they hit the water. But that was okay: Better to be under quota than over.

The tuna splashed its tail and raced away. We packed up the rest of the catch and set sails for home.

The *Californian* crew got their banner last season, and flew its red and green—power and fertility—from the top of the boat's mast for all to see. Elsie of the *Californian* was due to give birth in a matter of weeks. As soon as her pregnancy was confirmed, she stopped sailing and stayed in the household, sheltered and treasured. Loose hands resting atop mountainous belly, she would sometimes come out to greet her household's boat as it arrived. Nina would stare at her. Elsie might have been the first pregnant woman Nina had seen, as least since surviving puberty and developing thoughts of carrying a mountainous belly of her own.

Elsie was there now, an icon cast in bronze before the setting sun, her body canted slightly against the weight in her belly, like a ship leaning away from the wind.

We furled the sails and rowed to the pier beside the scale house. Nina hung over the prow, looking at Elsie, who was waving at *Californian's* captain, on the deck of the boat. Solid and dashing, everything a captain ought to be, he waved back at her. Their boat was already secured in its home slip, their catch weighed, everything tidy. Nina sighed at the image of a perfect life, and nobody yelled at her for not helping. Best thing to do in a case like this was let her dream until she grew out of it. Might take decades, but still . . .

My *Amaryllis* crew handed crates off to the dockhand, who shifted our catch to the scale house. Beyond that were the processing houses, where onshore crews smoked, canned, and shipped the fish inland. The New Oceanside community provided sixty percent of the protein for the whole region, which was our mark of pride, our reason for existing. Within the community itself, the ten sailing crews were proudest of all. A fishing crew that did its job well and met its quotas kept the whole system running smoothly. I was lucky to even have the *Amaryllis* and be a part of it.

I climbed up to the dock with my folk after securing the boat, and saw that Anders was the scalemaster on duty. The week's trip might as well have been for nothing, then.

Thirty-five years ago, my mother ripped out her implant and broke up her household. Might as well have been yesterday to a man like Anders.

The old man took a nail-biting forty minutes to weigh our catch and add up our numbers, at which point he announced, "You're fifty pounds over quota."

Quotas were the only way to keep the stock healthy, to prevent overfishing, shortages, and ultimately starvation. The committee based quotas on how much you needed, not how much you could catch. To exceed that—to pretend you needed more than other people—showed so much disrespect to the committee, the community, to the fishing stock.

My knees weak, I almost sat down. I'd gotten it exactly right, I knew I had. I glared at him. Garrett and Sun, a pair of brawny sailors helpless before the scalemaster in his dull gray tunic of authority, glared at him. Some days felt like nothing I did would ever be enough. I'd always be too far one way or the other over the line of "just right." Most days, I'd accept the scalemaster's judgment and walk away, but today, after setting loose the tuna and a dozen pounds of legitimate catch with it, it was too much.

"You're joking," I said. "Fifty pounds?"

"Really," Anders said, marking the penalty on the chalkboard behind him where all the crews could see it. "You ought to know better, an experienced captain like you."

He wouldn't even look at me. Couldn't look me in the eye while telling me I was trash.

"What do you want me to do, throw the surplus overboard? We can eat those fifty pounds. The livestock can eat those fifty pounds."

"It'll get eaten, don't worry. But it's on your record." Then he marked it on his clipboard, as if he thought we'd come along and alter the public record.

"Might as well not sail out at all next week, eh?" I said.

The scalemaster frowned and turned away. A fifty pound surplus—if it even existed—would go to make up another crew's shortfall, and next week our catch would be needed just as much as it had been this week, however little some folk wanted to admit it. We could get our quota raised like Nina wanted, and we wouldn't have to worry about surpluses at all. No, then we'd worry about shortfalls, and not earning credits to feed the mouths we had, much less the extra one Nina wanted.

Surpluses must be penalized, or everyone would go fishing for surpluses and having spare babies, and then where would we be? Too many mouths, not enough food, no resiliency to survive disaster, and all the disease and starvation that followed. I'd seen the pictures in the archives, of what happened after the big fall.

Just enough and no more. Moderation. But so help me I wasn't going to dump fifty pounds just to keep my record clean.

"We're done here. Thank you, Captain Marie," Anders said, his back to me, like he couldn't stand the sight of me.

When we left, I found Nina at the doorway, staring. I pushed her in front of me, back to the boat, so we could put *Amaryllis* to bed for the night.

"The *Amaryllis'* scales aren't that far off," Garrett grumbled as we rowed to her slip. "Ten pounds, maybe. Not fifty."

"Anders had his foot on the pad, throwing it off. I'd bet on it," Sun said. "Ever notice how we're only ever off when Anders is running the scales?"

We'd all noticed.

"Is that true? But why would he do that?" said Nina, innocent Nina.

Everyone looked at me. A weight seemed to settle on us.

"What?" Nina said. "What is it?"

It was the kind of thing no one talked about, and Nina was too young to have grown up knowing. The others had all known what they were getting into, signing on with me. But not Nina.

I shook my head at them. "We'll never prove that Anders has it in for us so there's no good arguing. We'll take our licks and that's the end of it."

Sun said, "Too many black marks like that they'll break up the house."

That was the worry, wasn't it?

"How many black marks?" Nina said. "He can't do that. Can he?"

Garrett smiled and tried to take the weight off. He was the first to sign on with me when I inherited the boat. We'd been through a lot together. "We'll just have to find out Anders' schedule and make sure we come in when someone else is on duty."

But most of the time there were no schedules—just whoever was on duty when a boat came in. I wouldn't be surprised to learn that Anders kept a watch for us, just to be here to rig our weigh-in.

Amaryllis glided into her slip, and I let Garrett and Sun secure the lines. I leaned back against the side, stretching my arms, staring up along the mast. Nina sat nearby, clenching her hands, her lips. Elsie and *Californian's* captain had gone.

I gave her a pained smile. "You might have a better chance of getting your extra mouth if you went to a different crew. The *Californian*, maybe."

"Are you trying to get rid of me?" Nina said.

Sitting up, I put my arms across her shoulders and pulled her close. Nina came to me a clumsy thirteen-year-old from Bernardino, up the coast. My household had a space for her, and I was happy to get her. She'd grown up smart and eager. She could take my place when I retired, inherit *Amaryllis* in her turn. Not that I'd told her that yet.

"Never. Never ever." She only hesitated a moment before wrapping her arms around me and squeezing back.

Our household was an oasis. We'd worked hard to make it so. I'd inherited the boat, attracted the crew one by one—Garrett and Sun to run the boat, round and bustling Dakota to run the house, and she brought the talented J.J., and we fostered Nina. We'd been assigned fishing rights, and then we earned the land allocation. Ten years of growing, working, sweating, nurturing, living, and the place was gorgeous.

We'd dug into the side of a hill above the docks and built with adobe. In the afternoon sun, the walls gleamed golden. The part of the house projecting out from the hill served as a wall protecting the garden and well. Our path led around the house and into the courtyard. We'd found flat shale to use as flagstones around the cultivated plots, and to line the well, turning it into a spring. A tiny spring, but any open fresh water seemed like a luxury. On the hill above were the windmill and solar panels.

Everyone who wanted their own room had one, but only Sun did—the detached room dug into the hill across the yard. Dakota, J.J., and Nina had pallets in the largest room. Garret and I shared a bed in the smaller room. What wasn't house was garden. We had producing fruit trees, an orange and a lemon, that also shaded the kitchen space. Corn, tomatoes, sunflowers, green beans, peas, carrots, radishes, two kinds of peppers, and anything else we could make grow on a few square feet. A pot full of mint and one of basil. For the most part we fed ourselves and so could use our credits on improving *Amaryllis* and bringing in specialties like rice and honey, or fabric and rope that we couldn't make in quantity. Dakota wanted to start chickens next season, if we could trade for the chicks.

I kept wanting to throw that in the face of people like Anders. It wasn't like I didn't pay attention. I wasn't a burden.

The crew arrived home; J.J. had supper ready. Dakota and J.J. had started out splitting household work evenly, but pretty quickly they were trading chores—turning compost versus hanging laundry, mending the windmill versus cleaning the kitchen—until J.J. did most everything involving the kitchen and living spaces and Dakota did everything with the garden and mechanics.

By J.J.'s sympathetic expression when he gave me my serving— smoked mackerel and vegetables tonight—someone had already told him about the run-in with the scalemaster. Probably to keep him or Dakota from asking how my day went.

I stayed out later than usual making a round of the holding. Not that I expected to find anything wrong. It was for my own peace of mind, looking at what we'd built with my own eyes, putting my hand on the trunk of the windmill, running the leaves of the lemon tree across my palms, ensuring that none of it had vanished, that it wasn't going to. It had become a ritual.

In bed I held tight to Garrett, to give and get comfort, skin against skin, under the sheet, under the warm air coming in through the open skylight above our bed.

"Bad day?" he said.

"Can never be a bad day when the ship and crew come home safe," I said. But my voice was flat.

Garrett shifted, running a hand down my back, arranging his arms to pull me tight against him. Our legs twined together. My nerves settled.

He said, "Nina's right, we can do more. We can support an extra mouth. If we appealed—"

"You really think that'll do any good?" I said. "I think you'd all be better off with a different captain."

He tilted his face toward mine, touched my lips with his, pressed until I responded. A minute of that and we were both smiling.

"You know we all ended up here because we don't get along with anyone else. But you make the rest of us look good."

I squirmed against him in mock outrage, giggling.

"Plenty of crews—plenty of households—don't ever get babies," he said. "It doesn't mean anything."

"I don't care about a baby so much," I said. "I'm just tired of fighting all the time."

It was normal for children to fight with their parents, their households, and even their committees as they grew. But it wasn't fair, for me to feel like I was still fighting with a mother I'd never known.

The next day, when Nina and I went down to do some cleaning on *Amaryllis*, I tried to convince myself it was my imagination that she was avoiding me. Not looking at me. Or pretending not to look, when in fact she was stealing glances. The way she avoided meeting my gaze made my skin crawl a little. She'd decided something. She had a secret.

We caught sight of Elsie again, walking up from the docks, a hundred yards away, but her silhouette was unmistakable. That distracted Nina, who stopped to stare.

"Is she really that interesting?" I said, smiling, trying to make it a joke.

Nina looked at me sideways, as if deciding whether she should talk to me. Then she sighed. "I wonder what it's like. Don't you wonder what it's like?"

I thought about it a moment and mostly felt fear rather than interest. All the things that could go wrong, even with a banner of approval flying above you. Nina wouldn't understand that. "Not really."

"Marie, how can you be so . . . so *indifferent*?"

"Because I'm not going to spend the effort worrying about something I can't change. Besides, I'd much rather be captain of a boat than stuck on shore, watching."

I marched past her to the boat, and she followed, head bowed.

We washed the deck, checked the lines, cleaned out the cabin, took inventory, and made a stack of gear that needed to be repaired. We'd take it home and spend the next few days working on it before we went to sea again. Nina was quiet most of the morning, and I kept glancing at her, head bent to her work, biting her lip, wondering what she was thinking on so intently. What she was hiding.

Turned out she was working up the courage.

I handed the last bundle of net to her, then went back to double check that the hatches were closed and the cabin was shut up. When I went to climb off the boat myself, she was sitting at the edge of the dock, her legs hanging over the edge, swinging a little. She looked ten years younger, like she was a kid again, like she had when I first saw her.

I regarded her, brows raised, questioning, until finally she said, "I asked Sun why Anders doesn't like you. Why none of the captains talk to you much."

So that was what had happened. Sun—matter-of-fact and sensible—would have told her without any circumspection. And Nina had been horrified.

Smiling, I sat on the gunwale in front of her. "I'd have thought you'd been here long enough to figure it out on your own."

"I knew something had happened, but I couldn't imagine what. Certainly not—I mean, no one ever talks about it. But . . . what happened to your mother? Her household?"

I shrugged, because it wasn't like I remembered any of it. I'd pieced the story together, made some assumptions. Was told what happened by people who made their own assumptions. Who wanted me to understand exactly what my place in the world was.

"They were scattered over the whole region, I think. Ten of them—it was a big household, successful, until I came along. I don't know where all they ended up. I was brought to New Oceanside, raised up by the first *Amaryllis* crew. Then Zeke and Ann retired, took up pottery, went down the coast, and gave me the ship to start my own household. Happy ending."

"And your mother—they sterilized her? After you were born, I mean."

"I assume so. Like I said, I don't really know."

"Do you suppose she thought it was worth it?"

"I imagine she didn't," I said. "If she wanted a baby, she didn't get one, did she? But maybe she just wanted to be pregnant for a little while."

Nina looked so thoughtful, swinging her feet, staring at the rippling water where it lapped against the hull, she made me nervous. I had to say something.

"You'd better not be thinking of pulling something like that," I said. "They'd split us up, take the house, take *Amaryllis*—"

"Oh no," Nina said, shaking her head quickly, her denial vehement. "I would never do that, I'd never do anything like that."

"Good," I said, relieved. I trusted her and didn't think she would. Then again, my mother's household probably thought that about her too. I hopped over to the dock. We collected up the gear, slinging bags and buckets over our shoulders and starting the hike up to the house.

Halfway there Nina said, "You don't think we'll ever get a banner, because of your mother. That's what you were trying to tell me."

"Yeah." I kept my breathing steady, concentrating on the work at hand.

"But it doesn't change who you are. What you do."

"The old folk still take it out on me."

"It's not fair," she said. She was too old to be saying things like that. But at least now she'd know, and she could better decide if she wanted to find another household.

"If you want to leave, I'll understand," I said. "Any house would be happy to take you."

"No," she said. "No, I'll stay. None of it—it doesn't change who you are."

I could have dropped everything and hugged her for that. We walked awhile longer, until we came in sight of the house. Then I asked, "You have someone in mind to be the father? Hypothetically."

She blushed berry red and looked away. I had to grin—so that was how it stood.

When Garrett greeted us in the courtyard, Nina was still blushing. She avoided him and rushed along to dump her load in the workshop.

Garrett blinked after her. "What's up with her?"

"Nina being Nina."

The next trip on *Amaryllis* went well. We made quota in less time than I expected, which gave us half a day's vacation. We anchored off a deserted bit of shore and went swimming, lay on deck and took in the sun, ate the last of the oranges and dried mackerel that J.J. had sent along with us. It was a good day.

But we had to head back some time and face the scales. I weighed our haul three times with *Amaryllis*' scale, got a different number each time, but all within ten pounds of each other, and more importantly twenty pounds under quota. Not that it would matter. We rowed into the slip at the scale house, and Anders was the scalemaster on duty again. I almost hauled up our sails and turned us around, never to return. I couldn't face him, not after the perfect trip. Nina was right—it wasn't fair that this one man could ruin us with false surpluses and black marks.

Silently, we secured *Amaryllis* to the dock and began handing up our cargo. I managed to keep from even looking at Anders, which probably made me look guilty in his eyes. But we'd already established I could be queen of perfection and he would consider me guilty.

Anders' frown was smug, his gaze judgmental. I could already hear him tell me I was fifty pounds over quota. Another haul like that, he'd say, we'll have to see about yanking your fishing rights. I'd have to punch him. I almost told Garrett to hold me back if I looked like I was going to punch him. But he was already keeping himself between the two of us, as if he thought I might really do it.

If the old scalemaster managed to break up *Amaryllis*, I'd murder him. And wouldn't that be a worse crime than any I might represent?

Anders drew out the moment, looking us all up and down before finally announcing, "Sixty over this time. And you think you're good at this."

My hands tightened into fists. I imagined myself lunging at him. At this point, what could I lose?

"We'd like an audit," Nina said, slipping past Sun, Garrett, and me to stand before the stationmaster, frowning, hands on her hips.

"Excuse me?" Anders said.

"An audit. I think your scale is wrong, and we'd like an audit. Right?" She looked at me.

It was probably better than punching him. "Yes," I said, after a flabbergasted moment. "Yes, we would like an audit."

That set off two hours of chaos in the scale house. Anders protested, hollered at us, threatened us. I sent Sun to the committee house to summon official oversight—he wouldn't try to play nice, and they couldn't brush him off. June and Abe, two senior committee members, arrived, austere in gray and annoyed.

"What's the complaint?" June said.

Everyone looked at me to answer. I almost denied it—that was my first impulse. Don't fight, don't make waves. Because maybe I deserved the trash I got. Or my mother did, but she wasn't here, was she?

But Nina was looking at me with her innocent brown eyes, and this was for her.

I wore a perfectly neutral, business-like expression when I spoke to June and Abe. This wasn't about me, it was about business, quotas, and being fair.

"Scalemaster Anders adjusts the scale's calibration when he sees us coming."

I was amazed when they turned accusing gazes at him and not at me. Anders' mouth worked, trying to stutter a defense, but he had nothing to say.

The committee confirmed that Anders was rigging his scale. They offered us reparations, out of Anders' own rations. I considered—it would mean extra credits, extra food and supplies for the household. We'd been discussing getting another windmill, petitioning for another well. Instead, I recommended that any penalties they wanted to levy should go to community funds. I just wanted *Amaryllis* treated fairly.

And I wanted a meeting, to make one more petition before the committee.

Garrett walked with me to the committee office the next morning.

"I should have been the one to think of requesting an audit," I said.

"Nina isn't as scared of the committee as you are. As you *were*," he said.

"I'm not—" But I stopped, because he was right.

He squeezed my hand. His smile was amused, his gaze warm. He seemed to find the whole thing entertaining. Me—I was relieved, exhausted, giddy, ashamed. Mostly relieved.

We, *Amaryllis*, had done nothing wrong. I had done nothing wrong.

Garrett gave me a long kiss, then waited outside while I went to sit before the committee.

June was in her chair, along with five other committee members, behind their long table with their slate boards, tally sheets, and lists of quotas. I sat across from them, alone, hands clenched in my lap, trying not to tap my feet. Trying to appear as proud and assured as they did. A stray breeze slipped through the open windows and cooled the cinderblock room.

After polite greetings, June said, "You wanted to make a petition?"

"We—the *Amaryllis* crew—would like to request an increase in our quota. Just a small one."

June nodded. "We've already discussed it and we're of a mind to allow an increase. Would that be suitable?"

Suitable as what? As reparation? As an apology? My mouth was dry, my tongue frozen. My eyes stung, wanting to weep, but that would have damaged our chances, as much as just being me did.

"There's one more thing," I managed. "With an increased quota, we can feed another mouth."

It was an arrogant thing to say, but I had no reason to be polite.

They could chastise me, send me away without a word, lecture me on wanting too much when there wasn't enough to go around. Tell me that it was more important to maintain what we had rather than try to expand—expansion was arrogance. We simply had to maintain. But they didn't. They didn't even look shocked at what I had said.

June, so elegant, I thought, with her long gray hair braided and resting over her shoulder, a knitted shawl draped around her, as much for decoration as for warmth, reached into the bag at her feet and retrieved a folded piece of cloth, which she pushed across the table toward me. I didn't want to touch it. I was still afraid, as if I'd reach for it and June would snatch it away at the last moment. I didn't want to unfold it to see the red and green pattern in full, in case it was some other color instead.

But I did, even though my hand shook. And there it was. I clenched the banner in my fist; no one would be able to pry it out.

"Is there anything else you'd like to speak of?" June asked.

"No," I said, my voice a whisper. I stood, nodded at each of them. Held the banner to my chest, and left the room.

Garrett and I discussed it on the way back to the house. The rest of the crew was waiting in the courtyard for us: Dakota in her skirt and tunic, hair in a tangled bun; J.J. with his arms crossed, looking worried; Sun, shirtless, hands on hips, inquiring. And Nina, right there in front, bouncing almost.

I regarded them, trying to be inscrutable, gritting my teeth to keep from bursting into laughter. I held our banner behind my back to hide it. Garrett held my other hand.

"Well?" Nina finally said. "How did it go? What did they say?"

The surprise wasn't going to get any better than this. I shook out the banner and held it up for them to see. And oh, I'd never seen all of them wide-eyed and wondering, mouths gaping like fish, at once.

Nina broke the spell, laughing and running at me, throwing herself into my arms. We nearly fell over.

Then we were all hugging, and Dakota started worrying right off, talking about what we needed to build a crib, all the fabric we'd need for diapers, and how we only had nine months to save up the credits for it.

I recovered enough to hold Nina at arm's length, so I could look her in the eyes when I pressed the banner into her hands. She nearly dropped it at first, skittering from it as if it were fire. So I closed her fingers around the fabric and held them there.

"It's yours," I said. "I want you to have it." I glanced at Garrett to be sure. And yes, he was still smiling.

Staring at me, Nina held it to her chest, much like I had. "But . . . you. It's yours . . ." She started crying. Then so did I, gathering her close and holding her tight while she spoke through tears, "Don't you want to be a mother?"

In fact, I rather thought I already was.

ABOUT THE AUTHOR

Carrie Vaughn is the New York Time Bestselling author of close to twenty novels and over seventy short stories. She's best known for the Kitty Norville urban fantasy series about a werewolf who hosts a talk radio advice show for supernatural beings—the series includes fourteen novels and a collection of short stories—and the superhero novels in the Golden Age saga. She also writes the Harry and Marlowe steampunk short stories about an alternate nineteenth century that makes use of alien technology. She has a masters degree in English lit, graduated from the Odyssey Fantasy Writing Workshop in 1998, and returned to the workshop as Writer in Residence in 2009. She has been a finalist for the Hugo Award, various RT Reviewer Choice Awards—winning for Best First Mystery for *Kitty and The Midnight Hour*— and won the 2011 WSFA Small Press award for best short story for "Amaryllis." Carrie lives in Colorado.

PUBLICATION NOTES

"The Best We Can" originally appeared at *Tor.com* July 2013 | "Strife Lingers in Memory" originally appeared in *Realms of Fantasy*, December 2002 | "A Hunter's Ode to His Bait" originally appeared in *Realms of Fantasy*, February 2003 | "Sun, Stone, Spear" originally appeared in *Beneath Ceaseless Skies*, March 2015 | "Crows" originally appeared in *Talebones*, Winter 2006 | "Salvage" originally appeared in *Lightspeed: Women Destroy Science Fiction*, June 2014 | "Draw They Breath in Pain" original appeared in *Paradox*, Winter 2005-2006 | "The Girl with the Pre-Raphaelite Hair" originally appeared in *Talebones*, Fall 1999 | "Game of Chance" originally appeared in *Unfettered* edited by Shawn Speakman, 2013 | "Roaring Twenties" originally appeared in *Rogues*, edited by George R.R. Martin and Gardner Dozois, 2014 | "A Riddle in Nine Syllables" originally appeared in *Talebones*, Fall 2000 | "1977" originally appeared in *Ravens in the Library*, edited by SatyrPhil Brucato and Sandra Buskirk, 2009 | "Danaë at Sea" originally appeared in *TEL: Stories*, edited by Jay Lake, 2005 | "For Fear of Dragons" originally appeared in *Weird Tales*, October-November 2006 | "The Art of Homecoming" originally appeared in *Asimov's Science Fiction*, July 2013 | "Astrophilia" originally appeared in *Clarkesworld Magazine*, July 2012 | "Bannerless" originally appeared in *The End Has Come*, edited by Hugh Howey and John Joseph Adams, 2015 | "Amaryllis" originally appeared in *Lightspeed Magazine*, June 2010.

OTHER TITLES FROM FAIRWOOD PRESS

Joel-Brock the Brave & the Valorous Smalls
by Michael Bishop
trade paper & ltd hardcover: $16.99/$35
ISBN: 978-1-933846-53-8
ISBN: 978-1-933846-59-0

Traveler of Worlds: with Robert Silverberg
by Alvaro Zinos-Amaro
trade paper: $16.99
ISBN: 978-1-933846-63-7

On the Eyeball Floor
by Tina Connolly
trade paper: $17.99
ISBN: 978-1-933846-56-9

Seven Wonders of a Once and Future World
by Caroline M. Yoachim
trade paper: $17.99
ISBN: 978-1-933846-55-2

The Ultra Big Sleep
by Patrick Swenson
hard cover / trade: $27.99 / 17.99
ISBN: 978-1-933846-60-6
ISBN: 978-1-933846-61-3

The Specific Gravity of Grief
by Jay Lake
trade paper: $8.99
ISBN: 978-1-933846-57-6

Cracking the Sky
by Brenda Cooper
trade paper: $17.99
ISBN: 978-1-933846-50-7

The Child Goddess
by Louise Marley
trade paper: $16.99
ISBN: 978-1-933846-52-1

www.fairwoodpress.com
21528 104th Street Court East;
Bonney Lake, WA   98391

CPSIA information can be obtained
at www.ICGtesting.com
Printed in the USA
LVOW12s1200040916

503165LV00008B/583/P